THE RULES OF YOU AND ME.

THE CHECKLIST ROMANCE SERIES.
BOOK 3

EMMA MILLER

Edited by
SABRINA GRIMALDI

Illustrated by
KASSANDRA CAMPONI

To the people who talk too much but never say what they really mean. Here's to knowing what you deserve and asking for it from now on.

TRIGGER WARNINGS.

Trigger Warnings and a note to my readers:

Parental death (mentioned)
Growing up in foster care
Open door sexual content
Conversations about mental health and seeking help
Therapy scenes depicted
Physical violence depicted (no gore)

This book is based around football but some of the contents within might not align with accurate football rules or college football regulations. Inconsistencies within the content may occur.

And lastly, every song within this book was completely intentional and deeply thought out before being included. To increase the emotion, and feeling while reading the book, I suggest listening to the songs placed within the story during or after you read the chapter. I took quite a bit of time selecting the perfect songs for the specifics in each chapter to increase plea-

TRIGGER WARNINGS.

sure and reading. Music has always been a giant step in my writing. It's inspiring and helps the intricate details come to life in a more vivid picture. Thank you for choosing my book and listening to my words.

PLAYLIST.

Theme Song: I Can See You (Taylor's Version) by Taylor Swift

1. exes by Tate McRae
2. Garden Life by Luke Hemmings
3. Fearless (Taylor's Version) by Taylor Swift
4. 2 hands by Tate McRae
5. When by Dodie
6. Superbloodmoon (feat. d4vd) by Holly Humberstone
7. Take Me There by Rascal Flatts
8. Sunny Disposition by Carol Ades
9. MUSCLE MEMORY by Kelsea Ballerini
10. imgonnagetyouback by Taylor Swift
11. Blindside by James Arthur
12. Madness by Muse
13. illicit affairs by Taylor Swift
14. I Can't Let You Go by Levi Ransom
15. I Guess by Lizzy McAlpine
16. BIRDS OF A FEATHER by Billie Eilish

17. The Alchemy by Taylor Swift
18. Juno by Sabrina Carpenter
19. Boyfriend by Justin Bieber
20. Best Friend by Conan Gray
21. Frisky by Dominic Fike
22. Ryder by Madison Beer
23. Down Bad by Taylor Swift
24. My Body by Young the Giant
25. All Falls Down by Lizzy McAlpine
26. Save A Horse (Ride a Cowboy) by Big & Rich
27. Treacherous (Taylor's Version) by Taylor Swift
28. Must Be Love by Niall Horan
29. Cowboys Cry Too (with Noah Kahan) by Kelsea Ballerini
30. Someone's Somebody by Levi Ransom
31. making the bed by Olivia Rodrigo
32. Linger by The Cranberries
33. Dreams by Carol Ades
34. Must Be Doin' Somethin' Right by Billy Currington
35. Dirty Little Secret by The All-American Rejects
36. Isn't It Obvious by Katherine Li
37. think later by Tate McRae
38. motive by Ariana Grande
39. Suddenly Okay by Blake Rose
40. Afterglow by Taylor Swift
41. Yours by Alexander 23
42. came to the party for you by Lexi Jayde
43. Constellations (Piano Version) by Jade LeMac
44. Novocaine by The Band CAMINO
45. girl with a problem by Amy Allen
46. You and Me by Lifehouse
47. Call Me (Piano Version) by The Franklin Electric

48. Bring Em Out by T.I.
49. Last Night's Mascara by Brynn Cartelli
50. My Girl by The Temptations
51. tired of healing. by Noah Henderson
52. More Than Just Tonight by Picture This

CHAPTER 1
EXES BY TATE MCRAE

Brianne Archer:

The guy talking to me right now definitely has a girlfriend. I don't know what it is about him that gives it away. Maybe it's the fact that he's constantly checking his phone. Maybe it's the fact that his two friends are on each side of him like bodyguards. Like they're watching for her or her friends to show up. Or maybe it's because of his insistent need for me to be interested in him. He's glanced at my chest a total of 16 times in the short time we've been speaking. Unfortunately for him, I'm lacking in that department, but it doesn't seem to bother him. He checks his phone and I sigh.

"Is that your girlfriend?" I ask, and he chokes on his beer.

A spatter of it hits the ground between us. I scrunch up my nose and look him directly in the eyes, pressing a very small smile on my lips—an incredibly fake one at that.

"I... I don't... She's not my—"

"Listen, Todd," I start.

"My name is Trey," he interrupts, and I sigh.

"Oops. Either way, I wasn't interested. I was hoping you

were planning on buying me a drink, but now that I know you're taken, I don't bite if your line is already hooked. Shoo."

I wave my hands and his jaw is slack. Most of the time, I wouldn't be this forward... But taken men in bars are an exception to that rule. He stutters once more.

I noticed his Seattle Pike University Athletics shirt the minute he started speaking to me. He's not a football player, but maybe... basketball? Baseball? I have no idea. That doesn't mean he won't know who my brother is. Everyone does.

"Fine, if that wasn't enough... Bellamy Archer is my older brother. Scared yet? Go away." I tilt my head and smile as his eyes go wide.

I wave my hand, and he turns away, almost tripping over his feet. If my brother knew I was here right now, he'd probably freak out. Overprotective is basically his middle name.

I sigh and turn from him, bringing the straw up to my lips as I sip my margarita. I survey the people around me, and my eyes land on a very familiar face. I almost choke on my drink. Ryland Turner, one of my ex-boyfriends, approaches. It's absolutely not a good idea that I'm near him. He might have been mediocre in every aspect of the relationship but he did have a nice-sized dick, and he actually knew how to use it which is more than I can say for most of the others. I haven't been with anyone for months. But right now, I have alcohol in my system despite the fact that I shouldn't have even been let in the bar. I can't get tangled up with him. I can't get myself into trouble before my freshman year of college even officially starts. I scan the room quickly and act fast as I jump in front of the only other freshman teammate that I have on the cheer team.

I have talked to him a handful of times. He's sweet from what I can tell but I haven't really gotten to feel him out. The only two people I've been around are him, and Valerie, the junior on our cheer team that has been tasked with making us

THE RULES OF YOU AND ME.

aware of traditions and fun stuff around campus. I wouldn't consider myself close or even on a first-name basis with either of them. That's going to change now. We're going to see if Dakota is a real one or not.

"Dakota... right?" I ask him, and his eyes scan me in a way that is anything but friendly.

I smirk. I guess I wore the right outfit. Or maybe he's not looking at me in that way, maybe I'm just amusing... Dakota is picture-perfect, I saw that from the start, but I also cheer with him... So the non-friendly way he's looking at me gives me bad ideas that I will be ignoring.

"Yeah... and you're Brianne, right? Rumor has it I'm going to be your stunt partner for the foreseeable future," he speaks in a casual voice, and I raise my eyebrows.

"I guess that means we should probably get to know each other..." I tell him, keeping the same casual nonchalant tone.

I lean against the bar, and he ditches any other plans he had to stand in front of me. This could go very well or very bad. I'm hoping for the former because if he's right, the next four years will be hell if I hate the man standing in front of me. I send up a prayer that he's not the absolute worst.

"Are you drinking tonight, Dakota?" I ask him, and he shrugs his shoulders and eyes me up and down once more.

"Whatever you're having... but I prefer tequila," he tells me.

His eyes are kind, pretty, and blue, and his facial structure is strong. He looks like a Ken doll. His muscle tone is mouth-watering, and the way his shirt hugs his chest like it was made for him makes it hard not to stare. I'm around 5 '5, but I look miniscule next to Dakota. He could be on the football team, not the cheer team, if we were basing things just on the way he looks. And the answer he just gave is music to my damn ears. Tequila should run through my veins instead of blood. I'd be far more tolerable.

3

I look over Dakota's shoulder to see Ryland staring at me like he was waiting for me to notice him. The second of eye contact is enough to make my ex move. It takes a few moments for me to register that he's making his way over to me, and then the panic sets in. I cringe and groan out. Dakota tilts his head and furrows his brows.

"What?" he asks, confused by my body language.

"Can I kiss you?" I ask Dakota, and he furrows his brows. "Yes or no, quickly please." I tilt my head, and he narrows his eyes.

"You want me... to kiss you? I just met you," he offers and I shrug.

"I've done worse," I fight back.

He looks at my eyes, then my lips, and then doesn't hesitate to pull me to him by the nape of my neck. His large hand splays over my skin and warms me all the way down to my bones. His lips are warm and persistent. My breath catches, but despite how skilled he is at kissing me, there's not a single spark that ignites. I keep my lips on him though, and I grip his shirt, sinking into the feeling... or lack thereof. I breathe in the scent of him and indulge in that too because this man smells like heaven.

This means nothing, not even slightly, and I hate that because what if fireworks are going off in his brain right now and I'm going to break his heart? *I should stop kissing him.*

I back up slightly, my body still in his grasp. I leave a distance between our faces so I can look directly at him. His bright blue eyes are staring down at me, a smirk pressed to his full lips. I'd be lying if I said I wasn't absolutely obsessed with his appearance but there are no feelings attached. He's a cutie and someone else will be damn lucky if they bag him.

"Are you going to tell me why you kissed me now?" he asks, his hand still intertwined in my hair.

THE RULES OF YOU AND ME.

"You kissed me," I clarify, and his smirk grows. He fights a laugh and backs up slightly.

"You asked," he offers with a shrug.

"Do you do everything strangers ask you to do in bars?" I ask him, and he shrugs his shoulders again, all of his motions subtle and calm.

Bellamy isn't going to believe it when I tell him what happened tonight.

"If they're as gorgeous as you then maybe. But... I don't think I'm interested in getting involved with someone I have to be this close to every day for the next four years, and from the way you pulled back, I think you're thinking the same thing, so tell me what that was for. Unless I'm wrong, then we can keep kissing, no strings attached and cheer together until our faces turn blue," he insists.

A smile presses to my lips.

"My ex-boyfriend was walking over, and the last time I talked to him, I ended up sleeping with him. I refuse to go down that road ever again. No more exes now that I'm in college, especially not when tequila is involved." I slightly raise the drink I have.

He raises his eyebrows and shrugs slightly, accepting the answer as a good one.

"Is he still looking?" Dakota asks, and I casually glance around and don't see Ryland anywhere. I shake my head slightly.

"Then we did a good job, didn't we?" he asks and lets go of me.

"You were an incredible kisser Dakota, but I think we should never kiss again," I tell him with a smile pressed to my lips.

I hold my hand out to shake his in agreement. I watch his

ocean eyes stare down at my hand, and then I see him glance back up to me, a grin on his lips.

"You're drop-dead gorgeous Brianne, but I think that's the best idea you've ever had."

He shakes my hand. I see his eyes leave my face and follow a tall guy across the bar as he walks past us. I realize now that the way he looked at me before was not attraction but curiosity. The way he just eyed the guy that's now past us... That was lust. Pure and obvious want.

"Are you gay?" I ask him, wondering if I just made a complete fool out of myself. *Hitting on a gay guy? Really Brianne? Welcome to college, you idiot. Now he probably hates you and—*

"Don't sound so surprised. I like women and men. I'm bisexual, not an alien," he laughs, and I sigh in relief.

"Oh, thank god. I thought I just hit on a gay guy. Which wouldn't be a problem, but if I hit on you and there's not even a single slight chance you might want to take me home then I totally just made a fool out of myself, you know? Sorry, that sounds dumb. I just didn't want to embarrass myself, which I'm doing right now by yapping. I'm like... A certified yapper."

He laughs as I continue to ramble.

"You definitely do talk a lot," he tells me, and I press my lips together and shrug.

"Sorry," I apologize, and he shakes his head slowly, now standing next to me, his back also to the bar top.

"I like it," he tells me. I smile to myself. *I like him.*

"You know, you basically hit gold being a male cheerleader. You get to stare at hot football players, and cheerleaders all the time," I tell him, and he holds his drink out to me. I clink mine to his.

"I'll drink to that," he chuckles and takes a long drink out of his glass.

THE RULES OF YOU AND ME.

My eyes bulge out of my head at the sight of another familiar face. I turn around, ducking my head closer to the bar. I close my eyes tight and cringe.

"Oh my god..." I whisper to myself. *Adrian. No fucking way did he actually choose to come to SPU... He said he wasn't and yet...*

"What?" Dakota asks.

"Would you believe me if I said another one of my ex-boyfriends is walking this way?" I ask him, knowing how it might sound.

"If you just want to kiss me again that's all you have to say. But we did just promise no more," he jokes, and I look up at him from where I stand with a glare of mild annoyance. "Which one?" he asks, and I peek over my shoulder.

"Long black hair, man bun..." I tell him.

"You're into man buns?" he asks me, and I shake my head.

"He didn't have it when we dated. No, absolutely not," I tell him.

"He's walking this way," Dakota tells me.

"Dakota, I don't know you well enough yet to know if you're fucking with me or if you're so dead serious right now."

"Absolutely as dead serious as I could be. He's cute, even with the man bun," There's a smirk in his voice and I want to crawl under the bartop and risk whatever disease is lingering on this disgusting floor.

It would be worth it.

"If I jumped over the bar do you think they'd kick me out?" I ask him, and Dakota laughs.

"We said no more kissing, and I've never been a rule breaker," he tells me, and I look at him.

"I've never been one to make rules," I admit, with rising panic as time runs out.

I need better tactics but for now...

"Fine, pucker up."

He brings me back into yet another kiss, and I still feel nothing, not even desire now that I know that there's a clear line drawn between the two of us. But damn, whatever guy or girl he makes a move on is going to be in for a fucking treat. He breaks away first this time and presses another small kiss to my lips before fully moving back. He looks around and relaxes back against the bar.

"He darted quicker than expected but he's gone," Dakota tells me, and I smirk.

"I like you in a weird way... Like the way where we could be platonic soulmates or something," I admit without dropping the lore about me and my lack of friendships in my life.

I've never been good at making connections with people. Not at bars unless they're meant to be casual and very short-lived. I'm scared of making friends. I'm scared of having boyfriends, too, but they're easier to come by. With him, though? The pull was instant. Whether that's because I asked him to kiss me after two minutes of knowing him, or because we actually blend well, I guess I'll figure out later.

"It's pretty soon for you to be throwing the soulmate word around, I don't even know your favorite color," he tells me, and I laugh. "I like you too, I figured I would have to, or else these next few years would suck. We're going to be the head bitches in a few years so it's better this way, I think. Oh, and my favorite color is green," he tells me, and I smile.

"So is mine," I admit.

"Never going to beat these soulmate allegations," he nudges me slightly and I smile with closed lips, not being able to hold it back.

"I guess not," I laugh through my words.

"Now, tell me how many exes you have, and how many we

THE RULES OF YOU AND ME.

might potentially run into before I have to kiss you a thousand more times," he tells me.

"There's Ryland who was the first one we saw tonight. I dated him for about six months. Then, you obviously saw Adrian. He was a year of my life. I had Jackson, he was cool, but he goes to college in Cali, so no chance of seeing him. There's Kade, he was a loser, but he was really hot. He didn't go to college, so no chance. Then, there was Ashton. He also goes to SPU. So... There's one more, but he probably won't be here tonight. He plays hockey. Either way, there's no way of us rekindling anything," I explain.

"And what about that guy at the bonfire? The one we all saw you making heart eyes at?" he asks me.

I did sit next to Dakota at the bonfire. We didn't speak much, to be very honest I was nervous which happens pretty often in social settings for me. The bonfire was... *Oh god, it was a whirlwind.*

I think about the exact moment Dakota is speaking of, replaying it on a loop. The beach bonfire was yesterday, it's annual and happens every year for the new cheer and football teams to hang out before the season starts. Everyone who's on both teams goes and brings their boyfriends and girlfriends which inevitably turns into a huge beach party.

We were all there, and one second things were fine, but the next a giant football player was crashing into me. A football player with perfect loose curly hair that flows and sits perfectly, even when it falls in his eyes. A football player that could have crushed me, but reacted so quickly that he wrapped his big arms, and hands around me, and took the brunt of our fall. I landed on his chest and locked eyes with him. Did I mention he has the prettiest hazel eyes? It was slow motion, and the way his eyes poured into me felt... Magical, almost. Like a Taylor Swift song.

9

He Taylor Swift'd me and didn't even know he did it. Then I realized we weren't alone, and that he was most likely one of my brother's teammates, so I backed off as quickly as I could. I've been doing my best to try and pretend it didn't happen. I'm failing though, especially when my teammate brings it up, reminding me again that every single person around saw it.

"Parker Thompson? No... not even a chance. He's... He's my brother's friend. They aren't the same age, but that doesn't matter. He's off limits," I tell him, diverting my eyes.

I don't like talking about what happened at the bonfire because I can't help but heat up when I do. That moment was straight from a movie which is exactly why it's dumb. That would be me being a silly little girl and a hopeless romantic which I'm not and never have been. So I won't be that here at SPU.

"Who's your brother?" Dakota asks me.

"Bellamy Archer. He's the quarterback on the football team," I tell Dakota.

"Your brother is hot," Dak tells me, and I chuckle.

"We have great genes, what can I say? He has hotter friends. You get used to it," I tell him.

I'm immune to all my friends thinking my brother is hot. It's inevitable.

"I don't think I'd ever get used to him and his hot friends. Remember that platonic soulmate thing? How about you keep that in mind so we can sleep over at your place more often than not," he jokes, and I scoff.

"You'd use me for my brother and his hot friends?" I ask.

"I would," he clarifies, and we both burst into laughter.

"I cannot believe you." I sip my drink, and he shrugs.

"I protect you from your five evil ex-boyfriends, you let me stare at your hot brother. I think it's fair," he explains.

"Deal, but Bellamy never finds out," I tell Dak.

THE RULES OF YOU AND ME.

"Best idea ever."

He slinks his arm over my shoulders, and I nestle into Dakota, finding it easy to talk to him. Laughter also comes easy, which is a plus. I have a habit of talking too much and scaring people away. But Dakota talks a lot too, more calm than me, but somehow matches my energy perfectly. I feel a warmth spread in my chest. School hasn't even started and I've already made a friend. That's more than I've ever been able to say before now.

CHAPTER 2
ALL FALLS DOWN BY LIZZY MCALPINE

Brianne Archer:

I count in my head and keep a smile on my face. Today is our first official practice as the cheer team and I am more than ready for it. At least that's what I keep telling myself even though I'm sweating buckets right now. It's not that hot in Seattle despite it being the end of July—I'm just freaking out. Leah Ashley is the cheer captain, and a female vulture, ready to pick the skin off your bones if you fail. Not only that but she's also my brother's ex-girlfriend. According to him, and Kamryn, his current girlfriend, they've smoothed everything over and they're cool. I, on the other hand, think she can smell my freaking fear. I've been scared since I made the team that she would be harder on me than everyone else. Today will be the telltale sign.

"Deep breath." I feel Dakota's hands on my bare waist, and his words are soft in my ear.

He was right last night at the bar. We were paired to be stunt partners for the season. It makes sense why.

Last night, I learned that Dakota is a year older than me. He's 19 and turns 20 on August 27th. I'm 18 and turn 19 on

THE RULES OF YOU AND ME.

August 29th. We're almost twins. That's what I said at the bar last night. He took a gap year in his learning so that he could figure out what exactly he wanted to do before he came to SPU. So we're officially the only two freshmen who made the cheer team this year. I've never clicked so easily with someone like I did with Dakota last night. It's like the minute we met we had that thing people talk about—like you've known someone forever even though you just met.

We're basically the same person in different forms. We both love Tate McRae and Taylor Swift. We have the same favorite color. When I asked what his favorite Barbie movie was he said Princess and The Pauper, just like me. Our lucky number is 13 which definitely took me by surprise. We both prefer tequila.

I focus back in, and do what he says. I take a deep breath, ignoring the slight headache I have from my very subtle hangover. Bellamy still has no idea that I went out to the campus bars last night. I don't think my brother has any idea what he's gotten himself into in wanting me to come to the same college as him. Honestly, I don't know what I've gotten myself into. I've got a reputation of my own solely because of him. That's how it's always been, though. Bellamy is the star of the football team and I'm his baby sister. Always the baby. It was the same in high school as well. Even after he graduated, I was his legacy.

Leah captures my attention by clapping her hands and counting us down out loud. I nod my head, and Dakota's hands tighten around my waist. He lifts, and hoists me up, making me feel absolutely weightless as I fly over him. I tighten every muscle in my body as Dakota's hands stabilize my foot. I smile, pom poms in the air, and feel completely secure in his grasp. I've never done much solo stunting, only during stunt lessons, but even then, it wasn't frequent. So the fact that it's seamless for Dakota and me makes me feel a lot better about this pairing and our friendship. We just work.

"Tighter!" Leah walks past each stunt duo. "Sloppy."

She moves on and looks up at all of us, but I keep my eyes straight forward, ignoring her completely as if she's not there, even as she approaches slowly. She can smell my fear, like a shark. Like a scary shark with blonde hair and a perfect manicure.

"Danvers, you're going to kill my flier if you don't fix yourself as base! Stable, grounded. You are her foundation," I hear her say.

She's in front of me now, I know she is. I can sense her below. I hear nothing and know that she won't attack if I just don't make eye contact.

"Good job Baby B, and Daks for not sucking. Drop 'em!" she shouts, and I swear my heart stutters for only a second.

Thank god. I prepare for my dismount, and Dak is perfect in the way he moves. I press my poms tight to my sides and double down until I'm safely in Dakota's arms and my feet are touching the ground. I stay standing close to Dakota, my back pressed to his chest as we watch Leah closely.

"You good, Baby?" he whispers in my ear, and I'm still not used to the nickname.

It makes sense and I love it, considering I am the youngest on the team. Still, it's normally romantic, but with my teammates, it's obviously not. Leah started it this morning and it's already sticking.

"All good," I whisper back, trying to catch my breath.

"We start scrimmages in about two weeks so I need all of you to be on your A-game! Do you understand?" she asks us.

We all reply in a form of yes, and she goes on, "We are going to be practicing three times a week. I don't care how perfect you think you are, you're not. The calendar is in the group chat. And as for all of you, you're hot, you're fit, you're perfect. Stay hydrated please, and keep your protein and calorie intake up. I

THE RULES OF YOU AND ME.

don't need any of you weak, or falling apart on the field. Don't make me have to worry about you."

She barks orders like it's second nature. For her, I'm sure it is.

"She needs to get laid," Dakota whispers beside me, only loud enough for me to hear.

I smirk, holding my laughter in, and I feel his breath whisper past me, and his chest moves like he's silently laughing.

"You're all dismissed! Except you two!" Leah snaps her attention to Dakota and me.

My lips instantly shut and the smirk wipes off of my face. I take back the shark comment. She's scarier than a shark. I'd rather face a Great White than Leah when she's in cheer coach mode.

"You are the only freshman on the team. These are your rules," she tells me, and I stare at her. She looks back at us and shakes her head. "Well, what are you waiting for? Write them down."

She motions and I scramble for something to write with. There's a notepad on the bench with a pen, both branded with SPU Athletics. I write a messy rule list.

"Number 1. If you drink, you better be absolutely careful. I'm not an idiot, I was a freshman once. If you ever get into any trouble call one of the upperclassmen. Not me unless you're severely in trouble or potentially dying. If you're not either of those things, I might kill you myself.." she tells us.

"Number 2. If you fuck a football player, you keep it to your damn self. Don't bring that shit onto the field or into practice, understood?"

"Yes sir," I speak quickly before I can think about what I'm saying, and then I panic. "I mean, yes ma'am. Captain. Miss... Leah." I stumble through the words.

I wish the field would turn into a hole and suck me in.

Dakota squeezes my side, and I bite my lip. I wish I knew when to close my mouth.

"God, you need help," she sighs, and I groan internally. *Yes, yes I do.*

"Sorry," I mumble.

"Last thing on that list is to remember that we take care of people. That was a big problem last year, the girls were out to get each other, and the guys on the team were not involved because they didn't want to know the drama. The team was a mess and we struggled. We cleaned all of that up. Cheerleaders and football players alike are a family. We lean on them, they lean on us. Don't fuck that up," Leah snaps, and I nod.

"Anything else?" Dakota asks.

"Yeah, don't get Baby B pregnant. I see you two..." She nods between us and my cheeks burn.

"We're not—"

"Ah, Uh huh... I don't care. I don't want to know. Don't include me in your drama, I'm not doing the drama thing anymore, no," she silences me.

"Wait." Leah stops me again and I raise my eyebrows. "You dance. I know that, and I know how cutthroat our dance program is. Do not burn yourself out. If you need a slight break or leniency, you tell me or coach," she instructs and walks away, not even letting me reply.

I wasn't expecting that from her. She's right, though. I am a dance major here, and my professor is cutthroat, which is perfect for my career and my goals. I turn with Dakota, walking away from our practice spot.

"One person already thinks we're together, should we keep a tally?" I joke.

"People are going to believe what they want to," Dakota taps his hand on my side and then walks around me.

"Can I come to your place tonight, maybe your brother will

THE RULES OF YOU AND ME.

be home... And his friend, what's his name? Lawson?" he asks, and I scoff.

"Stop objectifying my brother and his friends," I laugh.

I know he's joking, but it is funny seeing him fawn over my brother.

"What else are they good for?" he asks, which only makes me laugh.

"I actually have plans with Bellamy so I can't hang out but I can take you back to your apartment," I tell him, and he nods.

We both grab our things and make our way out of the stadium, and into the parking lot that's starting to clear out. My white Jeep has the top off currently, and she's sitting pretty in front of us right now. Dakota places his hand on the door and hoists himself up and into my car without even opening it. I roll my eyes at the boyish movement.

"You're such a guy," I groan.

"Considering I'm a man I'll take that as a compliment, I guess," he chuckles as I climb in.

"Wait, what are you doing tomorrow night?" I ask him, and he shakes his head.

"Whatever you're about to invite me to," he smirks, and I smile too.

"My brother is throwing a going away party for his roommate Griffin, he's going to the NFL. We're all going to Haven, it's a bar near campus. You should come with me," I tell him.

"Your brother invited you to Haven?" Dakota asks.

It's a fair question. I am very much an underage college student. But, I have a fake ID, just like Bellamy did when he was my age.

"No, he actually told me not to come because I'm underage, but I laughed in his face," I smile, and Dakota rolls his eyes.

"I'll be there if you are. And the entire football team..." He

17

wiggles his eyebrows at me, and now I'm the one rolling my eyes.

I turn on my playlist and Dakota groans as the sound of country music hits my speakers.

"I honestly don't think there's anything wrong with you, Baby. You're physically perfect, so hot. Drop dead gorgeous. You're a dancer, you're smart, and you're funny. But dear God, please stop listening to country music. It's your downfall," he tells me, and all I do is turn the Rascal Flatts song up.

I don't care who hates it. The country twang makes me more than happy.

CHAPTER 3
MY BODY BY YOUNG THE GIANT.

Brianne Archer:

I stand in front of Dakota's bed in my bra and underwear, staring at the three outfits I have laid out. I tap my pointer finger to my lips. I'm already ready besides my outfit. My hair is natural in waves down my back, and I did my makeup too. I hate doing makeup on days that aren't dance days or cheer days. I grew up wearing makeup for competitions and football games so I normally find myself not wearing any when I'm not required to—except for nights like this when I have no idea who I could meet or talk to.

Dakota walks out of his bathroom wearing only a towel, his chest dripping from his shower. My best friend is hot. That's all I can say in my head before turning back to my clothes. I don't miss the way he shakes his head at my lack of clothes before he turns toward his own dresser. I grew up a dancer and cheerleader, modesty isn't a word in my vocabulary.

"You know we're never going to beat the dating allegations if this is how our friendship is going to be," he tells me.

"Don't care. I can have hot friends that I don't want to fuck.

If people don't want to accept that, then that's on them. Like you said, people will believe what they want." I shrug.

Yes, Dakota and I grew really comfortable really fast, but we're so alike it feels like I've known him forever.

"Why are you not wearing any clothes?" he asks.

"Which one?" I ask, motioning to the outfits laid out.

Dakota stands next to me, his arms crossed over his bare chest as he looks down at the clothes. He brings his finger to his lips, tapping as he deciphers.

"Middle," he tells me.

I don't question it and put on the lace shirt. It's tight and black, and it's off the shoulders. I pull my hair out of my shirt and grab the black mini-skirt that matches. The skirt sits on my hips, showing my lower stomach, and my belly button. I brought my tall black boots that hug my calves. Dakota is getting dressed too. He's in black loose-fitting jeans, and shrugging on a black button-up. He doesn't button it all the way, leaving his chest muscles on display for all the lucky onlookers that I know will be staring at him.

"Wait, do your roommates think we're dating?" I ask him.

"Nope, but they do think we're fucking," he tells me, and I mimic a gag. He smirks and shrugs. "I told them we weren't. That we won't. They don't believe me," he explains.

He's not close with his roommates, They met on a Facebook group that was meant for searching for roommates. They don't play sports, according to him. He said he preferred it that way. I guess he has no intentions of being close with them, which is fine by me, more Dakota time for me.

"You look good," I smile, and he turns to look in his floor-length mirror.

"No one needs to think we're dating tonight. I want to get laid," he tells me, and I nod.

THE RULES OF YOU AND ME.

"I'll be the best wingwoman ever," I tell him, giving him a nod.

"You haven't slept with anyone since you got here. Why don't you keep your eyes open, and try to get lucky?" he asks.

"Because everyone that's going to be here is going to be a football player," I tell him, and he shrugs.

"So what? You can't avoid football players all year, Baby. And I promise you, even with your brother being who he is, they aren't going to pretend you don't exist when you look like you do. You're hot," he laughs, and I feel my cheeks burn red.

I never thought that any of them would look at me the way Dak is describing. Mostly because Bellamy's friends he brings around me are so close with him they're like my brothers too. Griffin and Lawson are the perfect example. They would never look at me that way but there are so many players that aren't close with him like that... so maybe Dakota's right.

"All I'm saying is that your brother never told you not to fuck his teammates. Maybe don't sleep with all of them, but also you're an adult who can make big girl decisions. Who cares if you sleep with a football player? Also, no offense, but what your brother doesn't know won't kill him. One day, when you're both married and older, you can tell him and it'll be a good laugh. Until then, who gives a shit?" Dakota shrugs, and I put my hands on my hips, smiling at him.

"You know, you're right. It does give me a rush thinking about sleeping with a football player. I never have because they all panic when they figure out who my brother is. Even after he graduated from high school, none of them would talk to me. They avoided me like the plague. Are you sure they'll see me like you say?" I ask and Dakota scoffs.

"They already do. They avoided you because they thought you were hot. Pay attention tonight and you'll notice them noticing you. You've just been blocking them out because of

21

Bellamy so you've never noticed it. Realize you're as hot as you feel, and run with it, Baby. I'm serious," Dakota tells me and I smile wide.

"This is why you're my best friend. Let's go."

I hold my arm out for him. He hooks his with mine, and we leave his room. His apartment is empty and we make our way out of it and to my Jeep.

"Please no country music," Dakota begs, and I roll my eyes.

"You have three choices. Country, Taylor Swift, or—"

"Tate McRae?" he asks, and I smirk.

"It's like you can read my mind," I sigh the words out.

I hit shuffle on her discography and pull out of my parking spot. We might have to Uber home unless Dakota gets his wishes and he goes home with someone. We drive all the way to Haven, and I look in the parking lot, and on the street where cars are lined, and don't see my brother's car or Lawson's yet. I park and Dakota and I walk in together, flashing our ID to the bouncer, not even getting a second glance as they let us in. I love living in a college town.

The bar is dark. I've never been in here but this place is a perfect mix of bar and club. There are tables pressed to the walls and a giant round bar in the middle. There is a dance floor and people are already on it. The music is loud and there are plenty of places to disappear in this building if you are looking for that. So many dark corners, and of course there are a lot of eyes, but it seems like no one would care if they caught someone in the moment. I sure as hell wouldn't bat an eye.

We both go straight to the bar and I sigh. I should make a rule that anytime I go out I shouldn't be buying my own drinks. I should add to Leah's freaking rule list and make my own for my freshman year...

"If you don't want to buy your own drinks, then get to flirt-

THE RULES OF YOU AND ME.

ing," Dakota picks up on my attitude right away and nods his head.

My eyes follow where he directs my attention, and I see Parker Thompson standing at the bar with a few hockey players and he is... mouthwatering. Absolutely drop-dead gorgeous. Why is he hanging out with hockey players though? Does he know my ex?

"I can't talk to him. He's too pretty," I tell Dakota, and he rolls his eyes.

"That's exactly why you should talk to him," he tells me, and I groan, my moral consciousness still peeking through.

A football player is one thing, there are plenty of mediocre players on the team I cheer for. But Parker? That's anything but mediocre. That's the exact opposite.

"Okay, Dakota, think clearly. Are you sure I shouldn't be straying away from guys my brother knows or could consider to be his friends?" I ask.

Bellamy hangs out with Parker. I don't know if they're actually close but I have seen pictures of them together on his Instagram. They were hanging out at the bonfire and they even rode together.

"Okay, fine. Theoretically, yes. You probably should stay away but also theoretically speaking, if Parker Thompson needed a dog I'd get on my hands and knees and start barking. That's how hot he is. Didn't Leah tell us that if we wanted to fuck football players that was fine, but to keep it to ourselves? She's your captain, you're not supposed to ignore what she says," he argues, and I groan.

I look over my shoulder toward Parker and I guess I catch his attention. His eyes hit me like a truck. He's got a straw in his mouth, and the only thing I know about Parker is that he's drop-dead gorgeous and that he doesn't talk much. I also know he's got killer reflexes considering how he plays and what happened

23

between us at the bonfire. He eyes me, his eyes moving up and down my body. I feel like I'm on fire at his glance. I guess he doesn't have any rules about looking at his teammate's sister... He has to know I'm Bellamy's sister, doesn't he? Maybe he does but he doesn't care. Or maybe he's drunk... Maybe he's trying to be the protective teammate for his team captain.

"He just undressed you with his eyes," Dakota tells me, and I wipe all emotion from my face.

Stay calm. Calm, cool, and absolutely collected. Hot guys talk to you all the time. Even though Parker isn't just hot. He's a Greek sculpture of a God-level beautiful but that's beside the point. I can handle pretty men.

"Hi..." I turn to see someone else approach.

Also attractive. He's got light brown hair and pretty eyes. He's smiling and his teeth are perfect. All good signs. Dakota smirks with raised eyebrows and walks away.

"Hi..." I speak to the guy that's now next to me.

I don't hesitate to join in conversation with him. Mystery man shifts, and I notice Parker's eyes are still on me, more serious now as he stares from across the bar. There's no hesitation or reservation in the way he's looking at me. I recognize the look in his eyes. It's protection and it annoys me right away. Yep, he's definitely playing the big brother card right now. *Great.*

"You look pissed... You should smile more."

I furrow my brows and fight the urge to scowl at the guy in front of me. He's smiling, as if what he said was a compliment. He also looks like someone who's never been punched in the face before. After the last comment he made, I wish that would change.

"And you should speak when spoken to," I snap back.

"Feisty..." He touches me, and I back away with ease, not wanting to draw attention.

"Hands off," I tell him. He rolls his eyes.

THE RULES OF YOU AND ME.

"You're one of those girls," he chuckles to himself, and I scoff.

"Someone who likes their personal space when speaking to random strangers they just met at the bar? Yeah, I am. And you're one of those guys, aren't you? The kind who don't like the word no, and don't care to listen when I say it?" I ask him, and I feel a heavy presence that the two of us are being surrounded.

I look around and see Parker standing behind me, his eyes on the guy. But he's not alone. There are three other large men standing around him. I've never been made to feel exponentially tiny but right now, I do.

The hockey players Parker was just standing with are now standing around us. There's a player with incredibly wide shoulders, a very strong build and dusty brown hair that's faded on the sides but long on top. His eyes look serious, but I can tell he's a nice guy. Then, there's the one standing next to him, who is only slightly shorter but not by much. He's buff with a prominent chest and arms and he's of Asian descent. Also hot, just like his friend. Then, there's one more, standing between me and the mystery man.

"Oh, come on..." The mystery man groans to the guys around him. He talks like he knows them.

"Back off, Barsky. She's a freshman and obviously not interested. Go away," the one next to me speaks.

He has dark black curls and is built in the same mouthwatering way both of his other friends are. I can see tattoos scattered on his arms and one on his neck. I eye him and look over my shoulder at Parker who's silent, and stern with his stare.

"She was—"

"Eyeing me, so you can go," Parker tells him.

When I look back at the mystery guy, he's turning away. All the other guys nod to Parker and then back away too. I look at Parker and furrow my brows.

"First of all, your eyes aren't innocent either. Second, who were they? Do you know them?" I ask and Parker asks for a drink from the bartender.

I watch him move with ease. He doesn't talk a lot but he's smooth. Mysterious. Maybe that works for him, I don't know.

"The guy you were talking to is on the hockey team. Apparently, he's a dick," Parker tells me.

"Apparently?" I ask.

"I've never met him. I don't know how he is," Parker eyes me as he drinks from his new beverage the bartender just provided.

"And the other guys that walked over here with you? Are they also hockey players?" I ask him and he sighs.

"Yes, and my roommates. Andrew was the one on the left. Then there was Nico next to Andrew. The guy on your side was Xander," he tells me and I nod.

"And why did you come over here?" I ask.

"Because I know you and saw that you felt uncomfortable. My roommates know that guy and he'll listen if his teammates step in. Most people would say thank you," he explains.

He keeps his answers clipped and to the point. His eyes won't leave my face to the point that I want to hide from his stare. His eyes are so bright that I almost can't. He doesn't seem like the joking type, but I am.

"Thank you for being my knight in shining armor," I say sarcastically. He rolls his eyes.

"Smart ass." He swigs from his beer. I smirk. "You're welcome, Princess," He jokes.

I continue on now that the thanks are out of the way.

"And—"

"No more questions..." he speaks, stepping closer to me, his eyes cast down on me, still burning through me. *Oh my god. Don't panic. Be calm.*

"What do you suggest instead?" I ask, smirking up to him.

THE RULES OF YOU AND ME.

He looks down, and I can see amusement in his eyes. But I see reservations too. He clears his throat, and shakes his head, stepping back. I don't know if he's anxious just like me or if there's another reason he backed down. I'm assuming it's the ladder.

"You're a bad idea, Brianne," he says softly.

"The reddest out of all the flags, right?" I ask, leaning into his joke.

"Your red flags look pretty green to me in this lighting." His eyes are roving over me.

"Have you had too much to drink, Parker Thomspon?" I ask him and he looks at his beer.

"Not too much, but I have had a few..." he mumbles, drinking his beer again.

"Maybe that's a sign," I raise my eyebrows, and he presses his lips together.

"You don't know anything." He doesn't smile, just drinks his drink, and backs away from me. "That's my cue to leave." he nods over my shoulder and turns away from me. I look over and see my brother and his girlfriend, and behind them, I see Lawson and his situationship Sienna. Of course, Parker was the one to point it out. Of course, he backed away the second my brother got here. He does care, even if I thought he didn't at first. Great, my fun is now dampened. But he said I would want him to leave. Does that mean he would stay if I wanted him to? And what would my brother say if he did see that... Me flirting with his teammate. He'd surely freak out. I sigh and walk away. Tonight isn't about me, it's about Griffin, and Jade, his girlfriend, and that they're leaving because Griffin got drafted for the NFL. I hug a wall and people watch instead.

I watch everyone else have fun. I watch everyone take shots and dance. Dakota was with a girl by the bar a little while ago and both of them have disappeared from sight. I see the joy on my brother's face as he stares at his girlfriend. He watches her take shots like she's hanging the moon and I think I'm in love with their love. I watch his instinct to protect her, and I smile, knowing I've met a few of my brother's exes, but none seem that special.

I also watch Lawson, and how he's not standing directly with Sienna, but he's definitely watching her like his life depended on it. Lawson isn't the dating type, but with the way he's looking at her, I have a feeling he wants to be. I feel a presence next to me, closer than most strangers would stand. My brother mentioned to me that Lawson had eyes for Sienna in a more than friendly type of way. I turn my attention to my side to see Parker next to me. His hand is in his pocket, his eyes scanning around.

"What? Do I need more protection? You know, everyone that's friends with my brother always does this stupid shit around me. Protect Brianne. Protect the little sister, follow her around, and make sure she doesn't do anything wrong. You can go take shots with your friends, go dance with a girl, stop watching me like—"

"Shhhh."

He shuts me up, and my jaw hangs slack. I turn my body toward him. We're standing out of the normal light so there are shadows casting over both of us. You'd have to be looking to really find us in this pocket of the bar. He's smirking and it's the first genuine expression I've seen on his face. Everyone has said he doesn't talk a lot, but he seems to be talkative around me, even if his replies are short. I should probably listen to him and stop talking so much or I'll scare him away.

"Did I talk too much?" I ask him and he shakes his head.

"No, I'd let you talk for hours if you were saying something worthwhile but you weren't. I'm over here because you're doing what I do. People watching. I am not over here on your brother's

THE RULES OF YOU AND ME.

account. He's my team captain, not my boss," he tells me, and I narrow my eyes. *Alrighty then...*

"I just don't really know anyone," I shrug.

"The guy you came with? Where is he?" he asks.

"Probably with his tongue down someone's throat," I admit, and Parker runs his eyes over my face, he tries his best to read me, I can tell. "You don't have to stay here with—"

"Not everyone needs to have a motive to want to stand next to you, Brianne. If you want me to walk away, I will, but I don't have any reason for standing next to a pretty girl except that I want to," he tells me, and I stare up at him with a tilt of my head,

"Is that why you're standing so close to me, because you want to?" I ask, and he casts his eyes down once more.

He nods softly, and my neck is tilted all the way back as I stare at him. I inch and my chest is against his. This feels wrong —standing this close to a football player that I know is friends with my brother. It feels wrong in so many ways. It feels wrong, but it also feels so good. I wanted this. I did, but... I shouldn't... We're just looking at each other, there's nothing wrong with looking at him. Who kisses random strangers in bars? Well... I do. I have but I shouldn't.

"You don't think this is a mistake?" I ask, and his eyes flicker from my lips to my eyes.

"I never said that," he speaks softly, and I feel my entire life hanging over my head.

He's been drinking. That's what this is. Parker plays football with my brother. It's hard to believe he doesn't care that Bellamy is my brother. But the way he's looking at me is not even slightly friendly. He doesn't know what he's doing and I do. So I should stop but I want it and him. I've never argued with myself this much over the thought of a measly kiss.

"Parker—"

My words are cut off by yelling and we break away. Parker

pushes past me and I move with him, not understanding why he's moving so fast until I see who is involved in the fight that's broken out behind us—my brother and, of course, Lawson.

"No, stay there," he tells me, and I open my mouth but he gives me that look. The one that makes me freeze in place. "Don't get yourself hurt, Brianne," he grumbles and moves toward the fight.

Parker, acting as a concerned teammate, tries his hardest to pull Lawson away from another guy who is screaming insanely vulgar things toward Lawson and both Kamryn and Sienna who stand behind him, mortified. I watch as the other guy, who seemed to start the entire debacle, aims his fist for Lawson but misses and hits Parker right above his eye. I cringe at the impact and scurry around them, waiting for the fight to officially be broken up.

In all the years that Lawson and Bellamy have been friends, Bellamy has always had stories to tell me about Lawson getting in fights. I don't know what he fights about or why it happens, I just know he does it. So seeing it in real life for the first time is no surprise to me but what is surprising is that it seems to be over a girl, and not only that but not even his friends can break him from the fight easily.

"What the hell is going on?" I turn over my shoulder to see Dakota has basically materialized out of thin air.

"Where the hell have you been?" I ask him and he smirks as he shrugs.

"Here and there," he tells me.

I roll my eyes. I turn my attention to the fight that's now broken up. Everyone is surrounding Lawson but not a single person is looking at Parker—not a single person gives a shit that he just took a punch for Lawson, one that obviously hurt by the looks of it. I contemplate what to do. I'm in front of everyone, my brother, his friends... Parker's not even concerned about

THE RULES OF YOU AND ME.

himself it seems. I look at Dakota and nod my head to Parker. I mouth the words 'what do I do?' to him and he looks between me and Parker then smirks.

"Talk to him," Dakota speaks beside me.

He wouldn't encourage me if he didn't think it was a good idea. I reach forward and touch Parker's elbow, pulling his attention to me.

"Are you okay? Can I get you anything?" I ask, and his features soften. "You took a really hard hit, and I just want to make sure you feel alright... Since no one else seemed to notice... Not that you aren't noticed. You are, I just mean—"

"I'm fine," he speaks softly but stiffly, shaking his head.

I furrow my brows, seeing that he's obviously not fine. The blood on his forehead is showcasing how not fine he is. I don't reach for him, but I do keep his attention, my hand still on his arm.

"What happened?" I ask, and he shrugs.

He said he doesn't know but Lawson got into a fight with some guy because of Sienna. It's not shocking. Lawson is prone to fighting, but not in specific defense of a girl he's sleeping with. So I assume it's more than that—more than him just sleeping with her. Bellamy told me Lawson isn't the dating type, but maybe she's different, special to him in some way. My brother looks livid as he talks to Kamryn, and I know he's pissed at his best friend. Lawson has disappeared and is nowhere to be found, and the bar is in complete chaos right now. I'm overwhelmed as I look around.

"You look like you're about to pass out..." Parker speaks now and I shake my head.

"This is just really chaotic, and everyone is screaming, and you're hurt and pretending you're not," I tell him, anger coating my words even though I'm not mad. Frustrated yes, but not mad.

"Why do you care?" he asks, and I frown slightly, my eyes meeting him again.

He's hurt, why wouldn't I care?

"B-because you're hurt. Of course, I care that someone I know is hurt. It seems like no one else cares, including yourself," I raise my eyebrows at him.

His eyes search mine, and he opens his mouth to speak, but I don't let him.

"Come here," I take his hand, feeling the exponential size difference between our hands as I do. I drag him through the crowd and he stumbles behind me.

"Brianne, what are you doing?" he asks, and I notice that he doesn't call me by a nickname.

Not by the names everyone else calls me. It's always my full name, and I like the way it sounds coming from his lips. I hope he doesn't change that either.

"I want to look at your face," I tell him and realize how it sounds. "I mean your cut. You... You're hurt, and I wanted to look at the..." I sigh and groan. "Just shut up," I tell him.

"I'm not talking, you are," he tells me, and I glare at him over my shoulder.

I stop abruptly in the hallway, and he presses into me as I turn around. I try not to let it affect me, but it's incredibly hard. I'm not the type to be affected by small things. Hand touches, or even kisses. But the sheer proximity of Parker Thompson is taking my breath away, and I don't know what's wrong with me. Maybe it's because he's like forbidden fruit. I'm only affected because I can't have him. I reach up softly and try to get a better look, but he turns his face.

"I said I was fine," he tells me, his voice set and slightly irritated. *Grumpy*.

"You're being annoying is what you are. Let me look at it, Parker," I insist, and he sighs.

THE RULES OF YOU AND ME.

"If I let you look at it, will you leave me alone?" he asks, and I furrow my brows.

"Asshole," I mumble.

"Not trying to be," It sounds like he replies through his teeth, and I pull him further into the hall, and toward one of the bathrooms.

I yank open the door and don't notice anyone inside so I pull him toward the counter.

"Just let me see if you're okay in this lighting," I tell him quietly.

I push myself on the counter.

"It's fine. I told you it's not a big deal," his voice is gruff.

He's being such a guy right now. A grumpy, moody man. I roll my eyes, and grab his hand, pulling him toward me. He nestles right between my legs, and I ignore just how intimate it feels. I'm helping him, then he's gone. Nothing else is going to happen. I'm deciding now that no matter how attractive he is, I can't make this mistake. Bellamy would be so angry. Even so, who knows if he's really interested. Part of me thinks I made this all up in my head. Or that he's more intoxicated than he's letting on which is why he's remotely looking at me like he is right now.

"You don't look fine," I tell him matter-of-factly.

I reach for his face, and he lets me this time. I stare up at his face, and brush his hair from his forehead, taking a wet paper towel to dab on his harsh cut. He sucks in a sharp breath between his teeth, and I press my lips together in a grimace. His eyes watch me like I'm the only thing that exists, and I'm pretending like it's not affecting me. I slow my movements and he stares at me so intently that I can't focus on anything but his eyes, then his lips. He hesitates but inches his face forward. My heart feels like it's about to explode. Like there's nothing that can keep it in my chest until we hear someone clear their throat.

Parker inches back, and to my horror, Lawson and Sienna both walk out of a bathroom stall.

"We were just..." Parker starts, but Lawson isn't having it.

I'm sure he's about to go play babysitter and tattle tale to my brother.

"Don't care. I didn't see anything, and this is a really shitty situation for all four of us. I didn't see you guys, you didn't see us," Lawson interrupts.

Lawson grabs Sienna's hand, and his eyes drift between Parker and me. I feel embarrassment creep up on my cheeks. This is like my own brother walking in on me. I've known Lawson for years... Parker and I weren't actually doing anything but I still feel caught. Lawson turns away, then stops himself, and I prepare myself for him to be angry. Not that he has any right. Nothing was happening, no matter what it looked like.

"And I would be a fucking dick not to warn the two of you that whatever the fuck you're doing could hurt Bellamy. And that it could also be a really shitty idea for the team Parks," he tells us, once again making me feel like a child.

That's Bellamy and Lawson's specialty. I'm not going to deal with this for the next year. The two of them sticking their head where it doesn't belong. Brothers or not, I can make my own choices.

"Nothing is going on. Forget it, Lawson, and stay out of my shit."

I push off the counter and then push past him. I was telling myself that nothing was going to happen. For someone like Lawson to act like a kiss is life-altering and world-ending is hilarious considering his track record. He has no room to speak on who I do and don't kiss. No one does.

Either way, I never even got the chance to stop the kiss before it started... If that's what was even happening. I don't know and I don't want to think about it. I want to leave. So I

THE RULES OF YOU AND ME.

search the bar, and when my eyes land on Dakota who is searching like a madman with his eyes until they land on me, I feel relief. We both surge toward each other, and he grabs my shoulders.

"Are you okay? Where did you go?" he asks, and I shake my head.

"I'll tell you later. Do you... Are you leaving with someone or—"

"You. I'm leaving with you. Are you ready? You can stay at my place tonight," he asks, and I nod.

He hooks his arm over my shoulders, and we leave, not another word exchanged with anyone else. Thank God.

CHAPTER 4
MOTIVE BY ARIANA GRANDE

Parker Thompson:

The way Seattle Pike University is set up makes me feel like I'm walking through multiple different universes to get where I need to go. To get from the football stadium to my apartment, I walk through the main part of campus where the science and math buildings are. I have to walk through the main fountain where a giant Hornet statue is showcased in the middle. I make sure to avoid the south side of campus, which means I have to walk west past the dorms, and straight through fraternity row. A street of frat houses that look perfect on the outside but I know are disgusting the second you walk through the doors. After I make it past all the frats, I am onto the final route. I tunnel north and end up at my apartment which is still considered student housing but is exponentially cheaper than what most people pay here.

I walk up the stairs all the way to the fourth floor, no elevator in sight. I walk through the messy hallway, cluttered with doormats, and trash cans overflowing with trash that the apartment building still hasn't collected. I sigh, making it to my

THE RULES OF YOU AND ME.

door. There are four papers stuck to the door by our hall manager, someone that's placed in our hall to keep us in line that does nothing to actually help any problems we have. The only thing she's done is this—make little paper stickers for our door. There are three hockey sticks crossed with each of my roommates' names—Xander, Nico, Andrew, then me. Parker. Instead of a set of hockey sticks, I have a football with a helmet. *How cute.*

I unlock the door and walk inside to complete chaos. My roommates have turned the living room into a makeshift hockey rink. Our apartment isn't even slightly big enough to be considered for this kind of sport, or for three grown men wearing rollerblades.

"Out of the way!" Nico yells.

I move out of the doorway as he barrels through it and out into the hallway. I didn't want to live with football players. I was paired together with Alexander for my freshman year in a dorm. Then, sophomore year, we all moved into this apartment together. I'm not sure why I thought hockey players would be any better than football. They're louder, bigger, and much more annoying. I keep my eyes down and walk past all of my roommates.

"Who shit in your cornflakes, Parks?" Xander asks, rollerblading in front of me.

He continues to rollerblade backward down our hall as I walk toward my door.

"No one," I grumble.

"Parker is always pissy, Xander. You know that," Drew states from the living room.

"What Drew said," I reply.

"You're never pissy with me, Thompson. What is it? Do you need a nap?" Xander stands in front of my door, spreading his arms out so I can't go in.

37

"A nap. Quiet roommates. I'll take either," I fake a smile and he scoffs.

"Grump," he mumbles, skating out of my way and around me.

"Try not to put any more holes in our walls," I tell them.

We're never getting our security deposit back. I close my door tight, wishing it was soundproof. We got this apartment for its privacy and space. Though it's not big enough for hockey practice, the shared living room space is pretty big. There's a connected kitchen and we all share a bathroom. It's set up like a dorm would be—you walk in and there are shower stalls, as well as three separate toilets and three separate mirrors. We all have our own bedrooms. They're not big enough for much but they do have space for just what we need.

My bedroom has a full-sized bed, a desk, and a single nightstand. I also keep a mini fridge in here with a microwave on top despite that it's a fire hazard. I have a closet, and inside, I have a dresser with drawers, but other than that, there's nothing. I read online somewhere that this place would feel more like home if I got decorations so, my sophomore year, I bought a pillow with the words "Yes you can!" written in script. On the wall behind my bed is a small triangular SPU flag I got at orientation. That about sums up the decor. My comforter is light blue, my room is clean, and I keep it just like this at all times. It's too small for me to let it get messy. I think I did pretty well considering I didn't have any help.

I throw my bag in my chair and kick off my shoes. I grab my towel and go into the bathroom across the hall. I strip down and shower in the lukewarm water, not waiting for it to get scorching hot. After I get the sweat from the gym off of me, I get out and wrap a towel around my body. I leave the bathroom and go back into my room, ignoring the reckless commotion coming from the living room. I get dressed once again in sweatpants and a hoodie,

THE RULES OF YOU AND ME.

my hair wet but pushed back and off of my face. I grab the book I'm required to read before classes start next week and open it. Not even two seconds into it, my phone vibrates multiple times. I contemplate ignoring it but get another text, and just from a small glance, I see it's from Bellamy so I pick up my phone. I haven't really seen him outside of our summer football practices besides when we all went to Haven a week ago. Since I almost kissed his sister... I look at the group message the idiots started and sigh.

Bellamy A: PARKY POO!!!

Lawson B: Parker mother fucking Thompson.

I SIGH at the texts between the three of us. Bellamy seems like the type to keep people around. Socially, he needs others to thrive. His tight-knit group was Lawson and Griffin, but after last week, Griffin is now gone. Bellamy and Lawson seem to want a new third member to join their party. I was acquainted with the trio but never close with them and I don't like pity invites. I also don't like feeling like I need to question people's intentions. I have no idea what Bellamy's are and being added into a group chat with these two... I don't know how I feel about it, especially considering I'm the opposite of Bellamy. I'm the one who strays away from a social situation. When I'm on the field, I wish I could wear earplugs so I don't have to hear the fans or the coaches. It would make my life a lot easier and a lot less stressful. I tap out a response quickly.

Hey.

Lawson B: "Hey" You're so boring.

Bellamy A: Lawson fuck off hes being mysterious leave him be

Lawson B: Okay, he can be mysterious around the ladies, but not us. We're his friends. Also, would it kill you to use correct punctuation?

Bellamy A: I'm texting so why would I need correct punctuation. Im going to incorrectly punctuate just to piss you off;

Did you guys need something?

Bellamy A: "Yeah" you should come over? Because! We're hanging out and I bet your roommates are being loud,

THE RULES OF YOU AND ME.

Lawson B: Your so annoying.

Bellamy A: You're*

Can't. I'm studying for classes.

Lawson B: Okay, well now you're coming to Bellamy and Lawson's apartment.

Bellamy A: I will show up to your place and stand outside of your window until you come over

I SIGH and push my reading off of my lap. There's no point in saying no because Bellamy truly would come to my apartment. He's persistent. I'm assuming he feels like he has to be my friend because of my position on the field. I get it, he wants us to mesh well, but I don't need him to pity me. Bellamy, Lawson, and I played together fine the last two years I've been at SPU. Now with the head receiver gone, I've moved up in rank on this team which means I've moved up in social status too. Lawson doesn't seem like the type to pity me, but he also doesn't seem like he really cares as long as it's a good time. I gather my shit and head out. Bellamy and Lawson's apartment is on the west side of campus which is on the nicer side of town. It's where most of the well-off students live.

"Where are you going?" Nico asks.

"Parker, why don't you hang out with us tonight? We're going to order pizza and—"

"I'm going to Bellamy's apartment. Sorry," I reply, and Xander wiggles his eyebrows at me.

"Didn't Brianne Archer, his hot sister, move in a few days ago? Is that why you're going over?" he asks and I glare at him.

"No. Brianne Archer is not the reason I'm going over there. Stop talking about her," I tell him.

I didn't even tell them what happened between Brianne and I, mostly because I knew they, especially Xander, would never shut the fuck up about it. Also, because nothing happened. Something almost happened and it shouldn't have, she obviously seemed hesitant. So, it's a good thing it didn't.

"Why? Because you two were making sex eyes at Haven a week ago?" Nico asks and I sigh.

"I was drinking and you're an idiot. Don't bring up Brianne Archer to me," I tell the three of them. "And don't bring her up to anyone else either. The last thing I need is a fucking problem."

Nico raises his hands in innocence.

It's true. I don't want problems. I was just... overwhelmed. She came out of nowhere looking drop-dead gorgeous. Not only that but she was the first and only person who's ever... noticed my discomfort. She picked up on it in a single second... Those few words, 'Are you okay?' Never have I heard them before in a situation like that and even if I've heard something resembling them, never has anyone sounded so concerned like she was. It

THE RULES OF YOU AND ME.

was... new. It was overwhelming. All of my roommates are staring at me.

"Just don't fucking bring it up, alright?" I ask them.

Nico and Andrew at least try to hide their amusement. Xander just shows his shit-eating grin anyway.

"Alright, Parks, say less," Andrew says.

I press my lips together and leave the apartment. My roommates might annoy the shit out of me, but they aren't bad people. They aren't going to cause problems for me, especially problems that have no reason to be started. Brianne Archer is off-limits... until she's not. Until she makes it apparent that she's not. I'm not looking for a hookup. I wouldn't be opposed to a girlfriend but I also don't think I have it in me to try and get one —to open myself up or take the time to get to know another person when half the time it feels like I don't even know myself. She's... interesting, though. She's someone to watch. But is she too interesting for me? I don't do much. I'm not much at all.

The look on her face when I stopped that douchebag hockey player from making a move on her—defiance and fire in her eyes—there's something about her that interests me. But she seemed hesitant. I might have been drinking at the time, but if it wasn't for her pulling away, I would have kissed the girl. Stupid or not, I'd still kiss her but I'm not going to actively go after her. Lawson's words play in my head anytime I've thought about it this past week—that it's a bad idea for the team. He's right. Which means it's a bad idea for my future, and my potential to be drafted next year. My senior year. To win The Heisman... I'd be one of the only people who's not a quarterback to achieve the award, but I have the stats. I have the skill... That's also why I don't have a girlfriend. Nothing can get in the way of what I've done to get myself where I am. Not even a girl.

My walk was uneventful, but the second I open the door to

Bellamy and Lawson's apartment, I'm greeted with screaming and yelling. Feels just like my own apartment.

"You're really going to look at me and tell me that mermaids don't fucking exist?" Bellamy raises his voice at Lawson who sits across from him at the island in the center of their kitchen. Bellamy is standing with his hands out, anger coursing through him visibly.

"I never said they didn't exist, dipshit. I said the probability of merpeople existing over Bigfoot is unlikely. It's fucking Bigfoot," Lawson argues back.

"The probability of merpeople existing over bigfoot is—Oh, grow up, Lawson. Bigfoot doesn't exist. You're telling me a giant man that lives in the woods hasn't been fucking discovered yet? He'd be hard to fucking miss, don't you think?" Bellamy yells.

"Are you fucking kidding? People have spotted Bigfoot. He hasn't gone undiscovered because there's proof he exists. In the wild! And it's not just one person, it's a species which makes the probability more likely. We literally live in Seattle, dude, woods everywhere and you're going to tell me there's no bigfoot out there?"

"Merpeople haven't been discovered yet because they're smaller and slippery. Do you know how much of the ocean hasn't been explored yet? Have you seen Aquaman?"

His first point was valid but the second was complete idiocy.

"THAT'S FUCKING FICTIONAL!" Lawson stands up, screaming at the top of his lungs.

I slam the door hard, hopefully announcing my presence.

"Hey guys..." I speak out and they both look at me.

Bellamy smiles and Lawson gives a small wave.

"Hey, Parky," Bellamy speaks first.

"Hey, Parks," Lawson chimes after.

"I just think that you don't have enough evidence to back up

THE RULES OF YOU AND ME.

what you're saying," Bellamy goes straight back into the argument, and I sigh, walking toward both of them, standing between the two of them.

"Evidence? I have way more evidence than you do. Have you heard of this thing called fucking Google? Read a fucking book, dude," Lawson crosses his arms and leans back into the high-top chair.

"Maybe you're both right, and they both exist... What about Vampires? Werewolves?" I ask.

"No chance," Bellamy tells me.

"There's no way," Lawson shrugs me off.

I stare between the two of them, wondering if they're serious.

"And either way, it's not about if they're both real, it's about which one is more likely to exist over the other. Bigfoot," Lawson tells me and I nod.

"Got it," I nod.

"Anyway, were you really going to spend your night at home doing nothing?" Bellamy asks me. I shrug.

"I went to the gym earlier," I tell him. They both look at me like I'm crazy. "What? Don't both of you have girlfriends to fill your time? Why do you care where I am?" I ask, shoving my hands in my hoodie pocket.

"Our girlfriends are hanging out tonight and we weren't invited. That's beside the point. We still do other things that don't involve them or football, like video games. Or drinking. Lawson reads books and we go out, and... and we do college. You don't do college," Bellamy tells me.

I roll my eyes.

"I do college just fine," I tell him.

"You haven't been sexually involved with anyone in the past three years, have you?" Lawson asks, and I look at him blankly.

45

I look at Bellamy and he raises his eyebrows, waiting for me to answer. I already wish I never came over here.

"He's right. You haven't gotten laid, have you?" Bellamy asks, crossing his arms.

"Why would I talk about my sex life with either of you?" I ask them.

"Because, we're your friends, and friends talk about sex stuff. I had sex last night. Lawson?" Bellamy looks to his friend.

"This morning," he tells both of us. They look at me.

"Doesn't matter. Maybe I'm not into the whole hookup thing," I tell them.

Yes, it has, in fact, been a while. For lack of trying, because I don't want mess and problems. I don't need to waste time getting to know people. I wouldn't want to, there's no point. Every part of our lives is in segments. College is a segment and all of us are going to go separate ways. Attachments aren't worth the hassle. Hookups aren't worth the mess. I'm not necessarily opposed but I'm not seeking it out. I'm not going to put excessive effort into it when no one usually puts that kind of effort into me either. My mind drifts to Brianne before I snap myself back. *What am I thinking? Her brother is right here...*

"Spill your guts, Parker. One year? Two?" Lawson asks.

"Probably freshman year? Maybe? I don't remember, and it doesn't matter," I admit to both of them.

I do remember. It was my freshman year and it was a mistake. Like I said, it turned into a mess. They always do.

"You not remembering is a problem, Parky. Sex is good, sex is a stress reliever, and you my friend are always stressed, and all panicky and alone. And you're grumpy. And on the field you get super angry and stuff," Bellamy tells me.

Like he even slightly knows me. I've never opened up. He knows nothing about me. He has no room to make these claims.

THE RULES OF YOU AND ME.

"Why does how I am and who I fuck matter to either of you?" I ask them.

I feel uncomfortable with the conversation, mostly because I have no idea if this is normal. Do guys talk about shit like this with each other? Or are Bellamy and Lawson weird?

"Wow, you have got it all wrong. I don't care who you fuck, I don't want to know, neither does Bell," Lawson tells me and Bellamy shakes his head.

"I don't want to know, he's right," Bellamy agrees, smiling his normal goofy smile like he always does. "But I care about you and the team, and I feel like all of your college experience has been inside of one box, and maybe you should potentially step outside of the box. There are no rules in college. It's about experiencing things, figuring shit out, messing up, and doing whatever feels good for you. I feel like you should totally do that this year."

I nod. I've never really been given advice from a friend because I don't know who I actually consider friends and not friends. I don't think I even understand the word myself. I've never really considered these two in front of me as friends. Just teammates.

"That's part of why we wanted you to come over tonight," Lawson tells me.

"Why, to tell me I'm a loser who doesn't get laid?" I ask and he rolls his eyes.

"No. But you are a loser who doesn't get laid..." he tells me and I glare at him.

"We asked you to come over because we wanted to ask you something that's kind of a big deal. So big that we convinced Coach Corbin to let us talk to you about it instead of him," Bellamy tells me, and I furrow my eyebrows.

That's ominous and kind of terrifying. I shake my head, waiting for someone to talk.

47

"You know there's always at least three Team Captains, and with Griffin gone this year, we need to fill his spot. Normally, it would go to a senior, but since you took our last captain's role on the field, we think it's a perfect time to move you up. You went from 2nd to 1st on the team so you deserve this because not only can you do it, but you need the confidence boost. The team will need a leader for next year, someone that's going to run the field. There's not a single senior that will be starting quarterback, it's probably going to go to that sophomore Samson," Bellamy explains.

I know the guy in the same position as Bellamy. He's got a lot of work to do but he's really good.

"I have confidence," I tell them.

"No, my friend, you do not. You have the confidence of a teddy bear. Which is weird considering you're grumpy and moody all the time. Are you sleeping enough?" Lawson asks, and I sigh.

"That's beside the point. Lawsy is right. You don't have the confidence on the field. You kick ass, your stats are off the fucking charts, Parky. But you act like you're nothing special when you've basically got a one-way ticket to the NFL after you graduate. You could even win The Heisman which is crazy considering you're not a quarterback," Bellamy tells me.

My chest tightens at the words. It's all I've ever wanted. Since I learned what the award was, I told myself I'd win it one day.

"All I'm saying is you deserve the spot, and you have the talent to be a little cocky sometimes. You never do a touchdown dance or celebration when you scored plenty last year, and you weren't even a first-string WR then. Parker, this is your year, take it," Bellamy tells me.

"Will you be our team captain buddy?" Lawson asks, and I nod, pushing down the excitement so I can play it off cool.

THE RULES OF YOU AND ME.

"Yeah, of course I will," I agree. "But I don't know what that has to do with me getting laid?" I roll the conversation back and Lawson pinches the bridge of his nose.

"It's like talking to a child," he mumbles to himself.

"It's about confidence. When you're getting laid, you're getting boosted. Plus you're in college, you need to act like it," Bellamy tells me.

Sex doesn't equal being in college in my head, but I guess Bellamy, Lawson, and I all have different definitions of what college is really about.

"So, using a girl for a confidence boost?" I ask them and both of them get defensive.

"No. Absolutely not," Bellamy cuts his hands through the air.

"Never use anyone unless it's a mutual benefit. You're not using said girl to boost your confidence without her knowledge. I've had sex to boost my confidence. Usually with a confident, badass woman themself, but I made sure that they knew this was just that. A small moment in our big lives," Lawson tells me.

"So don't use her without her knowledge. Platonically use her?" I ask.

"You're missing the point. It's not about necessarily hooking up. If you want to date someone, do that. Friends with benefits is an option. I love having a girlfriend. I've always been more of a relationship guy. It's about your preference," Bellamy tells him.

"Remember when we all used to say YOLO? You only live once?" Lawson asks, and I raise my eyebrows at him.

"Are you about to unironically tell me YOLO?" I ask him, and he nods.

"I am. Parker Thompson. You only do college once, do it right. Get laid, go to parties, go out to bars, hang out with us. We're awesome." He motions to Bellamy and himself. I nod.

"Whatever you say."

49

This is the easiest way to get them to quit. I don't want to get close to them or anyone else for that matter. Once again, disappointment is not something I'm a fan of. That's exactly what all of the things they're suggesting would lead to... even if the thought is somewhat inviting. The thought of having someone else warming my bed right beside me.

"Promise. Just try some stuff, have fun. I want to see you let loose this year. I'm hoping my sister does the same, and I gave her similar advice. You've been here for two years and this is your third, it's time for you to have fun," he tells me, and I nod with a sigh.

I can try. Trying is not promising. It's not saying yes. It's halfhearted.

"I'll promise to do whatever if you promise to end this conversation," I tell him, and he nods.

"Deal. Can we watch The Barbie Movie?" Bellamy asks, and I furrow my brows.

"Isn't that a girl movie?" I ask him.

"Movies don't have genders, first of all, and if you haven't watched it, you have to. It's actually really funny," Lawson tells me, and I realize now I have no room to argue, and I honestly don't care enough to. A movie is a movie, maybe I'll like it.

I'M NOT surprised Bellamy cried. He's a softie. I didn't but I did get that warm fuzzy feeling in my chest. It was good, I'll give it to Bellamy and Lawson. They were right.

"Okay, I have to go to bed or I won't make it to practice tomorrow on time," I admit.

I'm the type who doesn't do well without an obscene amount of sleep the night before.

"And you're going to have fun, and do fun things, and live

THE RULES OF YOU AND ME.

your life to the fullest?" Bellamy asks as he walks toward his bedroom.

"Yes, I will."

I shake my head, not knowing how, where, or who I will start with, but I will have to figure it out if I want him off of my back. I said I would try. I never said I would try really hard. Maybe if something pops up. Maybe if something falls into my lap... but it still feels like I'd be using someone. I don't want to do that. If I want anything, I want a connection. I want to be drawn to someone. I want them to want me first. Saying all of that feels foreign to even my own thoughts, but it's true, even if I don't like admitting that.

"Goodnight! Get laid!" Lawson tells me as he walks up the stairs in their apartment.

I walk myself to the front door as Lawson walks into his bedroom. They told me to get laid like it's easy. Who? If I'm going to have fun with someone, if I'm going to do what they say, and potentially start something with someone, I have no idea about who it should be, or where I should start. You have to be social to get laid and I'm the opposite of that, and don't want to change that. I'm not going to go out on my own volition. Invitations will be required.

I open the door and someone runs straight into my chest. I look down to see Brianne. She's smiling, her lips curving around her teeth. Her cheeks are perfectly rosy and bright, what I've come to know as the drunk glow that girls get. I stare down at her, and her lips part, the smile disappearing as she looks up at me. She's just as pretty now as she was the night in Haven. Not surprising.

"Hi," I say to her, her hands still on my chest.

"H-hi," she mumbles quietly.

She's perfect. Blue eyes, perfect lips, rosy cheeks, and the sweetest fucking voice. She's a bad idea wrapped in the most

51

irresistible package. I put my hand on her hip and nudge her slightly, her boyfriend approaching behind her. He'd be a problem—the only problem I'm seeing in pursuing Bellamy's sister. Like I said, I don't want to chase. I don't want to put in severe effort to get to know someone if they aren't willing. It feels like it might be easier to get to know Brianne. I feel like I already know her partially. She's already made the effort to care about me, even if it was a small thing... This could be a huge mistake but...

"Hey," her boyfriend speaks behind her.

"Parker, have you met Dakota?" she asks me, and I shake my head, holding my hand out to him.

"Nice to meet you," I say.

Shaking the hand of the guy whose girlfriend I want for myself... That's horrible for me to think about, but it doesn't stop my thoughts. Not even slightly. Yeah, this is a bad idea but I don't think I care.

"Same to you. Let's go, baby," he speaks, guiding her by her back.

I don't let my eyes roam, but I do let my mind wander. Maybe Bellamy is right. Maybe I should try something new... I don't think he meant his sister, but he also never said not to. Only if she bites first. If she does then... Then maybe I'll bite back. Maybe.

CHAPTER 5
DREAMS BY CAROL ADES

Brianne Archer:

My first day of classes couldn't have gone any better if I wanted it to. I jump down the cement stairs of the stadium and onto the field. I was wearing a cuter outfit to begin my day, but I've traded that in now for some dance clothes—a light pink pair of tights and a black leotard. I traded my pointe shoes for a pair of short UGG boots that are my go-to when I go to and from dance class. My hair is wound tight into a perfect bun and I'm wearing a sheer black ballet skirt on top of my leo to cover myself.

"Nice outfit, Bri," Lawson calls out to me as he walks with two of his teammates who are not my brother.

I give him a fake smile and then flash my middle finger.

"I came from dance, asshole. Where is my brother? He told me to meet him here," I ask, crossing my arms over my chest.

"I think he was the last one in the locker room," one of the guys next to Lawson tells me.

"They were cleared out. You can go back there and knock on the locker room. I'm sure he's there, he was on the phone with Kam when I walked out," Lawson tells me.

"Cool, thanks," I give a real smile now and walk away from them toward the underbelly of the stadium.

"Did you have a good first day?" Lawson calls after me.

He's walking backward, looking at me.

"Perfect!" I call back.

He throws a thumbs up in my direction and smiles at me. I'm left feeling thankful for my built-in second brother asking how things went. I love Lawson so much more than I let on. I can't wait to tell Bellamy about the day I had too. How much I loved all my classes, how scary but amazing my dance professor is. I love it here already and it's only the first day.

I walk into the underground hallways of the stadium and take a left instead of a right for the boy's locker room. The girl's are in the opposite direction for the cheer team, which is where I'm used to headed. I knock on the door and peek my head inside.

"Belly?" I call out and hear nothing in response. "Bellamy!" I shout to him but still hear nothing.

I decide to make my way in. There's no view of anything from the door as there's a giant slab of cubbies blocking my view. I turn the corner around them and run straight into not just anyone, but a naked, wet someone. I try to keep myself upright and hard hands stabilize me by my shoulders. My hands brush the naked chest in front of me. My lips make an O, my shock more than present as I look up to find Parker Thompson staring down at me. The only thing on him is shock and a very low-hanging towel.

It takes me two seconds. Two fucking seconds to see him before I feel heat spread throughout my body. Not only because I'm embarrassed but because he is... He's so gorgeous.

His perfectly trimmed facial hair is short and kept. His hair is wet and slicked back except for a few loose curls that are hanging over his forehead and around his strong face. Every line

THE RULES OF YOU AND ME.

of his body is perfect, rigid, and muscular. His jaw, his nose, his high cheekbones. His cheeks are slightly flushed from what I'm assuming was a hot shower. Shower. SHOWER! Parker is naked, covered only with a towel, and I'm standing here staring at the man like I want him to undress me and take me into the fucking locker room. I tell myself not to but just thinking about it makes my eyes flip down. His chest is perfect and so is the hard V that leads exactly where my mind wants to be. Speaking of, he has a tattoo. One I would never have known about unless I saw him like this. It's a fern on the right side of his body, curving over his hip, and diving below the towel out of sight. I slap my hand over my eyes and step out of his grip.

"Oh my god. I'm so sorry," I mumble as quickly as I can.

I move as fast as possible and almost topple over the sports equipment on the floor. I don't care if I fall. The only words tumbling through my mind are RUN! LEAVE! ESCAPE!

"Be careful...Brianne—"

I don't wait another second to hear any more of his words as I walk into the hallway. I take my hands off of my eyes and cover my mouth. *Oh my god.* Oh my fucking god! That was so embarrassing. I not only almost walked in on him naked, but I also unashamedly undressed that man with my eyes. That is my brother's friend and... Bellamy is going to freak out. He's going to be pissed because Parker will probably tell him that his little sister was... This is so bad. And on my first day of college? I need Dakota, but no. I can't tell him either. I sit in a chair across from the door and decide the only logical thing to do is wait and apologize profusely until he has no choice but to forgive me.

I need to think logically about this. Parker Thompson and I have had only a few interactions. All of which have been a little awkward but also tense and not in a weird way. Tense in the way that I don't know if I want to kiss him or run away. First was the day we met when he almost took me down on the beach at

55

the bonfire. He caught me and I couldn't have made up us locking eyes. I did not make up the way his defenses fell. I saw how pretty his eyes were. How kissable his lips were. But we were in public so we backed away quicker than we fell together. I didn't make that up, even Dakota noticed that happen.

Then there was two weeks ago at the bar for Griffin's going away party. He approached me. Yes, in a weird annoying way that all football players do where they try to protect me so that they get brownie points with my brother. At least that's what I originally thought, until he sought me out later on and he looked at me like... like he was really looking at me. Like he saw something that wasn't a little sister, but a person. A woman. I would have fallen victim to that look if it wasn't for the fight that broke out around us. So... So after both of those things, those two instances where he obviously looked at me in a way that wasn't necessarily friendly, is he really going to run to my brother? Are the two of them as close as I think they are or am I just faking myself out?

I shake my leg for what feels like a million minutes and I bite my thumbnail aggressively as I do. I'm going to be the laughingstock of the football team and the cheer team when everyone finds out that I walked into the freaking locker room. I stand up and pace in front of the door, switching thumbs, gnawing on the other one now. I need to talk to Dak. Screw my earlier plan, he's what will help me through this. I open my phone and click his contact.

"What's up, Baby?" he speaks in a calm tone and I groan into the phone. "Ow. Warning before you break my eardrums next time. What happened?"

"I'm the biggest idiot to ever exist, Dak. I was supposed to meet Bellamy at the

stadium and I ran right into someone else who wasn't my

THE RULES OF YOU AND ME.

brother and…" I hear the door creak open, and I turn as quickly as I can.

Parker stands in the doorway, staring at me. His eyes rove up and down until they land on my eyes. I shut my mouth right away.

"And then what? Who did you run into? Earth to Bri," Dakota talks on the phone and I stumble on my words.

"I gotta go. Come over tonight when I get home. Love you, bye," I hang up before he can answer.

"Your boyfriend?" Parker asks.

"Parker, I am so—Wait, my what?" I ask.

My brother obviously thinks that Dakota is my boyfriend because he's around but… Why would Parker think that? Is Bellamy really talking to him about it? Or do people just assume guys and girls can't be friends without wanting to sleep together?

"Dakota, the guy I met the other day. I'm assuming that was him on the phone," he asks me and I sigh.

"Not you too. Dakota is not my boyfriend. He's my best friend. We are not interested in each other like that," I tell Parker and he nods his head.

"I definitely thought you two were dating… You seem close," he tells me and I shrug.

I don't know how he is always so calm and chilled out, especially after a very un-chill situation.

"He's attractive, I have eyes, I can definitely see that, but if we were to ever get involved it would make things too complicated. He's my stunt partner and he would drive me crazy if he was my boyfriend. He makes a way better best friend. That's all he is and all he'll ever be. I keep trying to tell people that, but no one seems to want to listen," I explain, and he eyes me again, looking down at my clothes.

"Dancer?" he asks, completely bypassing the entire situation that just happened, and everything I just said.

"You're not going to say anything about what I just said?" I ask and he shakes his head.

"You said you weren't dating. I have no reason not to believe you. I also hate arguing with people," he explains and I sigh.

"Parker, I am so sorry. I should never have stepped inside that locker room. Lawson and some of your other teammates told me Bellamy was here and I called out and no one answered and I never should have done that. I can't believe how stupid I am, because how dumb can I be if I just walk into a men's locker room—"

"Hey Brianne..." His voice is calm as he stops my rambling.

"I'm sorry, did I say too much?" I ask, turning my face toward him.

He's looking at his feet as we walk but I don't miss the way his lips twitch into a soft smile as he looks down. Unfriendly thoughts are what's coursing through my head. I'm being unreasonable. I'm being absolutely crazy.

"No. I just don't think there's a reason for you to be panicking right now... It's not a big deal," he tells me and I open my mouth to talk, but then close it right away.

"It's... It's... not a big deal? I walked in on you naked and I... You're giving me the easy way out of this so I need to stop babbling," I tell myself more than him.

"Never said that. Everything is fine, Brianne. Small accident, we'll keep it between us," he tells me and I nod.

Keep it between us. Meaning he's not running to my brother. He's not whispering in his ear...

"Thank you. I'm so embarrassed. Honestly, I just thought Bell would be here and... and I'm just sorry. Now we can forget about it," I tell him.

He hums in agreement. He keeps his eyes forward and then

THE RULES OF YOU AND ME.

says nothing more. *Man of very few words.* That's definitely what most people say about Parker. He doesn't have a lot to say. We head for the field and I pull out my phone to find a text from Bellamy telling me he had to go check on Kamryn because apparently she wasn't answering him, and to meet him back at the apartment. What I'm reading is that all of this could have been avoided. I sigh and shove my phone back into my messenger bag. I look at Parker who is saying nothing and avoiding eye contact with me.

"I am, by the way... A dancer, I mean," I tell him, breaking the silence.

"What kind?" He asks the question most people do.

"All kinds," I smile, clasping my hands in front of me as we walk up the stadium stairs.

My tight bun is starting to make my scalp ache which means it's time to let it down. I will, the second I'm in the car.

"What's your favorite, though?" he asks, and I hesitate, not normally getting asked more than the first question.

"Um... I prefer ballet. I like balance and routine but I also love contemporary style. Fluid motion and feeling everything. Feeling the music through all of you and moving to it is just... It's like therapy," I shrug, not wanting to start rambling.

"I've never met a dancer," he tells me, keeping his eyes forward as we step out of the stadium now.

"Well, now you have. Nice to meet you," I extend my hand and he takes it, lightly smiling for the first time.

Instead of shaking it, he lifts it, spinning me around in front of him. I do one twirl and end on his other side, laughing next to him.

"Be safe," he tells me, then heads in the opposite direction as me.

"Thanks..." I stand for only a second, watching him walk away before heading to my Jeep.

59

I chose it because my brother also drives a Jeep—the one our dad used to drive before he passed away. I've always wanted one, just like his. So I bought a used Jeep when I turned 18 with some of the money my parents left me after they passed away. Mine is still far newer than my brother's, but not brand new either.

I climb in and my eyes lock on Parker who is now across the parking lot, not going to a car, but continuing to walk. He might not have a car... and it would be so rude for me to let him walk all the way to wherever he's going. Although, it also seems like a horrible idea because I can't stop staring at him when he's within a few feet of me.

I can be an adult. I can be in the car with one of the hot football players. I'll have to be around him all season so this is no different. It's obvious we have a mutual attraction, at least from what I can tell. I can leave it at that. I can be mature about thinking he's hot.

He's my brother's friend. He was drinking the night at Haven. Nothing has happened between us. Nothing can happen between us. Nothing will happen between us. This is just a ride home. I repeat all these things a million times as I drive toward him, and stop beside him. He turns slightly, his eyes landing on me.

"I can take you to your place..." I tell him, and he hesitates. "Come on, get in."

I move my duffle out of my passenger seat and into the back. He walks toward my car, and opens the door, climbing in with ease. As he situates himself, I do the same, pulling the pins out of my hair, and tucking them between my teeth. I loosen the bun and take out the hair elastic, letting my long hair fall down my back. I sigh in relief, and take all of my bobby pins out. I reach behind me and tuck them in the side pocket of my duffle

THE RULES OF YOU AND ME.

before turning back in front. Parker is staring at me and I can feel heat crawl up my cheeks.

"Sorry, I get really bad headaches if I leave them in too long, even after all these years," I tell him, tucking my hair behind my ears.

I turn my playlist on and my music up only slightly so we can both hear it.

"Thank you for taking me home," he tells me and I nod.

I keep both my hands on the steering wheel as I pull away from the stadium. His eyes are like weights pressing down on me. *Mutual attraction.* He appreciates the way I look. I do the same for him—that's all it is. Nothing else.

"I'll take you home whenever. You'll just have to deal with my music taste," I laugh.

He reaches for the dial and turns the volume up a little more. The sound of Prayin' For Daylight by Rascal Flatts plays louder in my car now. He nods his head.

"Country?" he asks.

"Sorry," I shrug, not actually caring if he cares.

"I like it. Country music. Any music. I don't listen to it much so I don't really mind," he tells me.

"You don't listen to music? How?" I ask back, trying not to turn to him for an answer.

"I'm always around loud noisy guys and cheering crowds and... and I grew up around a lot of noisy kids and people all the time... I prefer quiet when I can get it," he explains and I nod.

I guess he has a lot of siblings.

"So if you were to listen to music, what would you choose?" I ask. He shrugs.

"I listen to music without lyrics a lot. Calming stuff, classical stuff... and if I'm in the mood, then I will listen to rock or metal music, usually when I'm at the gym or working out," he tells me.

"I listen to a lot of classical... because of ballet and stuff," I tell him and he nods.

"Does all the noise not bother you?" he asks and I shake my head.

"I prefer it. No matter what, I want music playing. Because... Well, music is like a universal language, you know? It's one of the only things that everyone understands in their own way. It's a way to communicate and involve groups of people. It's a way to feel things and it's so interesting. Someone can write their experience down, exactly how they feel after a breakup or death, or anything really, and there will always be someone out there who can relate. There will always be someone who wants to dance or sing or listen to it. I just think there's something so special about..." I let my voice drop off, realizing that I'm most likely saying way too much.

"What?" he asks and I shake my head.

"Nothing, you get it... I just like music," I tell him.

"You don't just like music, Brianne," he laughs and I feel heat cover my cheeks. I know I'm blushing.

"I know I was rambling. I've just always had such a connection to it, maybe it's because I've danced my whole life," I shrug.

Maybe it's because my mom and dad always played music when they were home. We had a speaker system wired through our entire house so we could listen to music as loud as we wanted. My mom always used to sing to Bellamy and me when we were younger, and not only that but when she went away with my dad for work... She always sent me new music, or old to listen to. Music reminded my mom of me, and that made me feel loved.

"I get it. Other people's love languages are words, or spending time together... Yours is music," he tells me, and I smile, glancing over at him as I drive.

THE RULES OF YOU AND ME.

His face is so cool and calm as if he didn't just say something that made my stomach erupt in butterflies. I nod slowly.

"Yeah, just like that. It reminds me of my mom because she said music reminded her of me. She sent it to me when she was thinking of me," I tell him quietly.

"Why country?" He asks.

I tell him everything. I tell him that I loved Taylor Swift when she did country and got into other country artists when I was young because of her. As I grew up, I never grew out of it, even if Taylor Swift did. He instructs me quietly on how to drive to his place while listening to every word I say intently. He doesn't interrupt. He doesn't interject, and most importantly, he doesn't make me feel stupid for speaking about something I care about... even if I do feel like I'm rambling. He even promises me he'll listen to some of the artists I recommend.

I park in front of his apartment and he grabs his bag. He looks at me and hesitates before turning to get out of the car. I don't leave, I just watch him go and he turns back to me. I roll the window down.

"Brianne..." He approaches my car again, a fearful glimmer in his eye.

I have no idea what it means, but I like it—the eagerness on his face.

"What's up?" I ask, trying to sound as cool as I can.

But I am anything but cool. Parker makes my brain go haywire.

"Do you want to get a coffee... or dinner, or... or anything?" he asks, and just stands, no expression on his face.

My jaw slightly hangs, complete confusion probably laced through my entire expression. *Pardon?* This was just mutual attraction. I thought it was. I thought he just... I thought...

"Why do you look so shocked?" he asks me, and I shake my head slightly.

63

"You... You're..." I stumble on what to say. *Is he crazy? Or did he hit his head?*

"I'm? What?" he asks and I shake my head.

Maybe I'm the crazy one for not just saying yes?

"Nothing... I'd... I'd love to..." I admit. "Let me get my first week under my belt... My birthday is this weekend so I just... I've got a lot going on, but yes. I'd love to," I smile with closed lips.

He leans into my window, his large arms hanging into my car. He passes me his cell phone and I type in my phone number, still shocked. No fucking way is this happening. I was so wrong...

"When is your birthday?" he asks.

"Friday," I tell him.

"Friday... That's our first official game," he tells me, and I nod.

"The perfect way to celebrate. I think we might be doing something small afterward at my apartment. I'm sure you'll be there... with my brother," I add on, not wanting to ruin anything by mentioning him. Parker nods, with no hint of regret on his features.

"I'll see you later, Brianne," he nods, his eyes scanning my face before he backs out of the window, and turns away from me. I have no idea how to go about what the fuck just happened. I do know I can't talk to Bellamy about it. Not yet, maybe not ever. This could be very bad, but I feel really good about it anyway.

CHAPTER 6

GIRL WITH A PROBLEM BY AMY ALLEN

Brianne Archer:

Bellamy drives us back home from our childhood house and I sit with my head touching the window despite the chill it gives me. I keep quiet as Taylor Swift plays over the speakers. When it's just me and Bellamy, it's always Taylor Swift. He can say it's because of me, but I know he loves her just as much as I do at this point, especially now that he has a girlfriend who loves her too. Part of me knows he plays it this much around me because he knows it will make me feel more comfortable. Bellamy turns the volume down and nudges me with his elbow.

"Talk to me, B." He's soft with his words. I press a smile to my lips.

"I'm okay. Really, I can talk to Madeline about it this week," I tell him, mentioning my therapist to him.

I've only been seeing her this past year, but so far, I feel like everything we've worked through has stuck. I haven't been able to attend any of our video appointments the past two weeks because life has been too hectic, but I warned her it would be that way when I moved. I have a lot to update her on. I wonder if I should even mention Parker to her... She doesn't have to know.

"But I should also be there for you, B. I can listen. I might not be a licensed therapist and my advice might be shitty, but I can still be here," he tells me and I nod.

"I just get sad sometimes. It's normal to be sad," I admit.

The last thing I need is for Bellamy to worry about me. He goes into spiral mode when he thinks I'm not okay. I remember his sophomore year, I had a really bad episode. I was going through a rough time with an ex and I wanted my mom and... Bellamy wouldn't leave my grandparent's house, where I still lived, for a week. He refused. I don't need him doing that again.

"You miss Mom and Dad?" he asks and I nod.

"Always," I admit reluctantly.

Even when I do, I try not to bring them up to Bellamy. I know it affects him and I don't need to make his life harder. It's his senior year and he has a lot riding on this football season.

"Me too." He reaches over the console and grabs my hand.

He squeezes and I squeeze back. He doesn't normally play into conversations like this. I don't think he's told me he misses them in years. He coped with our loss easier than I did. He's still dealing with it better than I am all these years later.

"It's unfair," I say out loud and I feel selfish saying it.

I know there are worse things. Worse things could be happening to me and worse things are happening to other people all over the world. It's selfish to be upset but I am.

"It is but I know this is what they would want, for us to be together here at SPU," he tells me and I nod.

"They would. Mom and dad never talked to me about college, but I know that they knew you wanted to go here. I hope they imagined us here together," I tell him.

"I'm sure they did." He offers me a smile and I sigh.

"Is Kamryn coming over tonight?" I ask him and he nods.

THE RULES OF YOU AND ME.

"She's already over at our place. Sienna is with Lawson and I'm sure he's ready for us to be home so Kamryn will give him his girlfriend back," he tells me and I smile at the thought.

"I'm glad you have Kamryn," I tell him.

"I am too..."

I see that look in his eyes—that look that you see in the movies on the guy's face when you can just tell how in love he is. It's how I wish someone would look at me. Bellamy has always been a lover, he's always been a romantic but he's never had a girl give him exactly what he deserves and I know Kamryn is giving him that. I know she's exactly what he needs because I can see that she looks at him the same exact way.

I'm glad too because every week when he would come home to tutor me, I would never hear the end of it from him about her. I swear I thought my ears were going to fall off.

"I'm glad you have Dakota, but speaking of, I figured we could talk about that," he adds and I furrow my brows.

"If you're trying to have the sex talk with me, Gam already did, and either way, I'm not a virgin," I tell him and he cringes.

"I'm well aware... I almost got in a fight with that Ryland kid when you two broke up because of it... If you don't remember," he speaks sarcastically.

"Oh yeah, then what?" I ask, turning to my brother.

"I know you're in college now. I'm trusting you to make smart choices and I can't tell you not to have your boyfriend over because that would make me a hypocrite, but if you do choose to have sex with him, please don't be... loud."

He looks more than uncomfortable talking about it and I cringe as well.

"Dakota and me—"

"Are really cute... But I don't want to know. Just like you really don't want to know the details about me and Kamryn," he explains.

67

I want to argue considering he used to blab about her all the time to me so him not letting me even get a word out is slightly irritating, but I let it go.

"Don't worry, then. You won't hear a thing from me and Dakota, swear," I promise, knowing how easy that will be to keep.

When we pull up to the apartment, Dakota is waiting in his car. He gets out when I do, and all three of us meet in front of our complex.

"Dakota," my brother smiles as a greeting to my best friend.

"Bellamy," Dakota nods as he speaks. I stand between the two and walk with them.

"Brianne," I say my own name and Dakota slinks his arm over my shoulder, then covers my mouth.

"That was not as funny as you thought it was," he tells me.

I bite his finger and he winces, pulling his hand away from me.

"Ow, you little shit." He shakes his hand out and I smirk to myself.

"Play nice, B. He doesn't have to stick around like I do," Bellamy smirks as we get into the elevator. I roll my eyes and cross my arms.

"You're both annoying," I tell them, tapping my foot on the ground until we reach our floor.

I walk out first and pull my key out. I unlock and open our door to find the exact scene I was expecting. Sienna and Kamryn are talking on the couch together and Lawson is sitting next to his girlfriend being completely ignored as he sits with his head in his hands.

"Thank god," Lawson says. "Take her, please, I beg you." He looks at Bellamy and I laugh to myself.

"Hey, rude," Kamryn furrows her brows.

"Hey, you know I love you, but right now I want to love my

THE RULES OF YOU AND ME.

girlfriend. Respectfully, go away," Lawson pulls Sienna off of the couch, then lifts her up and over his shoulder with ease.

She squeals and he takes her up the stairs without another word.

"Caveman!" I yell at him.

"I've been called worse!" he calls back and makes it up the stairs.

"Goodnight, we have things to talk about," I loop my arm with Dakota and pull him toward the stairs.

"Night, Bri!" Kamryn calls.

"Night, B. I love you," Bellamy calls after me.

"I love you, Belly!" I say as I walk up the stairs with Dak.

The second we're in my room with the door closed and locked, I throw myself on the bed and promptly slide onto the floor. I groan all the way down and then roll over, my body now flat and my head turned up to the ceiling. Dakota stands over me and stares right down at me.

"Why are you being dramatic?" he asks. "Does this have to do with why you interrupted me earlier? I was very busy." I roll my eyes.

"Making out with a hot football player is not an excuse. Best friend trumps hookup," I tell him and he rolls his eyes.

"Get up and tell me."

He holds his hands out and I take them, letting him pull me forward. I stand and then turn him, sitting him on the bed. He leans back and looks at me as I start to pace my bedroom floor. I pull out my phone and pull up Parker's Instagram. He's got fewer followers than my brother, but still a lot in comparison to most people but that's what they both get for being sponsored as well as being on the best team in the nation. I click on what could possibly be the hottest picture of any man to ever exist. He's smiling, holding a football on the field in one of those stupid fucking compression shirts that guys seem to love.

69

"This. This is why I'm being dramatic," I tell him. He takes my phone and nods.

"Parker Thompson is drop-dead gorgeous, we've known this," he tells me and I sigh.

"Yes, yes he is, and you know what? Compression shirts should be banned in this country. They should be against the dress code. You're telling me I couldn't wear a tank top in high school because it's distracting but a man can wear one of those slutty little shirts and get away with it? Unfair."

I throw my phone onto the bed and cross my arms over my chest.

"Tell me how you really feel, Baby," he chuckles to himself and I turn to him.

I think about today and run my hands down my face, dragging my lips with me. I let my hands fall and Dakota looks at me with raised eyebrows with concern written on his face.

"You're hot and he's horny. What's the problem?" he asks.

I think about just how hot Parker is—how hot and hard his body was today in the locker room. Wet, too. It was also dripping wet...

"Brianne Emily Archer, why are you blushing like a whore in church?" Dakota asks me, a smirk on his lips. I gasp.

"Dakota, don't talk about whores that way. We have an ex-whore right down the hall," I tell him, referring to Lawson.

"Hey, I didn't mean it in a bad way. Jesus loves the dirtiest whores or... something like that. Anyway, tell me what you're hiding. What happened today?" he asks and I start chewing on my thumbnail.

"I walked in on Parker in the locker room today," I tell him quickly.

"What do you mean when you say you walked in on him? Did you see anything?" he asks and I shake my head.

"No. I ran straight into his half-naked body, then he grabbed

THE RULES OF YOU AND ME.

me and held me still so I didn't fall, and I basically removed his towel with my eyes. It was hard not to imagine what was underneath when I was staring at him like that, Dak. And he has this tattoo that goes down his V line and—" I explain and Dakota smirks.

"Please tell me you fucked Parker Thomspon in the locker room." He gets far too excited and I scoff.

"No!" I half-whisper and half yell.

"Did you give him head at least?" he asks and I roll my eyes.

"No. I ran away like an idiot and sat in the hallway, completely appalled that I did that. I was so embarrassed, Dakota... I called you then he walked out. He was super chill about it and didn't seem to care at all even though he was basically naked, and it was obvious that I wished he would have been. Then he asked about you and I told him we weren't dating... Then we had a good conversation and I dropped him off at his apartment. Then he... Dakota, he asked me out. Like asked me to go get coffee with him, or dinner, or anything. That was his exact wording," I tell my best friend and his jaw dislodges as he drops it.

"Parker Thompson asked you out on a date?" he asks me and I nod.

"He did," I tell him.

"And you said yes, right?" he asks me and I nod.

"I did, but accidentally like my mind wasn't thinking right. He's off-limits. I feel guilty because that's my brother's friend. I shouldn't go out with my brother's friends. At first, it was okay because I just thought he was hot, but him thinking I'm hot too? That's what changes things. I can't tell my brother, and this is the first thing I've never been able to tell him and I feel wrong," I tell him.

"Why? Your brother doesn't need to know. It's just fun, that's it. When it's serious, then it's something to worry about.

71

Until then, have fun. You can't meter your life on how everyone else around you is going to feel about it. Parker is hot and he's interested. Are you really going to pass that up because your brother might be a little weirded out by it? Did he say anything about Bellamy?" He asks and I shake my head.

"He didn't seem to care about Bellamy at all," I admit.

"Then neither should you. You're an adult. Live your best life but you better not go out with him on my birthday," he tells me.

His birthday is in two days. Mine is in four.

"I'm not going out with him until next week. That's what we decided on. Speaking of, we're going to be here for my birthday after the game... but I was thinking maybe something on Saturday," I tell Dakota.

"Baby... We've got it planned already. My birthday is Wednesday, then we're celebrating the next day. Thursday is my day, we're doing Thirsty Thursday with the team, whoever wants to come. Then, some of the team and I planned something for you on Saturday since you have plans with Bellamy on Friday," he tells me and I pout my lips.

I've never had anyone do anything for me for my birthday. Normally, it's left up to me.

"You planned something for my birthday?" I ask him.

"I did. Get your cowgirl boots out, country girl," he tells me and I clap my hands.

"Oh my god, are you taking me to a country bar? One with a mechanical bull? Please say yes!" I get excited and he rolls his eyes.

"I have never seen someone get so excited over a mechanical bull. Yes. They do line dancing. All of us got outfits to wear too and I'm not inviting your lame-o brother and his friends. You don't ever want to have fun when he's there so it's just going to be us and the team," He tells me and I nod.

THE RULES OF YOU AND ME.

"Deal. Ugh, I'm so excited now! Thank you." I wrap my arms around his neck and sloppily kiss his cheek. He shrugs me off and wipes his face.

"Get your ass off of me before I regret planning this for you," he tells me.

"I love you more than words, Dakota," I smile to myself and dance across the room to my dresser.

"Like a sister," he chimes.

"Like a brother," I reply back.

"Are you going to invite your new boyfriend to your birthday party?" Dakota asks me as he rifles through his bag.

"I don't know... I might," I smirk to myself, knowing there's potential for anything.

Dakota is right. This is silly and fun. It's not serious. Parker probably just wants something super casual. If it's casual, it doesn't have to feel high stakes. I'm doing this. I feel absolutely ecstatic about the thought of this weekend. First game of the season. Dakota's birthday, then my birthday. Cowboy club. Maybe seeing Parker. Things feel better than expected and it's only my first freaking day.

CHAPTER 7
BRING EM OUT BY T.I.

Parker Thompson:

"Today is your first game. Why do you look like you're sitting there moping?" Xander asks me, jumping over the back of our couch to sit right next to me. I sigh, staring at my phone.

"If I tell you something, will you not be... you about it?" I ask him and he narrows his eyes.

"I'm hurt. What does that even mean? I'm basically perfect," he tells me and I sigh, my jaw ticking. There's no way I can talk about this with him.

"Tell me, too. I'm better than Xander," Nico saunters into the room, eating a spoonful of what looks like noodles. It came from a package, to say the least. *Lunch of a champion.*

"Jesus Christ," I sigh, leaning forward.

"What is it? You're acting like you're in crisis." Xander kicks his feet up on our coffee table and pulls his phone out, nonchalantly scrolling.

I look between him and Nico who are barely paying me attention at all. Andrew is the most simple and level-headed. Of course, he isn't here right now when I could potentially use his insight.

"Brianne Archer took me home the other day and I asked her out," I tell them.

Noodle juice splatters across the living room and I see Xander slowly look up from his phone and forward to the wall across from us.

"I beg your finest pardon?" Xander asks, cocking his head toward me, his phone screen now dark.

"And I have her phone number. Today is her birthday and I want to text her, but I don't know how," I tell them and Nico's shock turns into a smile.

"Are you asking us for girl advice, Parks?" Nico sets his bowl down

"This is exactly what I didn't want. Don't get weird," I tell him and Xander shakes his head.

"Back up. This is your teammate's sister, no?" he asks and I nod.

"Yes, and?" I ask.

"Doesn't it bother you?" Xander asks and I furrow my brows.

"Should it? I'm not best friends with him or anyone on the team. I wasn't looking for you to chastise me, I wanted to know what to say to her without sounding... You know what, never mind," I start to get up and Xander stops me.

"No, no sit down... If you're not worried, then it doesn't matter. Maybe just text her happy birthday. Plain and simple?" he suggests and I shrug.

"I don't want to sound dumb. No emotion behind it, just happy birthday?" I ask the two of them and they both shrug.

"She won't read into it too much," Nico tells me, and I look at him and then back to Xander, and watch as the realization sets in.

THE RULES OF YOU AND ME.

"Okay, she probably will. Maybe don't say anything and just tell her in person," Xander tells me and the thought didn't cross my mind.

Telling her in person. That would most likely be more special anyway—showing that I've been thinking about it, that I remembered it. Right? Or am I being an idiot, overthinking this to the point of exhaustion when she doesn't even slightly care if I say it or not... Brianne is interested. *I think.* Part of me wonders if she likes the excitement of talking to a football player, not me specifically—that I haven't been the thing that impacts her but what I am and who I am has. I don't like that thought so I need to get it out of my head before I psych myself out. I'm supposed to be getting out of my head and going for things this year. This is me doing that, even if I'm not doing a great job so far.

"Okay," I nod and click my phone off. Then, I stand, push away from the couch, and walk toward my room.

"Okay, what? Are you going to text her? Parks!" Xander yells after me.

"I guess we'll see," I tell him and he follows me into my room.

"We'll see? Parker, you haven't gotten action in years and haven't had a real girlfriend since before I met you. No, that girl from freshman year does not count... Wait, have you ever had a girlfriend?" he asks me and I scoff.

"Yes, I've dated before. Go away," I grumble.

"Don't put your grumpy pants on yet. It's a valid question, you never talk about women. I swear, I thought you went celibate. This is exciting," Xander tells me and I look back at him, wondering how someone with a sleeve of tattoos, and large muscled arms as well as the most stern, 'fuck with me and find out' face can be so soft sometimes. He's like a scary-looking teddy bear.

77

"You shouldn't be this excited over my relationships," I tell him, checking my football bag.

"Says who? I care about my friends' love lives like I care about my own," he tells me and I raise my eyebrows.

"Last time I checked, we were both dry in that department. I gotta go," I tell him and he groans.

"At least keep me updated!" he calls after me.

"Don't wait up tonight. I'm going to Brianne's after the game," I tell them, and Nico and Xander both scoff.

"You dirty little—"

I close the door before I can hear anything else.

It's the first official game of the season and I'm panicking for some reason. I can hear the crowd even from under here in the tunnel. We're about to enter the game and head onto the field and my nerves are shot. I'm geared up in my uniform, all of us wearing the royal blue home game uniforms, which is my favorite out of all of them. Bellamy starts like he always does. Coaches are starting to walk onto the field and my heart is beating out of my chest. I can already hear the crowd outside of the tunnel that we're in.

"Who are we?" Bellamy screams and we all start our slow chant together, as tradition.

"S," Bellamy chants and we call back.

"P," he yells and every single team member calls back to him.

"U," he screams and we all chant.

"SPU!" we start. "SPU, SPU, SPU!!"

Bellamy, Lawson, and I, the three team captains lead the guys out of the tunnel, all of our team behind us. Our entrance song plays, T.I.'s Bring Em Out. It's the same entrance song this team has had for the past five years and it does what it needs to

THE RULES OF YOU AND ME.

do. I feel the bass of the stadium in my bones as we run onto the field. The lights are blindingly bright and as many times as I've run onto this field over the past three years, I've never heard the stadium louder than it is at this moment. The entire school is here right now, all decked out in blue and gold.

Bellamy and Lawson, along with our other teammates, turn into someone else on the field. Their confidence shoots to the sky, their adrenaline taking over. I'm the opposite. When my feet touch the turf, I've never been more in tune with myself. I've never been more focused. I block out the stadium. I block out the sound of the cheerleaders. The only thing I listen to is Bellamy as he calls plays to my teammates. I never focus on anything like I do on my game. My sport. Nothing else exists but me, and the field when I enter. But this year is going to be different. As Bellamy said, confidence is key on the field. I can do it too, just like them.

We run and my focus starts to click in, the anxiety dissipating in my bones, leaving out of my body slowly but surely. No distractions. No nothing... except that's not true. For the first time ever, that's not true. Because my eyes catch, not on something, but on someone. I've never lost my focus, never stumbled over my game, but as I make my entrance out past the baton dancers, and the band that stands on the field, I see the cheerleaders. They wear royal blue uniforms, their skirts glittering and shining under the lights. The tops they wear are long-sleeved and the same color blue with gold and white accents as well as a hornet on the front. Brianne looks stunning. That's the only word I can think of. She looks like a diamond under the lights. I've never seen her this way, done up like this.

She has red lips—perfect red lips—and her cheeks have that same blushing look as they always do. She's smiling so wide as she shakes her pom poms, looking at all of the players. Time slows, my head sounds like it's underwater, the music blowing out around me as I look at her. I slow down, not stopping myself, but making sure she sees me.

"Good luck number 13!" she shouts at me and I nod my head.

"Happy Birthday," I yell over the screaming, and to my surprise, the blush on her cheeks intensifies and I'm left speechless.

I jog backward slightly, only giving myself a few more seconds to look at her before I go back to my headspace. Back to the place I should be right now for games. God, she's gorgeous. I'm never like this. I've never been affected by someone because of their looks like I am with Brianne, but it's not just that. It's her gentleness. Her care. She's unique in a way I don't know how to describe. I don't have time to describe it right now. I need to focus. To lock in now before I lose my head altogether. We're just... Having fun. Whatever happens is casual, there's no pressure. Not on me, not on her. I need to remember that so I don't work myself up.

"What did you just say to her?" I snap out of my head at the sound of Bellamy.

I jump up and down on the sidelines of the field, the adrenaline and focus sinking into my veins.

"She dropped me off at my apartment the other day. Mentioned her birthday was today," I tell him.

"Yeah, she's really nervous right now since it's her first game. I should go wish her luck, shouldn't I?" he asks.

"Sure. She seemed fine. I just said happy birthday, though... I don't know," I shrug.

I totally just gave myself away. *That was weird, right?*

"Do you want to come over after the game? We're probably going to celebrate her birthday tonight," Bellamy extends an invite he has no idea that I've already received.

So, that's a good sign, he doesn't know anything.

THE RULES OF YOU AND ME.

"Sure." I nod, keeping my words short and clipped.

I'll think about that after the game ends. Until then, I won't be thinking about anything.

Bellamy runs to his sister and I wait with Lawson. Bellamy and Brianne hug and then the two of them start a handshake, a full blown intricate one. Her smile is vibrant and bright... I turn away, waiting until Bellamy comes back, and Coach Corbin pulls the three of us in, giving us a pep talk.

Coach Corbin doesn't hesitate to remind us we don't have Lawson playing on the field tonight since he is still injured from the first scrimmage. One of our competitors took him down on a play we probably shouldn't have done. His recovery is almost done but he won't be playing today despite still being in uniform. He's going to do the team captain coin toss with us anyway. I know he's itching to be back on the field with us. It sucks too because I don't want the loss of Lawson to be the reason we don't win our first game of the season.

I've never been a team captain on this scale. If I didn't already have a confidence booster, this is it. This is what I needed. Music booms over the stadium and we walk out, the three team captains in a line. I feel intense and badass. Like no one could even touch me if they tried. We meet at the center of the field, our opponents standing there with their team captains. I know this is being televised. I know everyone's watching and honestly, I don't care. For once, nothing affects me.

"Head captains, call it," the ref tells us.

"Tails," Bellamy tells the ref and we watch as he does the coin toss. I wait, then he nods his head toward us.

"Tails. Seattle Pike gets the ball," he tells us and we jog backward, and then walk off the field in a line still. It's time to do what we do best. Win.

$\sim$

There's 5 seconds left in the game. Not that any of that matters considering we're winning. Even without Lawson playing our first game of the season, we're up by 14 points. But it's going to be more if this goes the way we need it to. Bellamy holds his gloved hand out to me and I slap fingers, closing my digits around his in a subtle handshake as we get ready to set up for our next and final play of the game.

"Ready! Down set!" Bellamy shouts and we all get into position.

I keep my eyes locked in on my opponents. The defensive players are looking me dead in the eyes like they're ready to bury me in the turf under my feet. I wait, my heartbeat pounding in my ears, the sound of the crowd cheering drowned out by the sound of my own heavy breathing. I know there are cameras on me. There are people watching all over the country —people who know me, people who want to know me. Potential future coaches. I know all of this and block it out as I count down in my head, waiting.

Then, the whistle blows. I move, making sure I'm not blocked and free. I watch from my side, keeping myself open as I watch Bellamy hand off the ball to the running back stepping in for Lawson right now. He normally favors his right side anyway. He takes the ball and runs, but the second he looks like he's in trouble, he tosses it straight back to Bellamy. I run, darting down the stretch of the field, making it straight into the endzone as planned. I turn and watch Bellamy throw the ball directly at me. My heart thunders until I feel the leather ball in my fingertips. I'm taken down right as soon as I catch it, our opponent tackling me straight into the turf, but it doesn't matter. I caught the pass. My ears ring with the heavy guy on top of me but the second he's off, it's like a roar coming to life inside of me.

For the first time tonight, the sound thunders back into my brain, and I can hear the endless cheering as I come out of my

THE RULES OF YOU AND ME.

haze. I'm surrounded by my own teammates. I take one of their hands and he hauls me up. I lift the ball over my head and the crowd somehow gets louder. I let myself smile, knowing that this won't be just now, but a season of this. Wins like this. With me being the one they're cheering for, not just Griffin Jones. I didn't get as much play time these past few years because he was the top wide receiver. But now... now it's me.

Bellamy basically tackles me to the ground and when we make it to the center of the field, it's practically chaos. Lawson runs from the sidelines and shoves me side to side, congratulating me and so is Bellamy. Everyone is screaming and cheering, and I'm more than overwhelmed, to say the least. I'm swept up in it. I'm taken aback by it. I'm enthralled by it. I love it. I've never felt this type of adrenaline on the field, not once. But right now, I feel like I could conquer the world. A touchdown on my first game as a starting wide receiver....

The field takes some time to calm down, but once the chaos subsides, we're all ushered into the locker room. Coach gives us a short pep talk and congratulates us before telling us to get rest, and get ready for continued practice next week. Winning doesn't change anything. Normal Coach Corbin behavior.

We all shower and get our senses together but even after that, I don't feel like I've come down from my high of winning. My high of catching the last touchdown and being the one that was cheered for. I don't think anything could damper the feeling.

"You coming, Parky?" Bellamy asks me, pulling his shirt over his chest.

I stand, only in my briefs and I nod.

"I am. I can catch a ride from someone if you're ready now," I tell him.

"Kamryn is waiting. You don't mind?" he asks me and I shake my head.

83

He exits swiftly, heading out to see his girlfriend. I get dressed and leave the locker room. Once I make it down the hall and past the tunnel toward the back entrance of the stadium instead of the main one, I see a small group of cheerleaders leave the locker room. Brianne. She's the first one I spot. She's still got her uniform top on but instead of a skirt, she wears long royal blue track pants. Her cheer shoes are replaced with tennis shoes. Her hair is still the same—half of it is pulled up, but the rest cascades down her back in pretty waves. I watch as Dakota nudges her and nods his head toward me.

"I'll see you later, Baby." He kisses her temple and gives her a side hug before jogging off with one of the cheerleaders that's in my grade, Valerie. I don't know her well but I do know she's incredibly nice. She always has been.

"Bye, Baby B!" Valerie calls out. "Congrats, Parker!" She waves to me and then she and Dakota leave down the hall, leaving Brianna all to me.

"Do they all call you Baby?" I ask her and she nods, a smile prominent on her face.

"Why are we even talking about me? Go you! Parker that was... Oh my god!" She shoves me to the side, jumping around me, excitement very present in all of her movements. I smirk to myself. "Do not be humble right now." She raises her eyebrows and I see her get a Kamryn look on her face, the kind of face where she means business.

"It was pretty amazing..." I tell her, not just talking about the win but the feeling.

"This is why I came. This is why I'm here. I'm so excited for the next game already, that was. Ugh, that was amazing," she tells me and I remember this is her first college game. This is her first time cheering on this level.

"Answer my question now," I laugh, feeling her energy bouncing off the walls around us.

THE RULES OF YOU AND ME.

"Everyone calls me baby because I'm the youngest on the team. 19 now, but I'm Baby B," she tells me and I nod.

"I thought Dakota was a freshman too?" I ask her.

"He is, but he took a gap year so he's still older than I am," she explains.

"And is he not attending your birthday activities tonight?" I ask and she shakes her head.

"He planned everything for tomorrow. Tonight we're just going to hang out at the apartment like we always do on my birthday. Normally, it's just me Bellamy, Lawson, and Griffin, but now that my brother and Lawson have girlfriends, and Griffin is gone, things are a little different," she tells me and I nod. "You're coming, right? I can take you..."

I nod, "Sure."

I watch as she shuffles her feet. She's smiling still and I like that she's always smiling. Because her smile is bright, kind, and almost infectious. Almost. Because I'm not allowing myself to smile like an idiot despite the fact that I kind of want to.

We leave the stadium and make our way out to Brianne's Jeep. The second we get in, and she turns it on, the sound of Taylor Swift plays over the speakers and I smirk. She turns the volume up slightly and starts to drive. The word gorgeous is repeated so I assume that's the title of the song. As she sings it lightly, I can hear that she's actually not a bad singer. She taps the steering wheel with her manicured nails and I should probably stop staring at her, but I once again find it more than hard to take my eyes off. Once we pull down the main road, her music stops and her phone starts ringing. She opens the call and motions for me to be quiet.

"Hey, Belly!" she shouts.

"Hey, B," her brother has laughter in his voice and I keep my finger to my mouth, drawing on my bottom lip as I listen to the conversation.

"What's up?" she asks.

"We wanted to go out since it's the first game of the season. Do you need to get ready?" he asks her and I watch the smile on her face falter.

"I thought we were going back to the apartment? To play games?" she asks and Bellamy has a separate conversation, not with her, but with someone else.

"What did you say?" he asks her.

I know Bellamy isn't trying to be an ass, but right now, it feels like he is. It's her birthday... but he did just win his first game of his senior year. I understand both sides, I guess.

"I said... Never mind. Um, I think I just want to stay in if that's okay with you?" she asks him for permission and I narrow my eyes.

"Yeah, if you're sure you want to stay in. It's your birthday, you sure you don't want to come out with us?" he asks and she presses a smile to her lips, forcing it.

"No, I'm okay. But I love you. Have fun and please be safe. Call me if you need me," she tells him.

"I love you, happy birthday. I promise we'll be back to celebrate after," he tells his sister.

"Don't rush... and congrats on your win," she tells him.

Her brother hangs up. She grips the wheel tighter and sighs.

"Do you want me to take you to wherever they're going?" she asks and I hesitate.

"Why don't you want to go?" I ask her.

"Well, it's silly but it's kind of been tradition that I come to their apartment the past few years so I just... I didn't really want to go out tonight. It's fine though, really Parker."

She does that thing again where she forces another smile and I shake my head. There's an obvious difference from the smile she had in the underbelly of the stadium a few minutes

THE RULES OF YOU AND ME.

ago to the one pressed on her lips right now. It's very easy to spot when you really pay attention.

"That's bullshit. Why would he go out anyway?" I ask her and she shakes her head.

"Because you guys won your first game of the season and it's a big deal so he wants to celebrate. Seriously, it's no big deal. Where do you want to go?" she asks, leaving the offer open.

Well not necessarily open, but that's exactly what I'll take it as.

"I'm going back to your apartment like I planned to," I tell her and watch the shock swarm her features, and then leave them right away. She covers her emotions so well it's almost scary.

"You don't have to do that, Parker. It's seriously not a big deal. Birthdays happen every year," she tells me and I nod.

"And we've won the national championship three years in a row. We win games all the time too, doesn't make any difference to Bellamy, does it?" I ask her and watch her press her lips together.

"It'll just be us, and I don't want you to spend your Friday bored out of your mind playing—"

"Once again, Brianne, if I'm doing something it's because I want to. I think I told you that when we were at Haven... If you remember," I tell her and she nods.

"I remember fine, but to be honest I didn't think you did. I thought you were drunk," she explains.

"Drinking and drunk are very different things. I remember everything that happened and I meant my words. If I didn't want to come back to your place, I wouldn't. I'm not leaving you alone on your birthday. Stop fighting me," my words come out gruff and she scrunches her face up.

"You're grumpy," she mumbles.

"You're stubborn," I fight back.

87

"Awe, thank you," she smiles, and I smirk, but suppress the expression, chewing the inside of my cheek.

I look out the window. I'm spending my night alone with Brianne Archer, my teammate's sister, and somehow my new infatuation. I don't know how this happened. But if it wasn't meant to be happening, it wouldn't be this damn easy.

CHAPTER 8
NOVOCAINE BY THE BAND CAMINO

Brianne Archer:

I'm hiding the fact that I'm completely nervous out of my mind right now. Parker is calmly sitting next to me as we park and pull up to my apartment. Alone, with no one else there but me and Parker and every bad and dirty thought I've ever had about him. I need to talk to Dakota ASAP. I type him a quick text.

> Brianne: Hey, so Bellamy kind of canceled and Parker said he wasn't going to leave me alone on my birthday so he's kind of at my apartment with me... Alone.

> Dak: Brianne Archer this is a red fucking alert oh my god. Do you need anything? Do you have condoms?

> Brianne: Can't talk, just had to tell you. Love you, bye!

I click the screen off and slide my phone into my duffle bag. I feel a text vibration, then another. I ignore both because Parker is taking my bag from my shoulder, carrying it for me. He's a gentleman with ease. I was raised to expect nothing less, but I never actually get it from anyone except my brother so this is a nice change. I lead him into the elevator and up to our floor even though he's been here plenty of times and could lead me if he wanted to. I reach the door and unlock it, opening it for the two of us. I open up the door for him, letting him in first with a smile.

"Your phone is vibrating a lot," he tells me and I nod.

"It's Dakota," I tell him.

"Is something wrong?" he asks.

"With his head, yes. But in general, no. He's just being Dakota," I smile and close the door, locking it behind us.

"Which entails him blowing up your phone?" he asks and I nod.

"Yeah, you know how best friends are," I tell him and he shakes his head.

"I've never had a best friend blow my phone up," he admits and I shrug.

"Well, now I'm here, and I definitely will. You'll find out what you were missing out on," I smile and take my phone from my duffle. "You can set it down anywhere, thank you by the way."

"There's no reason to say thank you." He shakes his head.

I send Dakota's call to voicemail and immediately receive another text.

> Dak: Send me to voicemail again and I swear I'll leave your car on cinder blocks. <3

THE RULES OF YOU AND ME.

I sigh and another call comes through. I look straight at Parker with wary eyes.

"Dakota isn't going to leave me alone until he hears my voice so excuse me for five seconds," I tell him and he sits on the couch while I stand in front of the coffee table, pacing, my phone to my ear.

"Dak, I'm fine," I answer.

"You might be fine right now but what you need to be is a hoe. If this night doesn't end with you kissing him, Brianne, then you are useless, do you hear me? This is the chance of a lifetime. I've been digging and Parker doesn't usually do hookups. He doesn't even freaking talk. Literally, that was the only thing people said about him... So take your chance!" he tells me and I sigh.

"Not happening, Dak," I say quietly.

"If it doesn't happen, you're no longer allowed in my apartment. You're banished," he threatens and I scoff.

"You wouldn't," I fight back.

"Watch me. Kiss him. Fuck him. Live your damn life, please. It's Parker fucking Thompson. That's the only pep talk you need. I love you, be safe!" he tells me then he hangs up, and I just stare at my phone screen and then shake my head.

"Are you sure he's okay? Because if we need to go and—" I shake my head and cut off his words.

"He's definitely got something wrong with him but it's nothing to worry about and we aren't going anywhere. Are you ready to lose?" I ask him and bend down in front of the TV turning on the Nintendo Switch. I grab two controllers from the TV stand and bring them over to where he sits.

"Whatever we're playing, there's no way I'd lose," he tells me, taking a controller. "We're both athletes but I can promise you I'm more competitive."

I look at him with shock present on my face. I scroll over to Mario Kart with my controller and he scoffs.

"Yeah, you're going down, Archer," he shakes his head, preparing himself. I feel my cheeks heat up. We're close, intimately close, but I'm not even thinking about moving. "Why did you have that shocked look on your face?" He asks me and I shrug.

"Just shocked you outwardly admitted that you consider me an athlete," I admit.

"Do you not consider yourself one?" he asks and I shake my head.

"Of course I do. It's just normally a fight to convince other athletes that cheer is actually a sport," I tell him and he shakes his head slightly with a single shrug of his shoulders.

"You've got more stamina and drive than half the players on my team. Cheerleaders are built and badass. And for you, not only do you cheer but you dance too. The muscle you need to dance is... It's just crazy to me that anyone would fight that. I mean, look at your friend Dakota. He's got the same tone and definition Lawson, Bellamy, or I have. He's fucking built. It'd be dumb to diminish that for what reason?" he asks.

"Because we wear sparkly outfits and pretty makeup," I admit.

"Sounds like a perk... Staring at you while you do what you do best," he tells me, not even eyeing me.

I bite my lip to hide my smile. Parker scrolls through the Mario characters and picks Dry Bones which is oddly fitting. I pick Princess Peach and he slightly nods like he's impressed but also confused.

"I didn't think you were a Princess Peach person," he admits.

"I only pick Princess Peach when Bellamy isn't here

THE RULES OF YOU AND ME.

because he always picks her before I get a chance," I admit. "But when he is here, I pick Donkey Kong."

"So how did you and Dakota meet?" he asks casually.

My eyes drift to him only for a second and he looks away from me and back to the screen. *Smooth Parker...* I'd be lying if my confidence wasn't slightly boosted knowing he was staring at me.

"Well, it's actually a funny story. It was the day we both did our cheer orientation for the team. A lot of the new recruits went out to one of the bars on campus... I actually ran into one of my exes who I'd rather jump off a roof than speak to, so to avoid it, I kissed Dakota. There was some in between that, but that's the gist," I tell Parker and he coughs, choking slightly. "Then we decided that we were never going to do that again because we're going to be stunt partners for our entire college career, right? Then, I saw another one of my exes so we broke our rule and kissed again. Then, we swore that was it and it really was the end of that. But it was the start of our friendship," I smile and use my advantage in the game to throw a banana behind me.

I watch Parker's character slip on it and he curses under his breath.

"So you ran into two of your exes in one night?" he asks and I nod.

"Yeah, I knew one of them was coming to SPU but the other said he wasn't so I was shocked to see him," I admit.

"Do all of your exes go here?" he asks with a soft laugh present in his voice.

"Only three. The other two are in fact not in the state anymore," I tell him. "Why?"

"Just in case," he shrugs as if that was casual. *Just in case what?*

"So you and Dakota—" he starts but I don't let him finish.

93

"Are strictly friends. You're the only person who has actually listened to me when I say it. So, I'm promising you there's nothing between us besides a pretty strong friendship. We kissed, we swore never again, we moved on... The only feelings that are there are the friend kind. He planned something for my birthday tomorrow, so you should come. That way, you can see that we're just friends. Are you jealous, Parker?" I ask and he shrugs one shoulder.

"No. I'm just making sure I don't have a reason to be," he tells me.

I'm glad the only light that's on in the living room is the lamp in the corner and the glow from our game on the TV because I'm blushing more than I should be right now.

"This feels so wrong," I say out loud, almost blurting it out.

"Playing games in your apartment? Because that's all that's happening," he says so casually. My hands are sweating profusely. I'm sure if I wasn't using this controller, they'd be shaking.

"Being alone in the apartment. Of your friend. My brother," I admit.

"Nothing is happening, Brianne. I'm spending your birthday with you, just like he should have, because I want to. Not everything revolves around your brother. Things can revolve around you too," he explains and I go quiet. "Is that how it's always been?" he asks and I shake my head.

"It's not like that. We're equal in who things are about. I just... Like to think of everyone's feelings. After my parents passed away Bellamy..." I stop myself, feeling stupid for getting personal. He's not my therapist. I don't need to talk his ear off.

"Yes?" he asks, turning his face to me slightly.

We're so close. His face is directly next to mine when I look at him. I watch his eyes travel over my face, hesitate on my lips, then go back to my eyes.

THE RULES OF YOU AND ME.

"You don't have to talk about it if you don't want to," he tells me, turning his face back to the game even though my breath is caught in my throat right now.

"Um... After my parents... After my parents passed, everything was about me. That was when we really started getting close and he made everything about me and he was just so... So obsessed with making sure I was okay, and I just, I don't know. Sometimes I overcompensate by making sure it feels equal all these years later," I admit.

"Did your parents ever make you feel like..." he hesitates, trying to find the words.

"No. No. My parents weren't like that. Bellamy was close with both of my parents but I was closer with my mom. She was my best friend and Bell took that place when she was gone," I tell him. "You grew up with siblings, didn't you? So I'm sure you're close with one of them?"

"I didn't have siblings," he tells me and I furrow my brows.

He said he grew up in loud environments with other kids. That has to mean siblings. *Right?*

"I thought you... I guess I assumed. Sorry," I tell him.

That's what I imagined he meant—noisy kids usually means siblings.

"I mean, I could have siblings somewhere but I don't know who they are or if they exist. I'm... I mean, I was in the foster system. I lived in foster houses my whole life," he tells me and my jaw drops slightly, then I pick it back up right away.

"I had no idea. Was that hard?" I ask, not wanting to apologize.

That's probably my least favorite thing people do. When people learn something sad or tragic, they apologize like that will do anything. I appreciate the sentiment but I've just learned to hate it. I'm sure he feels the same. I don't know if what I asked him was what I should have asked. I don't know if

95

he wants to talk about it and if he does, why would it be with me? But he's opening his mouth so I guess he's answering either way.

"It wasn't easy. But it also... I mean, at first, I was kind of an asshole, so I got sent to a few different families. Then, after I straightened out, I wasn't moved around as much but it happens, even if everything is good. As good as it can be," he tells me and I nod.

"Have you played football your whole life?" I ask and he nods in response, jerking his hands with the controller to skate around the turn.

"That's why I got my act together. The foster system is unforgiving. And it's... It's shitty, but I know my story is one in a million, and even with my circumstances, I was lucky. I was also very privileged where I grew up..." he tells me.

"Washington?" I ask.

"No. I grew up in California. I moved up and down the state but I'm originally from the Bay Area..." I stay quiet and let him continue on.

"My school knew I couldn't afford to play but they needed me in something, some activity, something to keep me straight. It was some program that the area I lived in was doing with the students. My school board paid my way and I ended up loving football. After that, I got quiet and focused. I made sure I would be able to keep playing if it was the last thing I did. So, when I was in high school, I worked harder and I got offered a few big scholarships, one from California Sun our rivals... but I got offered a full ride and sponsorship from SPU. After that, I was... I mean it was—" He tries to put it into words but shakes his head, obviously at a loss. I nod.

"I understand. I mean I don't, but I do," I tell him. "I didn't know any of that. Does anyone know any of that?" I ask him and he shakes his head.

THE RULES OF YOU AND ME.

"My roommates do. Mostly because it got awkward our first year around the holidays, but it's never really come up. I don't need to talk about it anymore," he explains.

"So why talk about it to me?" I ask.

"If you want someone to feel comfortable around you, it's easier when you share things. Normally people feel comfortable because I never talk but I can't get you to like me if I don't talk so... I'm talking," he shrugs and I press my lips together.

"I already like you," I tell him and I see a phantom of a smirk in the dim lighting. "And I am comfortable around you," I add on.

The whisper of a smirk turns into a full-blown grin.

"Sure," he mumbles.

"And either way. You can't tell me the only reason you dropped your trauma lore is because you thought it would make me feel comfortable. That's a heavy thing to tell someone..." I shrug.

"Fine. No one usually asks. No one talks to me or asks me about it and you asked. And because neither of us have parents," he tells me.

"Trauma bonding." I move my fist over and he bumps it, shaking his head. I cross the finish line coming in second and Parker is right behind me on my tail.

"Dammit," he mumbles. "Beginner's luck."

He challenges me again and I smirk, setting us up.

"You're on," I tell him and start another game on a different track.

～

"Absolutely no way," Parker sets his controller down and I smirk, three for three.

"Just accept your defeat, P. I win," I tell him and he runs his

97

EMMA MILLER

hands over his thighs like he's rubbing the sweat off of his palms. "What? So I make you nervous, Parker Thompson?" I ask him.

"Yes, actually you do," he admits and I'm taken aback by the honesty that I didn't expect from him. He's more open than I expected him to be.

"Why are you so honest... So forward?" I ask.

"Because I have nothing to hide from anyone. Like I said, no one ever really asks so I never share. You ask and you pay attention... to me," he hesitates to add the last part.

My face softens at the thought. I think back to the bar—to the fact that he seemed so shocked and soft over me being concerned over his face and him being hurt. As if he's never been cared for before in that way. I don't like the thought of him feeling like no one has cared. It's an unsettling feeling, especially coming from a place where it feels like people almost care too much about what you do, and how you are.

"I'm sorry... If I ever push too far or pry I... I don't mean to, I just. You know I talk too much and I just ramble and never really know what to say so—"

"I'm glad you talk because I don't really like to talk, Brianne. It's okay," he admits and I look at him, my controller in my lap.

It's pitch black outside the windows and I have absolutely no idea what time it is. I have no idea where anyone is or when they might come back. I have no idea when Parker is going home or why he's staring at me like he's going to kiss me but I feel like my insides are mush, and my outsides are about to melt.

His eyes. It's dark but not dark enough for me not to see the green haze. It's not dark enough for me to not notice the way they're looking at my lips like they're the only thing he's ever wanted in his life. I'm terrified because I don't want him to back away. I don't want him to not kiss me. He hasn't kissed me yet and I already feel a burning hot fire in my stomach and

98

THE RULES OF YOU AND ME.

scorching lava in my veins. My chest is heavy, my head is spinning, and I'm just thinking about it.

I haven't felt that in... I haven't felt that ever. I haven't kissed him and I'm burning for him. He's one of my brother's best friends. This was supposed to be something silly. Something small. As of right now, it's still that. Silly and small. It means nothing. All that could change in a mere second. I need to be careful.

"Parker..." I mumble his name, trying to make sense of my thoughts and the words jumbling in my head.

I talk too much most of the time but can't seem to get any words out of my stupid mouth right now.

"Brianne, I'm gonna do something really reckless unless you, something, or someone else stops me," he tells me and I don't say a word.

I can't say anything. I should definitely say something but I won't say anything. Even if it's stupid and reckless and the dumbest thing I've ever done. Even if I just told myself to be careful, that word seems to have evaporated from my vocabulary. My eyes flutter closed when his hands weave into my hair and his tongue wets his lips. I wait only a second before the vibration of my phone interrupts us. I feel his breath on my face and his presence so close that I can practically taste him. I sigh and break away. The sign that he was looking for showed up in soaring colors.

"It's Bellamy..." I tell him softly, moving a little bit so I'm not as close to him.

Nothing happened. I have nothing to potentially regret. Nothing to hide. Parker says nothing, his hands in his lap, one of his legs pulled up and the other off the couch and pressed to the floor. I answer the phone and hear his laughter.

"Hey, are you alright?" I ask carefully.

"Hey, B... You're still up, are you okay?" he asks.

99

"Yeah, I'm perfect... I'm... I had a good day, a good night," I admit and my eyes glance to Parker.

"Are you home?" he asks.

"Um, yeah," I tell him.

"Is Dakota with you?" he asks.

"No, he had plans tonight because he thought I had plans, but it's fine. I'm fine Bellamy, you don't have to worry," I tell him.

"I will worry because my baby sister stayed home on her birthday instead of going out. By the way, did you happen to see Parker when you left?" he asks, having no idea that I'm staring straight at him right now that I had every intention of letting the man kiss me...

I don't want to lie but I know that if I tell him the truth it will be a million questions. I know Bellamy would also probably freak out slightly.

"No. I haven't seen Parker," I lie and Parker holds his hands up, shaking his head.

What did he expect? Me to tell my brother I was hanging out solo with his bestie? Fuck no.

"Weird. He said he was going to find a ride to our place. I told him we changed plans and to meet us at Haven, but he didn't respond..." he tells me.

"I'm not sure. Maybe he just went home. You guys played pretty hard today," I chew on the inside of my cheek, not looking at Parker anymore.

"I'll call him later. We're all about to head back home, though. Do you need anything?" he asks me.

"No, I'm alright," I tell him.

"I love you. I'll see you in a little, B," he tells me.

"I love you, Belly," I tell him, then we both hang up.

I throw my phone back on the table in front of us and sigh.

"They're about to be on their way home from Haven," I tell him.

THE RULES OF YOU AND ME.

"Did he tell you that before or after you lied to him about me?" I look at him and see him raise his eyebrows at me, waiting for an answer to his question.

"Parker. I know my brother better than you or anyone. I've also known him longer. Don't question how I should be going about this," I argue.

"Whatever you say, Brianne. I guess I should leave."

He stands up and I do too. I said I needed to be careful and that doesn't include me wanting him to stay. It includes me hiding this from Bellamy but my chest is tight at the thought of Parker not being happy about it.

"Let me take you home," I offer and he just stares at me.

"I can get a ride from Xander. I don't want them to get home and you not be here and have to explain," he tells me and I can't tell if he's mad or upset.

I watch as he moves around me, avoiding touching me at all. I watch as he grabs his phone and heads toward the front door.

"Parker..." I call his name and he turns, walking backward.

He's not mad. He's... I can't read his features. It's like he's... confused? Maybe?

"I'll see you tomorrow. For your actual birthday celebration. That is if you still want me there," he offers.

"I'd really like you there," I admit and he nods.

"Parker..." I call him, very obvious desperation in my voice. He looks at me, waiting.

"I'm sorry... I didn't mean to upset you," I admit.

This is not the way I wanted our night to end.

"I'm not... I mean, I... I get it. It's not a big deal, Brianne. I'll see you tomorrow, though."

He leaves and I find myself staring at the door for a few seconds after he's gone.

101

CHAPTER 9

SAVE A HORSE (RIDE A COWBOY) BY BIG & RICH.

Parker Thompson:

Xander drives me to Dakota's apartment, mostly because he refuses to let me walk. He said he wasn't going to let me show up at my "girlfriend's" birthday party late or sweaty. As if either of those things fucking matter because she is in fact not my girlfriend and probably won't be considering her response to her brother yesterday. She doesn't want him to know and she doesn't seem like she'd be keen on keeping a secret from him. I would never ask her to do either after what she told me yesterday. He's her best friend. He's her closest family member. I wouldn't want to jeopardize that.

"So, you're one hundred percent sure this is a good idea?" Xander asks me as we near.

I sigh deeply, trying not to get nervous. I don't think I've ever been nervous about seeing a girl in my fucking life.

"Nope," I tell him.

I don't own cowboy boots or anything country themed. I don't know why the hell I would, considering I mostly wear warm-ups or workout clothes. I did have a flannel so that's

103

exactly what I'm wearing. That, and plain jeans. I know she told me Dakota planned all of this so I'm assuming he went all out. He seems like that type of friend.

"But you're sure that you're going to try? Like... Like you might not think it's a good idea, but you're sure that you're going to do it anyway because you like her, right?" Xander asks and I shake my head, looking at him.

"I don't know what you're trying to say. I don't... I mean I do like her, but," I pause, trying to gather my thoughts. "Jesus Christ, Xander, I don't know. I just know that whatever happens, happens and that I know it will be worth it too."

"Don't get your briefs in a twist you baby. I support you in your sexcapades, even if they are with your head captain's little sister," he smirks to himself and I roll my eyes.

"You're so fucking annoying, Xander. I haven't had sex with her. I haven't even kissed her," I tell him, not looking at him while I do.

I don't need to blush in front of him or I will never hear the end of it.

"But you want to," he adds on.

"If you don't shut the fuck up I'm going to—"

"Okay, don't be your grumpy self. You're about to celebrate her birthday, so be the normal you," Xander interrupts me.

"I'm normally this way," I grumble, not even looking at him.

"Right. So don't be the normal you. Be the better version of you. The one that she liked in the first place... Can't imagine what side of you that would be." He eyes me and looks away with a judgmental stare.

I roll my eyes. Not everyone is fucking smiling all the time like Xander. The only time I ever see him with a mean mug on is when he's on the ice.

"I don't know what side of me it was either. I barely speak when I'm around her," I admit.

THE RULES OF YOU AND ME.

"Well, yeah, then it makes sense why she likes you. Women love when men shut the fuck up." I catch his idiotic smile which makes me roll my eyes.

"And you know that because you're getting so lucky?" I ask, knowing he spends most of his time at the hockey rink and if he's not there, he's at our apartment with our roommates.

"You have no idea about what or who I'm sleeping with. Well not what, but who. You get it. Either way, women love when I talk," he shrugs.

"Whatever you say."

I shake my head and he pulls up to the apartment. I open the door and walk away as quickly as I can before Xander—

"Be careful, and text me when you're on your way home, sweetie pie! Don't be too late either—"

I hold up my middle finger, turning around to look at him as he yells out of his window. He drives a car nicer than anything I've ever ridden in—an all-black Range Rover. I love riding in his car but I'll never tell him that. He'd take it as a compliment and I'd have to deal with his affection afterwards. I text Brianne and tell her I'm here. She gives me a floor and room number. I follow her instructions and head that way. When I knock on the door, Dakota answers, and we're basically wearing the same thing. Jeans and a flannel. His is red and mine is a dark green so we're different by that standard. He's also wearing a cowboy hat and boots.

"Howdy," he smirks at the sight of me and I nod.

"Hi."

I walk in as he motions for me to enter and I notice Valerie, a cheerleader who is also in my grade standing at the island in the kitchen with Leah Ashley, and two other male cheerleaders. They wave and say hello, I do the same. I don't miss the way Leah Ashley looks at me skeptically before turning back to the alcohol on the kitchen island. Bellamy's ex... Hanging out with

105

his sister. She is the captain of the cheer team so I get it, but also, I wonder how it makes Bellamy feel. More importantly how it makes Brianne feel. Does Bell even know?

"She's still getting ready," Dakota tells me and I shrug.

"I wasn't—"

"You were, it's fine. I can keep a secret," he tells me and I stifle a sigh.

I try not to let myself feel affected by everyone's assumptions and comments about what's happening between Brianne and me. Considering nothing has happened. Considering I don't know if anything ever will. Considering I refuse to push her in that direction because I refuse to separate her from her brother. If she's uncomfortable with that. With something between us besides friendship, then it's game over. No questions asked. But I would like something, even if it is only friendship. Because oddly enough, there's already a connection between us. I just hope it's not one-sided.

Everyone in the kitchen is in some sort of country or western inspired outfit. Leah wears an incredibly cropped white tank top that says cowboy killer on the front in red letters. She's got red cowgirl boots on and a white cowgirl hat. Valerie is in a jean outfit—a tight strapless top and the same color denim shorts with brown cowgirl boots. Both of them are polar opposites. Though Valerie is the dark one, with dark hair, dark makeup, and olive skin and Leah is the bright one, with blonde short-cut hair, blushy bright makeup, and blue eyes... their personalities are different. Valerie is smiling and Leah looks like she's always on the prowl, like she's in defense mode before anyone can even approach...

I feel very out of place right now, but I don't let on and I don't say anything. I just stand with all of them and I'm passed a shot. I take it without hesitation, liquid courage is probably the only thing that will get me through the night with a bunch of

THE RULES OF YOU AND ME.

people I'm not close with and never will be. I hope I get closer to her. Speaking of, the door opens, and Brianne enters the room with a blonde girl that I don't know and have no intention of meeting, especially not when I have eyes locked on Brianne.

Brianne is wearing all black. Black shorts—leather, and tight. Her stomach is flat and exposed due to the tight long-sleeve top she wears, just like in her cheer uniform. She wears a belt with a buckle on the front and gold jewelry to match. She's wearing black heeled cowgirl boots that make her tan legs look a thousand miles long. Her hair is in the same natural wavy curls it's always in, long down her back. The top of her head is covered with a black cowboy hat. My jaw would be on the floor if I wasn't in a room full of people.

Usually, danger is signified by red but tonight it's dressed in black and tugging on every want and need I've ever had. I need to stay in check. I know I'm going to have to keep reminding myself of that too. Restraint is something I never struggled with. I'm very good at telling myself no, but I think tonight might be the first time I fight with that part of me. I don't know what her friends know. What she'll want them to know... I don't know what she wants. What she's looking for. If anything happens at all tonight, it will have to be started by the girl in black.

"Did someone call the Uber?" she asks, joining in with everyone else at the island.

"I called one," Leah tells us.

"I called the other," Dakota tells her.

The two of them stand next to each other, and then she looks at me, her eyes catching mine. She freezes and then smiles, her rosy cheeks burning brighter. They are my favorite thing about her, I think. Her pink cheeks. Though, right now looking at her, it'd be almost impossible to choose the best part of her. I almost want to cringe at the thoughts in my head. I've never been very perceptive. I've never felt the need to take notice of what's happening around me unless it involves me. In technical terms, she does involve me. It's ignorance, I'm sure of it. I know I've probably missed out on a lot from having that mindset but I'm glad that I notice her, that I see her. That it's hard not to...

We all exit together, then haphazardly pile into Ubers when we get downstairs. I end up with Brianne, Dakota, and Valerie. The three of them are loud, just as loud as Brianne is alone. All of them match energy with each other, and I feel out of place but also like it doesn't matter like none of them care that I'm quiet or here because that's what they expect. They aren't trying to make me be something else or someone else. I keep my arm rested over the back of the seats and keep my eyes forward until we pull up to a bar called The Boot Scoot. I get out first and hold my hand out, helping Valerie and then Brianne out of the car.

"Why, thank you," Brianne dips her hat with her fingers and I smirk, following her into the bar.

She flashes what I assume is her fake ID at the bouncer and he barely looks at it because he's in fact staring at her. *Get in the fucking line, dude...*

I show my ID and continue behind her. My senses are completely overloaded the second we walk in. The bar is loud and absolutely packed. The waitresses and bartenders are all in country-themed attire. Men and women both walk around with trays of shots and bottles for the guests. The girls that work here wear assless chaps and tight ripped-up shirts that say The Boot Scoot on them. They wear underwear that covers only a small portion of their lower halves.

There is country music blaring and men and women everywhere—chatting, dancing, and drinking. There is also a mechanical bull off to the side surrounded by a ring. I've never been to a place like this. The music shifts from country to pop, but something with a good beat comes on, so the people keep dancing.

THE RULES OF YOU AND ME.

The lights are flashing too with colors popping up everywhere, making it hard to focus on just one thing.

Except her. She's smiling right now, more than I've seen her smile since I met her. Even in the dark with the flashing around us, I can see her blushing cheeks. She said she loved noise and music. This seems like the perfect place for someone like her.

"Is this what you wanted, cowgirl?" Dakota asks her, spinning her around.

Her hair whips around her and she laughs wildly, holding onto her cowboy hat.

"It's perfect!" she cheers.

"It's her birthday!" Valerie shouts over the music to the bartender.

"Shots on me, little lady," a man that's sitting at the bar winks at her.

He's probably freshly out of college. She smiles at him and he does what he says, not only buying her a shot but buying one for each of us. I just follow everyone else's lead, not wanting to object, but also wanting her to know that whatever she wants goes here. It's her birthday. That's how birthdays should be. We all settle and the group of us relaxes into the atmosphere of the bar as much as we can, considering just how rowdy it is. I look at her and she catches her eyes on me. I'm letting her lead this, if *this* is even a thing... but that doesn't mean I can't try.

"You look gorgeous," I speak loudly over the music and she smiles but furrows her brows.

Embarrassment over the compliment tries to sneak in, but I once again repeat the words confidently over and over again.

"What?" she asks, even though she's standing right next to me.

"I said you look..." I stop myself because she's still looking at me like she has no clue what I'm saying.

I know I have a little bit of alcohol in my system so I could

109

EMMA MILLER

blame it on that, or I could just blame it on the fact that I want her close to me like she was last night. I'm doing this because... because I need her to hear me. That's the only reason. I try to convince myself but I'm not very convincing. I hook my fingers through the space in her belt loop and tug her to me, bringing her in my space, into my orbit. She puts her hands on my chest and I lean down, my lips brushing her ear.

"I said that you look gorgeous, Brianne," I speak just loud enough for her to hear, even when I'm this close.

This is so out of character for me. Jesus Christ, I'm at a honky tonk bar if that isn't proof enough. My chest is thrumming with anxiety even with the alcohol in my system, but I'm doing everything in my power not to let it show. I want to play the calm and cool card like I usually do.

"And what about you, cowboy? You look..." she asks over the loud music.

When she leans back, she only does enough to look at my face, then she shakes her head with a smile on her face. Almost as if she can't believe what she's looking at. She takes her hat off and places it on my head instead. The way she looks at me, I decide right here and now that this is worth it. Honky tonk bar or not.

"Tonight isn't about me, is it?" I ask her and watch the smirk grow into a smile again.

Confidence will always be something I struggle with. Bellamy and Lawson were right about that but I can fake it. I can pretend for the time being. I muster up the feeling I have when I'm about to play or go onto the field. I burrow that in my chest...I bring my finger up, dancing it along her jaw, under her chin so her gaze stays on mine. Electricity shoots up my finger and through my body. This is the alcohol speaking. The music playing stops. It sounds like a record scratching and everything halts in the bar, including the moving lights. Brianne and I, as

THE RULES OF YOU AND ME.

well as everyone else, look around until an alarm sound starts playing on a loop over the whole bar and someone comes over the loudspeaker.

"Ladies and gentlemen, it's time to take it off tonight."

Whoever is speaking has a deep southern drawl and I couldn't tell you if it was real or fake, but it definitely fits and makes this entire place come together that much more. My hand is still resting on her hip, my fingers hooked through her belt loop.

"Are you going to dance with me or are you going to make me go at this all on my own?" She raises an eyebrow, stretching on her tiptoes to come dangerously close to me.

"I think you and I both know that I don't dance. I will buy you a drink, though, birthday girl," I tell her.

I get another shot for the two of us, knowing it's most likely a bad decision. We take it together. Despite the bite of the alcohol and the very small taste of regret, my insides warm.

"No dance?" she asks and I shake my head.

She narrows her eyes, purses her lips, and backs away slowly. The song that plays over the loudspeaker isn't one that I've heard in a long time—not since I was younger at a school dance I was most likely forced to go to. Take It Off by Ke$ha blasts over the speakers, and the employees move to the center of the dance floor, the bouncers in the club backing guests away. When the song picks up, the wait staff starts dancing, all in sync. A line dance of sorts and I see the excitement on Brianne's pretty face. I watch her, and the second the bouncers move, I see her hook her arm with the blonde she was with earlier.

They both have the same body type, small but incredibly fit. They're like carbon copies of each other except her friend is more pale and bright blonde opposite of Brianne's brown hair and tanned skin. Within a matter of a few seconds, and a few tries, Brianne and her friend have nailed the somewhat chal-

111

lenging steps and are dancing with the staff and a few other people in the crowd. Dakota is standing next to me and I catch him watching me as I watch her.

"What?" I ask, trying not to get defensive.

I don't need him thinking I'm an asshole. They're best friends. She surely listens to his advice.

"She's so out of your league," he tells me and I give a short laugh, and take a drink out of my bottle, ignoring the comment that's more of an insult.

"I'm aware," I grunt in response.

"Are you always grumpy?" he asks.

"Are you always nosy?" I ask back and he rolls his eyes.

"Who's that with her?" I ask him.

"Her name is Delaney. She's in Brianne's dance classes with her. Hence the fact that the two of them are naturals out there," he tells me. "You know, I looked this place up online and this dance is why I chose it. I saw it on TikTok," he tells me. I furrow my eyebrows.

"Why?" I ask over the music.

"Because a girl should have fun on her birthday, and God knows you don't have the balls to show her that kind of fun," he insults once again. "Watch... See the blonde guy, tall, cowboy hat?" Dakota asks me.

My eyes drift to the dance floor. I see him, directly next to Brianne, dancing to the Ke$ha song, with a cowboy hat shading his face. Well, everything but his smiling lips. He keeps turning his head to watch Brianne as she dances, as she swivels her hips and claps along to the dance, having the time of her life. It's hard to watch him when all I want to do is watch her.

"What about him?" I ask.

"Well, I don't know about him personally. I just knew the guys were hot, and that they were going to do this," he smirks to

THE RULES OF YOU AND ME.

himself, drinking out a straw, something that looks like a margarita.

He nods his head as the chorus starts to the song. The second that Ke$ha sings, "Take it off," the men on the floor who are employees do just that. They remove the flannels they wear. I have to give it to Brianne because she's a performer at heart. She doesn't falter in her moves much, but I can see her eyes drift as she stares at the blonde guy, his attention directed toward her. They're gravitating toward each other. It's obvious. I breathe deeply.

"So what?" I shrug.

"So, I knew that at least one of them, if not all of them would shoot their shot," Dakota tells me.

"You say it like it's supposed to shock me. She's fucking perfect, Dakota. She's going to get stared at and hit on," I tell him. "And we have nothing going on, so it doesn't matter. The guys out there aren't anything she can't handle." I tell him. I'm not lying.

"So that—"

He nods his head again and my eyes catch on the guy with his hand in her back pocket now, their chests touching and their bodies moving as a unit together. He leans down and whispers something in her ear, and she laughs like it's the funniest thing she's heard. I clench my jaw.

"Doesn't that make you a little bit jealous?" Dakota asks.

"I'm not the jealous type," I tell him, drinking my beer, wondering why it tastes more bitter than I remember.

If she wants him, then that's what she should get. It's her birthday. And we're just friends. If thoughts had a taste, that one would taste like black licorice. I clench my jaw. I'm only stating facts.

"Keep telling yourself that," Dakota pats my shoulder.

He moves like he's about to go out there too.

"Hey..." I catch his attention and he turns around.

"You're her best friend. If I'm so out of her league, why make it seem like you want me to make a move?" I ask him.

"Because she's totally into you and if you don't, she never will," he admits and shrugs his shoulders. "She's skittish sometimes but don't miss your chance, Thompson, because this is it!" he shouts at me and then turns around, and runs toward his best friend.

She's backing away from the male dancer, still engaging with him and Dakota runs onto the dance floor, sweeping Brianne by her hips and spinning her around. Her hair spins in ribbons around her and Dakota takes her in one hand and her friend Delaney in the other, spinning both of them. I watch as she leans into Dakota and whispers in his ear. Then, she pulls him with her and turns the guy she was just dancing with around. The second he turns, she backs away, leaving him face-to-face with Dakota. I watch as the two of them dance together and now, it all makes sense. I don't even think Dakota saw that coming. I smirk, those bitter thoughts tasting sweeter by the second.

The song ends after another minute and the person who was just speaking on the loudspeaker makes sure everyone knows the fun isn't over yet. They state it's ladies only on the floor and encourage the crowd to grab their girls and make their way down.

"Cowboys, keep watch of your little ladies tonight because things are about to get wild," the announcer says when a song comes on that I've never heard.

It's probably because it's explicitly a country song—so country that it's hard to do anything but pay attention to the southern drawl of the voices singing. It's like clockwork. The same female employees showcase the line dance steps and all the girls standing around join in. Leah and Valerie have joined

THE RULES OF YOU AND ME.

in with Brianne and her friend Delaney. They all look like they're having the most fun in the world like nothing could ruin this for them. The chorus of the song starts and I watch as the dancers move from the dance floor and climb onto the bartop on the edges of the dance floor. They continue their dance until the music pauses.

"Save a horse, ride a cowboy!" The entire floor of women cheers the words all together.

I don't look at the girls on the bartop next to me. I look straight at Brianne. She's perfect in the steps. She's moving with grace but also adding her own flare to every bit of it. This is her element. This is where she belongs and even if it's not the style of dance she's trained in, she's kicking its ass. She looks incredible while doing it. I finish off my beer and turn around to order another. One of the girls, a dancer, stops directly in front of me on top of the bar. I stare at her feet considering she's standing on the bar top, thinking she'll keep moving but she doesn't, so I look up. My eyes move up her legs until I reach her face. She's staring down at me with a wide grin. She holds her hand out to me, looking for assistance. I hold my hand out to her, helping her from the bar, and onto one of the barstools next to me.

"And what might your name be, handsome?" she asks, her voice carrying delicately but perfectly over the music. She's... Hitting on me... I'm not an idiot, but once again, I'm not perceptive. It's hard to notice the flirting unless it's flashing in bright red lights in my face. This is pretty clear... I think.

"Parker," I tell her, taking the beer from the bartop, my eyes barely glancing over her.

Not interested, even if she is gorgeous.

"Are you here on your own, or did you come with someone else?" she asks me, and my eyes slide to the dance floor, looking for Brianne but I can't find her.

115

I didn't come with someone but that doesn't mean I don't want her...

"Ummm," I hesitate. How do I explain this without sounding like an idiot, and why do I care how she perceives me?

"Ummmm," she mimics me, her finger drawing over my chest.

"I came with someone, but not in the way I want... Not yet," I nod to the dance floor.

"Which one is she, Parker?" The pretty girl in front of me asks.

I look for a longer while now and spot Brianne. She's shaking her hips, dancing with the rest of the workers who have now left the bartop and moved back onto the dance floor.

"The one out there in all black," I tell her.

"The one who dances like she works here," she laughs, obviously impressed.

"That would be the one."

I look directly at the woman standing next to me. She has dark black curls and bright red lips. She's pretty. Someone would be lucky to have her hitting on them but... My eyes drift back to Brianne, the wanting in my chest so heavy it almost hurts.

"Word of advice. Make her jealous and she'll have no choice," she tells me.

"Make her jealous?" I ask.

I don't want her to be angry, but... I also hardly know the first thing about getting with a woman or making someone like you. So if this is it, I'll have to be the one to try.

"She's looking at us, so look at me, be interested, and she'll be here in seconds... That is if she wants you the same way. If not, then you've got your sign..." she tells me, and I don't take my eyes off of the waitress, part of me wondering if she's going to be right.

THE RULES OF YOU AND ME.

Brianne hasn't expressed any form of wanting me. She agreed to one date. She didn't try to stop me last night when I almost kissed her... But... I go along with the employee's plan, staring at her face, then her lips. I don't lean into her. I don't touch her. I just look at her, smirking as I bring my bottle to my lips drinking. Her smile widens and a shit-eating grin forms on her bright red lips.

"5, 4, 3, 2..." The girl in front of me counts. Her finger is still dancing along my chest.

"Excuse meeee," Brianne sings the words, doing just what the mystery girl told me.

I watch her smirk before I turn my attention to Brianne who is standing in front of me.

"Yes?" I ask her, she smiles at the girl next to me, a genuine smile, then looks at me.

"Are you with him?" the girl asks Brianne.

"I could be," Brianne smirks at her.

"Say less," she winks at Brianne and then dances away, leaving her with me.

I guess it's time to play the part.

"And what if I was enjoying that?" I ask, using the waitress' advice and playing up this angle. I wasn't. I'm enjoying this exponentially more.

"Then I'd ask you why you came here to celebrate my birthday with me at a bar you'd never come to just to talk to other pretty girls... when I'm right here," she says, her voice suggestive. It's obvious she's got alcohol moving through her veins just like I do.

"I came because I wanted to celebrate your birthday," I answer simply.

"And?" she asks and she moves closer to me.

I'm sitting on a bar stool and she is now standing between

117

my legs, her hips nestled between my thighs. This is definitely a move—an intimate one that makes my chest tight.

"What do you want me to say? Because the second I say it out loud, it becomes something real, Brianne. I can't take it back," I tell her and her arms slide around my neck.

I just need her to bite. Once and then... then, it's game over. She takes the cowboy hat from my head and places it back on hers, shading her face from the lights.

"I don't want you to say anything..." she tells me, her voice heavy.

Part of me wonders if I should maybe be questioning this. Why now when last night she seemed so hesitant and skittish? I look at her lips and her rosy cheeks. Her bright blue eyes. The freckles spattered on her cheeks. Her thick lashes. I watch her as she looks at my lips too. I see her direct line of sight. She licks her own lips and nudges forward, her nose brushing mine before she tilts her head. I don't move. I don't even breathe. My ears are ringing, every single thing in the building surrounding us is drowning out. A bad idea has never sounded, felt, or tasted better than this supposed bad idea does.

Her arms are slung around my neck lazily and her lips are centimeters from mine. I look at her, almost positive she's not going to follow through. I beg in my head. Please kiss me. *God, please...* She hesitates, then melts, and so does every single thing inside of me. Her lips... Her lips are like buried treasure. Like a drink of water at the end of a race. Like the sun after fucking winter. They're slow and so tentative as they kiss mine and I'm so shocked that I indulge only now, closing my eyes. I take over now that her lips have given me permission. I bring my hands up to her. My left hand moves over the soft skin of her throat to the back of her neck. I weave my hand into her hair and grip the back of her thigh with my other hand. Her lips aren't tentative

THE RULES OF YOU AND ME.

anymore. They're crushed to mine like they were meant to be there until she pulls back.

"Do you think..."

"Whatever you're about to say, no, I didn't think that," I tell her, chills racing over my body now that her warmth is gone.

"I mean, maybe I should... No, I mean like I shouldn't, but I could just... Do you think that I should have another drink since it's my birthday?" she asks and I bring my hand out from her hair and wrap it around her neck. My fingers brush the bottom of her jaw as I bring her lips back to me—the lips I've been wanting and waiting for. I've only been waiting since the night at Haven when I initially wanted to kiss her... But it feels like I've waited a long time for this. For her. She pours into kissing me and I hold back the groan in my throat at the way she feels pressed between my legs right now. I pull back but lean in one more time, still not getting enough as I kiss her again, my teeth nipping at her bottom lip.

"That's what I think..." I tell her.

Her eyes flutter open, she's flushed a deep crimson I haven't seen yet but want to stay. I feel like I just scored the biggest, most important touchdown in a championship game. I have that much confidence right now. I'll be damned if I let it slip away tonight for even one second.

CHAPTER 10
THINK LATER BY TATE MCRAE

Parker Thompson:

"I think that I like what you're thinking," she smiles with her eyes closed, laughing to herself.

I don't talk to her anymore. I pull her back to me with my hand still on her throat. I can feel her pulse under my fingertips. It's like thunder through her veins. It's completely fueling me right now. My own ear-shattering heartbeat thumps through my own head. Her hands move now and my chest burns hot the second her fingers move under the hem of my shirt, touching my skin for the first time. She holds onto me, stabilizing herself. There's no point in doing so because both of us are in a whirl-wind of heavy breathing and mind-shattering kisses. I barely take a breath just so I can keep my lips on hers.

"Ahem," I hear next to us and I clench my jaw tight while she backs away.

She turns to the side and I glare when I look, wondering why the fuck anyone would interrupt. It's Dakota, that's why.

"Aw, hi, Dak," she smiles and I keep my glare trained on her best friend.

He smirks at me, "Hi, Baby. Hate to interrupt but the girls are about to come over and ask you to ride the bull. Didn't know if you wanted them to see you two getting... acquainted."

He looks between the two of us, and I don't think I would care if Bellamy Archer walked into the bar himself right now, I would've kept her lips on mine. Even if the world stopped spinning, I would've kept my lips on hers. Sounds like the perfect way to go out, kissing Brianne Archer.

"Good idea!" she cheers. "I want a margarita." She looks at me, and I nod my head.

"Yes ma'am," I mumble, my eyes looking at her lips before I press my thumb to her bottom lip. "Go to your friends, I'll meet you over there with a drink," I tell her, and she cheers, and scoots through the people surrounding us to her friends who are making their way over to us.

"How are you feeling, hot shot?" Dakota smirks leaning against the bar with me as I wait for the bartender.

I can't believe he's making small talk with me as if he didn't just interrupt the most important moment of my life to date.

"Homicidal..." I mumble.

"Get over it, grumpy pants. Take her home later, do that shit behind closed doors," he tells me.

"She made the first move. For the record," I tell him.

He raises his eyebrows, a smirk on his lips, "I'm sure I'll get the entire scoop in the morning. Don't worry, Thompson."

Dakota nudges my shoulder and the bartender approaches, taking another drink order from us. I get a margarita for Brianne, picking up on the fact that she prefers tequila just like her best friend. Once we have our drinks, I follow him over to the mechanical bullpen. The girls are in line, all of them waiting. I stand with Dakota who is shamelessly flirting with the blonde guy who was dancing with Brianne earlier. He's flirting back, his flannel shirt still unbuttoned showing off his muscles. I

THE RULES OF YOU AND ME.

pretend not to notice, but I have a feeling Dakota won't be leaving alone. Good for him. Maybe that means I'll get time alone with Brianne when we leave even if it's only for a little bit, like our ride home together.

I don't have to pretend to ignore the two of them when Bri bounces herself up to the bull. She's definitely intoxicated—she has the same red glow on her face she had the other day when I ran into her in the hallway of her apartment. She's smiling as she climbs onto the bull. The second it starts, its slow movement makes my face heat up, and so does my chest. She grinds into the bull, riding her hips, keeping them clutched to the mechanical bull. She rides the bull and I'm imagining things I shouldn't. The way she's moving, the way she's fluid in her motions, and the way she's smirking... She's doing it on purpose. A whistle comes from across the pen and then cheers come from other guys. I said I've never been the jealous type but that's because until tonight, I've never felt the need to be jealous. I need her off of that fucking bull.

"You better get your girl..." Dakota talks over his shoulder, his voice suggestive.

She's not my girl, but the way my jeans feel exponentially tighter around my groin than they did when I got here... I'm fucking acting like it. I clench my jaw and sigh deeply, watching as she rolls her hips one last time, then the bull turns and she falls, her hair whipping around her. She jumps up and moves back to the exit, surrounded by her friends.

"I'm serious, you better go over there because someone else is going to get to her first," Dakota tells me a little more seriously now.

I move toward the exit of the riding area, and there's already a guy standing there making eyes at her. I cut directly in front of him and pass her the drink she wanted, though I don't think it's a good idea. She'll probably regret it in the morning. She takes

123

the drink from me and smirks as she puts the straw between her tempting lips. I eye her, scouring up and down her body. Her hair is messier and tousled now. Her eyes are saying a million things and my mind is racing.

"Come on..." I motion for her to move away from the eyes surrounding us.

I move her in front of me, keeping my hand on her hip as we walk. Her butt skims over my groin as we walk, making this so much worse for me.

"Was it fun?" I lean down, talking right in her ear.

"I would have more fun riding something else," she tells me, and my cock physically twitches in my fucking pants as she looks over her shoulder at me, her round eyes staring at me like a fucking vixen.

I take a deep breath as I stare at her, and shake my head.

"You don't like that idea?" she asks, a fake pout on her lips as she turns around, her finger drawing down my chest.

I'm wondering if I should like that idea. I'm definitely intoxicated and she is too, but aren't I supposed to be gaining confidence? Having fun, sleeping with people? "Doing college" as they say? She's the only one exuding confidence in this situation and that's not going to work for me. Enough with the quiet, to myself bullshit. She wants me. I really fucking want her. That's reason enough.

"Finish your drink," I tell her and she smirks.

"Why, Parker?" she asks, her voice more of a purr than anything else.

"You know why, drink it down, cowgirl. Let's go."

She laughs as she turns around and I jokingly give her ass a soft tap. She squeals and moves quickly to the bar, not taking her lip off of her straw as she drinks down her margarita. She puts the empty glass down on the bar and turns around, her back to the bartop. I stand with my chest to hers, getting the

THE RULES OF YOU AND ME.

attention of the bartender to pay my tab. Her fingers roam under my flannel and I clench my jaw, trying to keep myself from groaning out loud at the feeling of her fucking fingers on my skin.

I'm going to need some serious restraint because it's been a long time and she's moving on me like she's ready to pounce. This was not what I had planned. I hoped she'd maybe suggest that she likes me—that she's interested. This is... so much more than that. My judgment might be slightly clouded. This might not be a very good idea but the feeling of her nimble hands on my body are switching up every signal my brain sends. My hands hold her hips and she stands on her tiptoes, her lips brushing my jaw as she leans up.

"Are your roommates going to—"

"Don't worry about my roommates," I tell her and move back to look at her.

She really doesn't need to consider the fact that I've had plenty of nights hearing all three of them having more fun than I'd like to know about. It's my turn and I'll be fucking damned if the thought of my roommates potentially hearing is what stops me. The only thing that will stop me is if she says the words herself. End of story.

"Dakota!" she calls out and the bartender hands me my card.

"I think we're going to head back to my place..." he tells Brianne, coming up to her with the employee.

"Howdy..." Brianne smirks as the worker nods his hat. "We were actually leaving... Um, just get an Uber, we can add two stops," she tells him.

"And where will you be going?" Dakota asks her.

Her eyes are hazy as she laughs, dragging me behind her.

"Don't ask stupid questions, Dak," She jokes. "What about the team?"

125

"I told them that Parker took you home because you got sick. I'm one step ahead of you, Baby," he sighs and we don't stop walking until we're outside of the bar and on the curb.

There's a line of unclaimed Ubers on the street as there usually is at popular bars in the city. We get inside a black Escalade. Brianne pulls me into the back and Dakota and his mystery man sit in front of us. I tell the Uber driver my address first since it's closer and Dakota starts talking too, but I zone out because Brianne has laid her head on my lap and is laughing. Her body shakes as she laughs.

"This is exactly what I imagined my life would be like when I moved here," she tells me and I smirk down to her.

"What's that?" I ask.

"Living for the moment. Living in the moment. Happy Birthday to me," she cheers and I stare at her.

I really look at the girl with her head in my lap. This isn't the traditional way. This isn't the way that I would normally do things because I normally don't hook up with people. I also don't normally make such a simple and easy connection. I never have. Not once in my life. I don't want to ignore the attraction I feel. I don't want to deny the attraction she's showing me. I'd be the biggest idiot on the planet if I did.

"Are you going to stare at me or are you going to kiss me?" she asks and I keep my eyes locked on her, bringing my hand up to her.

My hand is giant compared to her face, but I run my thumb over her cheek anyway.

"I have every intention to kiss you until you can't remember your own name, Brianne, but I have no intention of letting anyone else watch it happen," I tell her.

"You didn't seem to mind in the bar," she whispers, her eyes set on my lips.

"Maybe I like it when you make the first move," I tell her.

THE RULES OF YOU AND ME.

"Say less," she speaks, leaning up, closing the gap between us once again.

I indulge in her perfect fucking lips, inhaling deep as she kisses me, the smell of vanilla and citrus engulfing us. A perfect combination for a perfect fucking woman. I have never wanted anyone to break the law but I wish more than anything the Uber driver would hurry the fuck up. Speed, I don't give a fuck at this point. I don't intend to sleep with her tonight. I'd welcome it but I don't expect it.

I'll take whatever the hell she gives but she is going to maneuver us through this. It starts with her and it ends with her. I want her to choose how this goes. I want her to make the moves she wants to make. I want her to lead and feel good and... And I want it to be about her. About what she wants. She tugs my bottom lip between her teeth and I press my forehead to hers, trying to fucking breathe but finding it incredibly hard. It feels like there's not a single ounce of oxygen left in the entire car.

"Get a room," Dakota mumbles.

"Trying," Brianne tells him and kisses me again like she needs my lips on hers.

Kissing me as if she won't survive without it. I don't know if time stops or speeds up. I don't know what happens between the club and the car stopping in front of my apartment but the second we're there, both of us are moving with purpose out of the back seat and onto the street.

"I'll Venmo you for the Uber, bye," Brianne leans forward, pressing a kiss to her best friend's cheek.

Dakota leans over the guy he's taking home as we get out of the car.

"Bye!" She closes the door in his face and pulls me with her entire force so I'm moving behind her.

127

"Do you have any idea where you're going?" I laugh and she stops.

"Actually, no. Go." She moves around me and starts pushing me from behind.

I scan my key card into my building and lead her to the stairs. We walk up the flights of stairs until we're walking down my hall and to my door.

"Are you sure your roommates aren't going to... I don't know, be a certain type of way toward me? Are they going to say something or are they going to try and talk to me? Do I have to lie or pretend? Do I need to know their names before I—"

I cover her mouth with my hand and nudge her. She slightly moves back, her back against my front door.

"I don't think I want to hear another word about my roommates, got it?" I ask her and I feel her smirk under my hand.

"That was the hottest way anyone has ever told me to stop talking so much," she tells me and I smirk as I open my door, for once opening it to quiet.

"I'd never tell you to stop talking," I remind her and Xander is sitting on the couch by himself. Nico is sitting in the recliner and they are watching a movie that I don't care to pay attention to. They both look over the back of the couch, their eyes moving from me to Brianne, then back to me.

"Drew?" I ask them.

"Out with his almost girlfriend," Nico says.

I notice the smirk on Xander's face and he just turns the volume up on the movie as we pass. Brianne pulls me with her hand down the hall. *I'm never going to hear the end of this, but I don't care.* I turn her toward my bedroom. She walks in and closes the door behind me before I can even get a chance. She's on me faster than lightning. Her lips are more persistent and I didn't know that was possible.

"Bri—"

THE RULES OF YOU AND ME.

I can't even get her full name out.

"Shhhh," she mumbles against my lips, pulling me to my bed with her.

"Need consent, Sunshine," I groan and she pulls back now, a smirk on her lips.

"Okay, how's this?" She lets go, sitting on my bed with her legs crossed. She takes her cowgirl hat and places it over her heart. "I hereby swear to the sex gods that I allow Parker Thompson to... What was it... Kiss me until I forget my own name?" she jokes and I slowly walk toward her.

"You think you're so funny," I shake my head, approaching.

"I think I'm absolutely hilarious actually, probably the funniest person I know if I'm being honest." While she speaks, I close the space, standing with my knees touching my bed, my hands now turning her face toward me.

"I'm serious. I need you to tell me yes when it's okay and no when it's not. You've been drinking and so have I so I need to make sure that this stays... That we stay safe. That you feel safe," I tell her and watch her face soften.

"I do feel safe," she tells me softly.

She sets her hat down next to her and reaches for the collar of my shirt, pulling me down to her. With her lips on mine, I feel her kick off her boots. I kick my shoes off as she backs herself up onto my bed and I would sooner die than break from her one more time tonight. I move with her, my body meshing with hers, the heat between us not settled but completely scorching. I'd happily burn if it was by her flame. If it feels this good I don't know if anyone could turn it down...

She lays down full on my bed and I'm over her, my hand moving to the nape of her neck, keeping her lips attached to mine. My other hand moves to her waist and she arches her back against my chest.

"This?" I ask against her lips.

"Yes," she's breathless as she answers, her lips perfect as they speak the words I need to hear.

I move my knee between her legs, nudging them apart. The gasp she lets out against my lips sends every ounce of blood in my body rushing to my cock and I have never needed someone more than I need the girl underneath me. Sex wasn't important while I wasn't participating but with this feeling rushing through me, I feel like it's all I've ever needed when it comes to her.

"Yes," she says before I can even ask.

My lips are on hers, then her jaw, then her neck, and I can't stop because the little sounds coming from her lips are so addictive you'd think they were fucking illegal. I suck on her neck and she moves my chest back. I stop and she pushes me back onto my own bed, taking the lead in this situation.

"You're sure?" I ask and she settles her hips on my lap, heat radiating from between her legs.

"Are you?" she asks and I nod.

"I have a beautiful girl straddling me right now and you're wondering if I'm sure?" I ask her.

"When you put it like that..." she mumbles and reaches forward, unbuttoning my shirt with purpose.

"What are you doing?" I ask her.

"Something I've thought about for the past week..." she mumbles, taking my clothes off, rolling her eyes as she looks at my chest.

"What?" I ask, almost offended by the attitude I'm receiving.

"You're so hot it's annoying. Jesus Christ," she sounds genuinely annoyed and I lift my hands up.

"Sorry?" I question and she reaches for my belt buckle, not giving me a second to register anything before she gets it undone and also unbuttons my pants, tugging them down.

THE RULES OF YOU AND ME.

"This?" she asks, moving back up and I nod

"Yes," I tell her, then her hand moves over the obvious bulge in my briefs.

"This?" she asks, her hand palming my cock.

I throw my head back at the euphoria that courses through me, "Fuck yes, Bri."

I breathe, trying not to lose it. She undresses me and spits, letting her saliva coat my cock. She slides her hand over the head, making my body jerk.

"How about this?" she asks and my eyes roll to the back of my head.

"Yes," I push the words out.

"And what about my lips, Parker?" she asks.

"I don't even need to fucking answer that," I tell her and she leans down.

She kisses me right under my belly button. I lean up on my elbows to watch as she makes her way to my hip bone, one of her hands still working my dick, her other tracing over the fern tattoo I have on my hip.

"I like this," she tells me.

"How much?" I ask.

"This much."

She leans down and kisses my hip bone and then slides her tongue over the tattoo, all the way down the V of my muscles. I keep my eyes on her despite how badly I want to throw my head back and indulge in this. She moves back, bringing her tongue to the base of my cock. She licks from the bottom straight to the tip and I clench my jaw at how good she fucking feels.

"Oh my fucking—"

"Shhhh," she mumbles and takes my cock in her mouth, her cheeks hollow as she sucks the fucking life out of me.

"I'm going to need you to stop if you want to be fucked tonight, Brianne," I tell her, wishing I didn't have to.

131

"Who says I don't want to be the one fucking you, Parker?" she asks, moving from my cock to her knees.

"Touch yourself," she tells me and I just stare at her. "I'm about to strip for you, touch yourself, Parker."

I take my dick in my hands and pump up and down slowly, my chest tight at the sight of her as she takes the hem of her shirt and lifts it up, pulling it off of her perfect fucking body. She's wearing a fully lace black bra. It's completely mesh and see-through. There's extra lace covering her nipple, making a rose.

"Keep it on," I tell her, knowing she probably spent good money on the piece of lingerie.

"Yes, sir," she mumbles, a smirk on her lips.

She reaches for her pants and removes her belt, then her pants. She's wearing matching underwear with a rose right over her perfect pussy. I stare at her, taking her in. She's coated in muscle but still nimble, still delicate but absolutely perfect in every fucking way.

"Come here," I tell her, letting my cock go, wanting her in my hands instead.

She crawls toward me and straddles me once more. I lean up, my arm slinking around her lower back, pulling her to me.

"You wear this on purpose? Are you trying to ruin my life, Brianne?" I ask her and she moves her hair to one side, her body perfectly fitting against mine.

"Not ruin it, just slightly alter it," she jokes and I look up at her as I kiss her chest.

I kiss the center first, and then I bring both of my hands to her breasts instead, cupping her perfect handful of tits in my hands. She watches me, her eyes still hazy and dark.

"This?" I ask.

"Yes," she whispers.

"And my mouth?" I ask her and she smirks.

THE RULES OF YOU AND ME.

"I don't even need to fucking answer that question," she tells me, repeating my words from earlier.

I move the lace down, revealing her nipples to me, her perky tits sitting perfectly. I bring my lips to her nipple and she arches her back against me, a moan finally escaping her lips. I need her like fucking water. I need her now. I swirl my tongue over her hard nipple and then, bring my mouth to the other, sucking it, then pulling it through my teeth. Her moan turns into a pant.

"Please..." she speaks out, and I nod.

"Condoms are in the drawer," I tell her, having bought some after I was told I need to get fucking laid.

She leans over, opens the drawer, reaches for the box, and takes out a foil packet. She opens it herself, inspects the condom, and then leans back, rolling it over my cock. I part my lips and she leans up, placing herself and then sitting on my cock. Pleasure erupts all over my fucking body. My lips part at the feeling and she keeps her eyes on me, not letting them even close as she rides me just like she did the bull at the bar.

"This what you wanted?" I ask her, my hands moving simultaneously to grip her ass.

"Better than what I wanted. So much fucking better," she breathes, throwing her head back.

She rolls her hips with so much fucking skill, so much purpose. My mind topples over itself trying to keep up with her movements. I can't fucking do this. It's going to cause absolute insanity. Women like Brianne Archer are the kind that start fucking wars. She's fucking me like I paid for it and I have never been more appreciative of anything in my goddamn life.

"Look at me," I tell her.

She brings her face down to me, her forehead pressing to mine.

"I want to watch you. I want to see how good my cock

makes you feel," I tell her, that confidence I've never shown making its way to the surface.

If she can be in control, why can't I make her experience better?

"Keep talking to me, please," she mumbles, her lips brushing mine.

"You're fucking me so good, Brianne. So fucking good," I speak to her and she moans so softly I almost don't hear it. I feel her, the contraction, the clench of her walls around my cock. "So fucking wet for me. You're riding me so well. Good girl," I speak the words and she gasps, her thighs clenching around mine and she cums, her lips parted against mine.

"You like it when I praise you? When I tell you how good you take my cock, Brianne? Is that what gets you off?" I ask her and she nods, her forehead pressed to mine.

"You're so fucking big, you feel so..." she moans, still riding me and I can't help myself anymore.

"I'm..." I mumble.

"Oh my god," she moans, her orgasm still squeezing my cock.

I groan as I let my release barrel through me, knowing this would have lasted longer if I hadn't been celibate for so long but also knowing that I did my job by making her cum first. She's panting by the time we've ridden out both of our highs. She stops, my cock still buried in her. I rest my forehead on her shoulder, still trying to catch my breath.

"You are so fucking hot," she speaks through deep breaths.

"Likewise," I mumble.

I open my eyes and kiss her shoulder, her collarbones, and then I tilt her head down to me.

"Are you okay?" I ask her and she nods.

"I'm... I'm tired," she admits.

"Then lay down," I nudge her and she moves off of me.

THE RULES OF YOU AND ME.

"Pass me that..." She motions to my flannel and I hand it over, watching as she slinks it over her naked body and buttons it up haphazardly.

I discard the condom and don't bother turning on the lights. I turn back to her and she's curled up in my bed, hugging my throw pillow. 'Yes you can!' it reads. *Well, yeah, I fucking did.* My head is still cloudy and I don't know if it's from what just happened or the alcohol running through my system still. She blinks a few times, watching me pull sweatpants over my lower half, not putting a shirt on as I crawl over to her.

"You don't care that I stay?" she asks in a whisper.

"Of course not..." I tell her.

I'm not a fucking monster. I'd never kick a girl out after sex, especially not Brianne fucking Archer. I spread my arm under the pillow she rests her head on, the side I normally find myself sleeping on. I'm not going to tell her that and I sure as hell am not going to make her move. She turns her back to me but finds my hand under the pillow. She folds my arm over her chest. I angle my body to her, and within what feels like seconds, she's sleeping. I'm left to wonder how the hell I can make sure I can keep the girl lying in my bed...

CHAPTER 11

LAST NIGHT'S MASCARA BY BRYNN CARTELLI

Brianne Archer:

I inhale deeply as I wake up in such a cozy bed. I don't remember Dakota's bed feeling this comfy. I also don't remember Dakota cuddling me when we sleep in his bed... I crack one of my eyes open, realizing the cologne I smell is not Dakota's. It's definitely not. This person smells like... like a warm whiskey. They smell like how you might imagine a cozy coffee shop would smell... That's not Dakota. I look at the pillow I hold to my chest. 'Yes you can!' it reads. Well, I obviously did... I peek over my shoulder and then my night flashes through my eyes the second I see Parker behind me.

Oh my fucking god.

Oh my absolute fuck.

I fucked my brother's friend. I slept with my brother's freaking friend while we were both wasted and I enjoyed it... I have to leave. I need to talk to Dakota. I need to go to his apartment right the fuck now but I don't have my car. I don't have anything but my cell phone and the clothes I wore last night. I sit up and feel the throbbing of my head as well as the whoosh that signals I am more than violently hungover. Could this be any fucking worse?

I get out of his bed and pull my shorts on, keeping his flannel on my body for the time being. I slide on my boots and take the hair tie from my wrist to pull my hair back and out of my face. I also choke down the urge to throw up because the room is slightly spinning right now. It's also hard to breathe when I think about last night. When I think about Parker and how he... I can't. I can't. I start to unbutton his flannel when he shifts in his bed and I freeze.

"Brianne?" he asks and his morning voice makes my blood pulse. He does, in general.

"I'm leaving. I'm sorry," I tell him and he shoots up.

Regret and remorse hit my chest. I feel bad. Oh, fuck.

"What? Why?" he asks, alert now. His hair is messy from sleep but his entire demeanor is still devastating to my mental health.

"Because we slept together. Do you not remember?" I speak in a clipped tone.

"I remember every second of it. That doesn't explain why you're trying to leave in such a rush," he tells me.

"Because this was a huge, horrible mistake and I should have had enough sense to not sleep with my brother's fucking friend," I tell him and he starts to argue despite his face dropping. "I'm not talking about this and neither are you. If we talk about it, it gets messy and if it gets messy, then Bellamy finds out and that can't happen," I tell him, and leave, his shirt still on my body and the rest of my clothes still in my hands.

My stomach hurts and I really have to pee. I probably look like a wreck and a half right now but I don't care.

"Please..." The softness in his voice stops me before I walk out of the door. "Don't leave, please. Talk to me..." He's plead-

THE RULES OF YOU AND ME.

ing. My heart instantly lurches at the idea of this hurting him in some way. I close my eyes tight and sigh.

"I'm sorry, Parker," I speak softly and open the door quickly, walking as fast as I can to get out of here.

"Brianne!" Parker calls after me and I close his door behind me but I hear it open.

"Give me your keys, Xander," I hear Parker's voice.

"You are not driving my car," he fights back as I make it to the stairs.

"I will give you every dollar in my savings if I even make a scratch. Keys, now," Parker raises his voice and I hear keys rattle.

This is so embarrassing. This is so bad. I slept with Parker Thompson and it was... It was fucking phenomenal, but it was also not supposed to happen. I'm not allowed to sleep with him but I did. This was so dumb. I've made so many dumb choices, but this is by far the absolute worst one. A date with him was one thing. But sleeping with him? This is another level especially since we never defined what sleeping together means. Dakota said he did some digging and that Parker doesn't usually hook up which means this could mean something more to him than it should.

"Brianne!" He chases after me, running down the stairs.

"Go away, Parker," I say with my face turned forward.

I cringe at the tone of my voice. Jesus Christ, I'm being a bitch. I'm never a bitch. I'm not mean to people who don't deserve it and Parker definitely doesn't deserve it right now...

"You're not walking to Dakota's," he tells me and I scoff.

"We sleep together once and you're already bossing me around?" I ask, continuing to walk. "And who says I was going to Dakota's?" I ask, turning over my shoulder as he follows directly behind me.

"I'm assuming you're going to his place considering your car is there and so is your best friend. And I'm not bossing you around, Brianne. I'm not letting you do a walk of shame when you have nothing to be ashamed of," he tells me and I cringe again. *Just what I thought.*

"Speak for yourself," I tell him, walking quicker, wishing I could lose him. I wish he would just go back upstairs. I am ashamed. Ashamed that I'm the worst sister in the entire world.

"Ouch," he mumbles and I take a deep breath.

"Go back upstairs Parker, please," I start to beg.

"Not happening, Brianne," he argues.

I clear the last flight of stairs, and speed walk to the doors.

"Either you get in the damn car with me or I will drive next to you the entire way. Your choice," he tells me and I turn quickly.

"You wouldn't..." I mumble.

"I would. And the longer we stand here the more chance someone sees us together, which is obviously what you're trying to avoid. So, you make your choice. You're wearing my clothes outside of my apartment."

He paints a very clear picture and I clench my jaw. I fight the urge to scream. I'm such an idiot.

"Fine," I grind the words out and he doesn't smirk, he just nods his head to a very nice all-black Range Rover.

I move quickly, hoping there's not a single peering eye that will see us together. I climb into the passenger side and he sighs deeply.

"You are so fucking stubborn," he mumbles to himself.

I'm also sore and I feel like I might throw up... and I still really need to go pee.

I don't reply but I do look away from him because the sight of him driving with one hand on the wheel while wearing one of those stupid fucking compression shirts makes me think maybe I was smart for sleeping with him last night. I

THE RULES OF YOU AND ME.

don't remember how it escalated to that. I do remember snippets of the events that happened in his bed last night and how good they made me feel. I thought my exes were good in bed. Parker is another fucking story. He's an entire three book series...

"Are we going to talk about this?" he asks me and I groan.

"No. No talking, especially not about what happened," I tell him and he chuckles to himself.

I look at him and he's devastatingly pretty. So I look away, not giving myself a chance to stop regretting last night. I need to regret it. I need to regret him. That's the only way to make sure I don't do something stupid again. Or maybe I just need to sort out how all of this is making me feel and then I'll decide if I should or shouldn't do it again... or maybe I should talk to Dakota first and then choose what to do.

"I should have told you no," he mumbles to himself.

I press my lips together, a slight frown hitting my lips.

"So I was the one..." I start and then sigh, not wanting to finish.

Of course, I was. Because I want him. Sober or not, I wanted Parker. I just know better when I'm sober.

"Yes, you. I wasn't going to start anything because I knew... I knew you'd probably not want to because of Bellamy but you did it. I waited and you came onto me," he explains and I keep my mouth shut for a second, fighting the urge to continue talking.

"Well, I shouldn't have. I'm sorry I did it but I'm not sorry for walking away right now. I'm... I'm panicking, and this was just a downright bad idea," I speak after a few moments of silence.

He clenches his jaw, his fist tightening around the steering wheel. He gets to Dakota's apartment after a few more minutes in silence and I tighten my grip on my stuff. I look at Parker and

141

once again, my chest tightens at the sight of him. He looks... Sad. Hurt even...

"I'm sorry, Parker, it was a dumb hookup and—"

"If that's how you feel, that's fine, but speak for yourself," he grumbles and I stare at him in the car. His hair is disheveled from sleep and his face is distraught. *Am I an asshole? Am I a bad person? Am I wasting my time worrying about all of this when I need to talk to Dakota?* Yes, that's one thing I can definitely answer right now.

"I need to go," I say, then grip the door handle and open it.

"Call me when you actually want to talk about this, Brianne," he tells me and I ignore him, getting out of the car.

I slam the door and run to the apartment building. I get in the elevator and press the button a few times until the door closes and it takes me to his floor. My feet take me straight to his apartment. I type in the code and enter without even texting him a warning.

"Dakota!" I scream.

"Oh my god, it's 9 in the morning, Brianne," he groans from his open bedroom door.

"I don't give a fuck what time it is. I'm in crisis mode. Call the fucking cops, 911," I run into his room and there is another naked man.

I remember dancing with him but not his name. Dakota is rubbing his eyes and the other guy looks absolutely confused as he looks between the two of us. I look at the guy, then Dakota, and raise my eyebrows, waiting.

"Baby B, this is Henry. Henry, this is Baby B," Dakota yawns and I sit on the end of his bed, ignoring the naked man.

"I slept with Parker Thompson," I say quickly.

Dakota rolls over and sits up all the way.

"Full penetration?" he asks and I nod.

THE RULES OF YOU AND ME.

"I don't remember all of it because we were both drunk but I do remember most of it so yes," I tell him and his jaw drops.

"Are you sure?" he asks and I scoff.

"It feels like someone took a hammer to my vagina this morning so, yes, I'm positive. And I'm hungover and I need to pee, but more importantly, I fucking slept with Parker Thompson," I tell him.

"Who is Parker Thompson?" Henry speaks with a groggy voice.

"Brianne's hot football crush," Dakota answers.

"He's not my crush. He's a hot guy that also happens to be my brother's friend which is why this is so fucking bad, Dakota! Wake up! Get with the program!" I tell him.

"Oh my god, we are not back to this, are we? You said you'd go on a date with him. You were already going to give him a chance and you didn't seem to care last night," he argues.

"Wait, who's your brother?" Henry asks.

"Okay Henry, here's the rundown. My brother is a senior and the captain of the football team. He is friends with Parker who is also one of the other captains, but didn't become friends with my brother until over the summer so that's why we've never met until now. I met him then and thought he was hot because he is. He made a move on me and asked me out on a date, and then I made a move on him, and we slept together and now I'm screwed. Did I mention that my brother is like my best friend?" I ask and then take a deep breath.

"You talk a lot," Henry tells me and I groan.

"Ugh! Neither of you are helping!"

I get up and go to Dakota's bathroom, finally going to pee. The second it burns, I stare at the wall and absolutely know for a fucking fact this is a higher power punishing me for being the worst sister in the entire world. I probably didn't pee after sex last night. And now... Now I am almost certain I have a UTI, a hangover, sore muscles, and a throbbing vagina. I have to lie to Bellamy now. I can't face Parker until I figure out what I want or what I'm going to say. What else? What the fuck else? I finish and still feel like I need to pee, further solidifying the fact that I probably have a UTI. I walk out of the bathroom and feel mad, defeated, and so utterly frustrated with myself.

"Can I scream?" I ask.

"Scream?" Henry asks.

"She does this. Yeah, go ahead," he tells me, taking a pillow and covering his ears. I let out a scream and then settle into myself. I don't feel any better—not even slightly.

"I need to go to the doctor," I tell him and he sits up.

"Why? What's wrong?" Dak asks me.

"I think I have a fucking UTI," I mumble, stripping Parker's shirt from my body.

I take a shirt out of the pile of my things sitting on Dak's floor and pull it over my head. I shove the rest of my things in my duffle. I grab my keys and my bag, slinging it over my shoulder.

"Okay, maybe that is a sign of some sort," he tells me.

"Exactly. I'm being punished for being a slutty little whore. I'm leaving. I don't care what your plans are later, you need to cancel because this crisis is not over, it's just being postponed. Got it?" I turn around and point at him.

"Sir, yes, sir," he tells me, still lazily sprawled out in his bed. "I love you!" He calls out to me.

"Like a brother!" I shout.

"Like a sister!" he yells and I make it back to the front door. *I'm so fucked.*

~

THE RULES OF YOU AND ME.

I walk into my apartment feeling exhausted, defeated, and with an antibiotic prescription in my hand for the UTI from hell. This antibiotic isn't going to help with the throbbing headache or the fact that I threw up in the bushes outside of our building. I am not doing well, actually, I'm doing the exact opposite of that. I receive a look from Bellamy who's sitting on the couch by himself watching *Love, Simon*. I stare at him, our eyes locking. I know if he knew the truth of what is upsetting me right now he could hate me. But I need my brother now and always. I'm fighting with myself, but my lip quivers, and my eyes well up.

"Come here," he nods his head.

I scurry into the living room, ditching all my bags and things on the floor. I sit on the couch and he pulls me into him. "Tell me what happened," he mumbles.

He speaks in the same big brother tone he always uses when I come to him, warm and accepting. I don't deserve either right now considering I slept with his friend last night.

"I'm overwhelmed," I admit.

"Yeah, your first week is always overwhelming. It doesn't help that your boyfriend had a birthday and you did too. We won our first game... It's normal, and completely okay to be overwhelmed, B." He squeezes me tight. "What happened? To make you break?" he asks and I sigh.

I can't tell you... but I really want to.

"I'm hungover and I don't think I made all the right choices when I was drinking last night, Belly... I also have a UTI," I tell him.

"How did you get a UTI?" he asks and I pull back far enough to give him a look. "Oh. Oh... Ew," he scrunches his face up and shoves my head back down so he doesn't have to look at me.

"I just feel like I made so many mistakes and it's only my first week," I explain without giving details.

145

"That's what college is for. Mistakes. You'll get it right. You're not supposed to have it all figured out yet. As long as you're being safe... You kind of have to accept failure as much as you accept success while you're here. Not everything is going to be a win. Stick to doing the things that feel good, the things that make you happiest. I already know that's dance. I know you love cheer. Even if you don't know it yet, I know that you love Dakota. Stick to that..." he tells me and I nod.

I want to tell him about Parker. I think about it at first. I think about just coming clean now because keeping secrets from Bellamy has never been something I was good at, even when we were little... but I quickly decide against it. I still haven't sorted this out with Parker. I don't even want to do that.

"I'm also violently hungover," I admit. I can feel him nod.

"I can tell because you smell like throw up," he tells me, which only causes me to groan. "Go take a shower and I will make hangover food."

"You're the best person I know," I tell him.

"I know," he smirks,

I shove him and get up, going to the stairs inside of our apartment. I basically scorch my skin off in the shower and I sit on the floor for a while, letting the water semi-burn me until I get used to it. Maybe I'm going numb to it. All I know is that it feels good. I wash my hair that I'm almost positive has vomit in it. It's embarrassing but also laughable. I think about last night. I ran out like a crazy person. I panicked. Maybe I should have talked to him about it. He seemed like he wanted to talk but what about? Oh god, I'm so dumb. A hot upperclassman slept with me and I didn't even give him a chance to talk to me about it? I have no idea where he stands. He seemed upset but after I left the way I did... Would he want to talk to me again? Would he potentially want to sleep with me still? Or does he still want our date to go on? Dakota obviously thinks I should go for it.

THE RULES OF YOU AND ME.

Intoxicated me said fuck it. So... so maybe if he wants to continue this, then we do just that. Maybe we should see what happens, then maybe stop before it's too serious.

Once I'm out of the shower, I run a brush through my hair and Dutch braid it back and out of my face. The tail of my braid still reaches the middle of my back. I put on one of my dad's old sweatshirts. It's a ratty Miami Dolphins hoodie—his favorite team. The shorts I wear look nonexistent underneath my oversized hoodie. I don't feel better but I feel at least slightly more alive. I walk down the stairs and throw myself on the couch. My brother is shirtless with his back turned to me as he cooks in the kitchen.

"You alright?" he asks.

I groan in response, feeling like shit mentally and physically. I don't care if throwing pity parties is out. I am bringing it back in. I'm throwing myself a Hollywood-level pity party in my mind even though I'm currently facing the consequences of my own horrible and stupid actions. I should have listened to him this morning. Maybe I'll call him tonight if I don't talk myself out of it.

"Cover your eyes, and just... I don't know, try not to puke on our carpet. Actually, try not to puke at all," he tells me.

"If you stop saying the word puke it might help," I mumble with my arm now thrown over my face to cover it from the light.

The door to our apartment opens and I don't even look because I don't care.

"Hey, Archie... What are you making?" I hear Lawson's voice.

"Hangover food... For her," he replies.

"Oh my god, Brianne Archer's first college hangover!"

I move my arm from my face and look at him but barely see anything because he's jumping on the couch at me. He pulls me in and ruffles my hair, making me groan.

147

"I will throw up on you," I warn him.

"Throw up on Parks, not me," he jokes and my blood runs hot because I see him standing at the door, his hands shoved in the pockets of his sweats.

He eyes me, not a single hint of amusement on his features. There's not even a crack of a smile on his lips. Lips I've kissed... This is the first time I've ever felt awkward tension between the two of us. I want to talk to him now but I know I can't. Not yet. Not until the coast is clear. Maybe not at all because the look he gives me to the blind eye seems normal, but I can see in his eyes he's hurt by what I did.

"You guys want one?" he asks the guys.

"Of course, I want a burger. You make the best hangover burgers with—"

"I swear to god if you put an egg on my burger, I actually will vomit, Belly," I tell him.

"Burgers with eggs are masterpieces. They were made by gods. They were crafted by—"

"Lawson, stop talking," I tell him. He scoffs.

"Eggs on burgers are good. Right, guys?" Lawson asks both his friends.

One of which hasn't stopped looking at me since he walked into my apartment. He's showered now. His hair is still damp and absolutely perfect. He's perfect. I gave him the cold shoulder. Oh my god, I'm brainless. I fight the urge to groan at the fact that Parker is pretty and the fact that Lawson keeps saying the word egg just to piss me off.

"Yeah, I don't mind an egg on a burger," Parker shrugs.

"Because you're a guy," I mumble, following Lawson into the kitchen despite my body protesting with every step.

I sit at one of the barstools and I rest my head in my hands.

"Food doesn't have a gender. You can't say it's because he's a guy, that argument is totally invalid," Lawson fights.

THE RULES OF YOU AND ME.

"Though, I agree with you that food definitely doesn't have a gender. If it did for argument's sake... Burgers with eggs on them would be strictly boy food," I argue. "So would footlong hotdogs covered in sauerkraut. Sloppy Joe's. Meat lover's pizza. A rotisserie chicken. McRib from McDonald's. Do you want me to continue?" I ask them.

"You've thought about this a lot, haven't you?" Parker asks me.

"Yes. Considering I grew up with a brother, I know that I'm speaking facts," I tell all of them, not just Parker.

"Well, here you go. Burger with no egg, but still the perfect hangover food," Bellamy tells me, serving me a burger that does look absolutely delicious even though I'd rather go upstairs and crawl into bed than eat it right now.

If I know anything, I know that eating this will cure me or at least bring me back to life somewhat.

"Did you get meds, Bri?" Bellamy asks me.

"Yes," I grind my words out.

"For what?" Lawson asks, leaning against the counter.

"Bri has a—"

"Shut up, Bellamy! Don't air out my issues," I tell him.

"If he did that we'd be here all day, B," Lawson jokes, and I hold up my middle finger.

"What's up? Are we hanging out?" Bellamy asks his friends while we eat.

"I scooped Parks up. We thought we could go to the gym later since Kam is working and Sienna is with her mom," Lawson tells Bellamy.

"You want to come, B?" Bellamy asks me and I can hear the laughter in his voice.

"Haha, you're so funny. I'd rather die than go to the gym. Dakota is coming over. He is in fact the only man I'd like to be around right now," I admit.

149

Well, there's one other man I wouldn't mind being around but I can't say that out loud. My eyes drift to Parker for a split second. He's staring straight at me. I watch him clench his jaw, the muscles there feathering. *What does that mean?*

"Wait, Parker. Didn't you go out last night? With your roommates, right?" Bellamy asks.

I watch as Parker nods and my stomach clenches. He told them he was going out? *Interesting.*

"Did you get lucky?" Lawson asks and I choke on my food.

All three of them look at me like I'm insane. Bellamy passes me a cup with water in it.

"Jesus B..." Bellamy looks at me with concern and I choke my food down.

"I—" I start.

"It's none of your business," he tells them.

Why would they be asking Parker if he got laid? Why in the hell would they even consider asking him that? Did we get caught? Did one of Parker's roommates tell or—

"It totally is our business. We had a talk. Did you learn nothing?" Bellamy asks and I look between the three of them. *What? A talk?*

"What talk? What are you guys yapping about now?" I ask, the pounding in my head sadly not ceasing.

"Parker is boring so we made him promise he'd sleep with someone and have fun since it's college and he's such a snooze fest all the time," Lawson tells me.

My stomach bottoms out. I stop chewing for a second, not looking at Parker as the realization hits. I'm actually an idiot. A really big idiot.

"I told them no. They were making me mad over this whole thing and—" Parker starts.

Okay, so Bellamy pissed him off so Parker decided what? To sleep with his little sister to prove a point? Because it was that

THE RULES OF YOU AND ME.

easy... For once, I feel like I was used for being Bellamy's sister instead of being avoided as usual. I was picked because I'm naive and stupid.

"That doesn't matter. What he said didn't matter. He agreed. So Parker, what happened?" Bellamy asks. I don't look up as I speak.

"I don't want to hear about your sex lives," I warn them.

Especially not Parker's considering I already know it. What was he thinking? Is he really about to talk about this in front of my brother? In front of me?

"I don't care. Did you Parker?" Lawson asks.

"No," Parker lies through his teeth, his eyes bouncing between his friends, only hitting me once.

He's doing this for my sake as if he even cares about embarrassing me.

"You are lying. You're a liar. Parker, did you finally get some action?" Bellamy asks.

I wish someone would murder me in my kitchen right now. That would be better than this.

"I'm not talking about this," Parker shakes his head and I wish I could disappear.

"Just say yes or no, tell us the truth and we won't ask anything else..." Lawson promises.

Parker only eyes me once more with what looks like regret... I hate the look, but I understand it. He's at the same place I was this morning. Probably wishing it never happened. Now, I wish I never met him if I'm honest.

"Yeah, I did," he mumbles, and both the boys high-five and celebrate him.

I cringe at the thought that my brother is congratulating his friend on sleeping with me right now...

"You guys are gross," I mumble, not looking at any of them, but feeling a tight squeeze in my chest.

151

Dammit. I wish I didn't care. I wish I wasn't affected but I am. Right in the middle of my sternum, my heart is lurching.

"Says the one who's always with her boyfriend... We know what you guys do," Lawson argues and I glare at him.

"He's... You know what, whatever," I shake my head, not having the energy to argue with them.

I finish most of my burger and go upstairs, closing my door behind me. I turn the lights off in my room, lay my head down, and shut my eyes to the world, needing a reprieve from the headache and the stomach ache that Parker definitely is causing. I'm glad I didn't text him or try to talk to him since I left this morning. This was a horrible mistake. I was right in the first place.

"Wake the fuck up."

I shoot out of my bed toward Dakota, who is looking brand new and definitely better than me.

"You look like shit," he laughs.

"I feel like shit," I tell him. He sits on my bed, right next to me.

"So... Have your feelings changed at all? Where's your head at?" he asks.

"I feel like I broke the biggest rule I should have never broken. Not only that, I decided I should hear him out, and then he... Well, I found out that he had some weird thing with my brother and Lawson. They pissed him off because they made him promise he'd be more interesting and hook up with someone. So, Parker promised my brother he'd go out and sleep with someone... Then, he slept with me," I tell him.

"First of all, that's fucked up if that's the full story. But also, you probably don't know the actual full story. Parker is like... a

THE RULES OF YOU AND ME.

grumpy teddy bear. He's innocent until proven guilty. Maybe be angry for a few days and then still hear him out if you feel like it. As for what you said about the rule thing, we've been over that... There's no rule written for this. You're in the clear," he explains.

"I think I should just steer clear of him. It's gross that he was bragging to my brother that he slept with me even though Bellamy doesn't know that. I don't know, something feels wrong to me. I never said it was against the rules. I said it FEELS like I broke the rules," I admit.

"It's not on the rule list," Dakota fights back.

"Then give me the freaking rule list." I

hold my hand out. He moves, ruffling through my things before returning with the few rules I wrote down that Leah gave us. I lean over Dakota's lap and reach into the coffee mug on my nightstand that holds pens.

Bri and Dak's rule list.

1. If you drink, be careful. If you're ever in trouble, call an upperclassman.

2. If you fuck a football player, keep it to yourself.

3. We take care of our people. Football players and cheerleaders lean on each other. Don't fuck that up.

4. Don't let Dakota get you pregnant. (LOL)

I laugh at the last one and Dakota rolls his eyes. He looks at me expectantly and I stare at the list and then sigh.

"Well, what are you waiting for? What's number 5?" he asks.

5. DO NOT! Sleep with Bellamy's friends... Well, don't do it again.

6. Actually, don't sleep with any football players from Seattle Pike University ever again.

"Hey, I will not be doing that. I personally have no reason not to sleep with hot football players," he fights me. I fix it, putting in parentheses that Dakota is excluded from that rule.

7. Never let Bellamy know Brianne partook in #5.

"How about you add the fact that tequila turns you into a little slut?" Dakota asks and I scoff.

"Dakota you have to be nice to me, I'm hungover and suffering," I tell him.

"It's not on the rule list. I actually don't have to do that," he tells me.

"Fine," I grumble, putting my pen back to the paper.

8. Remember tequila makes me take my clothes off.

9. Dakota Milton has to be nice to me when I'm hungover and in crisis.

I stare at the rules and shrug.

"Seems pretty solid," I tell him and hold it out.

He opens my bedside table and ruffles through it until he gets the tape out. He rips off a piece and hangs it up in my makeshift gallery wall.

"Now you can read it every night before bed," he laughs and I do too, leaning my head on his shoulder.

"I feel like a horrible sister," I admit.

THE RULES OF YOU AND ME.

"You're not a horrible sister," he tells me.

"You have to say that," I laugh.

"No, I don't. I actually have every right to not say that. I'm always honest with you, Baby. You know that," he tells me.

"Enough about me. You need to tell me about your night with the cowboy," I angle my body to him and he smirks,

"Save a Horse (Ride a Cowboy) might be my new theme song," he starts and I throw my head back in laughter, feeling far better than I did this morning.

I'll just... avoid Parker. I'll pretend he doesn't exist unless I'm forced to be around him. Then I will be civil and act like nothing happened. Even if it was the best sex I've had. Even if I did enjoy it. I can never let it happen again. I can never let anything else happen between me and Parker Thompson.

CHAPTER 12
LINGER BY THE CRANBERRIES

Parker Thompson:

"Thompson, get your ass over here now!" Coach screams over the entire locker room from his office.

Everyone looks at me, literally the entire team. Heat hits my cheeks and I fight the urge to cringe. Bellamy taps my thigh as he sits on the bench in the middle of the locker room. He's probably tired and sore after the fight we just put up to win that game. We won by the skin of our fucking teeth. Coach was pissed. I understand why, I'm pissed too. That team wasn't one we should be worried about losing to. We should have wiped the ground with them but we didn't.

"You're going to be fine," Bellamy tells me as I run my towel over my hair once more, drying it as it curls up.

It's growing out, just now reaching my chin. What I had going on before wasn't doing me any favors so I figured I'd try something different. Maybe that will get Brianne Archer to talk to me again. It's been a week since she ran away from my apartment screaming and as much as I don't want to admit it to

EMMA MILLER

anyone, especially myself, it hurts. Her leaving the way she did and calling me a mistake hurt my damn feelings.

Bellamy looks at me expectantly and I clench my jaw. Reason number fucking one as to why I shouldn't speak to Brianne Archer is right next to me right now. I'm not crossing her boundaries. She set a very clear one and that was that we can't ever do what we did again, and Bellamy cannot find out. Staring at him right now, I feel like a dick for what I'm keeping from him. That's why I've been avoiding him all week. I also feel stupid for even letting myself surpass the single boundary I told myself I wouldn't cross until I was sure. I thought I was sure she'd be over the Bellamy thing. I was stupid to think that. That doesn't mean all of this isn't lingering around. If she texted me right now, I would be the fool that would run out of this locker room to meet her and talk this out.

"It's because I sucked tonight," I tell my teammate but he shakes his head.

"No. We all did. We all were somewhere else. There's no need to harbor all of the defeat on your shoulders. Maybe Coach Corbin has notes for you specifically," Bellamy shrugs as Lawson walks around the corner, a towel wrapped around his waist.

"Or he's kicking your ass to the curb," Lawson shrugs and turns around.

"I don't think I should listen to someone who's dumb enough to get a tramp stamp," I joke, eyeing the small butterfly inked on Lawson's lower back.

"My tramp stamp is sexy first of all, and second of all, it's Bellamy's fault I have it so blame him," Lawson hikes his thumb toward his friend who is smirking a mischievous grin.

"You better go before Coach bursts a blood vessel," Bellamy nods and I look over to see a red-faced Coach Corbin standing in his office, pacing.

THE RULES OF YOU AND ME.

I sigh and pull my shirt over my body, walking myself toward the office, dread present in my stomach. I really don't feel like getting yelled at right now. I shove open the door and he nods his head to the chair in front of him. His pointer finger taps his chin tentatively.

"Before you say anything, I know how bad I was tonight. I'm sorry," I tell him and Coach Corbin shakes his head.

"Be quiet son." He puts his hand out, almost like he's signaling for me to calm down.

"I—"

"I said shut it. I can hardly pull any words out of you normally, but the one time I need you to shut the hell up, you want to yap?" he asks.

I close my mouth instantly. *Well, that's one way to put it...*

"Yes, sir, sorry, Coach," I mumble, pushing myself back into the chair, wishing I could melt into the squeaky seat.

I take a deep breath and run my hands over my knees, wiping the sweat that's collected.

"I'm going to be honest with you here, Thompson. You know I've got your file. Just like every single one of my players I know your story, I know your life," he explains. I nod once. "You play like you're trying to win a fight," he tells me and I furrow my brows.

"Isn't that what I'm supposed to do?" I ask him.

"To an extent, yeah, you're supposed to fight to win. You're not winning a fight though, do you understand me?" he asks and I just look at him.

"You're the wide receiver. Your job is to do... Well, to do almost everything, you know what you're out there to do. Tell me." He motions for me to speak and I sigh, wondering if this is some type of trick question.

"I... I'm supposed to block players from the ball, run plays, run the ball. Outsmart, outmaneuver. Fight to win," I finish and he shakes his head.

"The win shouldn't be a fight if you're doing your job right, Parker," Coach Corbin shakes his head. "It's the way you were taught, the way you learned as you grew up and it's gotten you very very far in your career. But I want your career to move past here. I want you to go all the way. Like Griffin Jones. Like Archer is going to when he leaves here," he tells me.

The mention of continuing my career makes my heart jump. I nod.

"I want to keep going. That's all I want," I admit.

"I know, kid. I know and you can but you can't do it with the technique you have right now. You're on the right path. You just need a little bit of direction. You've fought your whole life to keep going, to stay afloat, to keep your football career. You don't have to fight anymore. You can enjoy it," he explains and I ignore the small sinking feeling in my chest.

"Yes, sir." I nod. "I'll do whatever it takes," I admit.

I truly would. Coach Corbin is right. I've fought for this my whole life. I have strived to be where I am and I'll be damned if I let something as minuscule as my technique on the field ruin that.

"You're the leader next year when Lawsy and Archie head out of here. I need you at the top of your game. You're at the top of your year but that's not enough. I had a lot of the other guys do this, separately, sometimes in the same classes. It shouldn't be an issue if you don't make it one. Do you understand?" he asks and I get a bad feeling.

"What is it?" I ask and he sighs.

"I need you to train with one of the head dancers over in the fitness buildings. Once or twice a week until I feel like you've improved. I've already talked to the dance professor. She's always on board considering she's helped me before."

THE RULES OF YOU AND ME.

I clench my jaw at his words.

"I'm not saying no, I just want an explanation as to why dancing will help me?" I ask him.

"Because you treat your body like a freight train. Sometimes I need a train and sometimes I need you to float... Like a little flower."

I stare at the big man in front of me and blink a few times before I open my mouth.

"You want me to be a flower on the field?" I ask him.

"Damn straight. Now agree and I will get your schedule set up. You aren't playing and risking an injury the next few weeks, so until you get your act together you're not stepping foot on that turf. Not until there's been time for improvement." He tells me. I sigh and shake my head.

"I said I'd do whatever it takes, I meant it," I tell him.

The thought of not playing is almost devastating but that means I need to prove to Coach I can really do this. Working on my game and working on my career is really what I should be focused on, not what Lawson and Bellamy want me to focus on. Not girls or parties or doing college the right way. I need college to end and everything else in my life to begin.

CHAPTER 13

MUSCLE MEMORY BY KELSEA BALLERINI

Brianne Archer:

I put my bag in a cubby hole and start to put my hair up. Professor Laurent offered an opportunity for one of the freshman dancers to earn credit hours if they taught technique to one of our athletic students. I wonder if she will be a lacrosse player, or maybe soccer? Maybe she and I will be friends... I turn at the sound of the door opening and I freeze in my tracks. Parker Thompson stares at me with a duffle bag on his shoulder. I clench my jaw.

"What are you doing in here? I'm about to have a lesson with a student-athlete and I don't need any issues before that," I say, trying to tame my annoyance, but failing miserably.

"I'm the student-athlete, Brianne," he mumbles and I swear my blood runs cold.

There are two ways I can do this. I can talk my face off, make this more awkward than it already is, and inevitably make myself wish I didn't exist anymore... Or I could play it professional and then get out of this teaching thing when I see

Professor Laurent tomorrow. I think that the ladder is the best option.

"Shoes off," I snap out of my stupor and he just stares at me.

I tilt my head and he kicks off his tennis shoes, listening to me.

"Sorry," he mumbles, not seeming to be enthused at all.

I wouldn't expect him to be. He probably thought he was done with me after our last encounter but here we are. I try not to let my thoughts of him infiltrate what I'm supposed to do here —teach him like anyone else.

"You don't have to apologize. If you're going to do these lessons, you have to respect this space. I'm not saying you wouldn't but there are rules to the dance studio. The floors are cleaned every day. If you track outside dirt and mud or whatever onto it, you could damage ballet shoes or anything of the sort. It's also dangerous, you could slip very easily," I explain, almost like I'm teaching a child.

"Understood," he speaks coolly like he always does.

That's Parker though. No thoughts, no feelings. If he had them, he wouldn't have done what he did.

"Where do we start?" he asks.

His face is unreadable but so damn handsome. His hair is longer. Even since my birthday, it's grown. I wonder if he's going to continue to grow it... I snap out of the thought and nod toward the floor.

"Never work your body without stretching first. I'll talk you through some of the things I've planned. I expect you to remember how you need to stretch your body to get the correct work done. I'm sure that you'll feel embarrassed doing this in front of your football friends, but if you do it, I'm sure it would make your game better," I tell him.

He nods and sits himself down on the floor. I lead him through stretches, keeping a completely straight face as I master

THE RULES OF YOU AND ME.

the stretch and watch him struggle. It's no surprise that he's not as flexible, but it does give me a sense of superiority over him. He reaches forward, trying to touch his toes.

"You can go a little farther," I push.

"Not all of us are human rubber bands," he mumbles and I smirk. "Press on my back."

I stand up and walk around him. I push down on his back lightly.

"Tell me when," I say behind him. I slowly push until I feel him let out a breath.

"Okay, when," he groans. "How the hell do you do this?" He sighs.

I fight the urge to do the same. It's easy to have a conversation with him, even if I'm fighting with myself over it. I want to give in.

"I've tortured my body for years to be able to get it to bend and contort the way it does. It doesn't happen overnight but you'll gain more flexibility as you work. You'll never be on my level because men's bodies don't move the way women's bodies do. But you know that," I explain and he nods.

"You know plenty about your body and how it moves and works in an intense and immediate way, but I want you to forget everything you know because this is different. For this... Your body is a vessel for movement," I explain.

"O-okay," he nods and stutters like he's overwhelmed.

"It's alright, Parker..." I tell him and he nods. "You can't really fuck this up. It's just us so if something doesn't go right, no one will ever know. You can make mistakes, I swear."

"Keep going," he tells me and I do, ignoring the uneasy feeling he's exuding off of him in waves.

"Ballet is all about symmetry. Your body is a line and it flows all together as one. The entire purpose of a ballerina is to appear graceful and elegant. You take up space, you elongate, you

165

connect every movement together to be moved as one. Fluid, like..." I hesitate.

"Water," he finishes. I hide my smile.

"Right, like water," I tell him. I face him and he stands with his back against the bars.

"I know the thought of it... Dancing and doing ballet is so silly to some, but it requires a lot of strength, mentally and physically. It's going to sharpen you up. It will enhance your focus on the field, your flexibility, balance, stamina, endurance, and honestly, your speed too. If you strengthen your knees and leg muscles through the practice, then you're definitely going to increase your speed."

"I don't think it's silly," he tells me and I fight a small smile.

"Then let's really get started," I tell him.

I walk him through the barre movement, that's mostly what we're going to do all night. Just barre practice. I take him through an entire course of plié, demi plié, and deep fifths. He doesn't complain, but he does start to sweat. I keep my smile to myself. When I have him turn away from the mirror and back to the front, I demonstrate.

"Rond de jambe à terre," I speak.

"Bless you," he jokes and I roll my eyes. I show him the movement.

"This. À terre means on the ground," I tell him, showing him the circles my pointed foot makes as I hold the bar and face him. "Now, you." I motion and he takes a deep breath.

"Don't complain," I mumble.

"All I did was breathe," he argues.

"In a complaining type of way," I fight back.

"I'm not complaining, I just suck," he admits.

"I sucked on my first day too," I tell him quietly, watching. "Can I touch you again?" I keep a soft tone to my voice. I know he let me push his back down but this will be different.

THE RULES OF YOU AND ME.

"I... Yes," he speaks quietly, continuing the motion.

The tension between us doesn't cease and it makes me want to scream. There are obviously things unsaid sitting between us. Both of us are failing at ignoring them. The minute he finds comfort in his movements, he will succeed here. If he puts his mind to it. I touch his stomach first and straighten him out, but keep my hand pressed to his hard muscles.

"Here. Keep it tight. I know it kind of aches, but when it feels uncomfortable, you're doing it right. In this art, everything comes from your core. If you don't keep it tight and straight, everything else fails to fall where it needs to," I explain. "Breathe. You have to keep breathing," I instruct, looking up to his face now. He's concentrated and focused.

"Explain," he tells me through trapped breaths that he's working to steady.

"Explain what?" I ask, tilting his chin down so he's looking straight ahead.

"Explain the breathing. In your words, explain it. Treat me like I know nothing," he explains, falling out of his stance.

I look up at him, my chin slightly tilted, "I'm confused. You're an athlete Parker, you know—"

"I know that I know. You said forget the stuff I know and I'm doing that. Even the basics. I want you to treat me like I know nothing about the body. Like I know nothing about what's happening. This is not a way I've ever moved myself. Even if I know certain things, they're going to be different in this... Art," he explains.

"Okay, start over. Get back into position," I instruct with my arms, angling them and stretching them exactly the way I need to so he can see me. "Tighten, chin up."

I do both movements myself as I face him.

"Done. Now, tell me," he breathes, trying to keep his exhale and inhale steady.

"When you work your body and your muscles, the amount of oxygen you breathe is important, especially in ballet. It keeps you calm and centered and like I told you before, finding your center and your balance is one of the most vital things. I remember my dance teacher back in my hometown. She was my teacher for years. She told me that when you make your breathing level and consistent, you're triggering a part of your nervous system that calms you and allows for your body to relax which will in turn relax your blood flow. All over, it makes you better in the field," I explain to him, keeping my breathing steady despite how hard it is with him this close.

My heart is haphazardly beating out of my chest. I'm standing at his front as he does the instructed move over and over again. He keeps his face steady, his breathing correct, and his form perfect. I can see the concentration and slight struggle in his features. It's hard not to fall victim to how devastatingly beautiful Parker Thompson is. I fell victim to it far easier than I had thought I would. He looks down, only with a glance of his brownish green eyes and I know that I can't do this again. The height difference between us is enough to make me fold, so I back away another step and nod.

"Um... If you don't regulate your breathing, the soreness of your muscles can increase. It's not ideal considering in ballet if we ever do it professionally, it's going to be an everyday kind of thing. Sore muscles don't help that. It's a build-up of lactic acid in the body that could have that effect," I tell him and his eyes haven't left me since he caught me staring.

He doesn't fumble in his near-perfect stance.

"Elongate," I tell him, sweeping my fingers around the curve of his arm, making sure it's perfect.

I step back, ignoring the screaming of my body as I step away from him. I don't care what I want. It's not what I need.

"And lastly," I nod down to his butt. "Tuck in your tail.

You're not a mommy duck. You don't have anyone following behind," I joke and watch as he falls into a perfect form.

"This sucks," he grunts his words out, his muscles trembling as I stare at them.

"I'm aware," I smirk to myself. "But you actually look perfect. Okay, relax."

He sighs and lets the position go.

"Now the other side," I tell him and watch as he clenches his jaw, but listens and starts on the other side. I can tell this is harder than he thought but I do see an appreciation for my sport growing in his features.

Parker and I finish and he sits on the ground, crouching to put his shoes back on. I stay, my body hovering toward the stereo system, not wanting to signal that I don't plan to leave anytime soon. The stress this one single lesson alone has caused me makes me want to stay and let it out. My body wants to reach for him but I question if I should. I want to step closer but I know it's not what I need. I should do it, to teach him better, I should. I... I need to control myself but it's hard when I don't know if it means something different. Parker Thompson only slept with me to prove something. I never should have slept with him in the first place. So this can't continue, these little lessons, I'll beg one of my classmates to take over.

"Brianne..." I turn to look at him. He's standing by the door, his shoes on, his duffle hanging from his shoulder.

"What's up?" I ask, trying to keep my voice casual.

"Can we talk when I walk you to your car? Please?" he asks and I look at my phone still attached to the stereo.

"I... I wasn't going to leave just yet, actually," I admit.

"Oh. Are you working on something?" he asks and I shake my head no softly.

"When something doesn't feel right, I get rid of that feeling and come here. Dancing never feels wrong," I explain in the simplest way possible.

"Doesn't feel right..." He breathes the words out, looking at me with kind eyes. I don't need this. This conversation, this... this potential argument.

"I know. I know that this is not what you had in mind and it's weird and hard and kind of awkward that I was the one who said I would help you, I know. I am going to go to my professor tomorrow and I'll get someone else to teach the class, okay? You don't have to deal with me or be near me anymore, I promise. This wasn't what either of us expected, honestly. I just thought the extra credits would be nice and my professor never mentioned it was a football player. She just said athletics. I'll drop tomorrow so—"

"Don't. Please, don't drop me," he cuts me off.

"Don't?" I ask, taking a single step away from the ballet room stereo.

"If... If it's not bothering you. If being my teacher isn't bothering you, then I'd rather you not..." he tells me.

"W-why?" I ask, confusion stumbling my words.

"Why? Because I need this. I told you a part of my story, I didn't lie. I...I needed football to survive and I still need this sport. I could lose it if I don't do what Coach Corbin says. He says I have to do this and if I can avoid any... issues, then I'm going to," I let him explain, but feel a sting at the way he looks at me when he says issues.

"I don't want to be an issue," I speak just above a whisper.

"I didn't mean it like that," he fights back but I speak right after.

"It's weird. For me, this feels weird," I admit.

170

THE RULES OF YOU AND ME.

"What can I do? To make this work, what can I do?" he asks, taking a step toward me.

I can hear the desperation in his voice. My heart clenches, the empath in me waking up. I can't let him suffer, even if it's a struggle for me.

"Pretend it never happened. Just move forward. I don't want to think about what we did. I don't want to think of you in that way ever again," I tell him, wanting to make sure he knows that nothing will be an issue. Considering that I was his idea to start with, it's annoying he'd see me as a problem but if he needs my help... Who am I to stand in the way of his career when in the long run, it can also help mine?

"Why can't it be someone else?" I ask him. "My classmates are good dancers. I can lie to my instructor. I can just tell her that my schedule is more hectic than I anticipated."

"If you really need to do that for yourself, you can, but I prefer you because I'm comfortable. Here in this unfamiliar space, I feel comfortable because I trust you. I don't know the others and I feel like it would be hard for me to... Do well if I... If I'm not comfortable," he explains. "But that doesn't matter if you... I mean if you're not—"

"It's fine. I'll be fine."

I shake out my thoughts, ignoring that nagging thing in the back of my head that's yelling at me. It's saying that just because he's comfortable in this space, doesn't mean I need to feel uncomfortable, especially since this is my safe space. This is my place to feel comfortable. But once again, isn't it ideal to push both of our careers further? Living in comfort has never helped anything or anyone, including me. I need to get over it.

"Brianne."

"No. It's fine. I'll do it. Just pretend. I know you said you didn't want to pretend it never happened but we have to. For this to work, we have to. This is strictly professional."

I slice my hands in a line but I smile. It's a fake smile that feels wrong and tight. Parker clenches his jaw.

"Yes, ma'am," he agrees.

"Okay, maybe not that professional," I joke but he barely smiles.

"Be safe."

He looks like he wants to say more, but he only looks for a second longer and then backs away, not saying another word. He leaves me to get every ounce of feeling I have out on this dance floor before it's cleaned and left for the next class in the morning.

CHAPTER 14

IMGONNAGETYOUBACK BY TAYLOR SWIFT

Brianne Archer:

I walk into my apartment and I see Bellamy's open bedroom door and his body sprawled on his bed. He's alone, for once. Lawson is lying across the couch and he looks freshly showered. He nods at me as I throw my keys in the bowl on the counter. I shove my duffle bag off and my backpack on the floor next to our table. I walk straight into Bellamy's bedroom and he eyes me from where he lounges.

"Hey, B."

He pushes himself up to a sitting position with his back leaning on the headboard behind him. He pulls his knees up to his chest and opens his arm to me. I kick off my shoes and pull myself onto my brother's bed. He gives me a side hug and I rest my head on his shoulder. I look at his TV and he's watching football tapes. I don't know if these are scrimmage videos or not, but we've only had two games officially so far. We've won both but barely scraped by on the last game so he's probably trying to fix that. Maybe that's what Parker is doing...

"Is Parker Thompson shitty at football?" I ask him and Bellamy pulls back to look at me.

"No, he's—"

"He's stellar, actually."

We both turn and Kamryn walks out of Bellamy's bathroom. Steam from the shower she obviously just took billows out from behind her, and a towel is draped over her body.

"You're actually the perfect person to ask," I turn my attention to her as she rummages through my brother's drawers.

"Rude. I play the sport," he argues.

"And I've been studying all of the prime players on SPU's football team for years including Parker. You know your stats. I'm sure you know some things about Parker, but you don't know everything," she tells my brother.

"Why do you want to know?" Lawson comes in, leaning on the doorframe of Bellamy's room.

He has a knowing look on his face. I know he witnessed what happened between Parker and I in the bathroom, but it wasn't what he was thinking at all.

"Because apparently, your coach thinks he needs ballet practice to make him play better. I'm just trying to figure out why," I admit.

Lawson chuckles slightly. "I had to do ballet when I was a freshman," he tells me. "That didn't last long.

"Why? Because you slept with the person who was teaching you?" I ask him and he scoffs and makes a face at me.

"No," he argues.

"Yes," Bellamy corrects.

"I didn't know she would stop being my teacher if we slept together. There's no hard feelings anymore. She's probably married with kids now and I'm in the happiest relationship I'll ever be in," he shrugs.

"Anyway..." I glare at Lawson and turn to Kamryn.

THE RULES OF YOU AND ME.

She walks out of Bellamy's closet wearing a giant t-shirt and what I assume is no pants. She has her hair wrapped in a towel still as she sits on the bed.

"Parker is really good. He was on scholarship even in high school at a really prestigious place in Cali. Apparently SPU, along with California Sun University, were fighting for him to come to their school. He was trained by the best before and he's being trained by the best now. The issue is, he plays with a lot of aggression. So, I assume that's what Coach is trying to eliminate," she tells me.

"What about Lawson? He's aggressive," I tell her.

"Yes, but the only times he lets that show on the field is if someone pisses him off. And even now, he tries to maintain it. Lawson plays like any player should. Parker plays like a battering ram. He's going to get himself hurt if he does that forever. His career will end the first injury he gets," she tells me.

"Wait, so are you..." Bellamy asks and I groan.

"Yes, I am. My dance professor asked if any of us wanted to get extra credit hours. She said that it would be simple so I said yes but she never told me it was a football player. It was so awkward," I admit.

I feel awkward now talking about it when none of them know how fucking stupid I was a few weeks back. But outwardly, none of them seem skeptical of my questions. Well, except Lawson but that first bit of suspicion seems gone now.

"Awe, Parky is probably embarrassed. I bet that's why he didn't tell us. I never had to take ballet," Bellamy practically brags.

"Yeah, because you don't have to prance down the football field like a wee little fairy like me and Parks do," Lawson tells us and I scoff.

"You are nothing like a fairy," I joke, looking at my brother's best friend.

175

EMMA MILLER

He's probably 6'4 and I know he spends more time at the gym than most which is why his arms are so large. Lawson is the opposite of a little fairy but he does shoot down the field like lighting. It's insane how fast he is, and now that I know he's taken ballet classes, that checks out. He's nimble despite being a giant.

"I just need to figure out what he needs to work on," I admit.

"Parker is always insanely tense. He's always got something weighing on him. That weekend of our first game, he was great, like he had his mind elsewhere, but this past game, he was back to his usual tense self. It's weird." Bellamy tells me and my stomach sinks a little.

"He got laid the day after our first game like he said. He was probably thinking about his booty call the next day and not over stressing the game," Lawson tells us and I control my breathing to a T, not letting any of their words panic me.

This is fine, they don't know. This shouldn't be awkward for me because Parker should be just another one of Bellamy's friends.

"I'm glad you're helping, B. He does need it," Kamryn tells me and I nod with a sigh.

"He needs to learn to relax more. He needs to get out of his head," Bellamy tells me.

"So, center himself and keep his head in the game. I can fix that," I tell him.

"I'm sure you can, you're bossy," Lawson tells me and I throw a middle finger in his direction.

"No, she just talks too much," Bellamy corrects and I scoff, pushing off the bed.

"I did not come in here to get bullied. I came for advice. Goodnight, Kamryn. The rest of you can kiss my ass," I reply.

"Your boyfriend can do that," Lawson tells me and we all have eyes on Dakota who is walking through the front door.

THE RULES OF YOU AND ME.

I run over to him and jump to hug him.

"Good morning!" I shout at him and he hugs me back with one arm.

"It's almost 11 pm," he argues.

"I'm so happy to freaking see you, let's go, now," I urge him up the stairs.

I have a lot to spill to Dakota and he has a lot to spill to me. Apparently, he knows something about Leah and who she's apparently been seeing. It shocked me that she was seeing anyone at all. Leah is private and to herself, so I don't know who he had to threaten to get this info but he's got it now.

I yank Dakota into my bedroom and start stripping my dance clothes.

"Tell me about Leah Ashley," I urge.

"No, you tell me about Parker Thompson," he commands.

"Say please."

"Brianne, I hate you sometimes."

"Don't say it too loud. It turns me on," I joke.

"Leah apparently is in some deep shit with her family. I don't know for how long but she's working at a bar on campus. None of us knew," he tells me and I gasp.

"What the fuck? Which one?" I ask.

There are a lot of popular bars for the students on campus but I've never seen her at any of them.

"I have no idea, I was just told all of this. Apparently, one of the hockey players saw her at the bar at the end of her shift and the secret kind of got out. I'm not asking any other questions. I'm just hoping if she's bartending that it will help her get laid so she can release some of that tension," Dakota shrugs.

"Interesting... Our hockey team actually requires its team members to be indescribably hot so I hope it's one of them. I hope she's okay."

I go through my laundry and throw the flannel I stole from Parker the second it touches my fingertips.

"You still have that?" he asks.

"Well yeah, what the hell am I supposed to do? Drive to his house and give it back? I'm not doing that so this is mine forever. I'll just... Get rid of it, I don't know." I tell him and put on one of my brother's old SPU shirts that's ratty and should probably be thrown away along with the flannel

"Tell me about Parker now. Is he cute in tights?" Dakota asks and I roll my eyes as I climb into bed.

"He wasn't wearing tights, idiot. He was wearing normal clothes and it was... it was hard," I admit, my voice dropping.

"Awe... Come here."

Dakota opens up his arm and I nuzzle into my best friend's grasp with a sigh.

"It was just weird. I mean I know that he had a reason for sleeping with me. It's college. Hookups happen, we move on. But it's just... It's not supposed to feel this unsettled. Yes, it's my fault that it feels like this, but—"

"Don't do that. Don't blame yourself. Seriously, Baby. It's not your fault. You hooked up with him and you left. You two are done. End of story," he tells me.

"I offered him the option for me to find a new teacher for him and he insinuated that I would be a problem," I tell Dak.

"Well, I'll make myself a problem for him if he's going to be a dick. I'm sure after a handful of practices together it will just feel professional and it'll be fine. Don't you think so?" He asks and I sigh.

"I hope. I'm just going to avoid him outside of rehearsing with him even if he tries. We both got sex. We both should move on and we can do it while helping each other in our careers. That's fair. It's just hard looking at him and not wanting to punch him knowing he slept with me because of some weird

THE RULES OF YOU AND ME.

agreement he made with my brother. And to top it off, he chose me for his game just because Bellamy was annoying him. It's gross. Parker is gross," I tell him.

"He's really hot for a gross guy," Dakota jokes and I groan.

"It's always the hot ones who are complete assholes," I make light of it but still

feel that sting and burn in my chest. Parker's cut definitely hurt.

"You could always hit him with your car," Dakota jokingly suggests.

"Part of me wants to do that, part of me wants to hurt him the way he hurt me and part of me wants to ignore the red flags and just hook up with him all over again," I admit, knowing how crazy I sound.

This is tough and sticky... but I know that this agreement needs to happen, even if it's not going to be easy.

CHAPTER 15
MORE THAN JUST TONIGHT BY PICTURE THIS

Parker Thompson:

I walk into my apartment to the sound of gunfire on the TV, very loud gunfire, and screaming between my roommates about the video game they're playing. I fight the urge to freak out but I can feel anxiety and anger welling up in my chest. I make a beeline for my bedroom, not even stopping to say hi to Xander and Drew who are on the couch. Since I started dance lessons with Brianne three weeks ago, my life has felt tight and awkward and completely derailed from everything it was before.

I close my door behind me and for the first time since I slept with her, I feel regret. Because I wanted her then and I want her now. I like Brianne and I am actively trying to not think of her or about her. It's really fucking hard when all I can think about when I look at my own bed is her and the way we were together in my sheets. On my mattress. In my bedroom.

I think about us and what happened and what could happen every single time I've been with her. Then, I think about her saying this was a huge mistake and that same hurt hits my chest. I put my bag down and before I can even take a seat, there's a knock on my door.

"Go away, Xander" I mumble and he knocks again.

"Open up, pouty pants. I will break the door down," he threatens.

"Xander—"

"Parker, open the door you little baby," he knocks again and I open the door with force.

"What, Xander? What do you want?" I snap and he, as well as my two other roommates, walk into my bedroom. All three of them sit on my bed.

"We're staging an intervention."

They all stare at me from my bed.

"I am not sitting through a fucking intervention. What do you mean by intervention?" I get defensive instantly.

Xander stands up and motions between my other two roommates, signaling for me to sit down.

"Sit. Now," he insists.

I do, considering my roommates have infiltrated my room and aren't leaving anytime soon. At least they won't until I listen to them or at least pretend to.

"You have been moping around our apartment for three weeks, and haven't talked to us. Not about where you've been going two nights a week and why you're sad when you get home. You haven't even talked about what happened in general with you and Brianne Archer," Xander says.

"I have talked to you," I argue.

"I said hi to you for a week straight and you didn't even look at me. That is a big fat lie," Nico argues.

"I didn't hear you," I lie.

"Doubtful," Andrew argues from my left side.

"Okay, maybe I just didn't want to talk. What's the problem?" I bark back.

THE RULES OF YOU AND ME.

"The problem is we, as your roommates and friends, are concerned for you. We also have no idea what's happening so we have no idea how to help." Xander crosses his arms over his chest.

I have a feeling if I don't talk about it soon, I'm going to blow up about it. I'm going to freak out on someone who doesn't deserve it. Someone who doesn't need to know I'm in deep shit like Bellamy or Lawson. I grind my teeth and Xander raises his eyebrows at me. There are worse people I could have to talk to...

"Come on, Parker... We want to be your friend. We can't when you... when you act like you," he tells me and I scoff.

"What do you want me to say? It's not easy for me to just talk about my feelings or feel like you guys are my friends when I've always thought of you as just my roommates," I ask, not knowing where to start.

"First of all, ouch," Nico starts. "But second of all. I know... Actually, we all know you're not keen on talking about your feelings. I get that. I respect your privacy dude, but... We're not just anyone," Nico shrugs and unfortunately, he's right. I'm not admitting that, though.

"What have you been doing at night on Tuesday and Thursday?" Xander asks.

"Coach Corbin is forcing me to take a dance fitness class with a student teacher to help my technique on the field," I admit.

"Wait, do you wear ballet clothes?" Andrew asks and I glare at him.

"No, you idiot," I mumble.

"Wait. Dance... Is Brianne your student teacher? Is that why you're all mopey when you get home at night?" Xander asks.

"I am not mopey," I argue.

"Dude, you're mopey," Andrew nudges me.

183

"How about you tell us what happened the night of Brianne's birthday party... That's where we should have started," Nico slightly shoves me with his shoulder.

"She... I mean I went because I wanted to celebrate her birthday. I had no intentions. She was drinking and so was I. She came onto me. More than once. She kissed me, she touched me, she suggested we sleep together. I wanted to so I took her home with me. We were both willing. She was completely into me and I was very obviously into her... Then, she woke up in the morning and... Well, you saw what happened," I tell them.

"What happened in the car? When you took her home?" Drew asks.

"She told me she wished it never happened and that she shouldn't have done what she did with me. She apologized too. She felt bad but her attitude has changed," I explain.

Xander sucks in a breath through his teeth almost as if he can feel the sting of rejection I felt that day and every day since.

"Damn..." he mumbles.

"Yeah, and she hasn't spoken to me in any of our rehearsals. We're there for three hours at a time some nights and she hasn't said anything at all except her stupid fucking ballet terms and to do better and tuck in my tail," I explain and shake my head when my roommates look at me like I'm crazy. "It's a ballet thing. Anyway, I'm forced to stare at her and watch her and be near her and it's painstaking not getting to even say a word. She hates me. She won't talk to me, it's just overwhelming," I admit.

"So, you haven't really spoken in a month?" Nico asks. I shake my head.

"How was her demeanor the last time you guys spoke? Is it tense in the dance studio?" Andrew asks. I shrug and sigh.

"Kind of. It's like the two of us want to be comfortable but what happened between us is playing in the back of our heads. She always stares at me... like she wants to say something more

THE RULES OF YOU AND ME.

but she never does. The way she left, like what happened meant nothing to her also hurt my feelings. I don't want to be the first person to make an effort," I tell them.

"So, it's not because she doesn't want you," he tells me, and I scoff.

"Considering how things went the night of her birthday, I could have assumed that," I tell him.

"I mean still. She still wants you," he tells me.

"Because you're an expert? This sounds delusional," I tell all of them.

"He's the only one out of us that has gotten any action and almost has a girlfriend so, yes," Xander tells me,

"Considering he's almost had a girlfriend for a month now and none of us know her makes me question if your logic is right," I fight back.

"Okay. I know more than you. She's still into you. There's a reason she's not wanting to talk to you," he explains.

"I know the answers already guys. She's best friends with her brother. She feels like she's... like she's betraying him by sleeping with me. She thinks I'm not worth the trouble," I explain, the last words stinging as I speak them out.

"You and Bellamy Archer are friends, sure, but it's not like you guys are attached at the hip. You're not like... Like Lawson is to him," Nico fights.

"I'm aware. That's why I went for it with her. I had every intention of going about it the right way, taking her to dinner or something because I had fun with her the night of her actual birthday but I drank alcohol and made a dumb choice and now she hates me," I explain.

"Wait, answer this. Does she know that you wanted to do it the right way? Or does she think... Does she think you wanted to smash then pass?" Xander asks. I roll my eyes.

"Don't know. Didn't really have a chance to talk to her.

185

Remember she ran away after that night? She didn't want to teach me either. I basically had to beg her to not go to her professor and drop me from dance lessons. We just don't speak," I explain.

"Right... So, maybe just be extra confident and more normal than you've been. Try your best to let her know that you're interested in her... Not her cooch," Nico tells me.

"Nico, if you ever say cooch again it will be too soon," I mumble.

"I was just being honest," he shrugs.

"So what exactly do you want from Brianne?" Andrew asks me and I sigh.

Be honest and they will leave.

"I want a chance to be more than a hookup or a regret. I actually like her—what I know about her, which isn't a lot, but it's enough to make me want to know more and that's never happened before," I tell them.

"Nico is right, then, even if he doesn't know how to say it. If you make it clear that you want her in more ways than just the one, that you didn't get what you wanted out of the experience and you think it could be more, maybe she'll come around to it," Xander tells me.

"But Bellamy—"

"Is not your problem. My mom told me once that I can't base my feelings on how someone else will feel. I think maybe you should take that advice. I'll tell my mom you said thank you," Andrew smiles. "Since you don't have one..." He adds on and I roll my eyes.

"Wow, thank you, Andrew. I had no idea," I nod.

"Just saying," he shrugs.

"So, I just butter her up until she talks to me?" I ask.

"Don't say butter her up like she's a chicken or something. That's weird. Woo her the old-fashioned way. At the very least,

THE RULES OF YOU AND ME.

make her want to actually talk to you. Do something to make her feel like she should at least clarify everything between you. A gesture, like flowers and... and I don't know, name some things she likes," Xander waves me on, expecting me to talk.

"Dance and cheer and... and music. She really likes music," I tell them.

"You don't ever listen to music. Come to think of it, you're kind of like a robot. Are you sure you were even born and not created?" Andrew asks me.

"Dude, fuck off..." I scoff. "I do listen to music. I started listening to some of the artists she recommended... I would... I mean I'd listen to more if it was something that brought us closer together," I admit, feeling stupid for even saying the words out loud.

"How cute. Little Parker has a big ol' crush," Xander smiles at me.

"I don't need you to make fun of me, asshole. This might be the first time I'm talking about my stupid feelings, but it could easily be the last," I tell them.

"Parker, one day you'll learn you can rely on us. Because we might be hockey gods, but we're also advice gods," Nico tells me.

"I'm a listening god," Xander fights.

"You're none of the above, except the hockey thing," I admit, knowing each of them can skate and play like no one's fucking business.

"Game plan... You woo the pants off of Brianne Archer. Bring her over, become the cutest couple known to man, and then invite all of us to be your groomsmen at the wedding," Nico tells me.

"What about her brother?" I ask.

"He can be a groomsman too," Nico shrugs and I sigh.

"That's not what he means Nico. Bellamy doesn't need to be a problem. Not yet. Cross that bridge when you get to it.

187

Don't worry about a problem that doesn't exist. You know, Bellamy is like an avocado," Xander tells me.

"What?" I ask, wondering what is wrong with my roommates.

"If you try to eat an avocado too soon, then it's hard and doesn't mush up or taste good. It has to be just right. If you tell Bellamy Archer too soon, he won't be ripe or ready. If you tell him too late, it'll be spoiled. You and Brianne being at a certain level, it will be hard for him not to accept it," he explains.

"This plan is foolproof. She's totally going to fall for you. Then you'll have a girl and a family for once," Andrew tells me and I slap him in the chest.

"Dude! Enough about the family jokes. I was in the foster system, we get it. Shut up," I laugh despite the seriousness of his jokes.

"Sensitive," he mumbles.

"Annoying. All of you, now go. I need to go to the gym and also I need to figure out what to do with Brianne first," I tell them.

"Flirt. When no one's watching, flirt. Duh. You know how to flirt, don't you?" Xander asks.

"Of course I know how to flirt," I roll my eyes. "I have shit to do. Get out. And turn the video games down," I tell them, ushering them out of my door.

I close it behind them despite their protests and I sigh, pressing my back to the door. I don't know the first thing about flirting and I have no idea how well this will go with her. My bet is on bad. Very very bad.

CHAPTER 16
BLINDSIDE BY JAMES ARTHUR

Brianne Archer:

I stand on the sidelines in full makeup and uniform. We're through the first quarter of the game. It's starting to get slightly windy in Washington but not cold enough while we're on the sidelines. When I'm continually moving like this, it's hard not to keep myself warmed up. I stand with Dakota on my left, both of us cheering together. Leah calls out a formation and Dakota's hands move to my body.

It's easy to find comfort in him. I trust him with my body. I trust him touching me because I know for a fact he's going to catch me if I fall. I know he's going to make sure I'm in the least amount of harm while we're on the field.

"Ready, Baby?" he asks, his lips brushing my ear.

"As I'll ever be," I tell him.

I double up and he holds me with one hand, easily. I truly have never had a better stunt partner than Dakota. My whole life, the only time I was ever able to practice solo stunting was with coaches at the cheer gym. So the fact that it comes second nature to Dak and I is a miracle. It's like it was destined to happen.

I shake my pom poms, waving with a smile on my lips. The entire stadium is full of screaming, fans roaring at us from the stands. It makes my adrenaline pump when I'm stunting. I really get a good look at them from up here and part of me is filled with nerves during these parts of games. Sienna is sitting close to the front with Lawson's mom and brother. She waves at me and I smile back.

A few weeks ago, Lawson got hurt during one of our scrimmages. He's been recovering and trying his best to get himself back on the field since then. This is Lawson's first game officially back. Last week, he played only in the last quarter to test the waters. He managed to get a touchdown and win us the entire damn game so he's definitely back. Parker isn't allowed to play right now. He's been on the sidelines since him and I started our practices. According to Bellamy and Kamryn, Coach Corbin wants him to improve before he's back playing to avoid injury or messing anything up for his future.

All of the girls that are up in stunts right now chant along including me. I clap my poms and when we finish, Dakota tosses me for dismount. I double down and land in his arms with ease. We stand facing the game for the time being since the quarter is almost over. My brother and Lawson stand in the center of the field, their teammates surrounding them as they point and yell. The team breaks and I sigh, my chest tight with anxiety and butterflies for some reason.

Since I started helping Parker in the dance studio, all I've wanted to do was see some type of improvement on the field. He hasn't played, so I can't. He's definitely going to carry the team next year if our lessons work and if he can handle it with his moody bullshit. I grind my teeth as I prepare myself for the next play. I yell at myself mentally for even caring about Park-

THE RULES OF YOU AND ME.

er's well-being but at the end of the day, if he doesn't improve, it's my ass on the line.

"Baby B!" I snap my attention to the side.

Leah Ashley is staring at me. She uses her hand and motions for me to smile. I snap back into attention and put a smile on my face.

"Why are you so flighty?" Dakota talks to me and I shake my head.

"I don't know what you're talking about."

"You're such a liar," he sighs.

"Pay attention," I talk through my teeth.

"You're gonna pop a blood vessel if you keep smiling that hard," he tells me and I roll my eyes, jumping into the cheer that Leah calls. We all turn back to the stands and away from the boys, chanting in complete unison.

"Tumble passes!" Leah cheers.

We all vacate, pushing our pom poms toward the stadium seats. We spread out in groups. Some of our less talented tumblers move toward the sides, stunting in groups or with partners. They all hold up blue and gold signs that say 'Go Hornets!' I'm the last to tumble because I'm the only girl on the team with the tumble skills I have, with the exception of Leah, who never tumbles because she's helping coach us.

I watch Dak go across the sidelines and his precision always impresses me. He's incredible and his smile is award-winning. I cheer for him along with everyone else and then, count myself down to ease my own nerves. I could do this tumble pass in my sleep. The team around starts clapping for me and I run to get power in this pass. Round off, full, whip, double. I land perfectly and turn to the front, snapping my hands on my hips. I wave and smile, doing what Leah told me to do after my pass. Sass and confidence—that's what she asks for.

"B, watch out!"

I turn over my shoulder at Dakota's yell, but there's physically no way I can move before there's a football player coming straight at me from the field. I can't do anything because I freeze. It's a blur of blue and gold. Whoever it is, their arms are wrapped around me. We roll once and I land underneath him. I hear shouts but my world stops when Parker stares at me. On the way down, we tangle. His hand found the back of my head, and his arm kept me from being absolutely crushed. There's a second player, one I don't know by name, that looks like they were pushed from hitting me, I'm assuming by Parker, but I have no idea.

I guess he's never beating the Spider-Man allegations because this is the second time he's completely caught me from being crushed. Or maybe he's just clumsy and needs to pay attention. Pay attention so I don't end up in his arms, staring into his completely panicked but absolutely stunning hazel eyes. Isn't that partially why I'm training him? So he's more... Dainty? Or something. I feel a slight throb in my arm and leg but push it to the side of my mind.

"Brianne, say something so I know I didn't just completely crush you, I... I was trying to help, I saw him coming and I tried to... To fix it," he says, keeping his hand on the back of my head.

He pushes us up and he puts his other hand on my face and moves me around, looking at me all over. His hair is messy and long and my stomach is heating up at the concern lacing through his features right now.

"How did you..." I mumble, knowing he wasn't playing.

"I saw the play and I tried to intervene and I messed up. I'm so sorry. Are you okay? Say you're okay..." he speaks and commotion breaks out all around me.

My senses are immediately overloaded when not just Parker, but everyone, surrounds me. Dakota, my coach, Leah. The football coach is running up with Bellamy, Lawson, and

THE RULES OF YOU AND ME.

Kamryn. My other teammates surround me as well. My eyes scan everyone else and I force a smile, immediately wishing for the attention to be anywhere else, especially not with Parker holding me the way he is.

"I'm fine guys," I speak out over all the noise.

"Brianne—"

"I'm okay, Parker," I smile and nod, nudging his hands off of my face, not liking how intimate it feels, especially as Bellamy approaches.

I don't know where the nickname comes from. I don't know where his concern is coming from either...

"Don't lie to me Brianne, did you—"

"I'm fine," I snap at him and he clenches his jaw.

Bellamy extends his hand to Parker and helps him up. Once Parker is out of the way, Bellamy moves to me but Kamryn pushes him out of the way.

"No, move out of my way," she huffs.

Kamryn is a sports medicine student. Her job is to decipher the situation, fix what she can, and send me to the hospital if I need to go. I don't need it though.

"I'm fine guys, seriously I promise," I smile.

"I think she might have hit her head, I... I didn't mean to, I tried to stop him because I saw where he was headed and—"

"I didn't hit my head!" I talk over everyone and Kamryn snaps her fingers.

"Everyone walk away except coaches, now! Yes, you Bellamy."

She turns over her shoulder to look at my brother and he looks at me with sympathy before listening to her. The football coach, my cheer coach, and Leah all stand around me. Leah crouches next to Kamryn and looks at me.

"You okay, Baby B?" she asks and I nod.

193

EMMA MILLER

"I promise, I'm fine. He barely brushed against me, look, no scrapes, no—"

I do have some scuffs from the roughness of the track but it's nothing that won't heal in a few days. I'm fine.

"Just let me check, then you're good to go," Kam tells me.

I give her a nod but try to stay smiling so no one thinks anything. So no one gets any ideas. I'm fine. I need everyone to think that, if I'm not, I can handle it. Bellamy is supposed to be focusing on his game and I'm going to fuck that up.

"Everyone else is gone, tell me the truth. What hurts?" she asks me quietly and I sigh.

"Right knee and left elbow. It's not a big deal, though," I admit. She rolls her eyes.

"You're just like your brother. I'll be discreet but I'm going to look," she tells me, picking up on the fact that I don't want any more attention on me.

Kamryn flashes her small light in my eyes, checking me out. She presses and rotates my joints, quickly doing her once over. She nods and puts her hand on my knee that's now slightly throbbing after only a few measly minutes.

"You seem alright. If you get lightheaded or dizzy, sit down and we'll send you to the hospital. You could have a concussion if you really did hit your head. As for your knee and elbow, it seems like you're just banged up. You'll probably have some nasty bruises but you're okay," she tells me.

"I didn't hit my head. Parker is just stupid," I tell her and she smirks.

"Her sense of humor is intact, I think she's all good," Kamryn gives me a wink and stands, extending her hand to me.

She helps me up and Leah gives me a single pat on the back.

"If you want to sit the rest of the game, that's fine. Don't pass out on me," she mumbles and walks back to her spot in our formation.

194

Kamryn and both our coaches go back to their respective spaces. Bellamy catches my eye before he runs back out on the field and holds up two thumbs, checking on me. I give him two thumbs and a bright smile.

"Just say yes or no if you're alright, we can talk later," Dakota mumbles, our attention on the football field.

"No, but I'll be fine. Overwhelmed, not hurt," I tell him and we continue on, doing what we came here to do.

Parker confuses me as I watch him on the sidelines with Bellamy and Lawson. He's completely snapped back into the plays and the game. But the second he was here, over me and looking at me, it seemed like not a single thing mattered. And he could see right through my smile and me trying to get the attention off of me. He's not been very perceptive the past few weeks, so why now? Maybe I'm just overthinking his every move and making it up in my head. Maybe I need to get Parker out of my mind because he doesn't care. He just didn't want to have the burden of flattening me on the sidelines on his shoulders. He made it obvious that I was a moment, not a chapter. I'd be dumb if I didn't pay attention to that.

Dakota and I get back to my apartment before the boys do and I'm thankful for that because I need to decompress in my room for at least two minutes before I'm bombarded by them and before they ruin the peace in the space. Well, I don't intend on peace either, but my noise is comforting, theirs is... It's a lot.

"I need to scream," I grumble to Dakota as I throw my cheer bag on my floor.

"I figured as much. Go ahead," he mumbles, setting his bag down softly.

I scream and stomp my foot, letting out... I don't even know what I let out but it feels good. I take a deep breath when I finish and nod. I start stripping, turning away from Dak as I walk toward my bathroom.

"Solo shower or do you need me to sit in?" he asks and I scoff.

"I have to talk to you. You didn't even need to ask that. What kind of best friend are you?" I ask, reaching into my shower to turn the water on.

I take my cheer skirt off, throwing the tight sequined skirt on the floor. Dakota kicks off his cheer shoes and when I get into the shower that is still warming up, he enters the bathroom. I can hear his voice from outside the shower as he sits on the toilet, a common setup between the two of us.

"Spill, Baby," he tells me.

"Freaking Parker. I've ignored him for three weeks and—"

"Why are you ignoring him? And don't tell me stupid reasons, only the serious ones..." he tells me, and I groan.

"They are NOT!" I open the shower curtain, peaking my head out. "Stupid!" I shout. "He's my brother's friend. That is reason enough—"

"Obviously not considering you fucked—"

I scream to stop his words, slamming the curtain shut.

"We said we weren't talking about that anymore," I argue.

"You said that. I never agreed to not talk about it," he laughs.

"Whatever. That's plenty of a reason but if you'd like more, he hasn't even tried to speak to me, even when we're dancing together. He got what he wanted, right? He came to my birthday to get lucky, considering he was talking to my brother and Lawson about how he needed to get laid. Why else would he come? He was flirting with that waitress, then me. Then my dumbass took him home and we slept together. That was what he wanted. Now, we're moving on. But during all of our dance

196

THE RULES OF YOU AND ME.

lessons and then today? It feels like there's something more... Like he cares, why?" I ask.

"Maybe... Don't shoot the messenger, but maybe it's because he does care..." Dakota mumbles and I roll my eyes.

"Don't be ridiculous. Yes, things have been tense, but he hasn't spoken to me at all and—"

"No, you're ridiculous. Maybe stop being skittish and freaky and just talk to him. He's a football player, not a bear, B," he tells me and I sigh.

"I'd rather be around a bear," I joke.

"I get it, but you're being dramatic," Dakota argues.

"I just don't think it's as deep as you're making it. He slept with me and scored. What are his intentions still talking to me? Friends with benefits? Does he want to hook up casually?" I ask. Is there something he wants? Besides what he sought out the night of my birthday...

"I'm not Parker Thompson. I don't know. Even if I did, I have a feeling you wouldn't listen to me," Dakota sighs.

"I'm sorry, Dak. I'm trying to listen, I just get in my head and then it's hard to listen to anything but my own voice. Because when that voice goes off in my head, it's nonstop and then, it's talking over itself. I have like twenty voices at once telling me different things and—"

"I get it, B. That's why I love you," he laughs and I sigh.

"Like a brother..." I mumble, turning off the shower.

"Like a sister," he replies.

I hold my hand out of the shower and Dakota hands me my towel. I take it, wrapping it around my body. Dak and I switch. He gets in the shower and I get dressed. I'm in the bathroom, talking to him and doing my skincare, brushing my hair, and then my teeth. The bathroom is steamy by the time he finishes and I leave my room to let him change. I hop down the stairs

197

and walk into the kitchen, ignoring Bellamy and Lawson in the living room. Kamryn and Sienna are with them.

"You okay, B?" Bellamy asks and I throw him a thumbs up.

"Fantastic, wonderful, swell. Congrats on winning by the way," I smile over my shoulder.

"All in a day's work," Lawson's smirk is present in his voice. I roll my eyes as I reach into the cabinet, grabbing for my Stanley cup.

"Do you ever use a different cup?" Lawson asks.

"No," I scoff.

"Good, if anyone ever fucks with you, you can use it as a weapon. That thing is like... Industrial," Bellamy chimes in, which makes me smile.

Someone knocks on the door, and I turn over my shoulder to look at my brother and the others on the couch.

"Who?" I ask and he shrugs, stands up and walks in from the living room.

The front door is directly next to the kitchen. I fill up my water cup from the fridge as Bellamy opens the front door.

"What's up, Parky?" he asks and my stomach bottoms out.

Don't blush. Don't panic. Don't freak out.

"I just... I wanted to make sure I didn't completely kill your sister. I feel like a dick. I'm not even playing and I—"

"Parker, she's good. I promise she's fine," Bellamy leans on the door and I look at my brother standing a few feet away at the front door.

"I just hit her pretty hard and I just want to make sure I didn't... I don't know, I feel like an ass," he admits and I watch my brother nod his head toward me.

"All good, Parky. We've all taken someone out on the sidelines before..." Bellamy's eyes are on me and Parker leans into the doorway. Then, his eyes are on me too.

"All good. All in one piece..." I speak softly, a small wave

THE RULES OF YOU AND ME.

toward Parker. Something like relief spreads over his features now that he's looking at me. "Just don't do it again," I joke and the corner of his mouth turns up, only slightly. Only for a few seconds.

"You wanna come hang out?" Bell asks Parker and I take that as my out.

"I'm going upstairs. Goodnight guys," I wave to everyone around us.

A chorus of goodnights rings around the room. My chest is hollow and full all at once mostly because I have no idea what to do or feel. He doesn't care... but he came all the way to my house to make sure I didn't lie about being okay. He definitely could have texted me or Bellamy. I probably would have never answered. But... the sentiment is there. The concern in his voice was deafening. The relief on his face when he saw me was hard to fucking miss.

"Dakota... I think I've got to talk to Parker again," I tell him as I walk into my bedroom.

He's lounging on my bed and he's smiling.

"As long as it ends in the two of you making out, I'm all for it," he jokes and I swat him as I climb onto my bed with him.

CHAPTER 17
SUNNY DISPOSITION BY CAROL ADES

Brianne Archer:

I sit in the middle of the dance studio, stretching myself as far as my body will go. I already had dance class and cheer practice today so I'm warmed up at this point, but it doesn't hurt to continue to make sure my body is ready to move. Parker walks into the studio, kicking his shoes off instinctively, his eyes are on me and then they're not. I haven't seen him since Friday night when he showed up at my house to make sure I didn't get crushed or hurt.

In perfect Brianne Archer fashion, every moment from Friday between the two of us has been on constant replay in my head like a horror movie. I'm picking apart every detail to see if maybe there's something I missed. Something that flipped Parker's switch to make him flirt with me or care about me. Maybe Bellamy was talking about me and it made him realize that he's got to take care of me now. Or maybe my brother threatened him... but that doesn't seem like Bellamy's speed.

"You're not in your normal..." he says first and I furrow my eyebrows.

"What?" I ask and he motions to me.

"You're not wearing tights and the black body suit thing," he tells me.

"Oh... Yeah, I came straight from cheer practice. Leah had called it randomly so I didn't have much time to change," I explain.

"If you need to do that you can," he tells me and I shake my head.

"Since it's not a normal dance rehearsal or class, I don't need to be in uniform. As long as you don't mind what color I wear," I joke.

I'm wearing a white sports bra with a black sheer workout shirt over the top and spandex shorts that are my favorite color green.

"I don't care... But do your professors really care?" he asks and I nod.

"Cheer practices that are called by our coaches are uniform based. We wear certain practice shirts and outfits on certain days. And as for dance, it's very strict, especially in the professional world... But it makes sense as to why," I admit.

"Why?" he asks, getting ready to stretch just like I am.

"As harsh as it may seem, ballet is basically about perfection. In the dance world, your whole being is supposed to be smooth, sleek, one line. So tights help with that, always pink, never black. Leg warmers on until you are warmed up, then you have to take them off. As for leotards, they require black or pink because neither color is distracting. Miss Laurent, my professor, prefers black. She said it moves better with the body and helps show the lines of our movement better. So, I strictly wear black leotards on ballet days but I have plenty of different colors for solo rehearsal or personal practice," I explain.

"Interesting," he nods and I can't tell if he truly wanted to know or not.

THE RULES OF YOU AND ME.

He sits next to me, starting his stretches, already more flexible now than he was a few weeks back.

"Is this helping? All of these classes?" I ask him, being the one to speak.

I told Dakota I needed to talk to him but this is a professional setting. We both decided on that and agreed, so I can't talk to him here. Maybe after... If I can bring myself to do it.

"It is... You are. Not that I get to play yet, but I still practice with the team every week" he admits, but doesn't let his look linger on me as he brings his body down to stretch his back.

I stretch myself too, easily splitting my legs and completely flattening my torso forward so it touches the ground. I hear an exasperated sigh. I look over my shoulder, my eyes hitting Parker, and his eyes practically devour me. He looks me in the eyes with hazy desperation.

"It's infuriating... This," he stares at me and I furrow my brows, pretending that his gaze isn't affecting me at all.

"What?" I ask.

"You. How easily your body just... does all of this," he mumbles.

Maybe I'm making this up. I have to be, right? The way he looks at me could be... Nothing. His eyes linger and I know I didn't make that up. I stare at his face. He looks at me and unabashedly smirks. It's subtle, but I do see it. I can't help but fucking see it. Like an idiot, I look away. Professional, like I asked. I stand up from my split, forcing my mind to focus on the task at hand—making Parker better.

"Okay, we're going to do some across the floor work after we warm up on the barre, okay? You know the same warmups we've been doing, so get into position," I tell him. "We're doing Tendu and Fondu."

"Like cheese?" he asks and I sigh.

"I've been over this," I remind him.

"No, we've never talked about cheese, I would remember that," he tells me,

"It's not about cheese," I tell him as the music starts. I face him, holding the barre gently. "Tendu, do you remember that?" I ask and he shakes his head.

"Teach me," he nods his head and I ignore his lingering stare that's far more intense today than it was at any of our past rehearsals.

His eyes scour my body and he clenches his jaw the farther down they go.

"Tendu, it's the extension of your leg, front side or back. I know we've done these before," I show him all three ways, every direction. "Your foot massages the floor like so."

I show how, my pointed foot brushing the wood dance floor under me, the satisfying scrape of my ballet shoe showing me how perfectly I've done the move. I bring my foot back into fifth position.

"And what about the cheese one?" he asks and I huff.

"It's not cheese. Fondu in ballet means to melt. So take your form that you were in with Tendu and," I demonstrate and he nods.

"Oh yeah, we've done that before," he tells me and I clench my jaw.

"You're infuriating today," I inform him.

"Just like you. Because you told me Friday that I didn't hurt you at all but I'm seeing now that you lied," he says as he practices the Tendu first, his form decent, but definitely needing correction. I walk around him, straightening his arm and I bend down, turning out his sickled foot.

"Guide with your heel when you move your foot forward. When you're returning it back, you guide with your toes, understood?" I inform him.

THE RULES OF YOU AND ME.

"Don't ignore me," he speaks, his eyes forward so he can keep his form correct.

I don't give him the satisfaction of moving to where he can easily look at me, knowing that's probably what he wants.

"I'm not ignoring you. We're not talking about this. We never talk during our lessons, so why start now?" I ask, keeping my arms behind my back.

"Because—" He starts to lose his form and I snap.

"Ah! No, get back into position," I argue but he doesn't listen.

He turns his entire body to me, ballet stance gone, but football player definitely in the room. He reaches for me, his rough callused hands brushing under my arm to lift it softly.

"Here," he informs me as if I don't know. "And here."

He bends down now, his other hand on the back of my thigh so he can look at my purple knee. The bruise is starting to turn green which means it's healing.

"Who says they came from you?" I argue.

"Did they?" he asks, looking up at me from the floor.

The innocence and intensity of his eyes send fire through my veins. My body is completely betraying me, but how could it not? Parker Thompson is on his fucking knees in front of me with his hands touching my skin. There's care and compassion in his voice. I'm ignoring the annoyance that I also hear but I can't ignore the confusion in my own head. *Why is he doing this?*

"Parker..." I clench my jaw.

"I want you to be honest with me. That's all I'm asking for. You don't have to like me or want to be around me. You can tolerate me but please don't lie to me, Brianne," he mumbles.

"Fine," I clench my jaw.

Parker doesn't really talk. He doesn't really do anything but what he's told. He keeps quiet and to himself, so for him to ask this of me, for him to be so persistent, I don't know how I could say no. I lift my shirt that I specifically wore because it was dark. If I had worn a lighter sheer shirt it would've shown the deep coloring on my hip bone that's also yellowing and greening around the edges. Parker's fingers touch my skin and send shockwaves through my entire body as the pads of his fingers graze my ribs.

"Brianne..." he mumbles, his eyes staring at the angry bruises.

"I said I was fine because I am. I've endured far worse bruising from being a cheerleader my entire life. Do you know how many times they've dropped me out of a stunt? I've broken plenty of fingers, and toes. I fractured my elbow. I survived. I'm okay," I tell him, only hoping to get his fingers off of my body because it's affecting me in every way it shouldn't.

"I did this though," he mumbles.

"It was an accident," I admit.

"One that I should have avoided," he admits.

"One that you made better by not letting the other player completely crush me. You were very quick in making sure that you protected my head and my back which were the most important things. I don't get padding as a cheerleader. It happens," I tell him and he clenches his jaw as I move back.

"I'm fine," I tell him, keeping my voice more firm. "Across the floor, let's go," I instruct, ignoring the way he stares at me.

I back away, his hand no longer in contact and my eyes still on him before I fully turn around. He follows me. I stand on one side.

"Grand Battement," I start and explain the movement, showing him.

I have lost my focus. I've lost my edge. I've lost every sense of control I had over this situation because he touched me. That alone is reason to run from him, to never give him another

THE RULES OF YOU AND ME.

chance. Parker is dangerous because he's practically undeniable. Now that my mind and my body know what it's like to be with him, to be touched by him, to be seen by him, it's hard to forget that. I'm still going to try, even if it's one of the hardest things I've forced myself to do. I told myself no because he used me for some weird fulfillment. I can't forget that, even if I do want to talk to him. Even if It's gnawing on me to figure out what the hell his deal is and why he's pretending to care so much. But if I know one thing, it's that even if my mind is made up now, it will change in an instant... I want to talk to him but I need to fight that urge.

CHAPTER 18
ISN'T IT OBVIOUS? BY KATHERINE LI

Parker Thompson:

I lay in my bed, my single throw pillow hugged to my chest as I watch Netflix on my laptop. If I'm honest, I've been zoned out and don't know what's going on, not even slightly. Not that I need to necessarily know what's going on in Criminal Minds. I don't feel like it right now. It's Sunday. I haven't had a moment of peace since my last dance lesson with Brianne on Thursday night. On Friday, I stole glances at her at the away game we had in Portland. We barely scraped a win again but we did and it didn't matter because I still can't play.

I really don't understand this attachment I have formed around her. Maybe it's the fact that I can't seem to be anywhere without seeing her or being reminded of her. Maybe it's her care and nurture, or maybe she's just a good person. I never really grew up forming any attachments to anything or anyone. I've been in the foster system since I was 4. My dad left before I was born and my mom passed away when I was too young to remember her. I moved around most of California up and down the coast all throughout elementary and then in middle school, they told me I could stay if I got my act together. The counselors and workers basically bribed me to get myself straight so I tried my best and then I ended up with a family near my private high school. That high school offered me a full ride to their school if I played football for them. That high school made me the player I am today.

That family was... They were alright. They had been fostering five other kids. Most of them were five years or more younger than me. They had their hands full and I wasn't much of a bother, mostly because I was scared to lose everything. I guess the only thing I've ever held onto was football.

For some stupid fucking reason, I can't shake Brianne either. After being in dance lessons with her, learning small things about her, watching the way she speaks, and seeing how easy it is for her to make me understand without making me feel like an idiot, I was hooked. Brianne is the most caring person I've ever met and she wants nothing to do with me.

When SPU recruited me and offered me sponsorship and a full ride to their school, I felt excited. Probably for the first time in my life, I felt like everything had been worth it. Then, when I got here and met Xander and he practically forced me into a friendship, I felt different. I could actually try my hardest at something normal. I could stick to a routine. I could stick to something. I was sure I would be getting a new roommate my sophomore year until Xander asked me to move in with him, Drew, and Nico. Rent is cheap. I had no reason to say no. I also had no one to stop me. I'm glad I moved in with my roommates but no one really knows my story, not the full thing or many details.

Except Brianne.

No, she doesn't know everything but the one time I mentioned growing up around a lot of kids, she remembered. She asked me about it. She listened when I explained and when

THE RULES OF YOU AND ME.

I did, she didn't apologize. She didn't look at me like you expect people to when you tell them you don't have parents. That's small but it's huge too.

I've also never really been around someone who doesn't feel awkward when I don't make conversation. She takes up the space that I don't feel comfortable filling but I know if I ever wanted to take up more space, she'd move to the side and let me. She's... She's just interesting. I have never wanted to know more about someone, mostly because I never want to pry into people's lives, but I want to know more. I want to ask. I want to find out everything about Brianne Archer.

I'm not doing a great job at that, though. The first person I've met that I don't just tolerate has to tolerate me. It feels like a joke especially considering the fact that I still see her in my head. The night we had. The sound of her moaning. The way her body fit against mine like a puzzle piece. The way she laughs. The way she doesn't fake a smile when she's with Dakota. The way her hands feel in mine. Flashes of our lesson on Thursday roll through my head like a movie. I'm not bad at what she teaches but I'd be a horrible liar if I said I didn't screw up on purpose sometimes so she'd touch me. It's intimate... It's safe.

"Pookie!" Xander crashes into my room and I jump, startled by his entrance.

"Don't call me that and go away," I grumble, tapping on my laptop to start my episode over considering I have no idea what's happening.

"Get out of your grumpy depressive episode," he groans, hanging on my door, moving back and forth. The hinges squeak with every single movement.

"No. Leave, now," I throw my pillow at him and he catches it right in front of his face.

"Yes, because Brianne is here," he tells me and I move with

such haste that I fall off of my fucking bed.

I move from the floor and Xander leans against the door-frame, his arms crossed over his chest, a smirk on his lips. I instantly get mad. He tosses the pillow onto my bed and I step forward.

"If you were fucking joking I'm going to be so fucking—"

"Not joking. I left her in the living room," he tells me and I would normally care how I'm perceived by my roommate, but right now, I don't care. I lean down to look in the short floor-length mirror in my room to make sure I don't look like a fucking idiot.

"What does she want?" I whisper and shake my head. "I mean. Why? What... Is she mad? Does she seem like she's going to yell at me?" I ask him and he narrows his eyes, his smirk unyielding.

"You're nervous," he teases and I sigh.

"Yes. Yes, I am. I admitted it, now get over it and help me. What should I do?" I ask.

"Change out of that shirt first of all because..."

He shakes his head and I strip it off of myself without hesita-tion. I reach into my closet holding up a hoodie.

"Sure, yeah. Anything is better than that ratty ass shirt," he jokes and I throw him a middle finger. He approaches me and pushes my lips up, revealing my teeth. I shove him halfway across my room and look at him like he's fucking lost it.

"What the fuck are you doing?" I grumble.

"Checking your teeth for food, duh," he reaches forward again and I shove him.

"Okay, fuck off. She's going to think we're doing something in here. Do I sit on my bed? Or should I—"

"Yes, sit on your fucking bed, watch your show, and calm down. Where did Parker go? Who is this?" Xander asks, pulling at my hoodie.

THE RULES OF YOU AND ME.

"Fuck off," I grumble.

I climb back onto my bed. My heart is thundering as I hug my pillow, wondering what the fuck is going on. I was balls deep in thought about her then she just... appears? I guess maybe I shouldn't start thanking God yet. She could be here to yell at me again... I turn when I hear her shuffle to the door.

She's the prettiest person I've ever looked at in my entire life.

Her brown hair is in wavy curls hanging haphazardly over her shoulders. She's wearing a dance studio hoodie and pink leggings that match the ballet slippers on the hoodie. Her face is covered in a blush that makes me wonder if she's just as nervous to see me as I am to see her. Jesus fucking Christ I've never had to pretend to play it cool until she danced into my life.

"Hi," she speaks softly. I feel the corner of my mouth twitch up into a smirk.

"Hi..." I speak back.

I don't know what else to say to her. I know what I want to say. Want and should are two separate things. *Hi Brianne, what the fuck are you doing here? What do you want? Why do you hate me? Can you give me a chance? Can you sit on my face? Can we kiss again? Can you stop making me feel absolutely out of my mind insane every time we're in the same room?*

"Can I..." she motions and I close my laptop,

"Always," I mumble and wish I could smash my head between my laptop. *Always? Really Parker? You're an idiot.*

She walks into my room. She throws her bag on my desk and sighs as she sits on the corner of my bed. I watch her carefully. My hands sweat as she looks at me, her big blue eyes staring straight through me. I'm pathetic.

"So—"

"What—"

We both start and I hesitate.

"You first," I nod my head and she sighs.

213

"I didn't want to talk to you at first but I have to talk to you after this past week because I'm confused and just need clarity so I know what to do. Actually, since the game when you almost crushed me really..." she explains.

"What changed?" I ask her, trying my hardest to mask my nerves.

"Dakota said this has been eating me up and if I don't talk to you he's going to drag you to me and make us talk... I know we did what we were supposed to, what you wanted. We hooked up and things ended after that, which is exactly what was supposed to happen. I heard what you were saying to Lawson and Bellamy and you had been trying to hook up with someone and get yourself out there, and I was that for you which is fine. Though, personally I want to know if I'm going to be a conquest or something to check off of a list before I help you complete that task. Either way, I get it. I see what happened now. I get why you came to my birthday stuff. That's over with, but what I don't understand is why you're still acting like you care about me. I thought it was the big brother type of angle but after our last lesson... After the past week, you caring about my injuries and the slight flirting you've been doing, or the fact that you're actually trying to talk to me. I'm confused what you—"

I have never felt or looked more confused in my life. I'm sure of it. I shake my head and sit up on my bed.

"Hey Bri, slow down," I tell her.

"—want from me. I've been racking my damn brain. At the game, you actually seemed concerned when I got hurt. And before the game you were... You were flirting with me. At least, I think you were flirting. I could be looking into it too much but you seemed flirty. Your roommates obviously know what happened because I've never met that guy out there but he knows exactly who I am which means you told them something. You wouldn't tell your friends things unless it was significant,

THE RULES OF YOU AND ME.

which I assumed that and I probably shouldn't be assuming things. I can't ignore the fact that I caught you staring at me and I want to know why. I'm demanding to know why even though I shouldn't—"

"Brianne..." I stop her finally.

"Did I talk too much?" she asks.

"Has anyone ever told you that you talk a lot but never say what you're actually thinking..." I mumble, trying not to smile at the blush that creeps onto her cheeks—her perfectly freckled cheeks.

"No... Most of the time people just say I talk too much," she admits.

"I'm fine with you talking as long as you're not saying something so completely untrue... Bri, I didn't come to your birthday party or hang out with you on your birthday so I could hook up with you," I tell her, finally making sense of what's been going on the past month.

I should have made my intentions more than clear. Crystal clear.

"You... But... I mean, I'm the little sister. I'm everyone's little sister and I'm an Archer, you know that, obviously. I was... I mean I ran out at first the morning after. I had thought about it and was going to talk to you that day but... Then you were talking to my brother about hooking up and he was encouraging you so I thought—"

"Can you stop?" I ask her and she does.

"Stop defining yourself by your brother. There's a lot of really cool things about you that have nothing to do with him. I don't think you're being very fair to yourself. Before Brianne, Bellamy's sister. You're Brianne, the dancer. You're Brianne, the cheerleader. Brianne, the teacher... You're Brianne, the country singer," I joke and she looks at me like I said words she's waited for her entire life.

The whisper of a smile hits her face. I say a quick prayer that I'll have the chance to make her smile like that again.

"I'm not asking you to be anything but Brianne. Can I explain and you listen with an open mind and also not interrupt?" I ask, talking now with more truth than I normally do in an entire day.

"You never talk. I think I can manage letting you do that for a little," she jokes.

"I was with your brother and Lawson, and they both said I needed to... To do college the way everyone else does. They said I didn't experience enough and they said that I was out of practice in the hookup department. They said it would help me on the field and they made me promise I would try to hook up with someone. That I would try casual sex or possibly the girlfriend thing. I agreed... but I also already saw you, Brianne. I had you in my head from the beach. Then the bar. You were already on my radar and when I agreed to hook up with someone, I had every intention of not doing it and lying about it. So no, I didn't hook up with you to check you off a list or whatever it was you were thinking," I explain.

"You said you were going to lie and tell them you hooked up with someone. Why?" she asks.

"Because I'm not the kind of person that will ever put myself out there to flirt or talk to girls at a bar. I'm actually not one to go out to a bar. I don't like being in a loud social setting unless I have to be..."

"So you just wanted them off of your back? Got it. What about my birthday? Why did you even come to my party?" she asks.

"I already told you why I hung out with you on your actual birthday. You can choose whether you want to listen or believe me this time. I came to your party because it seemed like you only invited the people you wanted to be around. So since you

THE RULES OF YOU AND ME.

extended that to me, I didn't take it lightly. I had no intention of... of bringing you here or sleeping with you. I'm happy I did. I mean I like... It was..." I stop myself and sigh. "Moral of the story, it wasn't my intention. Whether I enjoyed it doesn't matter. I would have been happy coming home alone," I tell her and she stares at me.

"So what... what is.... Why?" she asks and I shake my head.

"You really don't get it, do you?" I ask her and she just stares at me.

Honesty is tricky with me. It's not that I don't want to talk about myself or my feelings, it's that I never usually have an opportunity to. Even if I do, I never feel the need. I never feel safe doing it. Most people don't care, so I don't have to worry about how I feel or sharing that information. That's not going to be the case with Brianne, I can feel it.

"I like you, Brianne... I want to see you in and out of my bedroom. I asked you on a date, didn't I? Or did you forget that detail..." I ask, that blush returning to her cheeks. I fight the urge to let it appear on mine.

"Well, I thought you were doing that because you wanted to sleep with me... I've never really dealt with this kind of thing so that's what I've been thinking for the past month. That's why I didn't want to be in lessons with you and when you said I would be an issue—"

I shake my head instantly at her response.

"Jeez, now I get why you ignored me... That's a really shitty thing to do and I wouldn't do that. You aren't an issue and never have been, that's not what I meant. So, I'm sorry... that any of this has felt the way it has. That was never my intention, Brianne. What... What potentially happens between us, if anything, is between me and you. Even the date I had asked you on," I tell her, staring directly at her.

217

"Do you... I mean is that still..." she stumbles over her words.

"It's still on the table. If you're not going to reject me again," I tell her.

She looks at me for a long second, debating and deliberating over my words. I see the question swirling in her navy eyes but I cut her thoughts in half when I speak again.

"I'd like to have a chance. A real chance," I offer and wait for her answer, watching her think and deliberate.

I know her thoughts are most likely going a mile a freaking minute in that beautiful head of hers. I think I'd be scared to be inside of her head, but I appreciate it, mess and all...

"Slow. This moves slowly." she tells me and I fight the urge to smirk.

My heart thumps in my chest.

"Yes, ma'am," I nod my head.

"Don't do that," she tells me and I wipe the smile off of my face.

"Why?" I ask.

"Because it makes me want to ignore what I just said," she admits, her eyes trailing to my lips.

"We should probably talk to Bellamy before—"

"Are you crazy? No, absolutely not," she fights. "We do this on my terms. Bellamy doesn't know. He can't know, not until there's something to tell. You're taking me on a date, not proposing to me, and fathering my kids... We see... We see where things go. Then, we decide later if we tell. He still thinks I'm dating or doing something with Dakota like I said before. We have a cover, we should use it," she tells me.

I get a bad feeling in my stomach. No, he's not my best friend but he is my teammate. I trust him and he trusts me. I don't want to lie to him.

"Are you sure we shouldn't just—"

THE RULES OF YOU AND ME.

"I've known him my whole life. I'm sure. No stipulations. Bellamy doesn't find out. It's not lying it's... omitting the truth," she tells me.

"Isn't that just as bad?" I ask her.

"Semantics," she fights back and I look at her straight on.

Is it worth it? The potential of ruining my semi-friendship with the guy? Looking at her, I think it seems worth it but I also know that she never keeps anything from him. It can't go too far without her telling him. I can keep it quiet for a few weeks.

"I see where you're coming from Parker, but it's best that we keep it to ourselves. This isn't serious. Neither of us knows if it will ever be more than just fun. So, don't complicate it," she adds.

"Fine," I agree.

"Fine," she repeats.

"Then you'll be mine for a day?" I ask and she narrows her eyes at me.

"You get one date. One. Now that I know what I know, I think you deserve that," she explains.

"Alright. I'll text you then," I tell her.

"Alright then," she gets up and I do too, following her out of my room and to the front door. "Are you going to introduce me?" she asks, turning to my roommate sitting by himself in the living room.

"This is Xander. Xander, this is Brianne," I tell him. He nods and waves to her.

"When he fucks up, you can totally rebound over here with—"

"Shut the fuck up," I shake my head and usher her to the door.

"I'll see you..."

"Whenever... Soon, I mean. Definitely soon," I tell her, walking her out of the door.

"Bye, P," she mumbles.

"Text me when you get home," I tell her and she looks over her shoulder, a smile on her lips. I watch her walk to the flight of stairs and then close the door behind me.

"Text me when you get home. Oh, Bri. Be so safe, Bri," Xander makes fun of me and I shake my head, ignoring him. I pump my fist to myself, not caring if he sees.

"Wait, wait! Tell me what happened."

He follows me to my bedroom, not letting me close the door. I grab my shoes, a smile on my lips.

"I need a car," I tell him.

"What? What does that have to do with Brianne? What happened dude?" he asks.

"I have one date to impress the pants off of Bri. Not literally because she

expressed very clearly that we are going slow but I have a shot. I can't fuck this up. I need a car. Because what kind of loser doesn't take her out in his car on the first date? Dealership now," I snap my fingers.

"Man on a mission but she's not shallow. She's not going to care if you have a car—"

Xander follows behind me.

"I know that but it's about more than that. It's about the effort and she's worth the effort. I've been saving for one for a while anyway. It's time. If it's ever been time, the time is now. Let's go. Hurry up," I snap and Xander follows.

Now I get it when people say things like 'She's the kind of girl someone would move mountains for,' or 'She's the kind of girl someone would fight a war for.' I'm not moving mountains or fighting wars but I am going to buy a car... that's got to count for something.

CHAPTER 19
WHEN BY DODIE

Brianne Archer:

This week is a bye week which means we don't have a game on Saturday. I'm happy to have one Friday off. I'm happy to spend it with Dakota and Valerie. We're having a movie night. It's currently Wednesday, and though I agreed to go on a date with Parker this past Sunday, I haven't texted him since I told him I was home safe that night. I'm not going to reach out. I'm still bouncing off the wall nervous over this entire situation, knowing that he's actually interested in me. Also, knowing he doesn't care that I'm Bellamy's sister makes my head fog up.

I'm still swimming in my thoughts wondering if this is even a good idea. I'm about to start my Wednesday therapy session with Madeline, my therapist. She's been my therapist since last year and I like her alright. She's really good at listening to me but I'm scared to bring up Parker to her considering I never mentioned him in the first place. I never told her what we did on my birthday. I never mentioned anything having to do with my Parker sized fuck up. Do I really have anything to mention if Parker hasn't even planned our date? No, right? Because it prob-

221

ably won't happen... or it will and I'm being eager and crazy. My phone dings. Speak of the freaking devil...

> **Parker:** Saturday. Give me 24 hours...That's all I need.

> **Me:** 24 hours to sweep me off of my feet? You sure you can accomplish that, P?

> **Parker:** I think you should have a little faith in me, Sunshine.

My stomach bottoms out. Saturday... Saturday, Saturday, Saturday. No. Yes? No... I click my phone screen off and a call comes in on my laptop. I answer the call from my therapist and see her bright face on the other end once the video call connects. I turn my microphone on and I hear her start speaking.

"Hi Bri, how are you doing this week?" she asks me and I nod.

"I'm good. Great, some might say. Doing absolutely wonderful," I lie through my teeth.

Well, not fully. I'm having a fine week but a confusing one. I haven't been around Parker. I've avoided him whenever Bellamy has had him over. I ignored him while we were on the field for cheer practice. Even if it's bye week we practice. Parker was there with his teammates even though they weren't required to be. I obviously didn't text him so...

"Yeah, what's that about?" she laughs.

She's probably in her mid-thirties. I relate a lot to Madeline even if she is a lot older than I am. She's easy to talk to, of course, but it's hard to come out with it when I've completely danced around the Parker situation these past three weeks.

THE RULES OF YOU AND ME.

"So, I might have purposely not mentioned something that happened around a month ago... with a guy," I tell her.

"Okay. Are you ready to talk about it? Or him..." she asks and I nod. "What's his name?"

"Parker Thompson... He's... Well, he asked me on a date, then I agreed but we never made it on that date because he came to my birthday party and we both... We... I mean, I slept with... with him," I tell her and my cheeks heat up.

It's the first time I've admitted it out loud to someone that isn't Dakota.

"Sex isn't something to be ashamed of. It's alright if you're having casual sex, Bri. Is that what this is about?" she asks.

"No. I mean yes, but no. I've had casual sex before and it was never a problem. It was never deciphered what the sex was or what it meant, though... and the next morning, I ignored him and left his house. I didn't want to talk to him," I admit to her.

"Did he do something that set you off? Or something that bothered you?" she asks.

"He was perfect. As perfect as a guy could be honestly. Even took me home after I tried to leave his place... The problem is, Parker is a football player. He's on the same team as my brother," I tell her and she nods slowly.

"Are Bellamy and Parker friends? Outside of football?" she asks and I sigh.

"Yeah..." I cringe but still look at Madeline.

She's got sleek red hair cut into a perfect bob. Her glasses are animated and perched on her dainty nose.

"So, what's happened since then? Since you left that day?" she asks me.

"Well, I agreed to help out in teaching dance for one of our athletic players not knowing it was him. So I've been seeing him but not talking to him on purpose because of a misunderstanding. I thought he was hooking up with me purposefully. Like

223

he... he lied to me which wasn't true. But the other day, he flirted with me and I was so confused. Dakota convinced me to talk to him. I guess for the few weeks that I didn't talk to him, I assumed that he had gotten what he wanted. We had sex, we enjoyed it, we moved on... but then he was flirting with me and I almost got hurt at a game by him. He came to check on me... So, I went to his house in search of clarity," I explain and she nods.

"Good. I'm glad you went over there. Did you get the clarity you were searching for?" she asks and I sigh.

"No. I mean, yes. I got the clarity on why he was flirting with me and then it just made it all that much worse. He still wanted to take me on a date... He had never come to my birthday party to sleep with me, right? He just came because I invited him and he was trying to make a good impression. And he's really sweet even though outwardly he's very quiet and lowkey grumpy too. But all around, he's nice to me and he's just... I don't know... unique in a way," I tell her and watch her smile.

"Aw. Well, I'm happy for you, Bri. I am. I think it's good that you're giving someone a chance. It's been a little while for you and getting into something in college is always a whirlwind. I remember my first college boyfriend," she tells me. I furrow my brows.

"But shouldn't I be the one putting my foot down over this? He's my brother's friend," I explain.

"I don't see a reason why you should if I'm fully honest with you, Brianne," she admits. "How do you feel about going out with one of your brother's friends?" she emphasizes.

"I don't know. I feel good about Parker and everything except the fact that he's Bellamy's friend. Part of me is hoping the date goes horribly so I can just shut this down and never think about it again. But the other side of me..." I trail off.

"Hopes he sweeps you off your feet?" she asks and I nod.

THE RULES OF YOU AND ME.

"Well, how does Parker feel... about your brother, I mean?" she asks.

"When I mentioned it, he asked me why I had to be Bellamy's sister and why I couldn't just be Brianne to him. He doesn't mind it at all," I tell her and she gives an innocent shrug.

"I could ask the same question as him... As women, it's easy to want to define ourselves by those older, bigger, or over us in a way. Or by men. Though Bellamy is someone you love, you have had a habit of defining yourself by him. Correct me if I'm wrong, but from what I've seen and heard from you, Bellamy has let you do that for all these years. He's your brother, not your definition. You can just be Brianne. That's alright," she explains and I nod.

"I feel like I'm betraying my brother for going out with one of his friends," I admit.

"How long have you two known Parker?" she asks.

"Parker is a year younger than Bellamy. They didn't start being friends until recently," I admit.

"If it's going to tear you up, I don't suggest going. You should not have guilt for having feelings toward someone in your life, regardless of who they are to someone else. I know that's something we've been working on... So, if you can nudge yourself past feeling guilty over someone else's potential feelings, I don't see anything wrong with going out with Parker. It's like I told you. I remember the first college guy I talked to. He was just that, a college guy, not the man I married. This isn't forever, it's for now," she tells me.

"I just don't want this to be an issue. Later on," I explain.

"Don't borrow tomorrow's problems. It could be the worst date you've been on. It could be spectacular. You get to decide what happens after that, no one else. I think it's worth a try... Give yourself an experience, a chance to be Bri, not Bellamy's sister..." Madeline offers.

"This would be easier if I had a mom to talk to..." I admit, looking down at my hands.

"What do you think she would tell you? Remember her voice, remember her face and her touch, and close your eyes."

I do what she says and start to imagine my mom. I see her dusty brown hair and perfect smile. My mom had the same dimples that both Bellamy and I have. Her curly hair was my favorite part about her. I can almost smell the lavender lotion on her skin and the sweet perfume she would wear as I imagine her. What would she say to me... She would probably tell me she always imagined me with a football player... Just like my dad. She'd tell me to do what could make me the happiest and if I don't go for it, there's always going to be a what if. She never lived with a what if... Never.

She'd tell me all about her and my dad—how he was the star football player in high school and college. She cheered on the sidelines. They swept each other off of their feet and didn't stop loving each other until they... until they passed. She wanted that for me. I was young so we never talked about it, but she did. I know she did.

"She'd tell me to go for it..." I admit.

"Go for it, Brianne. Go for what gives you a shot at happiness," she tells me. "Everyone deserves a little bit of sunshine," she tells me and I nod.

I wipe away tears at the thought of my mom. She was full of dreams. Smiles, laughs, and hugs. She was human sunshine and she's all I've ever wanted to be.

"How's dance going?" she asks me, changing the subject so I don't have to.

I smile and jump into it. I jump into the harsh nature of the ballet classes but how much I love them. From here on out, it's as easy as pie to talk about what I love. It's easy to talk about the things I love, even if they are a struggle right now. What's

THE RULES OF YOU AND ME.

hardest for me is the want and need to talk to my mom but not being able to. My chest aches as I talk to Madeline, my heart lurching. I don't tell her, though. I don't even mention the pain.

~

Parker Thompson:

I sit in the living room of my apartment, with my head in my hand as I watch Xander lose once again at Call of Duty. He kind of sucks at this game, but I'm not going to tell him that. It might result in a controller to my head. I'm normally one to ignore him and my other roommates and head into my bedroom when I get back from weight training. But after I showered I... I didn't feel like being alone. So I sat on the couch, both Xander and Nico gave me a puzzled look then went back to their game, pretending this was normal. I'm thankful they did too because if they had made even a single snide remark or comment, I would have most likely parked myself in my bedroom and not left until morning. My phone vibrates on the table in front of us. I lean forward and snatch it, sliding to answer Bellamy's call.

"Hey," I mumble.

"Have you seen Brianne?" he asks and I hesitate.

"Um. W-when? I mean, no, I haven't. But... What happened?" I ask, wondering why he's asking. "Why would I have seen her?" I tack on. *Shit, did he find out already?*

"I don't know. I just... She's not answering me or Lawson and her location isn't on. I'm just worried. Do you have Dakota's phone number? Or do you know how I can find it?" he asks and I've never heard him so panicked.

"Calm down, Bellamy. Take a second and calm down because panicking is only going to make the situation worse for you and everyone else, okay? That's step one," I tell him.

227

Xander and Nico have now tuned into my conversation.

"She's never done this. I mean she wouldn't just disappear and not let me know what's going on or where she is. She was home all day after her classes. I said bye to her before I went to weight training and when I got home, she was gone," he tells me.

"Um... Did she have plans? Did she tell you that?" I ask.

"No. No, she had therapy tonight like she does every Wednesday. Lawson—" he starts mumbling to Lawson on the other end of the line and I sit up, my chest warming up with anxiety.

"Bellamy, do you need me to look for her?" I ask him, he snaps back into our conversation.

"We're going to look for her. If you have any ideas or know how to get in contact

with Dakota, that would be really helpful," he tells me.

"I can help... or try to. Can you send me Leah's number?" I ask.

"Yeah, sure, and thanks, Parky. My ringer is on. Call if you figure anything out," he tells me and hangs up.

I immediately try to call Brianne on my phone despite knowing she probably won't answer. As I assumed, it goes straight to her voicemail and I sigh. *Do not panic until there's reason to panic Parker.*

"What's going on?" Xander pauses his game and Nico turns to me. I text Leah, asking her for Dakota's phone number.

"Bellamy just called me freaking out. He can't find Brianne and hasn't heard from her in hours," I tell them.

"Why would he assume you know where she is?" Nico asks.

"I don't know. I think he's grasping for straws and doesn't know what to do. He asked me for help," I tell them.

"Well, has she told you where she is? Or at least where she was going?" Xander asks and I shake my head.

THE RULES OF YOU AND ME.

"No. I texted her earlier and she seemed fine. We haven't talked since," I admit.

Leah sends me a contact for Dakota and I click it and call right away.

"Hello?" Dakota answers almost immediately.

"Dakota, it's Parker," I tell him and he laughs to himself.

"To what do I owe the pleasure?" he jokes. I roll my eyes.

"Have you talked to Brianne? Or been with her today?" I ask him.

"I've been home all night working on a paper. Last text she sent was that she was about to start her therapy session. Why?" he asks me.

"Her brother called me and he can't find her anywhere. He says she isn't answering him. I called and it went straight to voicemail. He also said he can't see her location on his phone anymore. I was just wondering if you've got any idea where she could be?" I ask him.

"Damn. No, I have no idea. Do you need help? I can try to go and find her or... I don't know. Let me call Valerie..." he tells me.

"Text me if you figure anything out. I'm gonna go look around campus," I tell him.

"Likewise," he chimes back and hangs up. I sigh and put my phone down.

Think... Where would Brianne be?

"What did he say? Do you think something's wrong?" Xander asks and I stand up.

Probably. Something is most likely wrong with Brianne. She was in therapy, that's what Bellamy and Dakota had said. So what would she do... where would she go to work something out if she was struggling or dealing with something? The exact place she told me she goes when she feels wrong or out of place. Our first dance lesson she told me that. She goes to the one place it feels right.

"Can you take me somewhere? Or can I borrow your car?" I ask him and he rolls his eyes. "Come on, Xander. I wouldn't ask if it wasn't important. I think I know where she might be and if she's not there, then this could be bad. What if she's in trouble?" I ask him.

"Calm down. I just can't wait until your car is ready to be picked up..." he glares at me as he reaches for his keys. He tosses them my way. "Not even a scratch, Parks," he mumbles to me.

"Whatever," I mumble, shoving my feet into my slides, and throwing a jacket over my hoodie.

"Text us if you need something," Nico calls out.

"I will," I mumble, leaving without another word.

Where the hell else would she be if not at the dance studio? Dance is her football. It's her relief. Her escape. I wonder what's going through her head, what made her want to just disappear like this. That's all I can tell myself—that she wanted to disappear for a few hours. That she's okay, just escaping from life. I jump into the car and head toward the athletic education building. I have plenty of classes here so I know the way like the back of my hand. I try my best to drive carefully for the sake of Xander's car but not my own sanity. *What the hell was she thinking? Scaring the shit out of everyone like this?* She probably wasn't.

I pull up and barely even get the car parked and turned off before I jump out of it, rushing into the building. The only light is illuminating from the street lamps lining the building and sidewalk. There's no one in this building right now, no one except Brianne, hopefully. I scan my student card, gaining access to the academic building. I briskly walk down the empty, dimly lit hallway. I definitely could have looked in the student parking for her car but I'm already inside now.

THE RULES OF YOU AND ME.

I approach the main dance studio that we meet in each week. My eyes land on Brianne and I am flooded with relief. She's got her phone plugged into the stereo system and I start to push the door open but stop when she sets her phone down and moves to the center of the room. The music starts—a soft piano and a soft voice. A vulnerable voice. I don't move an inch, glad that she hasn't heard me.

I listen to the lyrics, my heart sinking at the thought of her relating to them. By the way she moves to the song—the way she's so dainty and purposeful like she's floating on air while she moves but at the same time so urgent and intentional—I know she means every move she makes. I know she feels every word the singer is saying just by the intensity of the way she's dancing. I'm frozen watching her, listening to the lyrics. My heart lurches. I've seen her dance in increments. Not long periods or for an entire song like this.

There's a build in the song, strings. An entire orchestra... Her body moves with the music like she's made of notes, songs, and melodies. I'm not a dancer. The past few weeks are proof of that. I'm used to impact, sweat, and screaming. Pummeling and dirt. I'm not used to the delicacy of this, even with the practice I've had in the past month. I still can't imitate the intricacy she possesses, the intimacy, the stillness, the quiet that is so loud it's deafening. I have never seen someone so entranced in themselves and what they are doing to the point that Brianne is doing right now. Every inch of her is buzzing with rhythm. I haven't seen her dance like this, but I could watch this. I could watch her for hours.

She's wearing leggings and a tight white shirt that clings to her skin. As she dances, as she bends and breaks to the music, I can imagine her in a flowing dress. I can imagine her with hair and makeup done. I can visualize candles surrounding her, their flames dancing with each breath of wind that her movements make. I bite my tongue, not wanting to even breathe wrong. I don't want her to stop. The singer in the song sounds ethereal as she goes up and down the scale. Brianne's facial expressions match the haunted yet melodic sound that comes from the loudspeaker. I can see her hurt. I can see her pain. I can understand it from the lyrics she just danced to.

I can feel the struggle she's feeling. It's one I've felt. It's one I've dealt with myself, the feeling of wondering when life will feel fulfilling. Wondering why I'm always wishing for something else, something different than what I've got. Wondering when I'll feel... normal. The fact that life is passing me by, that I'm young but not young enough. I fight the urge to relive those feelings. I fight everything in my head that tells me to let her be... but when the song ends, the only sound is her heavy breathing and the dim light reflects the tears in her eyes. She's on her knees at first and then she folds, sitting on the ground looking as though she might break at any second. I open the door the rest of the way and clear my throat. I don't want her to be alone, even if it's initially what she had wanted. She looks at me in the mirror, not turning to see me.

"What are you doing here?" she asks, her voice a whisper of her normal self.

"Looking for you," I admit.

I remove my slides, her words playing in my head about not wearing my shoes in here. My socks are slick so I move slowly so I don't fall. She watches me carefully and wipes under her eyes. She's not wearing any makeup and her hair is braided back, away from her face with the exception of a few strands that have escaped.

"You scared some people... Your phone is going straight to voicemail," I tell her and she nods.

"I put it on airplane mode, I didn't want to be bothered," she admits.

THE RULES OF YOU AND ME.

"I understand," I sit on the floor with her, pulling my legs up to my chest. "I can go in a minute... but I do need to know what to tell your brother because I think he might go to the police in about five minutes if he doesn't figure out where you went."

I try to crack a smile but she rolls her eyes.

"He's so overprotective..." she mumbles.

"He loves you. That's all," I tell her, a pang in my chest at the thought of someone caring that much.

"I know that..." she whispers, pulling her own knees up to her chest, hugging them to her small body. "Did you... Did you see all of that?" I nod to her question.

"I got here right before you started and I couldn't interrupt, I... I've never seen someone dance like you... Like that," I admit. "That didn't look like ballet. I mean, I recognized some of the movements you did but it looked so... so natural," I tell her.

She smiles at the floor, only lightly, barely there at all.

"It was improv. No routine just... just feelings. It's contemporary-lyrical if you need a name for it... But it was just... emotions, really," she explains and I nod.

"And the song? Why that song?" I ask.

"Because it felt... It felt personal," she admits.

She's looking away from me, not meeting my eyes. I hate the thought of it being personal but I do relate to the lyrics as well. Past me would have related more, but it still hits somewhere deep in my chest. I find the little kid inside my head. He's still there, not doing anything, not acting on his instincts but he's there, waving back at me. He's that part of me that relates but this isn't about me right now.

"What do you need me to do right now?" I ask her.

"Pretend you never saw any of that?" she asks, looking at me with tears in her sea-blue eyes.

"I don't think I could forget it if I tried, Brianne..." I admit.

"Could you tell me what happened? Only if you want to... Or I can go, you can talk to Bellamy or Dakota..." I tell her.

I served my purpose. I found her. She's physically okay. I can go.

"I... I had a therapy session today and it was a hard one. And normally when I finish with Madeline, my therapist, I just want to lay in bed. But today I... I just needed to get it out. To get the feelings in my chest out because it felt so heavy."

"Like it could crush you..." I finish for her and she nods.

"Just like that. I turned my location off because I knew Bellamy would try to find me and I put my phone on airplane mode like I said..." she admits.

"Why not go to Dakota or Bellamy?" I ask her.

"Because it's no one's job to make me feel better but my own. No one normally makes me feel better than music does. When I don't know if other people can relate to me in my own life I know that there are lyrics and melodies that will relate to exactly what I'm feeling. Hence the song choice. Hence the... the dance. The way I felt," she motions to the floor around her.

"Do you feel better?" I ask.

"Not really... but I will. I will feel better. You shouldn't have to see this either. I'm—"

I quiet her.

"What did the song call it? The sunshine disguise?" I ask her and she hesitates but then she nods. "I never fell for it in the first place... and I don't need it. You are sunshine-y. You're bright and kind but sometimes you fake it, and I can tell," I tell her. "You said you had never been sure if someone else could relate but you knew that music could... I can too. I can relate. And I can be here if you need it, if music isn't working..." I tell her.

She just stares at me, those tears still present in her perfect eyes. I want to look away from her stare, scared to be caught

THE RULES OF YOU AND ME.

under it... scared to know what it means. I'm fearful it means more to me than she intends it to... but there's something deep and meaningful behind it.

"Thank you..." Her words are just above a whisper when she says them.

We're interrupted by a phone call and I look to see Bellamy on my screen. I answer, my eyes locked on Brianne.

"Hey," I answer.

"I can't find her. I can't get a hold of her boyfriend. I think I should call campus police or—"

"I got Dakota's number from Leah and he's with her," I tell him and he sighs in relief.

"Jesus Christ. Did you ask him why she wasn't answering her phone?" he asks me.

She mouths the words 'thank you' and I nod.

"Her phone was dead. He said they wouldn't be out late. That's all he said, then she took the phone and told me to tell you to stop worrying so much," I tack on another lie and she smirks at what I just said.

"Whatever. She's going to hear an earful when she shows back up. Thanks, man. I owe you," he mumbles.

"Don't mention it. Seriously," I tell him. I hang up and click my phone off, looking up at Brianne.

"Is he mad?" she asks and I shake my head no.

"Not mad but he is worried. He said you were going to hear an earful when you get back so be ready," I tell her. She sighs.

"Are you going to talk to him... about all of this, about how you're feeling?" I ask and she shakes her head.

"No. Because it wouldn't be fair to him... to bring up how I feel. That's why I talk to a therapist because it's not his job to shoulder how I feel... especially when it has to do with our parents. I don't want to open wounds for him. I don't need him to know how much they still affect me when it doesn't... When

235

it doesn't hurt as bad for him anymore," she tells me and there's a hole in my chest that opens at her words.

Best friends. He is her best friend and she feels like going to him wouldn't be fair... even if she's drowning without it. I just nod because I spent too long not having anyone to talk to. Even still, I feel like that.

"You don't have to tell him. I just... I just thought I'd ask," I shrug.

"I should probably go back..." she sighs and starts to stand up.

I stand with her and take her hand before she turns back around. I don't know why I had to grab her, where the urge came from to touch her right now... but she doesn't pull away, so I keep hold of her while her eyes hold onto me.

"You don't have to... go back, I mean. You're here for yourself. You obviously needed it. I never... I never had an escape like this. If I had, I would have used it a lot," I tell her.

"Football?" she asks.

"Does a lot of great things for anger, but doesn't help much when I feel sad... Hopeless..." I admit.

"I'm sorry you felt that way," She tells me.

"I'm sorry you feel that way right now, Brianne," I admit.

She's sweet. Sickly sweet. Kind. Compassionate. Loyal. That's all I've gathered from barely knowing the woman in front of me... but there's one thing I know about trauma and pain and that's the fact that it doesn't cater to how kind you are. It hits everyone just as hard no matter who you are or what you do. And sometimes, it kills kindness and heart. Sometimes it wins... but I see her. I see Brianne. She's fighting, fighting to keep her head up and her heart on fire. I don't know all of her. Not even half of her, but I want to. More than anyone or anything thus far in my life. I think her fire and spirit would do well for me. I've

THE RULES OF YOU AND ME.

learned enough from her, but something tells me she's going to be teaching me a lot more than I had thought.

"Yes... To Saturday. I would love to go out with you Saturday but I can't do extravagant things," she tells me. I look at her straight on, my head tilted down toward her.

"Why not extravagant... if that's what you deserve?" I tell her, watching her already rosy cheeks flame.

"I'm... I can do it one day, I just can't do it... I'm, I can't do the pressure. I mean..." she sighs. "I just need to be casual right now, for my own sanity..." she tells me and I nod.

"Casual is fine, but don't expect me to go easy on you. It will be casual like you've never seen," I tell her. I let her hand slip from mine.

"Thank you..." she tells me as I move back from her.

"I didn't do anything," I tell her.

"If you say so..." she smiles to herself, turning back toward the stereo.

"Are you okay? Really?" I ask her and she nods.

"I will be okay. Promise."

"Okay," I nod softly and walk out of the room without another word.

I press my back to the wall outside of the door, my body out of view from her. I pinch my eyes shut and take a second to absorb all of that. All of her. Physicality is one thing—the obvious pull we have there is hard to ignore—but to me... It doesn't compare to the pull I have to her elsewhere. She is someone I want to know. I've never had someone like that. Not yet, anyway... Her feelings are so big and so avoided by everyone around her... because she doesn't let anyone see them. But I do. I have. I want to keep seeing them. I just hope she lets me.

CHAPTER 20
TAKE ME THERE BY RASCAL FLATTS

Brianne Archer:

I wipe an ungodly amount of sweat on my black dress as I stare at myself in the mirror and groan, shaking my hands out.

"You're going to be fine, B. You've been on dates before," he tells me, standing up from my bed.

"This feels different," I admit and regret saying it out loud.

That makes it more real. I turn to Dakota and he raises his eyebrows.

"Give me real best friend advice. I need it right now or I'm going to back out of this stupid date with Parker," I tell him.

He takes me by the shoulders and I have a pang in my chest, wishing I could be doing this with my brother. I push that thought away quickly.

"Bri, you look really pretty right now. Your outfit is cute and this is just a date. It can mean whatever you want it to mean. Stop putting pressure on it because there's no need," he tells me.

"Do you hate him? Do you think he's bad or—"

"I love giving him a hard time. I like him. He's cute and funny and he never talks which is great for you... Motormouth," he jokes and I roll my eyes, but a smirk etches on my face. He pulls me into a hug. "It's going to be fun and if it isn't, you can come over and we can make fun of him all night. I would never let you go on a date with a guy that absolutely sucks," he tells me.

I pick up my phone, check the time, and realize I need to leave to go to his place. Then, a text pops up.

> Parker: I'm here. Get a move on, Sunshine.

I stare at the text with furrowed eyebrows. *He's here? How?* Maybe he borrowed Xander's car.

"He's here," I tell Dakota.

"Alright, let's send you off then, B."

He grabs my small purse for me and I take it from him. We walk down the stairs and Bellamy and Lawson are... sword fighting? I stop at the bottom of the stairs to see Bellamy on the coffee table with a foam sword in his hand. Lawson is standing on the couch, holding a pillow as a shield.

"Where the hell are your girlfriends?" I ask.

"Kamryn got mad at me so she's in there," Bellamy points to his bedroom.

"Because you're annoying!" Kamryn yells from the open door.

"Sienna has lacrosse practice," Lawson tells me.

"Where are you going?" Bellamy asks.

"Date," I smile and Dakota puts his hand on my back.

Bellamy looks between the two of us.

"Have fun," he smiles.

"Have more fun than I'm having!" Kamryn yells from the bedroom.

"Baby..." Bellamy turns and Lawson wacks the shit out of Bell the second his attention is turned.

240

THE RULES OF YOU AND ME.

"You're such a dick, Lawson!" he yells and they start fighting again.

I take that as my cue. We walk to the elevator and go down. Once we're on the street, I look in the lot for Xander's car but I don't see it. Parker emerges from a truck, a very old Chevy. I smile at the dark blue truck with white stripes down the side and Parker who has a whisper of a smile on his lips.

"Your chariot awaits," Dakota jokes.

"When did you..." I mumble, approaching Parker.

"I thought if I had a chance, I better take it seriously... So I..." he hesitates.

"You bought a car so you could make sure you would impress her on a date?" Dakota asks Parker. I watch as he blushes slightly.

"Yep," he shrugs.

He jumps up on the ledge of the old car and leans through the open window. I'm still stuck on the truck in front of me. *He bought a car so he could take me on a date... Most guys don't even bring flowe—*

"For you..." He holds out a large bouquet of flowers, every color of the rainbow. I slightly gasp, still standing next to Dakota. He nudges me.

"I told you there was nothing to worry about. Have fun, Baby," he whispers next to me, and kisses the side of my forehead.

"I love you," I tell him as Dak walks around me and away.

"Like a sister," he mumbles, smirking to himself.

"Like a brother," I tell him and approach Parker, standing on the curb while he stands below. He's still slightly taller than me even though he's standing lower than me.

"Thank you," I take the flowers and hold them. My lips press into a smile.

241

"You're... Stunning," he shakes his head, like he was looking for the right word to say.

I blush. I feel it—the heat in my cheeks. I smile more, looking down on him. He's wearing loose-fitting jeans and a loose light-gray shirt. His arm muscles strain against the shirt, his shoulders looking broad and strong. His jeans are cuffed and he wears normal tennis shoes. He's cute and casual, just like I asked.

"We should probably get going... I don't want anyone to walk out and... and see us," he tells me and I nod.

I start to walk around the car but he follows, opening the door for me. He gives me a hand so I can climb into his truck and then he runs back around the front of the car, hopping in on his side.

"I know you obviously have a license but you're not a horrible driver, are you? I feel like you're out of practice," I joke as I buckle my seatbelt.

"I drove you home a few weeks ago," he argues as he puts the car in reverse and pulls out of the lot.

"Yeah, but I wasn't paying attention to your driving," I admit. He passes me his phone and I look at it.

"You can play whatever you want," he tells me.

"I'm surprised your truck has Bluetooth. What year is this thing?" I ask him.

"It's from the 80's," He admits. I smile at the thought. This is the cutest freaking truck. "And I had a new stereo put in... with bluetooth," he tells me. "Because I figured that you—"

"Oh my god, Parker," I stop him. "If you're about to tell me that you got a new stereo system put in your new car that you bought to take me on a date because you know I love music and wanted me to feel comfortable on our date I need you to stop."

He shuts up right away. He shrugs and zips his lips.

THE RULES OF YOU AND ME.

"Okay, I won't say that then," he tells me and my jaw drops slightly.

"Parker..." I mumble.

"Brianne," he looks at me.

"This is too much," I mumble.

"I have one date to make you like me. I'm not wasting it. So, yes. I got a stereo put in so you could listen to music. I figured it was important considering we're going to be spending time in the truck for a good portion of the night," he explains. "It's not too much. Stereos are used all the time," he tells me.

"You don't like music," I tell him.

"I never said that. I said I don't usually listen to it because I prefer silence but I could learn to. I've been listening to more music than I used to in the past few weeks," he mumbles, looking over at me for a split second before he turns to the road again, keeping his hands to himself. *Gentleman.* He's a quiet, sincere fucking gentleman. I'm going to melt into a puddle...

"So where are we going?" I ask him. He smirks and shrugs.

"Here and there," he mumbles and I scoff.

"Parker—" He cuts me off.

"Tell me why you like this song," he mumbles.

I just put a playlist I listen to on shuffle—a more mellow playlist without too much country on it. I chose it subconsciously even though I know that Parker wouldn't have cared either way.

"It's called Commotion by Young the Giant. I don't know. I really like all of their music, but this song is just smooth. It's like... Kind of like how I imagine falling in love would feel like," I tell him, my eyes catching on the sky and road in front of us.

"I like this song... Actually. It's simple and it's calming," he tells me.

I nod. It's a really good song, but they're a good band.

243

"Do you listen to this band a lot?" he asks and I shake my head.

"No. I like them, but they aren't my favorite," I tell him.

"Okay, play a favorite... Please," he adds.

I look at him and he glances at me. I don't share the music that I normally love mostly because people don't enjoy it. They don't get it, they don't understand it, which is fine because music is subjective, but it does feel like I'm sharing a part of myself that only I really understand.

"What? Are you scared?" he asks, not in a rude way. Not in a way like he's making fun of me. He's actually curious.

"Yes," I admit.

"I remember you said Rascal Flatts, right? You said that you really like them," he talks to me and my heart bottoms out. I nod. I mentioned it in passing, not thinking he would be listening.

"They are one of my favorites," I tell him.

"Well, then play one I like. Take Me There..." he tells me and I just stare at him.

He doesn't listen to music, especially not country music. I know he doesn't. He said he didn't so tell me how he knows this song. Tell me how he's aware of a song off of my favorite album by them?

"How do you..." I start and shake my head, butterflies flying around my stomach.

"I listened... You said you liked them and I wanted to understand it. I like that song. It reminds me of you," he tells me, and once again, I feel my heart lurch and stutter.

I press the song and listen to it quietly with him, wondering who the person next to me is. He's quiet and grumpy and very bossy. That's what people assume about him. That's what I assumed about him because it's what he showed me. He's not the kind of person who listens to music and says songs remind

THE RULES OF YOU AND ME.

him of me. Well, he wasn't that kind of person... Now... Now he is, I guess. Or maybe he always was.

"When did you become such a romantic?" I ask him.

"I don't know... I've never really had this chance with anyone so I figured I wouldn't waste it," he admits, keeping his eyes on the road. His words sink in and don't help with the nerves I'm already feeling.

We drive into the city and he keeps asking me about every song I play, his eyes drifting to me every now and then, just glancing. He still hasn't touched me once. I wonder if he's going to at all. I said slow and this is slow, but it feels really good. This is different from any date I've ever been on. Most of them weren't romantic and ended as any would. A Netflix and chill style, I guess. I'm not great at traditional dating. Considering how this started with Parker and I, I think that's proof. He parks his truck in a parking deck and he comes to help me from the car again. He takes a jacket from the car and throws it on before motioning me to go in front of him.

"What are we—"

"No asking. I won't tell you," he smirks to himself, his smile absolutely perfect.

I've never dated anyone with facial hair, mostly because I dated guys in high school and they couldn't grow any. Parker is only two years older than me, but he looks... He looks grown up.

We walk down the stairs of the parking deck and once we're on the street, he motions toward the right and I walk next to him on the street. Seattle bustles around us, a city I adore more than words. I look down at his hand hanging beside him. I decide that I can make the first move. That's alright. So I do. I take his hand and intertwine it with mine, electricity shocking every inch of my body and my mind. I push away the thought that I'm more reactive and in tune with my body when it comes to Parker,

245

mostly because I can't be thinking like that when it's only our first date.

He clasps his hand to mine. I look at him and see him glance down between us, his eyes looking at our joined hands. He looks forward and I pretend to not notice the slow smile that tints his lips. It's so subtle that it almost doesn't appear, but even if I couldn't see it on his lips, I can see it in his eyes. His hazel eyes are more green than brown right now. I look forward, a simple smile on my lips too as I look at my feet, walking with him. We turn off the street and there's a pop of life bursting off the block. They sectioned off the entire road, a farmers market living here for the time being. I smile, and look at him.

"They're doing a 'paint the street' down there. I thought it would be fun to... to paint and to walk around as well," he tells me and I squeeze his hand out of excitement.

To my surprise, he squeezes back and I pull him off the sidewalk and into the street. He follows and we make our way through pop up tents and small business shops set up on the street. I am completely taken away by all of it. Trying on hats at the small shops and sifting through artwork crafted and created just for this. Parker shows me art. He smiles with his eyes not just his lips and I feel my heart stutter when he looks at me with that warmth in his glance. I feel my entire body react when he reaches for me, taking my hand, walking us from booth to booth, his thumb grazing over my knuckles. A tiny tiny detail, but one that doesn't go unnoticed or unappreciated. I shiver and he takes off his jacket.

"This is so cliche," I mumble, staring at him and he shakes his head.

"Take the jacket, and stop complaining Brianne," he laughs.

"Why do you call me Brianne?" I ask.

"It's your name," he laughs through his words as I slide his jacket on my body.

THE RULES OF YOU AND ME.

It's a heavy Carhartt jacket but it's so warm considering the thing swallows me whole. I bunch up the sleeves so I can see my hands again, and we both reach for each other. My hand finds his. I bring my other hand over and hold onto his arm and lean into him subconsciously as we walk.

"I mean why do you call me by my full name and not a nickname?" I ask him.

"I like your name. I think it fits you... and..." he hesitates.

"What? Say it," I tell him, nudging him.

"You seem to have a really big attachment to your parents. You respect them and I feel like they named you that for a reason so I should... I should respect your name and call you by that. It's beautiful and it was the one gift your parents gave you that you can keep forever. If you want, of course," he explains.

I look up at him and a genuine smile filled with sentiment hits my lips.

"My mom is the only person that ever called me by my full name. Everyone else has a nickname for me unless they're mad at me, then it's 'Brianne Emily Archer! You're in trouble,'" I joke and he laughs. "You're very respectful."

"Did you expect something different?" he asks.

"I didn't expect anything. You're kind of mysterious. Honestly, you're quiet and lonely. You're an enigma. You're on the top football team in the country. You go to one of the best schools. You're best friends with the popular kids on the most favored sports team we have... Yet, you're introverted. So no, I expected nothing. But I'm... I'm happily surprised," I tell him.

"I had a few choices growing up. Do what I wanted and get punished, rebel and I would end up with consequences that were never worth it... Or respect others and get an easier draw in life. I was... I was really freaking lucky getting out of the foster system the way that I did. I know that and I know I have a lot of privilege in that sense. Who I am, what I look like, all of it

247

comes into play when thinking about how I got where I am currently. But... But I didn't have a choice in the respect part and once I started truly sinking into that, the quiet respectful persona, it was easy. I didn't really have to pretend because it just... It fit me. It felt better," he admits. I nod.

"You're respecting people you've never met and can never meet because they aren't alive. I think you've taken it to the next level, P..." I tell him and then hesitate. "Parker." I use his full name.

"You don't have to do that," he tells me and I nod.

"I don't but I will."

"The respect aspect isn't the same with my parents," he mumbles.

"But I think you deserve that same respect," I tell him and he actually looks at me now, his eyes roving my face.

He looks at every single inch of my face. He brings his other hand up, brushing his thumb over my cheek, then my bottom lip. I kiss his thumb and he smiles. Parker has given me glances and stares that I've never, not once, seen portrayed on his normally stoic face. He keeps his emotions, his smiles, and his feelings to a severe minimum. I don't take that fact lightly, that I've pulled something out of him. He only looks at me for another second before turning back to the street, guiding me to the paint section he had mentioned. There's actual artists painting portraits and masterpieces on the street in different sections. Then there are kids with parents. Couples. Every walk of life, painting on the streets. I clasp my hands together, getting excited.

We paint next to each other and I get so focused on the artwork that I don't talk much. I almost forget Parker is there for a few minutes as I sit on the cement and paint. I never knew this existed, this little farmers market, but I'm having a lot of fun. The food is good. The weather isn't that bad besides the small

THE RULES OF YOU AND ME.

wind chill breezing through the air. Parker is... He's perfect which makes my stomach heat and sink. I had... I had hoped he wasn't going to be perfect at all. I actually hoped for the opposite but I was rudely awakened from that dream and brought a different kind of dream. The kind of dream where you can hear Taylor Swift songs playing in your head when you look at the guy you're with. That's never happened before, not with my luck.

"A bouquet." He looks over at my painting.

"My favorite flowers. Peonies," I tell him, looking at what I created on the street.

It's been a few hours since we got here and we had gotten here later in the day so the small shops are starting to shut down as I finish my drawing, some still alive. The sun has sunk slightly lower and though we ate a bit throughout our walk, I'm actually hungry now.

"Ready?" he asks me.

He stands and gives me his hands, helping me from the ground. I turn back and look at our artwork. His is pretty. It's a sunset. He did decently well. I take a picture of the artwork and he smirks.

"Yours looks good," he tells me.

"So does yours. I had no idea I was on a date with Picasso," I tell him.

"Aren't Picasso's paintings kinda ugly?" he asks and I turn to look at him.

"It's a saying... So why would his paintings be ugly?" I ask.

"I had to take an art class once and from what I remember, the people in his paintings weren't the best looking," he tells me.

"Well, your painting was pretty. Is that what you need from me? To boost your ego?" I ask.

"You can keep going if you want, I'm enjoying it," he smirks to himself and I roll my eyes.

249

We walk back through all the tents and shops we passed along the way, but he stops at a flower stand and walks up, picking up an already arranged set of pink, red and white peonies. He hands his card over and I just stare at him.

"You already got me flowers," I tell him when he comes back, handing me the beautiful bouquet.

"I got you flowers, not your favorite flowers. There's a difference," he mumbles, his hands in his pockets as he walks beside me.

"But—"

"No but. If I want to get you something, I'm going to do it, even if you say no. Stop arguing." He instantly gets that bossy protective voice and I smirk to myself at the defensiveness.

"Sir, yes, sir."

"You're..." he shakes his head and I furrow my brows.

"What?" I ask and turn to him. Then, I bounce around him. "What? Say it!" I urge.

"It's nothing," he shrugs.

I don't push because I notice the shy, quiet nature returning to his features. He's retreating. *Maybe he'll say it later.* He brings me back to the car, two bouquets and lots of memories sitting between us now.

Parker drove us to get fast food and slushies to eat in his car and then he pulled up to Alki Beach, a beach I've frequented but never sat and watched the sunset at. It's definitely too cold to get out of the car, but sitting in his truck while the sun disappears... Finishing our food and sinking into one of the easiest conversations I've ever had. Parker Thompson listened to me when I asked for casual, but still took it the extra mile and is giving me an absolutely perfect date right now.

THE RULES OF YOU AND ME.

"First kiss..." He nods his head toward me, pushing for an answer.

I feel like a middle schooler playing 20 questions right now, but I honestly don't mind. I dig through the ice in the bottom of my slushie and think about my answer.

"My first kiss was with my first boyfriend named Ryland. He actually goes to SPU. It was very awkward," I admit and Parker smirks, digging through his slushie.

We've both gotten comfortable in his old Chevy. My legs are crossed and my back is leaned against the door so my body is facing him. He's angled to me, his legs spread, his gaze flickering between me, the sunset, and his drink.

"Tell me," he nods his head and I sigh.

"Okay, we were freshmen in high school. I was a cheerleader and he was actually a basketball player. Back then, the football cheerleaders did basketball cheer too. So, we knew each other through sports. It was after a game and we weren't even dating. He was very sweaty and I was not expecting it. He kissed me so hard that I actually hit my head on the wall behind me. Then, he apologized because he was an idiot and didn't mean to do it. Then, he kissed me for real and it wasn't as bad... but I wasn't dating him and at the time, when you're young and stupid... Well, I thought that made me some sort of slut or something."

A soft laugh bubbles in Parker's chest at my words.

"Then we started dating a week later. I subconsciously think it was because we kissed, but either way, he was my first kiss, first boyfriend, and also he took my virginity," I tell Parker and he raises his eyebrows.

"You let him take your virginity?" he asks and I shrug, mixing up my slushie.

"Virginity is a social construct. It can mean whatever you want it to mean and for me, it wasn't... It didn't need to be special. For some people, it does. Also losing your virginity is always awkward and weird," I laugh and shrug. "You're awfully quiet. What about you? Was your first time awkward?" I ask him and he smirks.

"I was at a party I was definitely too young to be at. I was also with a girl who had no business being around me. She was a freshman and I was an eighth grader."

I gasp at his words, faking shock.

"Parker, you dog," I joke and he rolls his eyes.

"Yeah, it was awkward. If you must know, I lasted about two minutes, and she pretended she wasn't mortified." He shakes his head and I cover my face.

"Okay, that wins," I laugh and he does too.

"You said you had multiple exes that go to SPU. Is there... Is there history?" he asks and I press my lips together.

"Ashton Gardner. He's my longest relationship to date. There's not much history left there to worry about but he is... I mean, he was important to me," I tell Parker.

"Did you love him?" he asks me and I shake my head right away.

"At the time when you're there and you're in it, I think it's easy to try and convince yourself you are but I wasn't. I've never been in love," I admit. Parker raises his eyes.

"Neither have I," he admits.

"And do you have any crazy exes I should be worried about?" I ask, feeling extremely relaxed in the passenger seat of his car.

"I've never had a girlfriend. I... I almost did. Her name was Sarah and she never wanted to commit. She also hated any gesture. She was... She was hard to be around and when I look back at it, I wonder what I was even doing. My entire freshman year, she was my almost kind of girlfriend. She broke it off when

THE RULES OF YOU AND ME.

I told her about everything with my family or lack of moreso," he tells me.

"What a bitch..." I mumble.

"You could say it louder, actually," he smirks and I do too.

"But she's not in your life anymore?" I ask and he shakes his head no.

"No. She left SPU after our freshman year. I don't know where she is now. She was... We weren't dating but I was still trying to be as all in as I could be," he explains.

I nod and look at him, a smile forcing its way onto my lips.

"Thank you... For trusting me with everything you've shared," I smile and he shakes his head.

"I can't really help myself from talking around you... It's weird," he admits and I look at him, a blush coating his face. He looks at me with a quizzical expression that melts into warmth.

"You are so pretty, Brianne," he mumbles, just above a whisper and my cheeks burn hotter. "That's what I was going to say back at the farmers market but it seemed cheesy. It felt like you might think I was trying too hard so I didn't say it but I just... I have to say it," he finishes and I laugh to myself, covering my face.

"You are cheesy and I really like it," I tell him.

"If you tell anyone I'm being cheesy, they won't believe you," he jokes.

"Oh, I know I can count on that," I laugh.

That's something I've noticed. Laughter is second nature with him. It's easy to let it bubble out of my chest in the midst of his words and our conversation. I've laughed more today than I have on every other date I've ever been on combined.

"How long have you been in therapy?" Parker asks and I smirk.

"Since my parents passed away. So, I was 10 years old when

I went. At first, it was Bellamy and I in there together for sibling therapy. Then, when I was old enough I went alone, and Bellamy never needed to continue. I mean, I say that but everyone needs to be in therapy if I'm honest. Even the most sensible people can use it, even the people who seem like they have everything all together could benefit from it, but Bellamy stopped going and he seems to be doing okay. It's odd too because Bellamy was older when they passed away so it seems like he—"

I stop talking when I look at Parker and he's giving me a look of confusion... I think that's what he's looking at me like.

"Sorry," I mumble to myself.

"Stop apologizing for talking. I enjoy listening to you talk, Brianne," he smirks and I feel a smile spread on my face.

"I talk a lot about me. I don't want to talk over any stories you have about you," I tell him, speaking truthfully. If I can learn something... anything about Parker it feels like a small gift that has a giant meaning. Most people know the basics, but even now with the little bits I know, I'm above average on Parker knowledge."

"I don't have many stories... Not many that compare to whatever you could say. Not in a sad way but in an honest way. I didn't grow up like you," he admits and I nod.

"Why did you change... You said you were kind of a punk as a kid so what did it for you? Was there something specific?" I ask, knowing it's a blunt question but wanting to understand him. He chuckles softly, the wheels in his head turning.

"Uhm... Honestly, I was... I was sad. It was just a deep unhappy feeling and I see it that way now. Back then, I didn't fully grasp that and I realized what I was doing was most likely the cause. I didn't have many options. So, I had to either take the opportunity given to me or continue on the path I was on. I didn't know what I wanted with my life because I didn't... I mean, I didn't know I could want things for myself at that

THE RULES OF YOU AND ME.

point," he admits and I can feel my heart swell and tighten at his words.

A kid that can't want things because he didn't know he even could.

"And do you know that now... That you can want things and that it's safe to do that?" I ask him softly.

He nods a few times, sheepishly at first. He reaches over the console and takes my hand and my entire chest shatters and breaks apart.

"I think I do. Yeah..." he admits and I can hardly breathe with the tension in my chest and the car.

This is so dangerous for me because I don't want this date to end and... and I had come into it hoping it would be horrible. Instead, I've lost track of time. The clock has ticked away the past few hours and it's felt like nothing like no time at all. I have two bouquets of flowers. I keep laughing and my cheeks have basically been stained red from how much he's made me blush tonight. My phone vibrates and there's a text from my brother, just checking in. I tell him I will be home decently late tonight, knowing that I don't want the date to end, and if it does, I'll be going straight to Dak's to spill all of it. I tuck my phone into my messenger bag on the floor.

"Bellamy?" he asks and I nod.

"Yes, just checking in," I tell him.

"Growing up with a brother, did he ever... I mean did you two ever fight?" he asks and I shake my head.

"I mean, yes, we fought every now and again, but honestly, Bellamy is the best brother. He's usually pretty level-headed. I'm the dramatic one most of the time or the one that's having a freakout or snapping at him. If I ever did, he would always just calm me down and settle me," I admit. "And without siblings? How did that feel?" I ask.

"I'm glad I didn't have siblings because we probably

255

wouldn't have been able to stay together. I do wish I had someone like what you're explaining. I'm sure a sibling would make life a hell of a lot easier," he explains.

"What about your roommates?" I ask.

"What about them?" he asks back.

"Do they not feel like your brothers this many years in? You spend almost every day with them... You're bound to be somewhat close with them by this point," I explain.

"I don't know. I mean life would be..." he pauses for a second and then furrows his brows. "I don't really know what my life would look like without them. They don't know that it would be really hard for me to adjust, especially without Xander. He pulls me out of my shit a lot. When I get upset, weird, or moody, he calls me out, helps me up, and dusts me off. So, I guess you're right in a way. They are kind of like the brothers I never had."

"Aw, three hockey players meet a football player and they make a family. How cute," I joke.

"Never tell Xander I said that or he'll be more insufferable than he already is," he jokes and I hold my pinky out.

"Promise," I tell him. He looks forward and I shrug. "What, you've never made a pinky promise?" I ask.

"No. I've never made a promise in my life at all," he tells me and I raise my eyebrows.

"Wow," I admit.

"Do you have a habit of making promises?" he asks me and I shrug.

"If I do, I always keep them," I tell him, but I lower my finger, not making him promise this. He'll promise something if it's actually important.

Time is spent, even longer than expected, continuing our conversation. We talk about nothing and everything. I tell him about how I got into dancing and all of my competitions for

THE RULES OF YOU AND ME.

cheer as well as dance as a kid. He asks if I have time for friends or sleep and I laugh. I laugh a lot. He wants to know more and more about me and I keep telling him, letting him know whatever he wants and surprisingly, if I ask him anything, he tells me. Parker spent his younger years playing football, going home, doing his schoolwork, and going to bed. We had similar childhoods but very very different ones at the same exact time.

I look at the clock on his dashboard and it's 11 at night. He eyes it and looks back at me. I sigh.

"I think this means we should—"

"I don't want it to end yet..." he cuts me off and I stare at him.

"Then, what?" I ask and he runs his hand through his hair, his eyes diverting from mine.

"Come home with me..." he suggests and I open my mouth to protest. "I won't pull anything. I just... I want to be around you. I can bring you home later, you just have to say the word. P-promise," he mumbles the last word and I raise my eyebrows.

"Promise?" I ask and he rolls his eyes and shakes his head.

"Don't make this—"

I lean forward, my face close to his shoulder as he turns forward in the driver's seat.

"Am I stealing your promise virginity, Parker Thompson?" I ask him and he sighs deeply but there's a smirk on his lips.

"Will you? Come back with me?" he asks and I debate it. *Will I?* I guess I shouldn't be asking myself that question. The question I should be asking is, should I? Should I go back to his house when I told myself he had one night...

"What are you worried about, Brianne?" He asks me and I sigh.

"Everything," I admit.

"Do what you want to do. Whatever it is you're wanting the most, do that," he urges.

"Then yes... I'll come back with you," I tell him and glance for a second to watch his smirk settle on his perfect lips.

It's dark outside. We can't see anything that's not illuminated by the street lights but I don't care. I'm doing what makes me feel good and I feel really good about spending more time with Parker.

CHAPTER 21

SUPERBLOODMOON (FEAT. D4VD) BY HOLLY HUMBERSTONE

Parker Thompson:

I drive us home and the drive now back toward my apartment is so much more... Free. Brianne is singing along to the music that she's choosing and my heart is... I shake the thought, not wanting to bring it to fruition in my own mind just yet. The minute I think about it, the more real it becomes because I don't know where she stands right now. I don't know if she's ready to give this—this obvious thing between us—a real chance. Or if it's not as obvious as I think it is and I'm just a fucking idiot. I wouldn't be surprised if I was being the biggest idiot right now, blinded by my own feelings.

"I love it when it rains," she tells me, pulling me from my thoughts.

Her eyes are trained on the light drizzle of rain outside the car that I hadn't noticed until right now. I'm not surprised she loves the rain. She seems like the kind of person who appreciates everything. I feel like when she lost her parents... someone so important to her, she learned at a young age to never take things for granted. The small things, at least. She's perceptive. She's honest and she's so ungodly pretty that it's hard to believe.

"How do you feel about it?" she asks me as the weather makes its angry appearance in our conversation, pelting my car.

"Um... I mean, I grew up in California. It rained a little so... it's fine," I shrug.

"Have you never played in the rain, Parker?" she asks me and I shake my head.

"Why would I play in the rain?" I ask her.

"Rain is the biggest gift because it washes away bad things and it grows new things and... It's just perfect, especially when the water is warm," she explains, watching it fall on the windows.

"I just never really thought about playing in the rain. Actually, it stuck with me for a long while. One of my foster families told me I'd get sick if I played in the rain... I never paid much attention to it after that," I admit, hearing just how bleak the thought is. The bleakness is definitely outshined by her colorful thoughts.

I pull into my apartment and park my truck across the lot. I don't even put the car in park before she jumps out of the truck and into the rain. Part of me could feel it coming—her going into the rain like it's where she belongs. I smirk to myself, carefully putting my truck into park and turning the engine off. I get out of the car, trying to understand the feeling she's talking about. The rain isn't warm, it's cold, prickling my skin as well as the chilled air outside. She dances through the parking lot, spinning and splashing and... and she's like a kid. That's what this is, child-like enjoyment. I wish it was daytime so I could see the pure joy on Brianne Archer's face.

"Choose the rain, Parker!" she shouts and I can't help but break into a smile.

THE RULES OF YOU AND ME.

This is my choice. All of this, every bit of her and this date—the rain, my truck, every last ounce.

Bri is jumping around me, dancing to music she's created in her own head and I smirk at her, enjoying the rain, sure, but enjoying her more. I reach for her hand, catching her off guard. She falls into me.

I move her in circles. I watch as she pushes to her tiptoes, letting me spin and twirl her around. Her once-perfect hair is now in wet ribbons, water spiraling off the ends as she dances in the rain without a single care in the world. She takes my hand too and spins me around. It feels awkward at first but I laugh as she crumbles to my chest, her fingers on me, holding the soaking t-shirt between her now cold fingers. We're laughing in the rain —a thing I've lived in my whole life, but never played in. I've never enjoyed it.

I imagine the little kid in my head, that little version of me. I see him now and he's no longer just there. He's smiling as he watches me do this. He's definitely a little confused as to why and shocked that I'm this... That I'm this happy. I don't remember smiling much as a kid... but that little kid is smiling now.

My heart. Once again, I think about what I wanted to think earlier. I allow myself to now. Now that I'm watching her become a part of the rain and the weather. I watch her take the Earth and the atmosphere and somehow make it her own, something I didn't know was possible. I feel my heart for the millionth time today, but for the first time in my existence, it beats with excitement. Not for a game. Not for an award or an achievement. Not for something that I worked for. I didn't work for Brianne to be here. She chose to and it fell into my freaking lap. My heart is beating because it's excited... for life. That's what it feels like, anyway.

"We're going to get sick..." I pull her to me, only allowing

261

myself simple soft touches, knowing good and well that if I don't restrain myself, I'll be putting both of us through torture.

"I guess you might be right," she says through a small chatter of her teeth and I nod my head toward my building.

"Come on, Sunshine. There's no explaining it if both of us wake up tomorrow with the same symptoms. Let's go," I smirk and she runs back to my car, rain splattering all around her.

She leans in carefully, grabbing her flowers and purse, and when she rounds the bed of my truck, I sweep her up and she squeals as I carry her, honeymoon style toward my apartment building. She laughs so wildly it's like it is begging to be free from her chest and her lungs and I smile to myself. Once we're in the building that I wish was warmer, I set her down and she curtsies in front of me.

"My prince charming, thank you," she jokes and I bow, replicating her regal stance which only makes her laugh again.

I guide her forward by her hip and then we walk side by side up the stairs. I fight the urge to smile at my feet but she doesn't. She's smiling from ear to ear, like she just learned how to do it which only makes it harder for me to keep mine from breaking free. We pass each landing until we reach the top of the fourth floor and round the stairs, walking down the hall. She steps in front of me and turns around, walking backward so she can look at me.

"Can I tell you something?" she asks, mischief in her sea-colored eyes.

"Always," I watch her, flowers cradled in her arms.

"I wanted you to kiss me. All night, I kept wondering, 'Will this be it? Will he kiss me now?' and it never came... But especially out there. I really, really wanted to be kissed by Parker Thompson," she tells me and I feel my heart bottom out and sink to the pit of my stomach. Then, my stomach sinks straight to my ass. I stare at her, keeping the strongest poker face I've

THE RULES OF YOU AND ME.

ever had in my entire life so I don't smile like that inner child is in my mind right now. Don't break... She stops when her back brushes my front door and I don't stop, coming close to her, close enough for our chests to touch.

"I'm doing this the right way, Brianne. The right way means the slow way," I hold her face in my hands, her skin cold from the rain and her heavy wet clothes weighing her down.

My thumbs graze her cheekbones, brushing over her freckles. Her makeup is slightly messed up, some of it pooling under her eyes. I don't look at her lips, knowing that if I do, I'd question if I should be doing this the slow way. She doesn't stop herself though. She looks at my lips without shame which makes me smirk.

"Turtle's pace... as you said," I remind her and she presses her lips into a smile.

I don't look at them, but I do see it in her eyes.

"You know rules are meant to be broken." She tilts her head, leaning into my touch.

"Not a chance, Sunshine."

I straighten her head and kiss her forehead, the only kiss I'll be giving tonight. She groans and I smirk once my back is turned to her. She wants to kiss me... Fucking score. I open the door to all three of my roommates sitting in our living room playing a very loud game of Sorry. I look at all three of them and give them a warning glare to not embarrass the shit out of me but Xander smirks so wide I already know I'm so fucked. Brianne stands beside me, a smile still on her lips. She waves one single time and then clasps her hands together in front of her and rocks back and forth only once on her feet, obvious nerves taking over her. I rub the back of my neck, looking at my roommates and then at her.

"Guys, this is Brianne. Brianne, this is Andrew, Nico, and you've met Alexander," I mumble.

"Dude, really with the formalities? You can call me Drew, just like he does," Andrew tells her.

"And you know damn well he calls me Xander. Doesn't he? When he talks about me?" Xander pushes and Bri just smirks.

"Hi. Nice to meet you and nice to see you again... And he doesn't talk about you, actually," she talks to all of them but directs the last part to Xander, a smirk on her lips as she says it. She winks and he scoffs, rolling his eyes.

"What were you two doing? Going fucking swimming? Isn't it like 50 degrees outside?" Nico asks.

"We actually just finished with your community pool, you guys should try it out next time..." she spouts off.

"Really?" Drew asks.

"No, not really, dumbass," I mumble and laugh.

"What did you do with our roommate?" Nico asks and I watch as Brianne furrows her brows.

"What do you mean?" she asks.

"I've never seen him laugh in the four years we've—"

"Shut the fuck up, Nico," I groan and put my hand on Brianne's back, guiding her from the living room.

"There he is... Jeez, you had me worried for a second," Nico holds his chest like he's gasping for air.

"Have fun, use protection!" Xander calls out.

"Xander!" I yell and Brianne laughs.

"What? I'm just being a good friend," he shrugs innocently and I grind my teeth, trying to keep my cool.

I'm in a good mood. Well, I was, and I don't want that to stop because my roommates don't know how to be normal functioning humans. Brianne steps into my room and I remember that we're both sopping wet. She shivers and I hesitate.

"Do you want to... I mean do you need a warm shower or a change of clothes or... What do you need?" I ask, feeling like I'm coming up empty in this department.

THE RULES OF YOU AND ME.

What do women need?

"A change of clothes would be fine... and face wash if you have any so I can take my makeup off," she tells me.

"Of course I have face wash. What kind of guys have you been around to ask if I have face wash?" I laugh to myself as I turn around and go to my drawers.

I pass her a long-sleeve t-shirt. It was one of our training shirts from last season, the number 13 on the sleeves is the only thing that signifies that the shirt is mine. I hand her a pair of my sweatpants and socks too so she can hopefully warm up a little bit. I lead her out of my bedroom and into the bathroom across the hall, telling her where my shit is so she can use it. I leave and go into my bedroom so I can change too. I wear a hoodie and sweatpants, shivering as I towel dry my hair the best I can. After a few minutes, she walks back into my room with wet hair but a clean face, her freckles far more prominent now. She smiles and that dimple... I reach forward, my finger grazing the divet in her cheek.

"I didn't know what to do with my..." She holds out her wet clothes. I take them and pile them on top of mine.

"I'll dry them so you can wear them home or... Or whatever. If that's okay," I tell her and she nods.

I take them from my room and walk down the hall to the nook in our apartment with a washer and dryer. I open it up and notice not only a bra, but underwear too and I clench my jaw. I wonder if she did it on purpose. Considering what she said in the hall and our track record, I wouldn't be surprised. But the thought of her not wearing anything under that stupid fucking shirt and those sweatpants makes me wonder how far my restraint will go tonight. She said slow. So I'm going slow. I sigh as I put the clothes in the dryer and start it. When I walk back down the hall and into my bedroom, she's sitting on my bed with her legs criss crossed and my decorative pillow in her lap.

"Can you please give me a backstory here?" she asks, turning the words 'Yes you can!' to me.

I sigh and climb onto my bed, lying on my side and propping myself up so I can look at her.

"I moved to college with nothing to my name but my clothes... God, it sounds pathetic when I say it out loud," I shake my head and she lays on her stomach, lying all the way down, resting her head on her crossed arms.

"Tell me," she smiles.

"I looked up online what would make a dorm room more home-like. It said throw pillows. So I went to Walmart and got that for cheap. It's a soft throw pillow so don't hate on it," I argue.

"It is very comfy, but you couldn't have picked a more exciting quote?" she laughs.

"What do you suggest? My choices were, 'Live, Laugh, Love' or 'Blessed,' so I chose 'Yes you can!' It seemed the most positive for me in my situation," I laugh back at her, stealing the pillow. "You know what? You don't deserve to hold my pillow." I cuddle my body to it and she smiles at me.

"I'm glad I said yes to going out with you," she admits and my cheeks warm up.

Have I ever blushed in my life? Am I seriously fucking blushing right now...

"I am too," I admit.

"You know, when you're around me, you're different," she tells me and I shrug.

"I could say the same for you, Sunshine," I mumble.

"Did you always play wide receiver or did you switch positions?" She asks and then rolls on her back. "It always interests me, honestly. It's pretty mixed with the cheer team whether we actually like football or not but I love it. I mean, I had to if I wanted to spend any time with my dad and Bell when I was

THE RULES OF YOU AND ME.

younger, but... it's just interesting to me," she rambles on and I listen to every word, watching her as she talks, her eyes trained on my ceiling.

"I was a quarterback my first few years playing but as important as the quarterback may be, I hated the thought of not being the one to run that ball in the end zone. Lucky for me, too, because I was a terrible quarterback," I tell her.

She smiles, and I watch as her freckles stretch and move across her perfect face. My eyes lingering, wishing I could count them all.

"And who made the choice, did you go to your coach or did they come to you?" she asks.

"They came to me. I had played quarterback until I was in eighth grade. We had games where scouts and people would come. A high school coach watched me play and said I wasn't where I needed to be and that I belonged in that end zone. He wasn't in my school district. I moved to that district to play for him because he said I had too much potential to waste. His name was Coach Wiesner. I honestly think about him a lot. He was right. When I made my first touchdown, even on such a small level, the feeling it gave me was the feeling of finally being successful at something and... I don't know. It made me realize that I needed to do this. That football was my out of all the things that I hated in my life. I knew it on some level but in that new position, being the one who can actually win the game for us, that was what made me really really put everything into the sport," I explain to her.

"Hearing you talk about football is different than with everyone I'm close to and everyone I've been around. Bellamy is dedicated to football, of course. It's his first love but I feel like a small part of him only stuck with it to feel close to my parents and me. He loves the sport more than anything but I think he grew to love it. Lawson... Well, I can tell after meeting Sienna, after seeing that there's other shit in life than playing games, I don't know if he'll stick with it or move on or what... But with you, it's like you're... Well, you're like a shark," she explains and I furrow my brows, watching her lose herself in thought.

"Explain," I smirk.

"Sharks are intense, but also super misunderstood and—"

"How do you know so much about sharks?" I ask, only interrupting this once.

"I love shark week," she shrugs. "Anyway, sharks are really misunderstood. They're actually really docile creatures but they're still intense. They can't stop moving. Physically, their body won't let them. It's life or death. Keep moving or die. I think that's you. From today, from learning about you and listening to you, I feel like you've had to keep moving or you'd... Metaphorically, of course, you'd die. You'd drown. With football, you're the same. Keep moving, keep getting better. Without it, you'd cease. You'd stop. You wouldn't be you because it was all you had," she explains.

For the first time in my life, I realize that there is intimacy in understanding. There is an affinity when you feel seen the way I am right now. I'm fully clothed, lying in bed with her and I feel more naked than I ever have. She knows. Without knowing me fully, without knowing every in and out, every part of me, she still understands a piece of me that I didn't even truly understand myself until recently.

"Football was the parents I didn't have, the siblings I never got, the friends that I didn't allow myself to make," I tell her.

A lot of my life was just that. Not allowing good things because... Well, a part of me felt like I didn't deserve them. I had a habit of telling myself if I got comfortable or felt happy or good that everything would take a turn—that feeling those things would cause me to lose it all. I spent most of my life not letting myself be proud of the things I had accomplished. I'm reminded

THE RULES OF YOU AND ME.

of Bellamy and Lawson and what they had said when they asked me to be captain. They said I deserve to be cocky sometimes. I realize now why I've never let myself be...

"I get it," she nods.

"You grew up with friends. Didn't you?" I ask and she shakes her head.

"There are the friends that are forced and the friends that are found. The friendships I had on cheer teams and dance teams were forced friendships. They needed to be nice to me and I, them. You know? I didn't find them. I didn't choose them. They were chosen for me. It was different with Dakota, though. Yes, we're on the same team, but I really met him the night before our first official practice. He got me right away. It was easy, sliding into the way we are right now. It was instant. There was connection and commitment in our friendship right away," I tell him.

"Connection and commitment?" I ask.

"Yeah, it's like... Well, your whole life you're going to connect with people. No matter what. Even if it's on a level you don't understand, connection is different than commitment. I can connect with a random guy at a bar and never commit to seeing him ever again. The ones who matter are the people who are worth the commitment. Connections come a billion times a life. Commitments are special and unique. When Dakota and I met at that bar officially, it was an instant connection and pretty soon after, a commitment. He protected me, he cared, and he made me feel safe. There was not a single part of me that wasn't ready to choose that friendship and that has never happened in my life," she admits.

I realize the only person I've felt that way about is... Well, it's her. I've never felt the need to commit myself to someone or had a connection with them like the way I feel with her. Our bodies and our minds seem to be on a track with each other in a way that I didn't know existed. And I met her three months ago, by chance at an annual bonfire I didn't even want to go to.

"What about a third C... What about chance?" I ask her.

"What about it?" she asks.

"Don't you think the chance of two people that are... Well, two people that are meant to meet that actually cross paths. Isn't that important too? Just as important as connection or commitment?" I ask.

"I guess chance is important. I met Dakota that night by chance. He caught my eye by chance..." she mumbles.

"I ran into you on the beach by chance," I tell her.

"You did that on purpose," she jokes and I smirk, taking a strand of her hair, twirling the end around my finger.

"I'm serious. I was mortified at first and I tried so hard to make sure I didn't crush you even though I had no idea who you were... Then you... Then I saw you," I admit and I watch her cheeks.

"Then you saw me..." She turns her head to look at me, her back still pressed into my mattress.

"Yeah, and I wondered who you were, why I'd never seen you before, and why the only sound I could hear was my heart beating. You looked just as shocked as me, and then the spell was broken because you looked mortified that we were lying on the beach," I laugh.

"My brother was watching," she admits.

"Then, there was that. I found out who you were and decided that fate hadn't intervened there. It was a stupid accident until the bar, of course. Then, it felt like there was no mistaking that something had to give but I don't do the feelings thing. If you couldn't tell... I think everything between us has been by chance," I admit.

"I agree... What about the connection? What do you think about that?" she asks me.

THE RULES OF YOU AND ME.

"We definitely have a connection. A lot of connections," I admit.

"As for the last one, I think it would be bold for you to ask me to commit tonight... Maybe our second date," she jokes.

"Are you telling me that you'll go out with me again?" I ask and she smiles.

"I guess I am," she says softly and I could actually jump up and down with excitement right now but I just smile instead.

We keep talking so much that when I look at the clock, it's 4:30 in the morning. I tell her to go to bed and she does just that, not curling into me but staying close enough that I can still feel her warmth. I don't know if this is going to ruin me or wreck me... but I've got another date and I'm going to take it and run with it...

CHAPTER 22
FEARLESS (TAYLOR'S VERSION) BY TAYLOR SWIFT

Brianne Archer:

My laugh sounds more like a cackle as I sit with Dakota at brunch, the two of us having perfectly cleaned up from when he picked me up this morning. I woke up when the sun was shining into Parker's room. He was really peaceful when he was asleep even though he was angled in such an uncomfortable position. He was very obviously trying to make sure he stayed on his side of the bed which was very cute. I wrote Parker a small note and left it on the pillow next to him then I blew Dakota up until he came and got me so he could bring me back to my place. I got myself ready when I got back home, avoiding every single question that Dak asked which brings us to now, hours later at the cutest brunch spot Valerie recommended.

We've been at the bar drinking mimosas for the past 30 minutes and I can't stop laughing because of him. He's giving every guy who passes by a new nickname. The last one was Silver Dick. I asked why. He proceeded to say that he looks great clothed but he's sure his dick would be as old as he is. My phone buzzes and I continue to chuckle to myself as I look down and check the notification. Parker...

I open the text, sip my mimosa, and promptly choke on it once I view the text. Orange juice and champagne partially come from my nostrils. I grab my napkin and wipe my face, ignoring the abhorrent look on Dakota's face as he stares at me.

"What the hell did you just look at? Did Parker send an unsolicited dick pic? Let me see," Dak leans over and I click my phone off and turn it face down on the bar top.

"Dakota, I have to tell you all about my date and you have to be super super honest with me okay?" I ask.

"Thank God you're going to tell me. I thought I was going to have to beat it out of you." He sips his mimosa and I shake my head.

"I knew you'd be all... Dakota about it.

"That's hurtful, but beside the point, tell me about all the dirty, sexy fun you had."

"We had no such thing. Not even a single kiss," I tell him.

"Oh, so he's a gentleman? Well now, he wasn't a gentleman when he took you back to his place the first time and—"

"SHHHHHHH. That never happened," I lie.

"It definitely happened," he smirks.

"Yes, but we're pretending that it didn't so we can start over. Clean slate and all that jazz," I tell him.

"I don't care about jazz. I care about Parker's dick," he informs me and I roll my eyes.

"Okay, well, I care about both. Well, no. I care about jazz and I'm going to care about Parker's dick... One day? Maybe? If we ever get there again. Ugh! Dakota, you're confusing me." I sip my drink and Dakota takes a bite out of his waffle.

"Talk! Talk! Tell me what kind of magic Parker has, spill," he jokes.

"He took me on a date and I usually feel one of two ways on

THE RULES OF YOU AND ME.

a date. I either feel like they're trying way too hard or they're not trying at all. It didn't feel like Parker was trying at all. It felt so natural and common but also, he's not the dating type. I mean, he's just not really experienced so I wonder what was going on in his head the whole time. Does he think I'm annoying? Obviously not because he invited me back to his place and—"

"Pause. That's what I want to know. How the hell did he propose inviting you back to his apartment and then also proceeded to not kiss you or touch you at all?" he asks me.

"Well... We talked. Literally all night. Like I said, it all felt easy. It was just amazing. Basically, he did everything the right way. He said all the right things. He bought me not one but two bouquets of freaking flowers. He got a car so he could take me on a date and he also made sure they put a stereo in the old car so I could feel comfortable and listen to music. That's insane, right?" I ask him.

"What's insane is the fact that the picture-perfect dude just walked into your life and is metaphorically sweeping you off of your feet—"

"Well, he did that too. We danced in the rain and he swept me up off of my feet and then carried me into his apartment," I interrupt and Dakota groans, then gags.

"Oh my god, barf. You guys are so cute, it's gross. There's no reason to be complaining right now. Why are you complaining and being ungrateful that the boyfriend gods blessed you?" Dak asks me, flipping his palms to the ceiling, begging for an answer.

"I'm not complaining, I'm explaining. I told him this story about my mom a while ago. I told him about how when my mom was away on business trips, she would send me whatever song she was listening to or music that she knew I would like because she was thinking of me. It was just really special because my mom was the only person who loved music like I do. Basically,

275

she just understood. Better than Bellamy, better than anyone," I tell him.

"That's such a sweet story, but what does that have to do with Parker?" Dak asks, turning his body completely to me now.

"Well, he hasn't texted me this morning. I was wondering if maybe he was waiting for me to text him first but he just texted me. Look..." I open my phone again and show him the text from Parker.

The song is Fearless by Taylor Swift. The correct version of the song too, Taylor's Version.

"Aww, Baby." Dakota puts his hand over his heart and pouts his lip. "That's the cutest thing. Cuter than bunnies and babies.," he tells me and I just stare at the text.

"But what does it mean? Did he hear it and think of me or did he just think about what I told him about my mom and... And maybe he was just thinking of me so he sent me the song he was listening to. Well, he doesn't like music so probably not but... I don't know. I think navigating this is going to be so weird because I know this is wrong, but it feels right," I explain.

"Backtrack, what the hell do you mean he doesn't like music?" Dak takes a bite of his waffle and raises his eyebrows at me, waiting for my reply.

"I mean, he prefers things quiet, so he doesn't choose to listen to music. I get it. If you've been surrounded by noise your whole life, you want peace..." I tell him.

"So wait," Dakota starts chuckling to himself. "You're telling me that the loudest, most talkative person I know is bonding with the broody, 'I prefer silence' kind of guy? This has to be some joke," he smirks and I shove a middle finger in his face.

"No, opposites attract. Hence me and you, I'm perfect and you're a loser therefore we're the ideal combo." He rolls his eyes at me and I sigh, looking at the text.

THE RULES OF YOU AND ME.

"What are you going to say? Flirt with him," he tells me. I type back a quick message.

> Thinking of me?

I set the phone between Dakota and me on the bartop. We watch as the three dots appear, then disappear. The action happens at least four times before I smirk.

"Damn, he's got to think long and hard, doesn't he?" Dakota asks. I bite my thumbnail and his reply appears.

> Parker: Always

I stare at it, ignoring the burning in my chest.

> Always? I don't know if I can believe that.

I'm trying to pull something from him—flirting, a conversation, anything—but he doesn't reply. He doesn't even start to type a message.

"So, are you fully on board the SS Parker?" Dakota asks.

"No. I'm still on the dock and the ship has not sailed. We've been on one date, and—"

"Screwed each other's brains out," Dakota smirks, downing the last of his mimosa.

"Beside the point, Dak. We've been on a date and had sex once, that's not a marriage proposal. It's a mix of lapsed judgment and hormones. I don't know what this is or what it could be. I had fun, but tying myself to it, putting a label on it, feels dangerous. I don't want to tread those waters yet so I'm not going to," I explain.

"Whatever you say, Baby," Dakota shrugs. "I think you're

277

playing your cards right. Pretend like he doesn't flood your basement and have him on his knees for you before the week is up."

"My basement is not flooded," I argue.

"Your insurance company just dropped you from their service because your basement flooded so bad the second you met Parker Thompson. There's no use lying to me. Now, drink your champagne so we can get to practice on time." He waves me on.

"Was it a smart decision to drink our weight in champagne before cheer practice?" I ask, drinking the rest of my glass.

"No, but what Leah doesn't know won't kill her," he tells me and I smirk, taking out my card to pay for everything.

CHAPTER 23
GARDEN LIFE BY LUKE HEMMINGS

Brianne Archer :

I sigh out a deep breath as Parker, Bellamy, and Lawson walk out of the apartment. It's been three days since my brunch with Dakota. It's also been three days since I've spoken to Parker. He never replied after the text I sent which in turn, sent me into a spiral. How are you going to send me a song, melt my heart on our date, then leave me high and dry? The silent spiral continued when the first text I received from him wasn't anything sweet or cute. Not even a check-in. He canceled our Tuesday dance lesson because Coach Corbin was panicking about the Friday game that we have. I thought that it was dumb that he made Parker practice considering he isn't even allowed to play but I didn't argue.

I know a phone works both ways but there's got to be a rule somewhere that when you text him, you can't be the one to text again. I thought maybe he'd send something by now, but my phone has been bone dry with the exception of Dakota, obviously. Dakota would never let me spiral alone. He pulled me right out of that panic and said that Parker is moody and broody and to give him time to deliberate his feelings and thoughts. It's crazy though because I've needed that time too. I don't know how I'm feeling or what is actually going on between us. I like him, sure, but that's just it. There's obviously a connection. I want to see him again, but in the back of my mind, there's Bellamy. The thought of him continues to nag at me so I wonder how Parker feels.

I walk into the kitchen, my feet smacking on the cold tile floors. It's not freezing yet, but it's getting colder in Washington. Halloween is not this weekend but the next and I still don't have a single clue about what I'm going to wear. I'm sure Dakota and I will plan something together. Considering Bellamy and Lawson have decided they're throwing a party here, I know I will need to pull out all the stops. I'll probably piss Bellamy off when I show up in next to nothing for the holiday. There's a knock on the door and I pad over, opening it without checking who it is.

Parker doesn't wait for me to open the door to him all the way before he steps into my space. He takes me by the hips and moves me over and out of the door frame before kicking the door closed. I open my mouth to speak but he puts a finger to my lips before I can speak.

"Shhh," He tells me.

"I thought you—" I speak, despite his finger pressed to my lips.

I ignore the rush in my heart.

"I said shhh," he tells me, his face serious. I close my lips and he takes his finger away, still keeping his other hand on my waist, his finger brushing my skin. I don't speak and look at him expectantly, waiting for an explanation.

"I left my key behind on purpose so I could run back and come get it but I only have a minute..." he tells me and I furrow my brows.

THE RULES OF YOU AND ME.

"For what?" I ask.

"To ask you to play hooky with me tomorrow and go away with me all day," he tells me.

"All day? I have classes and—"

"I don't care," He admits.

"You're a bad influence," I argue.

"Say yes," he tells me, his words rushed but his face expectant and so adorable.

"What are we going to do?" I ask.

"None of your concern. Just make up something so Bellamy thinks you're not going to be home tomorrow night and bring an overnight bag with warm clothes," he tells me and I look at him, contemplating.

I stare at his face, very aware that his finger is drawing small lines on the exposed skin on my side. It's almost painful how aware I am. His eyes are sea-green with rings of brown. His lips turn up into the smallest smirk, the kind of lopsided grin you see those guys do on the movie screens. I fold instantly.

"Don't make me beg, Sunshine," his voice turns low and soft.

I was already going to say yes, but now I'm about to melt into a puddle before I can.

"Fine. Now go before Bellamy thinks you got lost, go..." I tell him.

He brings his hand up and away from my waist to touch my face briefly. His thumb grazes my cheekbone, then he reaches over me to grab his keys from the countertop. Before I can blink, Parker is gone and I sigh a deep breath, my chest still feeling constricted like it's beating a million miles a minute. I lean against the door and press my head back with a sigh. I'm going to end up having a heart attack before I even get to kiss Parker again.

I wake up to a text from Parker telling me to wear clothes I can hike in. Are we going hiking? Are we doing something dangerous or... Well, he wouldn't put me in harm's way. Though, I've never really been hiking. It was something I wanted to get into. Considering I live in the perfect place to camp and hike, you would think I might have tried my hand at it. I haven't given myself the chance yet. It's early, to the point where the sun hasn't risen yet, but Parker gave me a specific time and now a dress code. I'm sticking to it.

Since it's early, it's chilly enough that I'll need some extra layers if we're going to be outside. I dress in my fur-lined leggings, with a baby pink t-shirt. Over that, I wear a sweatshirt and a raincoat as well as a pair of tennis shoes with my furry socks on too. I'll be warm and cute. I braid my hair back into two Dutch braid pigtails. I pack an overnight pack too like Parker said. I'm nervous but excited, more so the latter. I hesitate at my bedroom door before starting out of it. I have everything I need except the confidence I had the first night I got with Parker. Is he going to make a move today? Does this count as a date? What are we going to do? Is it going to be better than the first?

I walk down the stairs quietly and notice Bellamy and Kamryn both sleeping on the couch in what looks like a very uncomfortable position, which tells me it was accidental that they fell asleep that way. I sneak to the front door, grabbing my Stanley cup off the drying rack. I'll make Parker stop on the way so I can fill it up. I head down the hall and to the elevator, feeling a pang of guilt for sneaking around my brother. I push the thoughts away harshly though, knowing that I don't want them affecting my mood today. This is just a fun time. This is easy, new, and fun.

I take my car to Parker's place to cover my tracks. Bellamy

THE RULES OF YOU AND ME.

won't believe I'm at Dakota's if my car is still in the parking lot of our apartment complex. I cross all the T's and dot all the I's. My drive is short and quiet. It's one of those car rides where you purposely turn your music off so you can sit and marinate in your own thoughts and words. Consider it panic. Consider it whatever you want. All I know is I have a habit of overthinking and I've come to accept that. Once I pull up to Parker's apartment, he's already outside waiting for me with a giant backpack on his back.

I furrow my eyebrows at the sight. *Does he hike a lot? Maybe he enjoys it. Maybe one of his roommates does or maybe—Oh, shit he's walking over here.* I put my Jeep in park and turn off the engine, watching as he opens my door for me. He holds his hands out.

"Give me your bag," he tells me and I reach over, grabbing my backpack to pass it to him.

"Was there a specific reason we had to do this before the sun came up?" I ask him.

"Because it will be worth it when you see what I've seen. Come on," he nods his head. I groan and he scoffs.

"You're supposed to be sunshine-y and happy," he clarifies.

"Can't be sunshine-y when the sun isn't out, can I?" I ask.

"Brianne Archer is not a morning person, got it," he laughs to himself and opens his truck bed which now has a hard top over the back of it. He slides his bag, as well as mine, into it.

"Are you taking mental notes on me?" I ask, walking to the door. He follows and opens it for me.

"Have been since the moment I met you," he admits and reaches over me, buckling my seatbelt for me.

He stops so he can look directly at me, taking my breath away with the sheer proximity of his face to mine. I look straight into his eyes, at his lips, then back up to his eyes, cursing myself for being a damn traitor. He smirks before backing away from me and clicking my seatbelt in. I take a deep breath the second he closes my door and walks around the front of his truck. I need to play his game. I also need to chill. This date hopefully will top the last one, which is a hard feat to accomplish. Though, Parker seems pretty determined considering he's got me up this freaking early.

Parker drives and he turns on music himself this time. It's The Beatles... I look over at him and blink, my eyes adjusting to the very dusky light that just barely peeking through the muck of clouds. His eyes briefly glance at me and he gives me a skeptical stare.

"Is there a reason you're looking at me like that?" he asks.

"The Beatles?" I ask, the song Here Comes The Sun playing on the radio.

"What about it? Bad choice?" he asks.

"Not at all. I just didn't expect you to pick it," I admit.

"The last family I lived with was the Campbell family. The dad, he listened to them a lot. The wife also loved the music but I never really paid much attention. Until now," he mumbles, turning the song up.

He starts singing to the song lightly, his voice definitely not up to par. I cover my face, laughing. He motions to me at the lyrics, referring to me as the sun.

"You should stick to football," I speak through laughter and he just smirks to himself, continuing to look forward.

That was straight out of a movie—one of my favorite movies. I ignore the racing in my chest at the thought.

We pull up to the bay and Parker seems to know where he's going and what he's doing. I watch him carefully as well as everything surrounding me. The sun is encroaching on us, teasing the horizon with its presence. He doesn't take our bags out, but he does meet me at the front of his truck, putting his hands under my hood so he can hold the collar of my raincoat.

THE RULES OF YOU AND ME.

"Ready to watch the sunrise?" he asks and I take a deep breath and nod.

"I guess I am," I smile to myself.

The first date was magical and now we're watching sunrises together? This feels impossible. I quickly text Dakota and let him know that this is not a drill and I am in fact living in a fairytale. I walk only slightly in front of Parker because that's where he's keeping me, his hand on my hip, guiding me where he'd like me. He keeps me at arm's length, not letting me get far. He talks to the tour guide, to the kayak company, to everyone. He's straight to the point, blunt, and quiet. I'm sure to smile at all of them, knowing it's just me overcompensating for Parker's grumpy nature. The kayaks are brought out and we're all at the edge of the bay getting ready to depart. There's only a handful of other people that will be going out with us.

"Why do you keep smiling so much?" he asks with furrowed brows.

"Because you're being grumpy and I'm trying to give them a little bit of happiness. I don't want them to think we're mean," I explain.

"I wasn't being rude," he tells me.

"No, but you could be casual and normal. You've got your grumpy face on and it's going to make people think you're mad. You're not, but... You kind of look like it," I explain and he rolls his eyes.

"You're just doing what you always do," he explains.

We get into our kayaks and it takes me a second to get used to the feel of the paddle in my hands and the freezing water underneath me. This is intense when it shouldn't be but that's because I'm ignorant to it. I've never done this nor prepared to do it. We start into the bay, silence and quiet, our tour guide speaking in a low calming voice. I hear them saying that sunrise kayak experiences are meant to be peaceful, calmer, and quieter

285

than informative and loud. It makes sense why Parker chose this. I ride next to him, plunging my paddle into the water to keep up with the rest of the group.

"What do you mean I'm doing what I always do?" I ask him quietly.

"I mean you try to make up for everyone around you. You do it with Bellamy constantly," he explains.

I furrow my brows, feeling heat in my chest at his words.

"Shit. I'm not trying to be rude. Was that rude?" he asks quietly.

"I don't really understand what you're trying to say," I admit.

"You do this thing where you take the burden of other people's choices. Like today, I'm just the way I am. I'm not rude, I'm not mean. I just... I don't know these people. I was just talking. You took it upon yourself to smile for me as if it wasn't my choice," he explains.

"I just like the idea of being able to be kind... when I can," I tell him.

"And I really like that about you," he tells me. "It's not bad. I just... Notice it. That you do that," he tells me and I nod.

"You're perceptive," I admit out loud.

The only other sound is the water when our paddles connect to it and the tour guide a few feet in front of us, talking softly. There's mumbling and chattering amongst the other people on the tour as well. Everything is... peaceful.

"I don't talk a lot. You'd be surprised by the things people say around you when you're quiet all the time and I notice a lot because I don't talk. Like small things about you," he explains.

The sun is actually arriving now. I turn back to look at the city behind me that's getting smaller and smaller with each movement I make. I focus on my own movements, my breathing, and the way my body heats up the more I move. I've never in my

THE RULES OF YOU AND ME.

life surrounded myself with this much... quiet. I feel uncomfortable in it, only because I'm so not used to it. I do love it. The sky surrounding us is painted in the warmest light, orange and yellow with hues of pink and purple. It doesn't even look real to me.

"Look behind us," he tells me, and it feels like forever since he spoke.

When I glance at my watch, I notice it's been almost thirty minutes of silence. I look at him for only a second. He's staring at me as I turn to look behind me. The city. My city is so small. The city that feels larger than life is only a skyline in my sight but it looks ethereal in this light. In the quiet.

"Wow..." I breathe the word out, staring at it.

Everyone on the tour has stopped to look too but they're an afterthought as I stare. I force my gaze away from the skyline to find Parker staring at me, an intensity in his eyes. I smile with closed lips and notice the softening in his entire demeanor.

"What?" I ask. He shakes his head.

"Nothing," he mumbles and I let him have this one.

Just like our last date, I'm sure if it's important enough he'll come out with it. My heart stutters at the thought of everything I know and love being right there in front of me, but all of it looks so minuscule and small. I stare at the skyline and take a deep breath, the chilled air coursing through my heated body. I have been incredibly worried for weeks now. About everything. About my brother. About school and the thought of messing any of it up by potentially wanting to be with Parker... but looking at it all from this angle, seeing that even the biggest issues in my own headspace can look and feel like nothing when I look at them from farther back... When I stare at the bigger picture, I wonder if that was the whole point. If Parker wanted to give me perspective on how big life feels, but how small it looks...

"Everyone is moving on," Parker speaks to me and I nod.

"I'm coming," I tell him, not looking at him but the skyline still.

This is what I needed. To see it all. To feel it all.

The kayak tour was two hours of constant movement and my arms are insanely tired. Parker packed us up and started driving again, taking me away. We stopped at a diner, farther south than Seattle. The thing about Washington is that most of it is woods, trails, and nature. Over half of the state is covered in forest. I feel like it's safe to say we'll never run out. As much as I loved kayaking and the hour we took to drive to this small hole-in-the-wall diner, I am more in love with the idea of eating a burger. I don't care if it's 11 AM.

"Did you like kayaking? Or did you hate it?" he asks and I nod, looking at the burger that's being set in front of me.

"I loved it. I've never been before," I admit and dig in.

"I assumed," he speaks softly.

"Have you? You seemed like you knew what you were doing," I acknowledge.

"I have. It was a team-building thing we did when I was in high school. I grew up in California so it was very different. I thought it was dumb and then I did it. Not the same experience, it wasn't during sunrise but the way it made me feel was why I chose it for our date," he explains and my heart plummets in my chest at the thought of what he means.

"How did that first kayak experience make you feel?" I ask him.

"Small..." he admits and I stare at him, my eyes trained on him, my hands empty so I can focus solely on him as he talks.

"In a bad way?" I ask.

"In the best way. In a way that makes you feel normal again.

Like, I'm so much smaller than I think. My life isn't as big and scary and hard to hold onto when I see everything in front of me," he explains and I nod.

It's not exactly what I had felt but it's so similar.

"I was feeling like... like everything that I loved, everything that was a problem or a panic in my life was sitting in front of me, so small and far away that it... It matters but it's not what I had originally thought... It's not something I need to make bigger than it actually is," I admit.

"I was almost positive you'd understand that... I could see it when you didn't want to leave the view. I saw that look on your face," he tells me.

"Are you a mind reader?" I ask.

"Basically... Your everyday superhero," he jokes with me and I smile to myself, digging back into my food.

After we finished our meal, we continued south to the mountains. To the forest. To exactly where my mind was telling me we were going since this morning. Hiking. Another thing I've never done. I completely follow Parker's lead here. There's a hikers center at the beginning of the trail. He parks his car there and takes our packs out of the truck bed. He helps me put mine on, strapping the backpack to my chest.

"Have you been hiking or camping before?" he asks and I shake my head no.

"I brought you a beanie to cover your ears for when the temp dips, okay? I have everything we need in my pack. If you need it, ask," he tells me and I nod.

"Okay," I agree.

"Hydrate. You have your cup." He pats the cup that's perfectly nestled into my backpack pocket.

"If you need more water I have more, okay?" he asks, putting his hands on my shoulders.

"Aye, aye captain," I smiled at him.

"And speak up, please. If you need to stop, if you want to stop to look at everything, tell me. Also, if you feel tired and you need me to carry your pack, let me know," he instructs.

"Anything else I need to know?" I ask and he shakes his head.

"Nope," he tells me.

"What's up with all the nature? Kayaking and hiking? I didn't know you were an outdoorsman," I joke.

"When we got caught in the rain the other night, it showed me that you really appreciate everything, even the small stuff... So, I figured this would be something you'd understand the same way I do. I love hiking," he tells me.

"I had no idea," I admit.

I don't know a lot about Parker though, that's the entire point of being here with him.

"I just figured you'd be happy doing this... That you'd be open to it and appreciate it in a way that I do," he tells me.

"Like you with music," I tell him, both of us starting on the trail.

"Exactly," he mumbles to himself.

He walks in front of me and I ignore the burning in my muscles as time passes because as it does, the same feeling encroaches inside. I warm up, my body getting used to the movement, the chill of the wind, and the coolness of the air that I breathe. It feels clear like there's no filter of film over everything here. It is beautiful. All of it, even the simplest of things on the trail are brought to a better light. It's brought into a new perspective that I hadn't seen before. There's no city surrounding us anymore. No more Seattle Pike. No more friends. Just the two of us on this trail in the middle of nothing

THE RULES OF YOU AND ME.

but feeling everything. I watch Parker move with ease and intention on the path. He's very comfortable here in the quiet and the comfort of nothing.

It's contradictory. He is, in general. Being in a profession where he will constantly be surrounded by screaming loud men and fans, in a contact sport where he's being pummeled to the ground. Grass and dirt, blood and sweat. That's what he's chosen for himself but he loves this. Quiet that's so silent it's almost loud and I love it. I love the quiet that's surrounding us right now. I've never spent so much time being quiet. Not in my entire life. But this whole day, I've barely spoken anything at all. I... I don't feel like I have to. For once, I feel like I don't need to fill up the space with my voice to make things feel right. This is just right.

CHAPTER 24
TREACHEROUS (TAYLOR'S VERSION) BY TAYLOR SWIFT.

Parker Thompson:

My hands are sweating as we finally sit down. The sun is sinking and creating pretty colors in its wake. I knew I wanted to come to this specific spot to watch the sunset. Snow Lake is pretty no matter what time of day you show up. I knew that but the whole day was full circle. We woke up early enough to watch the sunrise and we'll settle in early enough to watch it set too. It's perfect. Brianne, for the first time all night, picks up her phone and I watch as she holds it up and shuffles through it. She presses it to her ear after a few moments. I sit quietly and listen.

"Hey, Belly," she says. "Can you hear me? Sorry, the reception is really spotty right here."

"Oh, I'm with Parker..." She instantly looks at me and then panics. "At the dance studio for our dance lesson. Then, I'm going to meet with Dakota and stay with him like I told you," she catches herself and I don't let myself smirk as I look down between us, getting ready to start a fire for the night.

"Yeah, sure," she mumbles. "Parker, you're on speaker now."

I freeze, hoping the shuffling noises surrounding me don't

make it obvious that we're not in a studio on campus right now but instead in the middle of the damn woods two hours away from SPU, and no one but us knows that.

"Hey, Parky. So, no arguments. We're all going on a mini vacation to Vegas. Since Griffin's a newbie, he doesn't have set guest passes for anyone and everyone except his mom, dad, and Jade, but he scored an extensive amount of VIP tickets for me, Kam, Lawson, Sienna, Bri and he said her boyfriend, but I'm sorry, B, the extra ticket is going to Parky. He's got more to learn from being on the sidelines at a Raiders game," Bellamy speaks out to all of us.

"Oh, that's fine. I'm sure Dakota wouldn't really care much about it anyway," she admits, her eyes not looking toward me.

"How much?" I ask and Bellamy scoffs.

"Everything is paid. Hotel stays and flights, Griff pulled some strings. He said he had prospects that will be on the sidelines, potential future Raiders players if you will. I don't know what he had to do to get this to happen, but it's not negotiable. We have our game tomorrow night, then we're leaving Saturday to spend the day and night in Vegas. We'll go to the game the next day and then head home before we have to be in class on Monday, sounds good?" Bellamy asks.

"I... Yeah, that sounds perfect," I mumble, not having another option, but also shocked he'd waste his extra pass on me. "Thank you," I extend my gratitude and he chuckles.

"It wasn't me, it was Griffin, but either way, this is going to be perfect. Brianne, as much as I don't encourage it, make sure you have your fake ready. We're all going out Saturday night to the Vegas strip, so bring something to wear," he tells Bri but she looks at me to make sure I'm listening. I nod toward her.

"Okay," I agree.

"Okay, I love you, but I have ballet to teach so..." Brianne hurries the conversation up and Bellamy chuckles.

THE RULES OF YOU AND ME.

"What I would give to see these lessons. You two have fun but not too much fun," he tells us and I watch Brianne furrow her brows.

"I love you," she speaks softly, her voice so different now compared to most days, compared to every other time I've heard her speak.

"I love you," Bellamy hangs up first and she just clicks her phone off and looks up and out, her eyes set on the sunset surrounding us.

We're on a soft peak that overlooks one of the many lakes. The mountains are surrounding us now fully. I'm surprised Brianne got service at all let alone enough to call Bellamy.

"What's wrong?" I ask her and it takes a second for her to force her gaze away from the view in front of her.

"Nothing. Why would anything be wrong?" she asks, a small smile playing on her lips.

I eye her, catching any and every detail in this perfect light. She's unexplainably pretty in any light, but this one... What do they call it? Golden hour, right? This is her best look. Slightly messy hair and bare-faced so I can see the plethora of freckles Brianne Archer wears like medals with so much pride and grace. I stare at the girl in front of me who normally talks more than she breathes, but she hasn't spoken in hours since our hike started.

"You've been silent... And you look... I don't know, you're just not the way you usually are," I explain.

"This is peace... Being out here. This is what it's meant to be, silence and nature and beauty. This isn't my space and I don't need to impose on that. Not only that, but..." she hesitates and I look up at her, I'm sitting, trying once again to start our fire.

She's standing, her ears now covered with the dark blue beanie I brought for her that almost matches the oceanic color of

295

her eyes. Her cheeks are rosier than normal because they're wind-bitten.

"What?" I ask and she shakes her head.

"I just haven't felt like I need to fill the space. A lot of the reason why I talk all the time is because like I told you, I'm not a fan of silence. So when I'm anywhere or with anyone, I'd prefer the time to be filled with conversation. No time wasted, no words unsaid," she explains. "Today, the past few hours especially, I didn't need to say anything. At first, it felt odd but that weirdness melted away. I was comfortable with the quiet... with you and just being here. It felt right."

She shrugs and then sits across from me. She cuddles into herself, wrapping her arms around her body.

"Are you cold?" I ask.

"Slightly," she admits.

The fire is burning, the embers setting under the logs in the center. I get up and reach into my bag, taking out one of the sherpa blankets I brought. I packed some of my bag, but Xander was in charge of most of it. I enjoy hiking but his family was anal about going hiking as a family hobby, according to him. He said he could pack a camping pack better than a professional, so I let him. He was happy that I was allowing him to help me. According to him, that's twice in one week which is a personal record. I rolled my eyes at that comment, to say the least.

"Here." I wrap the blanket over her shoulders. "I probably should have asked you if you even wanted to go camping before I just brought you out here," I tell her, a little bit of embarrassment hitting my cheeks.

"You're not trying to kill me, are you?" she jokes and I smirk.

"How'd you figure it out?" I joke back.

"But why? Actually, why did you want to go camping?" she asks.

"Well, I thought the idea of being able to stay in the same

THE RULES OF YOU AND ME.

area as you without our friends, roommates, or potentially brothers, around sounded appealing. Not that anything is going to happen, because it's not. I just liked the idea of privacy, seclusion, and... and quiet," I admit.

"Awe, you wanted to be alone with me," she picks on me and I keep my face the same, no smirk or laugh even whispering my features.

She lets her smile fall and I raise my eyebrows at her.

"I'm serious. Of course, I want to be alone with you. Thinking about the other night, being with you the way that we were, and everything that happened, I wanted to kiss you too, Brianne. One of the hardest things in all of this is—"

"Keeping it from Bellamy," she answers and I shake my head.

"Not even slightly. Lying to Bellamy isn't hard for me because I don't speak to him about my personal life. I don't even think your brother knows about my family history or my roommates' names. Bellamy knows nothing about me so, no. It's not hard because it feels normal being secluded from him in that part of myself," I admit.

"So, what is it?" she asks, shifting in front of the fire that's finally starting to bloom in front of us.

"It's remembering to have control and restraint. I've never been a physical person. Like having a person I try to reach for, that I actively want to touch when I'm around them. I don't reach for people to hug them when I greet them. I don't instantly want to swarm and hug my teammates when we win... But with you, it almost feels like second nature to reach for you, touch your hand when we're walking. To kiss your forehead when I say goodbye or touch your cheek before I walk off. And I've worked so hard to keep soft small touches like that," I admit, feeling insanely vulnerable. I instinctively crack my knuckles and she watches me do it.

297

"Is it because I said I wanted it to move slow? Is that not what you want?" she asks.

"I refuse to indulge in you until I'm sure that I'm worth that risk. Bellamy knowing about what I do in my free time is none of my concern but you and him are different. I respect the relationship you have with your brother. I know how important it is. I'm not going to cross that line again until I know that you're sure about me. If he finds out and gets upset, I don't want to be the reason in your head. I can't be the person you blame if this goes south, so I want you to be sure," I admit.

"So, it has to do with Bellamy?" She asks.

"Indirectly, yes, but more so you. I don't want you to regret it. I think explaining what happened the night at the bar on your birthday would be a little bit easier than explaining it happened again and again. Of course, I know you're going to tell him when you're sure but I want you to be sure of me, and this before I let myself touch you in that way again," I explain.

"What if I want you to though?" she asks.

"Then I'd say you're a liar because it's only our second date and turtles don't move that fast," I tell her and she smirks.

"Maybe when I said that I was hoping you would be horrible and not interesting or exciting," she tells me.

"Surprise, I guess?" I joke and she laughs to herself.

"A happy surprise but I'm okay with you touching me... Or kissing me," she tells me, her words soft over the crackling happening between us.

I don't say anything, I just look at her head on through the flames. She stands up from where she sits and walks around the fire, planting herself next to me. I place my arm around her shoulder, pulling her small body into me. She looks at me, her face inches from mine. I shake my head.

"Not even one kiss?" She nudges her face forward, tilting her lips toward mine to give me the easiest access.

THE RULES OF YOU AND ME.

"Not even one," I tell her.

"Do you need a title to be able to kiss me? Boyfriend?" she asks and I feel my lip turn into a smirk.

The idea of being her boyfriend or anyone's for that matter feels so juvenile to me but I absolutely burn at the thought.

"I like the sound of that," I tell her.

"What if I've never been too keen on labels?" she asks me.

"Then I'd tell you that I understand that but it's important to me to know that you're serious. I'd tell you that we'd both be doing a lot of things out of our comfort zone too," I admit and watch her cheeks turn a deeper crimson.

"What if I told you... That I have a rule list and one of the main things on there is to not let myself be with you?" she admits and my jaw drops.

"You made a rule to not speak to me?" I ask her.

"Okay, to be fair, I thought that you used me at that point so, yes. I made a rule to never sleep with you again," she tells me and I scoff, backing up so I can look at her in full.

"Brianne, I'm hurt. I want to see this list, hand it over," I tell her.

"It's hanging on the wall in my room thanks to Dakota. So, sorry," she shrugs but I can tell she's not actually sorry.

"Moral of the story, I'd like to make you my girlfriend... at some point. When you feel comfortable with that word, when you feel comfortable with me," I tell her.

"I've never had something so... sweet," she says the word like it's foreign on her tongue.

"That's surprising," I admit.

"Why?" She asks.

"I don't know... I guess it's hard to differentiate what I see other people as compared to what they might see themself as. I see you as deserving of all of that and more... I don't know," I shrug.

299

"I think I deserve something sweet and cute. I just haven't had it yet. Why do you think I've had so many boyfriends? I watched my mom and dad when I was young and how absolutely perfect they were and wanted that. Then, as Bellamy grew up, he was the perfect example of how a guy should treat someone he cares about. He was always the perfect person to every girl he was with... He got hurt so many times putting his heart on his sleeve for people who didn't deserve it. I told myself that I wanted someone who loves like my role models. My parents and my brother. I deserved that. I've tried looking for it obviously and it hasn't gone so well considering most guys are douchebags. I'm very hopeful that one day I'll have what I want. What I deserve," She tells me.

I've never wanted anything more than to prove to her I can be good... I've strived my whole life to be perfect. To be good, to be enough... I want that now. With her, I want it more than ever.

"I understand that but why don't you like labels if you want something like what your parents have or Bellamy? Last time I checked, husband and wife are titles. And Bellamy is Kamryn's boyfriend. Label," I argue.

"Semantics. I have commitment issues to a degree. I have to be... Very sure. The first few boyfriends I had were horrible judgment calls," she laughs to herself and I open my mouth to talk again but she stops me.

"And you, we skipped right over something. Physical touch. You... you don't like it?" she asks me and I shake my head.

"Not usually, no. I never really grew up being hugged much. I mean, a lot of kids grew up with hugs and kisses and love from parents or caretakers or whatever. The most I really got was a pat on the back from a coach or a hug on the first day I met a foster family... So there's not much room to grow up enjoying something you don't understand. I never really understood why

THE RULES OF YOU AND ME.

it was so sought after until you," I admit, feeling my own cheeks burn.

"Is that a pickup line or are you being serious? Because it sounds like a pickup line," she smiles up at me.

"It's not. I'm serious. It was like a magnet. And it didn't feel uncomfortable because with the exception of running into each other at the bonfire, every touch you gave afterward was intentional but careful and kind. It was on purpose and it was... sweet," I use her words, watching her blush at the intent of it.

"So, I haven't overstepped?" she asks and I shake my head.

"No. It's not that I don't accept physical touch. I understand that other people love it or strive for it. I just... I don't. It doesn't feel unintentional and weird when you touch me or hug me. Not like you're doing it out of obligation. You're doing it of your own free will," I tell her.

"I don't usually do things I don't want to," she tells me and I nod, despite how much I disagree with that statement.

She seems to be constantly doing things for everyone else, whether she wants to or not is a separate conversation, but she does. She's a giver, sometimes more than I think she can handle. She's got a very fake smile and a very real one. When I first met her, I didn't know the difference. Then I went to her apartment for her birthday and saw the stark contrast. I saw what it looked like when I made her smile versus when she was pretending to be interested in something her brother was doing or her classmates said. I've seen her smile like that with Dakota. I'm sure she does smile like that with Bellamy too, but I haven't seen it. I don't think she sees or understands that there's a differentiation.

I don't blame Bellamy for that side of Brianne either. It's her. She's playing a part she thinks she needs to play. She pretends she needs to revolve around other people... like a moon. The moon doesn't have its own light, it reflects the sun, but Brianne isn't reflecting everyone else's light. She is the

301

goddamn light. I want to tell her that but I don't want her to think I'm completely shitting on her brother. That's not the intention but I do wish she could see what I do.

Being so quiet, it's easy to pick up on things people don't normally want you to see or know. People say things around you because they don't remember you're there or don't care. They don't think you're listening, they don't think you care at all. It's interesting people watching when you portray yourself as a background character, or a place setting. There but not necessary. It's made life simply easy and interesting in a slight way. I've noticed exponentially how much everyone around Brianne with the exception of Dakota underestimates her, including myself. She carries more talent in her pinky toe than I carry in my entire body. That's not a simple feat. Brianne is a fucking force that's done everything in her power to live in her brother's shadow her entire life. And he doesn't even see that she's doing it...

"Why are you zoning out? Am I boring you?" she asks and I pull her into me tighter, putting her head on my chest.

"Not even slightly. This is exactly what I was hoping this would feel like," I mumble.

"How is that?" she asks.

"Perfect," I tell her.

"Perfection doesn't exist," she fights back.

"Whatever this is feels like perfection to me. It feels perfect and I've never felt perfect before," I admit.

"You're a romantic and a closeted dreamer," she tells me and I snort a laugh.

"I guess that's fine. I'll accept it," I shrug.

"No arguments?" she asks and I shake my head no.

"None. I'll be whatever you want me to be, Brianne, especially your boyfriend," I tell her.

"Is this you officially asking?" she asks and I nod.

THE RULES OF YOU AND ME.

"Yeah, it is. Be my girlfriend?" I ask her and she sighs, leaning into me.

"The title is appealing but not my speed. Turtle." She motions two walking fingers.

"Turtles don't kiss," I tell her.

"I disagree," she smiles up at me and I fight every urge to kiss the smile right off of her lips.

I wish. I want. I need. I can't... I shake my head and lean over into the cooler part of my pack, pulling out our dinner for the night.

Brianne not feeling the need to fill up the space or silence gives a sense of comfort I never felt before now. I also feel comfortable in my quiet. I never really care at the end of the day how my silence or seriousness makes others feel. If they don't like it, they don't have to be around me. But knowing that someone is comfortable with it, with how I am, and finding comfort in that, it's reassuring.

Brianne is not even slightly helpful when it comes to setting up the tent for the night. She does look incredibly pretty while she watches me do it, though. She said that she never asked to come camping so I shouldn't expect her to do any of the work and she's very correct in that sentiment. This was the activity I chose, so I don't mind doing the work. She obviously doesn't mind watching either considering the smirk on her lips as she does.

"Are we going to get mauled by a bear in our sleep?" she asks and I chuckle as the two of us climb into the tent, the fire simmering to nothing now.

"It's a slim possibility, but it's not a no," I admit and she laughs to herself as she crawls into the corner toward her bag. She lifts her shirt over her head and I divert my eyes.

"Are you looking away?" she asks.

303

"If I'm not letting myself kiss you, do you think I'd let myself see you naked?" I ask her, my face turned away from her body.

"Prude," she jokes.

"Tease," I mutter back.

I'm sure if I looked at her, she'd be smirking to herself. Thank God I'm not looking at her because I might have folded. I keep my body turned away from her as I grab my own pack and reach into it for the sleeping bags I asked Xander for. I pull the first out and reach back in, but feel nothing. I take the rest of the contents out of my pack and use my flashlight to look inside.

"Are you fucking kidding me?" I mumble under my breath.

"What? What's wrong?" she asks and I look over my shoulder, see her skin and turn right back, groaning.

"Jesus Christ," I sigh, pinching the bridge of my nose.

I'm going to have an aneurysm, I think.

"Sorry, sorry, there. Pants are on, sorry," she tells me and I turn.

"Xander is fucking dead tomorrow when I get home," I tell her and she furrows her brows.

"Why? What did he do now?" she asks, sitting criss crossed on the floor of the tent that's padded with all of our blankets. I shake my head as I unroll the sleeping bag and find a note.

Have a great night Parks, thank me later (;

I crunch it in my fist and sigh.

"He purposely packed one sleeping bag like the dick he is," I tell her.

"That was your first mistake. If I let Dakota pack my back for tonight all he would have packed was condoms, lube, and lingerie. Our friends have good intentions but the delivery is off," she laughs it off like we don't have an issue.

THE RULES OF YOU AND ME.

I clench my jaw, the muscles ticking as I stare down at the pack.

"You take it, I'll just—"

"Is it not big enough for both of us?" she asks.

"I'm not..." I sigh.

"You'd rather freeze half to death than sleep next to me?" she asks.

"I'd sacrifice myself to sleep next to you if that's what it took, but it's about morals," I remind her.

"You can't have morals if you die of hypothermia," she shrugs, taking the sleeping bag from me.

She unfolds the thermal material and crawls inside, showcasing that two people can comfortably fit inside. It will be close quarters, of course, but I know my stupid fucking roommate did that on purpose.

"You're not helping," I stare down at her and she shrugs.

"I only see one solution. Come on in, P..." she smirks to herself and I put every ounce of restraint I have to the forefront of my mind.

She's not yours, you can't kiss her. Remember that, you horny motherfucker.

I swallow, my throat feeling like sandpaper as I crawl into the sleeping bag, the heat growing exceptionally high. I'm not sure if it's from the thermal material or the fact that my body is centimeters from touching Brianne's in this stupid fucking sleeping bag. I grind my jaw and she stares at me.

"Cat got your tongue?" she asks and I clench my jaw and take a deep breath.

"You're evil," I mumble.

"I'm not doing anything." She gets a hazy triumphant look in her eyes and I shake my head, staring at her.

"Goodnight, mind if I roll over?" she asks.

"Be my guest, just don't—"

Before I can even speak, she turns her body, her ass brushing my groin before she scoots the single inch forward she can so she's not touching me anymore.

"Oops," she mumbles and cuddles into herself.

I try with every bit of power I have to stay exactly where I am because I know the second my fingers brush her skin, electricity will be coursing through my body. I feel her shiver beside me and I clench my jaw tighter. I'm just being nice. There's no other intention behind this. I care about her and I'm being nice.

"Come here, you're freezing," I mumble.

I rope my arm around her torso and alleviate the distance between us. Her warm lush body is pressed to mine, her ass perfectly pressed against my dick that I am practically begging to stay exactly where it is. If we don't move, I'll be fine.

"So cuddling is fine but kissing is a no?" She looks over her shoulder.

"When you're shivering in the sleeping bag and I'm burning up, then yes, cuddling is fine. Don't pester me." I reach around and turn her chin so she's facing forward. She moves, rubbing her ass against me and I groan.

"Brianne Emily Archer, if you don't stop..." I mumble against her ear and she giggles.

I feel myself hardening despite how much I wish I wasn't and I pinch the bridge of my nose.

"You going to punish me?" she asks in a mischievous voice.

"Not my speed," I grind the words out.

"I think you might have left the flashlight in your pocket... Something hard is pressing against me," I can hear the joke in her voice which only ticks me off more.

"You're pushing it," I mumble, trying to focus on her scent and the softness of her breathing to calm myself down.

"I'm trying to," she tells me.

"I'm well the fuck aware," I mumble.

THE RULES OF YOU AND ME.

"I'll stop," she laughs to herself.

"Thank fuck," I mutter and she gives us a tiny millimeter of space relieving some of the pressure.

"Goodnight, Parker," she breathes out, turning herself around so her forehead is against my chest, her arm draped over my side and her legs tangled with mine.

Despite the fact that she's innocently draped around me now, I'm still thinking about the way the curve of her ass felt pressed to me and I regret the choice I made that led me to this moment. Xander is getting punched tomorrow, to say the least, because while Brianne's breathing evens out and she falls asleep... I can't stop thinking about what it would have been like to kiss her until her lips felt numb. To touch her until my mind went fucking haywire... And I won't know that. So now, my mind is a mess due to the girl tangled around me in our shared sleeping bag.

CHAPTER 25
BOYFRIEND BY JUSTIN BIEBER

Parker Thompson:

"Okay, you can't still be mad at me."

Xander lays across my bed and I don't talk at all as I pack my carry-on sized suitcase. Brianne and I woke up yesterday morning in the mountains and it was a picture-perfect moment... Except I had morning wood and she found it hilarious. I don't care that she knows I want her but it does give me less of an edge. She tried again to get just a kiss, or anything from me. I said no and she closed herself off. I wanted to fight it, to fight her initial feelings on the matter but it's not my place. She's allowed to feel upset but she has boundaries and so do I.

I don't want to convince her to date me with the incentive of getting kisses or physical rewards. I don't want that to be her reason. I'm sticking to my word. I'm not doing anything with her until she's sure she wants me in that way. I have no intention of just being casual with her. It would sound a lot better to Bellamy if he knew that we were serious and not just screwing around. Brianne hasn't spoken to me since I dropped her off. She didn't even look at me once at our game and she completely ignored me after, even when I texted her. Which is exactly why I'm still mad at Alexander fucking Marino for being the biggest cock block ever. He wasn't trying to be but that's exactly what he did.

"Get out," I mutter, packing my two nights' worth of clothes into my suitcase.

"Come on, Thompson. You know I meant well by it. Besides, online it says girls love that shit. *The one bed trope,*" he tells me and I slowly turn my attention to him.

"In fucking books, sure. This is real life, you idiot. She wants to sleep with me. I want a relationship with her. You ruined that," I tell him.

"I did nothing of the sort," he argues.

"Well, now she thinks I'm pushing her into a relationship or something," I mumble, focusing on my suitcase.

"She does not, you haven't even talked to her," he argues.

"Because she hasn't talked to me," I explain.

"You're the guy. You text first, idiot," he tells me and I shake my head.

"Since when is that even a thing?" I argue back.

"Since always, you dipshit. Nico! Andrew!" he calls out.

"Jesus Christ, no, please," I speak to myself and just sit down on the floor in defeat.

"What?" Andrew comes out first.

"Why are you guys always screaming?" Nico asks and I scoff.

"Says you," I speak under my breath.

"Why is grumpy being grumpier than normal?" Nico asks.

"Who texts first?" Xander asks.

"Us," Andrew tells me.

"The guy usually," Nico agrees.

Then, Andrew's door opens. A stunning blonde walks behind the two of them, hair all the way down to her waist.

310

THE RULES OF YOU AND ME.

Andrew's hockey jersey hangs off of her body. She peeks her head into the room.

"Your roommates are right," she tells me and looks up at Andrew. "Are we getting food? Come on." She smacks his ass and walks around him. My jaw hangs open slightly at the subtle blush on his cheeks.

"Since when was she in there?" I ask.

"Since last night. And her name is Diana," he tells us.

"Diana is hungry! Let's go, hockey puck," she groans and I smirk as Andrew hurries out of the room and after the girl that I guess is his almost girlfriend.

"She's pretty," Nico speaks out.

"Agreed," Both me and Xander reply.

Good job to Andrew, considering how much of a loser he is.

"That's beside the point. You need to text her. Something besides a song," Xander tells me.

"I'm never taking advice or help from you again. You're on cautionary probation from helping me," I tell him and he scoffs.

"You're being dramatic," he argues.

"You basically ruined my life," I tell him and go into the bathroom. Both he and Nico follow me.

"That was a little dramatic, Parks," Nico argues.

"So what?" I shrug and grab all of my toiletries.

"Just forgive me. I'm sorry, I won't be an idiot again," he promises and I laugh to myself.

"If I'm going to forgive you, you can't lie to me," I look at him, walking into my bedroom backward.

"Are you calling me an idiot?" he asks and I nod.

"Mean." He crosses his arms.

"I'll forgive you if you take me to the airport so I don't have to park my truck there overnight," I offer.

"Really? Deal." He holds his hand out.

"So, does this mean you and Brianne are going to sleep

311

together again? Vegas for a night, that's so romantic," Nico wiggles his eyebrows.

"No, I'm not sleeping with her again until I'm ready and I'm not. I'm doing this the right way. I didn't last time and it ended badly for both of us. As much as I don't want to admit it to either of you, it really hurt when she ran out after that first night. It definitely made me feel like shit, so I'm trying to avoid that. Brianne is... flighty. She runs at the first sign of trouble and I'm not letting that freaking happen. She wouldn't look at me at the game last night at all," I tell them.

"Maybe she forgot you existed," Nico shrugs.

"Maybe you should shut your fucking mouth?" I suggest and he scoffs.

"She's probably just scared that she wants you the way you want her, dude. Just text her that you're excited to see her this weekend, even if it's not romantically. I bet she'll appreciate that. Have you even told her what you want?" Xander asks.

"Yeah, I did," I shrug.

"In what way?" Xander asks.

"I said I wanted her to be mine before I kissed her," I admit.

"AHHHHH," Xander makes a buzzer noise and crosses his arms.

I cringe at the loud sound. "What the hell was that for?" I ask.

"You're going about it wrong. Women never want to feel like a piece of property and I know that's definitely not your intention. Try something else," Xander tells me and I roll my eyes.

"He's right. You should definitely go about it in a different way, and not only that, but you should text her," Nico offers and I sigh, pulling my phone out, texting her the words Xander said exactly, knowing there's nothing to lose at this point. She immediately texts back.

THE RULES OF YOU AND ME.

> Brianne: Excited is an understatement.

I don't know what that could mean. Excited to see me? Or excited to be around me maybe? Excited for Vegas in general, probably. I sigh and tuck my phone into my pocket. I need to go or I'll be late... and I guess I need to listen to my roommates and get my shit together.

"Let's go," I nod to him and he clears his throat.

I look at Xander and he nods his head toward my bedside table.

"Forgetting something important?" he asks, nodding to the table again. I sigh deeply.

"I'm not sleeping with her. I told you that," I tell him.

"Okay, but what if she tells you she wants to be your girl-friend, and the hot makeout turns into something else and you're not prepared? Wouldn't you rather be over-prepared than underprepared?" he asks me.

"The likelihood of her saying she wants to be my girlfriend is so slim it's—"

"Oh shut it, Parker. Could you just hope for good things to happen to you? I get growing up and not being hopeful in your situation and I'm sorry you grew up that way, Parker... but you're not there anymore. You can hope for good things. You can wish for things. That's okay. Take the damn rubbers and hope for a girlfriend and good pussy. Come on, man," Xander urges.

I clench my jaw and hold my hand out, oddly feeling a rush in my stomach as I do.

"Fine. Hurry up," I grunt out.

He smirks and opens my bedside drawer, grabbing a handful of condoms. I take them and tuck them in the front pocket of my suitcase. Xander claps his hands and hops off my bed, charging out the door. I roll my eyes and follow after him.

I'm quiet as I shuffle onto the plane with the entire crew. Kamryn, Sienna, and Brianne are bare-faced and wearing a plethora of leggings and SPU athletics wear. They practically match. Lawson, Bellamy, and I aren't much better, all of us wearing football hoodies and sweats as we board the flight. Bellamy takes his seat next to Kamryn and Lawson takes his seat next to Sienna. I stare at Brianne as she sits behind the two couples, the window seat open next to her. We're in the nice fancy seats, the ones I have never flown in before. The only time I have ever been on a plane is for football, traveling to other games and other states, never for leisure like this.

She raises her eyebrows at me and I feel heat in my stomach at her stare. I take my bag and lift it over my head, putting it in the compartment above us. I take Brianne's bag and do the same with hers, not even waiting for her to ask. I take my seat next to her and pretend that she's just a person sitting next to me, not the biggest infatuation I have in my life at the moment. She's doing a great job at keeping it casual and cool just like me.

I buckle up, knowing we'll need to for takeoff anyway. I feel her gaze on me so I look at her and she looks away casually as if I didn't just slightly catch her staring at me. Her words are still hanging between us—that she's more than excited. I make a move first, testing the waters. I take her hand very softly and casually. I squeeze once and she looks at me, then relaxes her hand in mine until the two people in front of us shift and she moves her hand as quick as lightning. She wipes them on her leggings and looks at Lawson who's looking between us.

"Nervous or something?" he asks her and I swallow as I look at him.

"Slightly," she mumbles.

"Parker will die first if the window pops off," Sienna tells us.

THE RULES OF YOU AND ME.

"Gee, thanks," I mumble.

"Morbid, Si." Lawson holds up a high five and she claps her hand into his, both of them laughing now.

I pull out my phone as we wait for the rest of the plane to board and smirk at myself when I see a text pop up from Brianne.

"Quickie in the bathroom to ease my nerves?" she sends.

I bite the inside of my cheek to keep from smiling too wide, knowing if Lawson or Bellamy saw it, they would never stop bugging me about who it was about. I decide to go on my Spotify and pick a song from the playlist that Xander has sent me to get brushed up on music I should know. Boyfriend by Justin Bieber. I send it to her, knowing that Xander would be proud considering he is a self-proclaimed Belieber. I hear Brianne laugh next to me and a smirk curves onto my mouth but is wiped away instantly the second Lawson and Sienna turn around.

"Texting your boyfriend?" Lawson asks her and I look out the window of the unmoving plane.

"He's her situationship, not her boyfriend. Get it right," Sienna corrects.

"Thank you, Sienna. He's not my boyfriend. But yes, I am texting him," she tells Lawson, and heat burns in my chest knowing she's not talking about Dakota.

They have no fucking clue. I look back forward and Lawson is looking at me now. He gives me a single look that makes my stomach sink. He doesn't have a clue, does he? I eye him up and down and shrug.

"What?" I ask.

"You're being quiet," he speaks out.

"I'm always quiet," I shrug.

"Parker never speaks. It's like pulling teeth during our lessons," Brianne crosses her legs and shrugs. "Fuck off,

315

Lawson." She smiles and he points his middle finger in her direction.

I look at her, her hair down in long beautiful waves like curtains around her face. Her bare face is rosy and bright, those perfect freckles speckled on her cheeks. I give myself one second and then the plane starts to move and the flight attendants move toward the front of the aisles to start their demonstration. I decide not to look at Brianne for the rest of the flight out of fear that Lawson may or may not catch me staring.

CHAPTER 26
2 HANDS BY TATE MCRAE

Brianne Archer:

I hate plane flights as it is but riding for two and a half hours next to the guy you kind of like without even being able to get him to look at you probably takes the cake for the worst flight I've ever had. I clench my jaw as we all get out of the Uber and head into the massive hotel. The entire street is swarmed. The hotel is swarmed. Everything is insane and loud and completely overstimulating. I've never been to Vegas and I feel like I will never in my life want to come back considering that this trip has been shitty thus far. I sigh as we step inside and at least the hotel has nice music... And I'm not talking about the loud blaring music and mumbling coming from the casino about twenty feet to the left of us. Jesus Christ, is it always like this here?

"Okay, we're going to check in then we're going to get ready and Griffin is coming to get us so we can go casino hopping and to bars," Bellamy tells us. I nod, walking with him silently.

"What's wrong?" Bellamy asks, closing in next to me.

"Nothing," I mumble.

"You're never quiet for this long," he tells me and I roll my eyes to myself.

"I feel out of place here with all of you. I miss Dakota," I admit.

It's partially true but also, I don't feel like I can fully be myself right now which has never been the case when I'm around Bellamy, even with his friends around. I know it slightly has to do with Parker and my not knowing how to act around him.

"Well, I'm sure Parker feels the same. You guys are kind of friends. Stick with him. I will try my best to make sure you feel included. Seriously, try to have fun, B."

He nudges me and I bite my tongue at the thought of Bellamy pushing me toward Parker. My so-called 'friend.' My friend who I want to kiss and punch all at the same time. He can't and won't know that. Either way, I don't like the feeling of being the baby, the one Bellamy has to watch over and make sure isn't left out. I feel like hiding away right now.

"Sure, whatever," I mumble.

"Bri needs a nap," Lawson mumbles.

"And you need a muzzle," I speak back and hear Sienna chuckle.

"God I love you," she speaks to me and I smirk to myself as we approach the front desk.

I stand behind Bellamy as he checks in. Parker stands beside me and I feel the brush of the back of his hand on my wrist. I feel the weight of the air between us as he continues to casually brush my skin with his. I know he's doing it on purpose. I internally question why the hell he didn't even turn in my direction the whole flight, even when no one was paying attention but now, he's being casual and subtle like this. I move my arms and cross them over my chest, my interest piquing when the woman at the front desk says we have three rooms.

THE RULES OF YOU AND ME.

"Three?" I ask, stepping forward.

"Shit. Griffin was assuming that Dakota was coming with you so he..." Bellamy looks at Parker and sighs.

"Me and Parker can stay together and you and Kam can have our room," Bellamy offers instantly.

"No. That's stupid. Stay with your girlfriend," I fight.

"And what, let you share a room with my friend and be a horrible brother? No," Bellamy tells me and I feel my cheeks turn red.

I know to them it looks like I'm just the embarrassed little sister, but right now, I feel like I've been caught even though no one knows anything. I feel my throat tighten and I don't know where all the emotion comes from. I force a smile.

"No," Parker speaks up, his eyes on me. Persistently on me. He shakes his head.

"Parky it's—"

"Fine. It's fine. I'm going to just get a room for the two nights we're here. Whatever room you guys have available," he tells the woman at the front desk.

"It's going to cost a fortune if you—"

"Nothing I don't have," Parker fights me, shutting me up instantly.

I roll my eyes and walk away, tired of both of them at this moment. Yay, two nights in Vegas with a situationship that no one can know about who wants more but also gives me mixed signals, a bossy brother, and a skeptical Lawson who is going to be on my ass worse than Bellamy is most of the time. To top it all off, I don't have Dakota.

"Bri, just calm down, we'll get it figured out," Bellamy has an edge to his tone and I just roll my eyes.

"I just told you I feel out of place and now I'm the reason things are getting screwed up. Excuse me if I'm not happy about any of this," I speak to my brother and he furrows his brows and just sighs.

Parker gets his situation figured out and I only pay attention when I'm handed a room key by my brother. I storm away from everyone else and head up to my room. Bellamy texts me the time he wants to leave the hotel. I don't reply. I text Dakota a quick message about how much I miss him and he tells me I need to call him after our outing tonight and spill everything in the fluffy robes that the hotel probably has for us. I agree. I get a text from Parker with nothing but his room number...

I don't bother changing or taking anything but my phone and my room key. I leave and follow the hotel signs that point to his room. I knock on the door and wait a few seconds before knocking again. There's no response so I check my phone and make sure I have the right room number. The door opens and the second I see it's him, I'm swept inside and pinned to the door that's closing behind me. I stare up at him, my back pressed to the door, his hard and perfect body pressed to mine and his left hand pinning me to the door. His right hand is resting above my head. He leans over me, his eyes peering down.

"Be my girlfriend," he practically begs. But the moral of it stings in my chest.

"Kiss me." I urge, wanting the distraction, but also needing Parker.

"No." He fights himself, I can see it in his expression.

"Then no," I argue back.

"Why not?" he smirks and I nudge his chest back, overwhelmed by the whole day and tired of the game Parker is playing.

I thought his text this morning talking about his excitement meant that he let go of the boyfriend thing. I thought he was ready to just enjoy this thing between us, but no.

THE RULES OF YOU AND ME.

"No, you're annoying. Stop smirking at me," I fight. "Why do you want me to be your girlfriend so bad?"

"Because I really want to kiss you right now," he tells me, more bold than he's been before.

"That's a horrible excuse to want me to be your girlfriend," I tell him.

"It's not an excuse and it's also not my only reason. Say yes," he urges.

"The more you want me to say yes, the more I have the need to say no," I tell him.

"You're infuriating.," he tells me like I'm not trying to be.

"And you're giving me ultimatums. What if I don't want the title of girlfriend?" I ask.

"Does my lover sound better? My partner? My person?" he asks.

"No, no, and this isn't Grey's Anatomy. It's real life... where people are allowed to kiss without putting labels on it," I tell him.

"I like labels and these pressed to you in any way I want them," he explains, holding both of his massive hands up. I put my hands in his and push them down between us.

"And I like kissing. And sex. And mutual respect," I tell him.

"I respect you," he fights.

"No, you respect my brother, so you won't sleep with me again or kiss me or even freaking touch me just to save your ass in case he finds out," I fight and Parker is instantly quiet.

He stares down at me, his eyes now dark and completely unreadable to me. It's true what I said and I don't take it back. He wants me to be his girlfriend to cover his tracks, not because he wants me for real and it's all clicking into place. I said I wanted to move slowly and while kissing and sleeping together isn't moving slowly, neither is jumping into a relationship... We're both wrong. Parker's lips part but before he can get a word out, there's a knock on his door.

321

"Parky? Are you there?" My brother's voice is booming outside the door we're pressed against. My eyes go wide and Parker cringes. I move outside of view and panic. I look at Parker looking for anything and he shrugs and motions around the room.

"Hello?" Bellamy knocks again and before I can move from where I stand, Parker opens the door and I press my back hard against the cold wall right next to where Parker stands.

He could reach out and touch me meaning if Bellamy takes even a single step forward, he would see me and we'd be fucked. I don't even breathe. Parker puts his arm up, his hand splayed right next to my head, blocking Bell from stepping inside.

"What's up?" he asks, his voice completely casual, not husky and dry like it just was when we were alone.

"Have you talked to Brianne since we were downstairs? She wasn't in her room when I knocked," Bellamy says and I cringe.

"I haven't. Maybe she's showering or something," Parker lies like it's the easiest thing in the world and I quietly take out my phone and start texting him, hoping it will get this to move along.

"You look pissed," Bellamy tells him.

"Yeah, I just failed an assignment but I've got an A in the class so... I'll get over it before we go out," Parker explains, once again lying like it's second nature.

"Oh, shit. Bri just texted me and said she went to get a Starbucks from the one in the lobby. Thanks anyway, Parky, and sorry about the room situation," Bellamy apologizes.

"It's not an issue," he mumbles.

"I just feel bad. You know Bri doesn't have many friends and she's... She's my sister. I have to protect her so I'm glad you guys are kind of friends in a way and that you can make her feel comfortable and protected. It's cool. Kind of like Lawson is to her, in a way," Bellamy tells him.

THE RULES OF YOU AND ME.

"No problem, but your sister seems like she can take care of herself," Parker defends.

"You just don't know my sister like I do. Growing up, I always protected her from guys, mean teachers, or anything. Anyone. It's what she needed and what she still needs."

I hear the intent behind Bellamy's voice, the care, but it does sting because Parker is right. Not my brother. I hold in my sigh and Parker moves his hand down, his finger tracing my skin until it hits my hand. He hooks his pointer finger with my middle finger, keeping it there, so subtle Bellamy won't notice.

"You're right," Parker clenches his jaw and I stay as quiet as possible.

"Well, I'll see you in a few hours at the casinos, alright?" Bellamy walks away and Parker waves, then closes the door and I let out the biggest sigh I have ever held in my chest. Parker shakes his head and walks away.

"I don't like sneaking around," he mumbles.

"There's nothing to even hide because nothing is happening between us," I admit.

"Lie," he argues, turning back to me so quickly that I run into his chest. He stares down at me. "There's something happening between us. Both of us are just too stubborn and too in our own ways to give in to the other. You first." He tilts his chin up slightly, his hands holding each side of my face.

"No." I cross my arms. "I stand by what I said. About you respecting me and my wants and wishes."

"It has nothing to do with him. Once again, not everything revolves around Bellamy fucking Archer, Bri," he uses the nickname that he never does and I look at him with a straight, deadpan face.

"I wish that were true but you have to understand where I'm coming from considering the only reason you gave me is that

323

if Bellamy finds out, it won't be as bad if we're dating as opposed to just 'messing around.'"

Parker clenches his jaw.

"What do you want me to say? Are you waiting for me to say that I want you to be my girlfriend because I really like you? Because I search for you in rooms and crowds and I watch you when you're not looking so I can see you smile? That when we're alone or when you're asleep next to me I try to count every freckle on your face just so I can know something about you that no one else in the world could possibly know?" he pauses, catching his breath slightly. He reaches for me, holding my face between his hands.

"I have never had anything but myself and football. I have never wanted to have anything. Not friends, not family, or girlfriends because all I've known is that those things are temporary, and without a label, I feel like this is temporary. Do you need to hear that I want you to be my girlfriend for my own fucking morals because I like the thought of knowing that I have something that's even slightly mine that no one else can have for the time being? Is that enough? Or do you just want to focus on your brother?" he asks me and my lips part at the confession.

My heart stutters and stops then starts and beats out of my chest.

"I like you, Brianne. I don't know what else you need me to do to prove that to you. Do you want me to take you to the chapel down the street and let Elvis have his way with us? Because I will," he throws the words out there and my parted lips close and press into a smile.

I try to choke the laugh down and his face turns into a slight smirk too.

"I'm not going to force you to be my girl. That speech wasn't to make you feel pressured or bad for me. I don't own you and I never will but I want a part... A piece that's just mine. I can wait

THE RULES OF YOU AND ME.

as long as it takes you to feel comfortable but I don't want you thinking that I only want the label because of someone outside of this bubble. Here, when it's us, that's all it is. No one else is affecting it, no one else matters to me," he explains and I nod.

His thumb strokes over my cheekbone. I grab his wrist and hold him as he holds me.

"Do you really try to count my freckles?" I ask and he laughs and shakes his head, his eyes looking away from me and around the room.

"Yeah I have and I fail every time," he explains and I smirk.

"Keep trying. I'll be here tonight," I tell him and lean up on my tiptoes.

I press my lips to the side of his mouth, not quite his lips. I back off and slowly back away, our eyes locking for only a second before I dart away and out of the door. This feeling is something I should run from. Absolutely. It scares me, but it's exhilarating at the same time.

CHAPTER 27
JUNO BY SABRINA CARPENTER

Brianne Archer:

I shrug on my black leather jacket and run over to the mirror to look at the complete outfit. It's not as cold in Vegas as it is in Washington right now, but the jacket really adds to it. The red top I have on is the lowest cut I've probably ever worn, right down to my sternum. The material around my ribs hugs tightly and laces together in the back. I'm wearing a black skirt to match as well, low rise with sparkles spread throughout the material. I wear black knee-high cowboy boots that are the same leather as my jacket. My hair is all the way down as I normally try to keep some of it out of my face but I don't have a need to tonight.

I'm wearing red lipstick, which is something I never do because it reminds me of cheer and dance competitions. But tonight, it looks like it's meant for me. I take my phone out and take a picture in the mirror, sending it to Dakota right away. I click my phone screen off and scurry into the hallway feeling like I'm already late to meet everyone downstairs. I head down on the elevator and make my way into the bustling lobby. Now that it's nighttime, it's more crowded and so loud. There are people passing by a million miles an hour, so fast it's like a blur. I look around for my brother or his girlfriend, for the top of Lawson's blonde hair or—

My eyes don't find anyone but Parker and his eyes have already found me. He's staring at me with the most serious expression I've ever seen him wear. It looks like he shaved, trimmed, and shaped his facial hair. It's perfect and his hair is just the same, tousled and pushed back out of his face with the exception of a few strands. His hair is just past his ears now, longer and wavy and messy but in a purposeful way. He's wearing slacks and a satin shirt that looks so soft that it might melt in my fingertips. I make my way to him and the second I'm in view with my leather jacket draped over my arm instead of on my body, his eyes rake over me. They devour me, telling me that he's letting his imagination reign free right now. I open my mouth to speak and I'm interrupted right away by my brother clapping Parker on the back and everyone else coming into view. I force a smile and look at everyone as they surround me.

"Bri, put your jacket on," Lawson tells me and I glare at him.

"Agreed," Bellamy tells me and he nudges Lawson.

"She looks fine," Parker shrugs and looks at both of them.

They look at him like he's crazy for not just agreeing.

"What? I've seen both of you defend your girlfriends against douchebag guys who demean and diminish them to nothing but their bodies and all that shit. It's hypocritical for you to act just like that because she's your sister," Parker defends me and my jaw slightly drops.

"Oh, I like you. You're coming with me," Kamryn hooks her arm with Parker and Sienna does the same on the other side of my... Of Parker. I smirk and walk with the trio, turning over my shoulder to see my brother and Lawson staring at all of us with

328

THE RULES OF YOU AND ME.

shocked expressions. I shrug my shoulders and skip slightly to catch up.

"You guys coming?" I ask and Bellamy shakes his head, his face melting into a smile.

"My baby sister is all grown up," Bellamy hooks his arm over my shoulder and I groan.

"It's crazy. I'm in college, I have sex, go to parties, and drink alcohol," I say everything that normally makes him cringe.

"Don't push it.," he shakes his head.

"I absolutely love pushing it," I remind him.

"You're on thin ice," he warns.

"Well, dammit, I should have brought my tap shoes," I fight back and Kamryn laughs in front of us.

"You're also my favorite person." She grabs my hand and pulls me up with her.

We all look really good. Kamryn is decked out in sparkles—a black low-cut dress hugs every single inch of her body. The dress looks like it was infused with diamonds with the way it shimmers in the lights. Her fishnets also have diamonds just like Sienna's do. Sienna is wearing a white corset top that makes her boobs look absolutely stellar, to the point it's hard for me not to stare. The boobs are rhinestoned and her black skirt hugs her perfect curves. I absolutely love Sienna's style. She's wearing chunky heels to match her outfit, unlike Kamryn who's wearing taller, more dangerous footwear.

Bellamy is in head-to-toe black, a button-down with black pants and Lawson wears a short-sleeve shirt that's somewhat see-through showing off his body and his arms. I don't look into it much more because I'll start laughing. All I can imagine when I look at him is what Dakota would be saying if he was seeing the same thing. I make sure to text him a description of Lawson's outfit just so I can feel like he's present.

Griffin doesn't meet us until a little later into our night. I am

329

only two margaritas deep while everyone around me, with the exception of Parker and Lawson, has had plenty. I'm not sure why Lawson isn't drinking when his girlfriend is definitely drinking enough for both of them. I can feel Bellamy's eyes on me with every sip I take of my drink. I clench my jaw, my body tense at the thought. I know he continues to catch my glares in his direction too. Everyone is having so much fun, as much as I feel like I should be having. It's hard when you feel like everyone around you is in their own world and you're just floating in their orbit. When I'm with Bellamy alone, it doesn't feel that way. When I'm around him and his friends. It feels like I'm an afterthought. I get up from the bar and try to get my brother's attention but he's in his own world so I just leave, not minding the feeling of being alone.

The best part about Vegas is that no matter where you wander, there's always another bar. There's another room of slot machines. There are too many people for anyone to really care what you're doing or how you got there. So I can blend in and become a part of the bar I approach now, opening another tab and ordering myself a shot of chilled El Jimador with an orange instead of a lime.

"Put that on my tab."

I turn to my left and see a man who must be double my age but is absolutely fine. I stare, my eyes roving over him taking in every single expensive thing about him.

"Sure thing, boss," the bartender speaks out.

"Boss?" I ask him.

"I'm not the boss. Just a frequent flier which is why I've never seen you here," he raises his eyebrows at me. There's peppered white hair in his beard and hair.

"I'm here with my friends for the game tomorrow. Our friend plays for The Raiders," I admit.

"Ahh, well, welcome to Vegas..." he starts, then waits.

THE RULES OF YOU AND ME.

"Brianne," I tell him.

"Brianne," he purrs my name and then a hand is placed on my back and wrapped all the way around my waist.

"What are you doing? Are you okay?"

Parker is on me like white on rice and I look up to him, my hands on his chest, mostly from shock. I notice now that he didn't approach because of the man talking to me. He hasn't even noticed the guy behind me. He's actually concerned.

"I wanted to get a drink without being stared at by my brother," I mumble.

"Well, let me know next time so I don't turn around and notice you went missing without a word. You scared me half to death," he tells me and lets me go, putting some space between us.

Then, his eyes land on the man behind me who's smirking from ear to ear.

"Are you going to introduce me to your friend?" he asks.

"This is Parker, Parker this is..."

"Dimitri," he tells me.

"Nice to meet you," Parker relaxes by the second, shoving his hand in his pocket.

"What are you drinking, Parker?" Dimitri asks.

"Nothing tonight, thank you though," he tells him.

A man approaches the stranger next to me and brings him an iPad and papers. I watch the interaction, watch Dimitri make orders, and I smirk at him as the employee walks away.

"I thought you said you weren't the boss," I mumble to him.

"Semantics," he shrugs and stands up, adjusting his suit.

"Your girlfriend is gorgeous. You're gorgeous," he speaks to Parker first and then me.

"She's..." Parker hesitates. "Someone to be proud of," he corrects himself instead of correcting Dimitri.

"Take care of yourself, you two, and have fun at the game

tomorrow," Dimitri winks at me and I smirk, turning back to my shot.

"I can't take you anywhere without someone wanting you, can I?" He asks.

"Last time we went out together, you were the one who wanted me. Remember that," I pat his chest for him to step back.

"Earlier when I said you look fine I—"

"Thank you for that, for standing up with me. I know Bellamy means well but it can get to be very annoying," I tell Parker.

"I don't care about that. I just needed you to know you look more than fine, you look..." He doesn't say anything, he just looks me up and down and then shakes his head like he can't think of the word.

"I think you're looking for the word fuckable," I tell him and he rolls his eyes and then sighs.

"Unfortunately for me, yes," he mumbles to himself.

I throw the shot back and set the empty glass on the bar with the orange rind.

"You took that like a champ," he smirks down at me.

I feel my nerves ease slightly but I shake my head and then my hands out.

"Hey..." He grabs my chin and tilts me back up so I'm looking at him.

"I think I want to go back to the hotel or... Or maybe just call an Uber and do something else. You don't have to come and you don't have to be around me or feel bad. Honestly, it would probably be suspicious if we both left at the same time but it's not like Bellamy would even care considering he doesn't even notice that I walked away. Tonight, you were the one who did and I know it's so silly to be getting this way about my idiot brother but it just... It stresses me out and—"

THE RULES OF YOU AND ME.

Parker takes my shaky hand and puts it on his chest.

"Take a deep breath," he instructs.

"It's just so infuriating being talked to like—"

Parker kisses me. My world disappears. It explodes. It implodes. I don't know where I am. I don't know what is happening. I don't know who's speaking. I don't know who's around. Everything ceases when I'm reunited with the one person who can kiss me and create enough heat to burn the goddamn world. I melt at the plush feeling of his perfect lips on mine, so soft and careful in such a reckless place. The tickle of his full facial hair. He pulls back and moves my hair from my forehead, his eyes searching mine.

"That was a really great way of telling me to shut the hell up," I mumble.

"Not shut up, calm down," he tells me, his hand brushing over my knuckles as my hand is pressed flat to his chest.

"I'm assuming that was a one-time thing," I speak up and take a step back, the world coming back into play in my mind.

I forgot that we are in fact in public and anyone could be watching.

"For now but I couldn't help myself tonight," he smirks and I know my cheeks are burning red even through my makeup, considering how hot my face is.

The rowdiness behind me makes me stiffen, knowing who's about to approach.

"Parker, are you smiling right now?" Bellamy asks and Parker puts space between us.

"The bartender is funny," he shrugs.

"Where did you go?" Bellamy asks.

"What's it to you?" I ask, shocking myself. *I did try to tell him, though...*

My brother stares at me with shock and somewhat annoyance. I shrug, not taking back my words. I don't feel bad for saying them even if I am surprised I did. He promised to make me feel included, not only tonight but living with him in general, and though I have been trying, it obviously hasn't been working. Bellamy isn't keeping his promise.

"Come on, I'm done losing money. I want to dance. JADE!" Kamryn grabs her friend.

"Where are you going?" Bellamy calls after her, his attention no longer on me within a split second.

"Dancing! Come on Bri!" Kamryn look at me as she yells but then is pulled off by her friends. I'm left with the guys.

"I think I want to go back to the hotel," I admit. Lawson, Bellamy, and Parker stare at me.

"I'm going after them, meet up with me in a second when you figure this out with her," Lawson suggests and walks away.

Bellamy looks like he's going to argue but finally, he turns back to me. Parker is standing between us, almost like a barrier.

"It's fine, seriously," I nod and put a smile on my face.

Parker shakes his head and looks away. I know he knows exactly how I'm feeling which is why that response hits him differently.

"What's going on with you? You've been MIA all night. Come on, don't you want to have fun?" he asks, lightening up and I shake my head at my brother.

"I have felt completely left out all night and you asked me to bring my ID yet judge me every drink I order. I don't want to be with you guys. I'd rather just go talk to Dakota and go to bed," I argue.

"You'd rather FaceTime your boyfriend in the hotel than just give it another shot with us at a club?" he asks and I shrug, my eyes drifting. "Is there something else bothering you? Do you need me to come back and—"

"No, nothing is wrong, I just want to go back. You don't need to ruin your night for me," I offer, thankful he offered at all.

THE RULES OF YOU AND ME.

"Are you sure?" Bellamy puts his arm around my shoulder.

"Always. I wouldn't say it if I didn't mean it," I tell them and I can see the slight clench of Parker's jaw.

"I want to go back too. Is it okay if I catch an Uber with you?" Parker asks and I roll my eyes.

"Not you playing the protective alpha male too. I already have Bellamy and Lawson... but thanks," I joke and only part of me is being honest.

I don't need him ruining his own night by babysitting me.

"He's right. You shouldn't be wandering around Vegas alone, but Parky, I don't want you to go back just because she is. Don't ruin your night," Bellamy tells his friend.

"It's not ruining my night. I wanted to go back to...." he stops himself and looks at me, then Bellamy, and shakes his head.

"Are you... Oh my god. You wanna call your new girlfriend or something, don't you?" Bellamy asks and I shift my weight and sigh, annoyed that he's trying to be so involved in Parker's relationship status.

"No. Stop asking," Parker snaps.

"Just tell me if it's someone I know," Bellamy pushes. "Is it a hookup or are you together?"

"None of your business. Don't ask again because my sex life is that. Mine, not yours. For the record, she's not my girlfriend yet but I damn sure want her to be. Keep her name out of your mouth for the time being," Parker looks at Bellamy sternly.

"I can do that easily considering I don't know her name," Bellamy argues in a joking tone.

"Let's go, Bri. Your brother is pissing me off," he nods his head so casually, I almost convince myself that he wasn't just talking about me.

"Same here," I mumble.

"Don't be mean to me," Bellamy calls after us.

335

"Stop being annoying, then... And stop letting your friends babysit me!" I shout back and look at Parker.

We continue outside and Parker puts his hand on my back once we're far enough away, guiding me. I nudge him off and cross my arms.

"Not faking a smile now?" he asks and I sigh deeply.

"You seriously don't need to follow me back to the hotel. You're ruining your experience by—"

"You might be crazy if you think I'd rather be in a club or casino instead of being with you in one of our quiet and large hotel rooms. You're even crazier if you think I'd let you leave in a random city all by yourself. Seriously," he shakes his head.

"Fine," I mumble.

"Fine," he grumbles.

"Don't be grumpy," I nudge him.

"I'm overwhelmed and all I've wanted to do since I had to pull myself away from you is kiss you again. So, add frustration to that list," he chimes, his voice tight.

"So I'm frustrating now?" I ask.

"More than you'll ever know, Sunshine, but that doesn't mean I don't want you," he mutters and I smirk.

"Am I frustrating enough that you won't come back to my hotel room when we get back?" I ask.

"Never that frustrating," he admits and I smile to myself while Parker books our Uber.

CHAPTER 28
MUST BE LOVE BY NIALL HORAN

Parker Thompson:

Brianne leads me into her hotel room and I follow her with not a single expectation but warmth in my chest that I'm here. Thank God that the others didn't pester me into staying and let me leave with her.

Little did any of them know, I'd be standing here watching the girl of my dreams take off her cowgirl boots and throw herself on her bed like she just spent the last few hours running a marathon. I smirk as I look at her sprawled out like a starfish.

"I'm pooped," she tells me.

"Hi, Pooped, I'm—"

"Do not dad joke me right now." She points a finger at me and I stop talking.

"Sorry." I hold my hands up in surrender.

She breaks into a smile and I walk toward her. She leans up on the bed and I kick up my restraint to an all-time high. Her hands press back into the mattress and she looks up at me, her legs slightly parted where I've now wedged myself. My knees touch the bed as I stand close to her.

337

"I want to kiss you right now. More than anything, that's what I want," she tells me.

I swallow. Hard.

"Be my girlfriend," I tilt my head back.

"I... can't. Morally, I won't let myself," I clench my jaw.

"Are you ever going to say yes?" I ask her.

"Can I lay it out plain and simple for you?" she asks and I nod.

"I like plain and simple," I encourage her.

"Alright. I'm not ready to put a label on it. I'm also not ready to break it to Bellamy and when I'm ready to do that, I'll be ready to label it. Until then, I don't understand why it can't just be what it is. Fun and free and the most refreshing situationship I've ever been in," she explains. "I understand why the label and the word is important to you but I can tell you that you have something that is yours. I can promise you that this is real and it's here and that I like you and want to continue with whatever is going on. But I can't give you a label yet."

"I understand," I agree.

Her words break apart inside of me. *This is real.* It's here and it's real. It's something I can touch. It's something I can definitely feel. Definitions are things you find in books, not real life. I don't need a definite. I need a right now. Right now, she's here in front of me looking absolutely fucking phenomenal. My tongue darts out of my mouth to wet my lips and she watches me do it.

"We can just—"

I lean forward and kiss the girl in front of me, just like she wanted me to and it feels better every single time our lips touch. I didn't know kissing someone could make your entire world fall to pieces but that's exactly what this feels like. It feels like when I break apart from her, there's not going to be anything left but the two of us. I want to rip apart anyone else who's ever had the

THE RULES OF YOU AND ME.

chance to do this—anyone who's ever felt her lips on theirs like they are on mine right now. Brianne Archer is magic. She's light and water and air. She's everything you need and something everyone wants.

She grabs both of my wrists as my hands hold her face. The kiss was hot and warm at first but has now melted into something sweet and kind. I nip at her lip and she laughs. That sound is what I hope I hear when I enter whatever afterlife I'm destined for. I want it recorded. Taped. Replayed over and over again so I can feel that eruption in my stomach when I hear it. I break the kiss first, needing to breathe more than anything. She scoots back and nods for me to follow her. I kick my shoes off and I do.

I won't let this escalate. We said slow. I'd like to take my time with Brianne. I'd like to explore every part of her body in the most meticulous and caring nature I can. Right now, I choose her lips. Her perfect fucking lips. I want to know every single inch of them inside and out until I can kiss a room full of strangers and know which one she is with my eyes closed.

She crawls on top of me, her perfect body meshing with mine. She straddles me, her legs on each side of my waist. She leans down and her hair is a curtain surrounding us, blocking out every inch of the room as if any of it could distract me from her.

She kisses me now which is a different sense of euphoria. I don't know if I could put this into words that would make sense to her—the feeling of being chosen, being selected. There's an exclusivity to Brianne's intimacy as well as my own. Actively allowing someone into this space, not only this one but every space in their life, is a privilege that I don't take lightly. I feel favored and lucky and on top of the fucking world right now. Elated. That's the perfect word.

"Why are you smiling?" She stops kissing me and I look at

339

her as she backs away, her long hair all pushed to one side as she sits down on my lap, looking down at me.

"We're making out in bed like two teens that have never been kissed before. You're fucking perfect so it's kind of hard to believe that I'm in your bed right now. That's all." I put a hand behind my head and reach up, wrapping a single strand of hair around my fingertip.

"You're an idiot," she smirks.

"A very, very big idiot," I agree.

She covers her face, breaking out into a small fit of laughter. I take her hands off of her face, pull her down, and situate her so she's lying next to me. She stares at me and I start to look at her face, under her eyes, and around her nose. She watches me as my eyes move. I try not to blink so I don't lose track. My mind running a million miles an hour until—

"Are you trying to count my freckles?" She stifles the smallest laugh.

"You just made me lose track," I admit.

"How many did you get to?" she asks.

"Only 31," I admit, my voice is just above a whisper.

"You're never going to count them all," she warns me like I don't already know.

"I'll try until I can't," I admit.

We sit with that, in silence, something I'm so used to but have never been so comfortable in until I sat with Brianne.

"I should probably go and shower. We both smell like cigarette smoke and casinos," I tell her.

I see a small look of disappointment on her face. Then, I watch as she hesitates and stumbles over her own mind.

"That's fine," she nods and I stare at her, then she presses her lips upward.

I shake my head.

THE RULES OF YOU AND ME.

"Don't do that with me," I tell her. "Please..." I almost beg. "What is it? What do you want?"

"I want you to stay with me... but I didn't say that because it's probably not a good idea, is it?" she asks me and I know it's not a good idea.

It's a very bad idea if she wants to keep this hidden but the look on her face and how absolutely irresistible she is are two things that make saying no almost impossible. Red flags are green around her.

"I'll grab my things and be back in a few minutes." I reach forward and stroke my thumb over her cheek. "Promise," I tell her and watch her lips instantly smile with no hesitation.

No faking, either. I push off of the bed.

"Take my room key. I'm going to shower. Just let yourself in when you get back," she tells me.

I grab it off of the dresser and see myself out. I practically run to my room to get my things. I grab only a change of clothes, my toothbrush, and a charger. I could shower here but the thought of being away from her for longer than needed is not one I like. So I rush, also not wanting to potentially run into Bellamy or any of the others as I head back to her. I move through the hallway so quickly it's like I wasn't even there and let myself into her room again. Sound instantly fills my ears with music and her singing.

There's steam coming from the open bathroom. I smile to myself as I kick off my shoes. If neither of us made any rules, I could absolutely join her in there, but we can't. Not yet. I'm not bold enough to break the rules even though Brianne gives me the vibe that she absolutely loves breaking them. Not that I don't push her to do so... I shake the thought from my head and sit down on the edge of the bed, wondering if it will be a few minutes or way more.

It doesn't take long for the water to shut off and her singing

341

to stop. She does hum though. I listen softly, my eyes catching on her as she walks out of the bathroom, her hair twirled in a towel turban, her body wrapped with the warmest looking robe I've ever seen. She smiles, her face completely bare now, her cheeks so warm and bright that I feel butterflies swirling in my stomach.

"You wanna use my shower?" she asks me and I nod.

"If that's alright. I just didn't want to get caught in the hallway when everyone gets back," I tell her.

"All yours," she smiles and I move past her.

I hear the sound of her robe falling to the ground and I clench my jaw as I walk into the bathroom and crack the door. I strip and once again, shower as quickly as I can, not wanting to be away from Brianne for any longer than I have to.

I hurry from the shower with only a towel around my waist and I smirk to myself at the thought of teasing and testing her the way she has with me. Just like she did the other night with me in the tent. I start to brush my teeth and open the door, my toothbrush hanging out of my mouth as I stand in the doorway.

"Did you care if I use another towel for my hair... since it's longer it's just easier if I..." I lock eyes with her and she is staring at me, her lips slightly parted.

Once I meet her eyes, she closes her lips. I watch her throat bob as she swallows deeply. I hold the urge to smirk at the obvious attraction present on her face. Even if Brianne doesn't want a label. She'd be an absolute liar if she said she didn't want me.

"What? Do I have something on my face?" I ask her and look down at myself. She narrows her round eyes at me and I smirk. "Not that your eyes were on my face to begin with," I joke.

She gets off of the bed, only her robe on. She approaches me and crosses her arms over her chest as she stands chest to chest

THE RULES OF YOU AND ME.

with me, her body leaning against the door frame. I lean toward her, basically casting a shadow over her considering our height difference.

"What angle are you playing at, Thompson?" she asks, using my last name which she's never done before now.

"The same one you played the other night... Just having some fun, Sunshine."

The side of my mouth turns up despite how hard I fight it. I can't help it. I start brushing my teeth again and turn away from her.

"If you really want to play that game, then you should keep your shirt off all night. You know, for the effect," she tells me from outside the bathroom.

I smirk and jokingly roll my eyes at her blatant flirting. I've never had someone tell me these things, openly talking about my body or about the way I look. Hearing it from her feels... refreshing. Every other person I've been with in a hookup sense hasn't had to say it. We're about to sleep together so, obviously, we find each other attractive. Brianne finds a need. I love it. I do what she says and keep my shirt off, but pull sweats on my body. I walk out of the bathroom and my mouth goes dry.

"Two can play this little game you've got going on," she tells me.

"A game you started..." I remind her, staring at the absolute masterpiece in front of me.

She's in a light green set. The top is low cut and it's painfully obvious she's not wearing a bra right now. The shorts that match are more the shape of boxer briefs but obviously are meant for a woman. They fit her perfectly, bunching up at the sides of her hips to show off the subtle shape of her body.

"What? Do I have something on my face?" she asks.

She sits back on her knees on the bed, the most innocent look on her face as she starts braiding her hair back and out of

343

her face. Two pigtails on each side of her head, a normal look for her.

"Not that you were looking at my face..." She uses the exact words I did and I shake my head.

"Neither of us are winning this game... Because we're both torturing each other at this point," I remind her.

"I won a few kisses. That's more than you can say," she smiles and I shake my head.

"You didn't win. I gave you that," I fight.

"Semantics." She shrugs. "Do you want to do face masks?" she asks and I open my mouth and then close it right away, having no idea how to respond.

"I... Do you want to do them?" I ask.

"I mean, yeah. That's why I asked but it's fine if you don't want to. I just figured I'd ask because I want to do one and I don't want to do it if you don't because that would be weird if you just sat here alone while I did stupid skincare when we both said we were going to spend time together. I mean... It's... It's fine if you're not cool with it." She nods, finishing the other half of her hair. I smirk at her senseless ramble.

"Nervous?" I ask.

"Flustered," she admits, her eyes drifting down once again, taking my body in.

I feel my chest tighten at the thought of being perceived but allow her eyes to roam, enjoying it all the same.

"Cute." I nod my head. "I'll do your mask thing."

She moves off of the bed and goes to her suitcase, pulling a jar out of her things.

"Lay down. I'll put yours on first," she tells me, excitement pouring out of her now.

"Yes, ma'am."

I throw myself back on the bed, my hair still damp but my body feeling instantly relaxed in the cloud of a bed. It feels so

THE RULES OF YOU AND ME.

similar to the one I sleep on at home. She comes into my vision, her body climbing on mine. Before it was dangerous, her in the tiny skirt... But there's something about her this way—fresh, clean, and so soft. Her body is bared to me while being hidden, my imagination reigning free above me with this tiny thing she calls an outfit on.

"You sitting on me while wearing that is not a great idea," I inform her.

"Why?" she smirks to herself, opening up her jar of goop.

"I don't need to tell you why," I groan, my face incredibly serious to show the extent of my wanting for her.

"Grumpy," she jokes and I clench my jaw, not letting myself speak up.

I don't think I have it in me to say no to her right now looking the way she does and whatever would come out of my mouth would make both of us lose composure. She starts applying this stuff to my face. It smells fresh and feels cold as she evenly spreads it over my skin. I smirk at her as she concentrates, her tongue poking out the side of her mouth.

"What?" She moves back to look at me.

"You're cute," I tell her, feeling my own cheeks burn with blush but thankfully, she can't see it through the mask coating my skin.

"You're full of it and your face is perfect. Now, my turn."

She hands me the jar and I sit up, grabbing her back so she doesn't fall off of me. I keep her pressed to me with one hand and set the jar down with the other, taking my free hand to scoop some of the product on my finger. I do what I assume she did and start putting the green shit on her face, spreading it evenly so it coats her perfect skin.

"Is this why you always look like you're glowing?" I ask her and she pouts.

"You think I'm glowy?" she asks.

"I call you Sunshine, don't I?" I ask her and she rolls her eyes and I hold her chin.

"You're a horrible canvas. Stop moving," I instruct and she smirks.

"Yes, sir," she insinuates with her words and I ignore the pass, continuing to paint her skin.

Once I finish, I help her off of me and we both go and wash the stuff off of our hands.

"How long do I have to keep this on?" I ask her.

"Ten minutes. I told Dak I'd call him when I was in my room with a face mask and a robe on, so I need to do that. You don't have to be in it, though," she tells me and I shrug, not caring.

I throw myself back down on her bed and stare at my phone, scrolling through the various apps as she calls him. Brianne lays on her stomach, her legs kicked up behind her. She is so different from most women I've met but just like so many of them in other ways. Like right now, I feel like we're a scene out of a movie... I've never felt that before.

"Hey, Baby," I hear her best friend's familiar voice and try to tune out the conversation but find it incredibly hard.

"Hi, Dak. I'm obviously back in my room, I just wanted to check in," she tells him.

"Why are you back so early?" Dakota's voice sounds pouty and sad for her.

"Bellamy was being a—"

"Annoyingly possessive and overprotective brother per freaking usual?" he asks and I keep my agreement inside.

"Something like that. I just didn't want to be around him anymore because... Well, you know why. It makes me feel bad and when he's with his friends, it feels like I'm not his sister. I'm just there. I don't know, I'm being dramatic but I'm back at the room, though I'm pretty sure Bellamy is mad at me for leaving,"

THE RULES OF YOU AND ME.

she chimes, seeming like she's not upset by that fact but I know she is.

"Too bad... I was hoping things would go the right way and you'd end up in someone else's bed or have someone else in yours," I hear and I smirk, my eyes traveling to her.

She eyes me and raises her eyebrows almost as if she's asking if it's alright that she shows that I'm here. I step it up and reach for her phone, taking it out of her hands.

"What was that?" I ask, putting a hand behind my head, holding the phone above me.

"Even with that green shit on your face, you're lickable."

Dakota doesn't shock me anymore, considering the way I've heard him talk before. I just stare at him.

"Lickable, Dakota? Really?" Brianne leans into the frame.

"What? Didn't you lick him already? Down that tattoo of his. I'm just stating facts," he smirks and Bri's jaw ticks. I eye her, wondering what else she told him about our night together.

"Dakota..."

"Did I say too much?" he asks.

"For once, I'm going to say yes. Shut up. Wish Parker a goodnight," she tells him.

"I don't need to, I'm sure you will," he jokes and she snatches the phone from me.

"You're done. I love you. Goodnight, you idiot." She doesn't wait for his response and hangs up on him.

"What was that you told him?" I ask.

"Nothing." She gets defensive and I raise my eyebrows.

"Any other details you shared about what you did to me that night?" I ask and I know if I could see the color of her cheeks, they'd be neon red.

"No," she instantly closes up and I crack a smile.

"I'm not mad that you told him. I'm not going to tell my... friends, but if it's something you and Dakota do, then that's

347

fine. Just don't tell him how big my dick is," I urge and she scoffs.

"Who says it's big?" she asks and I just stare at her. "Fine, for argument's sake, let's say it is big. What would you say if I told you that I might have already shared that information with him because it was one of the first things he asked and I didn't ever have any intention of being with you after that one night?" she explains and I shake my head.

"Being with me?" I ask and raise an eyebrow.

"You hear what you want to hear," she tells me.

"I heard the words that came out of your mouth. We're together," I tell her.

"We are, in a way, just not the boyfriend-girlfriend labels kind of way..." she tells me, and turns away, looking at her phone as it vibrates. I watch her face drop slightly.

"What?" I ask her, feeling like I already know who it is making her smile leave.

"Nothing... It's nothing. I don't want to ruin our night or—"

"Tell me, Sunshine, please," I urge, reaching forward, hooking my finger to hers, tugging her hand toward me. I brush my fingertips over the palm of her hand and she sighs.

"I was right. Bellamy texted me and said he was upset that I left and that you felt the need to walk me back," she tells me.

"Little does he know this is where I would rather be... Ignore him," I tell her.

"Easier said than done... I should apologize," she tells me and I snatch her phone.

"No. You should ignore him because he doesn't get to tell you what to do. You're an adult making adult decisions. Besides, he never wants you out using your fake ID anyway. He's indirectly getting what he wants."

"Indirectly or directly, it's not going to go well if I just ignore him," she tells me, her hands in her lap.

THE RULES OF YOU AND ME.

"You're pretty when you pout," I compliment her, and she fights a smile.

"You're changing the subject," she argues.

"Am I? Is that what's happening Brianne?" I lean forward.

"Uh! No. Don't mess up my mask." She points between our faces and I shrug.

"I couldn't care less, Brianne. Kiss me," I urge, and despite her original protest... She does.

CHAPTER 29

CALL ME (PIANO VERSION) BY THE FRANKLIN ELECTRIC

Brianne Archer:

I walk into the apartment from dance lessons with Parker and I pull my jacket off of my body, moving to hang it in the closet that's by the door. It's Tuesday now. We got back really early yesterday morning from Vegas and despite the want and need to go and sleep for the rest of the day, I actually made it to all of my classes and my cheer practice with the team. Griffin won his game. He is new in the NFL so he didn't get to play for long, just at the end of the last quarter, but he did in fact score the final touchdown which was a major win for him.

We celebrated after the game with the Raiders team at an official NFL afterparty. Bellamy, Lawson, and even Parker were swept up in all of it. One thing I've noticed about Parker is that he's a silent dreamer. He's the kind of person who doesn't want to say what they want or hope for out loud because they're afraid of something. I think Parker is scared someone could maybe take his dream from him... I know how important his sport is to him. It's probably always going to be the most real and important thing in his life and I get that. It's one of the things I respect the most about him.

I didn't text Bellamy back, per Parker's request. The entire last day we were in Vegas, Bellamy was partially pretending I didn't exist. Not that he didn't notice me because he did, but it was like he was walking on eggshells like he couldn't speak to me unless he had to and it was odd. Since we've been home, I've hardly seen him but even when I did, we didn't really talk. I feel like Vegas was a small tipping point since I've gotten here. For weeks his behavior has been unacceptable to me. He doesn't see me as an adult. I don't like the tension, but there's nothing I can do unless he talks to me—

"Hey, B."

I whip my head around and my brother walks into the kitchen. He looks tense like he's not had the greatest day.

"Hey, Belly."

I walk into the kitchen and offer a smile, hoping he'll return it, but he doesn't. I see him standing there still and feel the somewhat awkward tension in the air. I wanted him to come to me. He said hey, so maybe I should just act normal?

"So... how was your day?" I ask with a smile, trying to alleviate that weird feeling.

"Fine," he mumbles, keeping his tone clipped. I clench my jaw and sigh.

"Awesome..." I whisper, not knowing what else to do but say something to him.

"It's obvious you have something you want to get off of your chest. So, if you have something to say, can you please say it?" I ask him, trying to keep my voice calm even though it's shaking.

Bellamy and I don't fight. Not before. Not ever. I don't understand how to navigate a disagreement or tension with him.

"You want to have this conversation?" he asks and I nod, my arms crossed over my chest.

352

THE RULES OF YOU AND ME.

"This is not us and that isn't you. Just asking each other how our day is and you acting like you barely know me or can barely talk to me anymore. It's infuriating." His voice is still stiff and clipped. I furrow my brows.

"Your tone is accusatory. Like I'm at fault here..." I mumble, not liking the thought of standing up to him or hurting him, but hearing Parker and Dakota in my head telling me that I don't deserve anything but the best from everyone else but especially myself.

"Because it's not me. You spent most of the Vegas trip in your hotel room and you snapped at me constantly. The second you moved in, I feel like you've just made your own life and your own everything and I'm not your brother or your best friend, I'm your roommate. You didn't even speak to me all day yesterday," he tells me and I feel an irrational anger boiling in my chest.

I try to be reasonable. Bellamy normally isn't the one to be confrontational. He's very level-headed on most occasions but right now... This feels like a joke. He was the one barking orders at me like he's my dad, then he turned around and decided to ignore me but wants to blame me for that?

"I'm the one? Bellamy, you..."

I close my mouth, not wanting to snap at him or say anything that could hurt his feelings. My mom told me to never say things when your emotions are heightened and my therapist said the same damn thing. The urge to just spew every thought is so prevalent.

"I'm what? If we're going to fight it out, then we need to put everything on the table. Tell me." He crosses his arms and I scoff at the cold look he gives me.

Bellamy is always warm. I never see him go angry and cold, of course, except now when he's speaking to me.

353

"You're being an asshole and a hypocrite," I mumble, trying to move past him and away from the situation.

I've never been one to call my brother out when he's being unreasonable because he usually never is. Normally, this type of behavior passes... but I've noticed more now than ever that Bellamy treats me very differently than he treats anyone else he's close to. I knew he was protective but the way he's been since we started living together again is unacceptable.

"You get a boyfriend and you make friends on the cheer team so now I'm nothing? I hardly know what's happening in your life, Bri." His voice is louder now and I snap, whipping around toward him.

"Because I don't want to tell you!" I don't think before I say it. Silence spreads between us and he stares at me. "It doesn't feel like it used to. You don't feel like you used to. You don't treat me the same and the way you treat me is a direct reflection of how I've started treating you," I admit out loud for the first time and as much as I wish it wasn't true, it is.

"Who's fault is that?" he asks me and I don't know what his goal was with that question.

I can't tell if he was asking to put it on me or if he's asking because he really doesn't know or understand it.

"Our parents are gone. That doesn't mean you need to parent me. Remember that." I shove past him.

"God, you're being... Bri, seriously? If Mom and Dad were here you know they'd be disappointed in—"

"Do not!" I snap and stand on the second stair as I turn toward him, tears in my eyes at the mention of our parents from him. "You don't have a right to tell me anything about Mom and Dad and how they would feel about me or any of my choices. Especially when you don't even know half of them. Bellamy, you're never the person to point fingers but you are right now, look in the mirror, please."

THE RULES OF YOU AND ME.

"You've changed." He shakes his head.

"Because you're supposed to. For the record, I absolutely adore the person I am. If you don't even want to try to get to know her, that's on you," I choke the words out and turn around and walk past him.

I grab my things, not even going upstairs to pack a bag.

"Where are you going?" he snaps and I shake my head, snatching my keys from the bowl on the island.

"Anywhere but here," I snap back.

"Run to Dakota, that's fine, but just know—"

I slam the door and don't hear another word. I hold in my tears and don't let myself get upset over him or anything else in my head right now. I don't want to prove my brother right but my first instinct is to call Dakota. I do, but there's no answer. He told me he was going to be with a girl tonight, someone he met over the weekend. I have no right to ruin that with my own shit. I can get in my car and drive around. I get a text from Parker right then, telling me he made it home. I shouldn't call him and bother him. Maybe I can go back to the dance studio...

> Parker: Are you okay?

I normally text him when I get back. I put my phone down, cover my face, and sigh. I'm overwhelmed. I'm beyond pissed but more than anything, I'm hurt and I'm upset. I start driving, not answering my phone or looking at it. It's not like anyone, including Parker, would understand this. It almost feels like a betrayal. Things haven't felt right for a while with Bellamy, but I never expected that to be the conversation we had to smooth it over.

Bellamy and I don't fight. Not ever. Not since it was just us. He's there for me, always, and yes, I have pushed him out and not told him about my relationships but one of the first things he told me when school started was that he didn't really want to know details. So, how is that my fault when he set that precedent so early on? The very light hum of music in my car is silenced when a call comes in over Bluetooth. I answer it and wipe my tears that I didn't realize I had started crying.

"Hello?" I ask quietly.

"Hey... You alright, Sunshine?" His voice is soft and kind. I choke up even more.

"I'm fine. I uh... I made it home," I tell him, not lying. I did make it home, I just left again.

"Then why does it sound like you're in the car?" he asks.

"Because I left again," I admit.

"Brianne..." he calls my name in a sing-song voice.

"It's not something you have to worry about, Parker..." I speak in a weak voice, barely able to get the words out.

"How about, instead of driving wherever you were planning on going, you start toward my place? Please?" he asks in the nicest voice possible.

"I don't want you to have to—"

"I'm going to just stop you and tell you now that I'm not being forced into anything. I don't know how many times I have to tell you, but I'll keep doing it until you understand. There's no gun to my head. There's no ulterior motive. I'm obsessed with you because I choose to be. I'm inviting you over because I want to. I called you because I actively care about you. So much," he speaks out, the romance and sensitivity pouring out of him and still I'm shocked by it.

"I..." I can't form words.

"Brianne Archer, if you are driving around in your car crying because of something, I suggest you stop and come here before I have to come find you," his voice turns serious and my chest burns at the timbre of it.

THE RULES OF YOU AND ME.

"Okay..." I agree and turn my blinker on so I can turn toward his apartment. I sniffle and he sighs.

"Was that mean?" he asks.

"No, it was a little scary but kinda hot," he laughs at that and I somehow crack a smile despite how foreign the action feels to me in moments like this.

"Just get here... Carefully and in one piece, please," he urges and I nod.

"Okay," I agree.

Parker hangs up first and I drive myself there just as he said. Carefully. It's not raining but it is cold. I was stupid too and didn't grab my jacket on the way out again. I just left. Though the heat is blasting in my Jeep, it's not doing enough right now. I shiver and park in front of his apartment, right next to his truck. I get out and rush to the door, letting myself in and wish the warmth that greeted me was a little more drastic. I climb all four flights of stairs and hesitate before knocking. I sigh, knowing my face is swollen and puffy from crying and the cold. It's too late to care about that right now. I knock anyway. There's an obvious struggle and shuffle behind the door.

"Seriously fuck off, Xander. I'm not kidding," I hear Parker's voice and I take a step back, waiting for the door to open.

It does and Parker hasn't even showered or changed out of his practice outfit that he was wearing at the dance studio.

"Hi," I speak up and don't smile because I know Parker would call me out for faking it.

"You're freezing. Where is your jacket?" Parker opens the door for me and moves into his apartment, reaching for the back of the couch.

He snatches the blanket and shoves Nico off of it. Then, he rushes to me to wrap it around my shoulders.

"I'm fine, it's fine," I tell him.

"Do we need to go beat someone's ass?" Xander asks.

357

"Shut up, Xander," Parker grumbles.

"Be careful or your girlfriend will see how much of a dick you are," Andrew warns.

"Seriously, Bri. I would go beat someone up if they fucked with you. Are you okay?" Xander leans on the edge of the couch and I shake my head.

"You're sweet. Thank you," I lean up and kiss his cheek.

"Jeez, you're so much nicer than Parker. You know you don't deserve all of that right?" Xander asks Parker as we start walking toward his bedroom.

"I'm well the fuck aware, Xander. Don't bother us," Parker grumbles behind me, following me into his bedroom.

"You need to be nicer to them," I chastise, kicking off my boots.

"They need to mind their own business," he argues and approaches me. "Are you okay? Are you hurt?" He tilts my head to the side, looking all over my face, my neck, my body.

"I'm fine. I'm not hurt, Parker," I urge and he shakes his head.

"What happened? Was it..." he hesitates and my face breaks, my lips shaking. "Was it your fucking brother? Was it about Vegas?" Parker instantly gets defensive.

"It was a stupid fight," I shake my head and sniffle. Parker wipes under my eyes consistently, catching every single tear as it falls.

"It obviously wasn't stupid, what did he say?" Parker pulls me down to sit on his bed.

"You need to shower and change and I'm holding you up, seriously it's not a big deal if you—"

"Brianne—"

"No! It would make me feel better if you didn't... If you did what you needed to do. Do that first. Don't put me first right now, please. Please go and do what you usually do. I will

THE RULES OF YOU AND ME.

feel like shit the whole time, please," I beg and he clenches his jaw.

"You're frustrating," he mumbles.

"You wouldn't be the first person to feel that way toward me tonight. Go," I usher him and he shakes his head, leaving me in his bed.

After about fifteen minutes, Parker comes into his bedroom with damp hair and loose gray sweatpants hanging around his waist. He crosses his arms over his chest and stares at me head on.

"Can I care about you for a second now? Or is it not allowed?" he asks me and I open my mouth and then close it and cover my face.

"I'm sorry," I apologize and I hear his feet approach.

"Don't apologize, Sunshine. Just look at me and tell me what happened," he speaks so casually as if he didn't just melt every part of me and my body with a single word.

I hesitate and he looks at me with concern and confusion.

"What?" he asks and I shake my head.

"Nothing..." I whisper. "Bellamy basically attacked me the second I walked through the door. Asked why I treat him like a roommate and not a brother. Then, he brought up Vegas and how I didn't talk to him yesterday. He blamed it all on me and acted like he had no part in the divide between us. I told him he wasn't my parent, he was my brother, and he... He said insinuated that they would be disappointed in me which is really what cut deep," I admit.

"Because it's a shitty thing to say and it's also not true." Parker reaches forward and brushes his thumb over my cheekbone. He shakes his head and keeps his eyes locked on mine.

"He just said that I've changed and I know we would have fought either way, even if I did reply to him when we were in Vegas. I want to say it's out of character for Bell, but I wouldn't

359

know. We don't ever fight. Kamryn wasn't there. It was just him and Lawson but he was upstairs with the door closed."

"He hasn't said anything to me," Parker starts. "About any of that or what happened to make him explode but what happened in Vegas was on him. He painted it like he wanted you to have fun and then pulled his usual big brother protective shit. You wanting to leave and your reaction is justified. His response is... He's your brother... I never... I mean, I never had a real sibling, obviously, but I do know that that's not the way he's supposed to act. Telling you that they would be disappointed in you was a low blow, like he was trying to say something to hurt you," Parker admits and I shake my head.

"Bellamy wouldn't say something just to hurt me. He's not like that, he's... Well, he wasn't like that. I feel like I don't even know right now," I admit out loud.

"I'm sure Bellamy and I will talk it out tomorrow. I'm... I know you hate it when I fake stuff but I'm not faking it when I tell you I'll be fine. I just... It took me by surprise. I didn't want to be home because I didn't want to say anything to hurt his feelings or that I didn't mean," I admit.

He looks like he wants to say something, like he wants to fight me on my thoughts but he holds his tongue.

"You're okay?" he asks softly.

"I'm okay," I nod, my tears dry on my cheeks.

"Can I get mad at you for a second now?" he asks and I furrow my eyebrows.

"You want to get mad at me?" I ask and he nods.

"Yes. I'm asking for permission to get mad at you right now, Brianne." He turns away from me and starts pacing.

"I mean, you don't really need permission to be mad at me, normally people just... do it," I shrug once, criss crossing my legs as I stare at him from his bed.

"Well, I'd like to give you a warning and treat you like a lady

THE RULES OF YOU AND ME.

and give you the option to tell me you can't handle it or need me to hold it in until later," he explains.

"Can I have a sweatshirt or something first?" I ask, still only wearing leggings and a leotard.

He passes me one of his plain hoodies, it's stark white and so oversized it will swallow me whole which is perfect for right now.

"Okay, go ahead," I give him the floor and he shakes his head.

"'You're infuriating, Brianne and you're also... you're selfish." He points at me and my mouth drops in a slight gasp.

"Not in a normal way, in a way where you... you hide everything and keep it all to yourself and don't ever share shit because you don't want to burden anyone else and it's selfish. I want to know. I want to hear it. I'm begging you," he fights and I open my mouth but he shakes his head.

"I'm not done," he stops me and I close my mouth and fight the urge to smirk. Mr. Never Speaks is talking a hell of a lot right now.

"You call me. Always. Do you understand that? When there's something wrong, call me. When you just feel like talking, if you're driving and you just want to feel like someone is with you, call me. I don't care if we sit in silence on the line and don't say a damn word, you call me always. Got that? I told you this... when I found you in the dance studio that night. I told you. Call me. Text me, be with me, or show up, I don't care, because you're the most selfless selfish person in the world. You don't want the world to revolve around you so badly that you can't see when someone is happy to revolve around you. I'm fucking stoked that you're the sun and I'm any other damn planet there is rotating around you. So stop." I watch him stand in front of me, freezing in place.

"Could you say please and maybe I'll consider?" I ask and

361

he looks at me with disbelief and then he breaks into a soft chuckle as he shakes his head.

His hands are on his exposed hips, the hard muscle that curves and creates his perfect chest is rising and falling as he tries to catch his breath after that.

"You're such a brat," he shakes his head.

"You've called me a brat, selfish, infuriating, and frustrating in the last hour," I tell him.

"Well, that's how you're being," he argues.

"And you're being grumpy and mean to me which you never are..." I argue.

Parker's jaw ticks.

"I'm not trying to be. It's frustrating, you are..." he sighs and I hesitate.

"I—"

He cuts me off. Not with words but with a kiss. I breathe in his scent, kissing him back with harshness and all the want that's been building inside of me for weeks. He breaks apart and puts his thumb over my bottom lip, touching me there.

"I'm sorry. If that was harsh or mean or too stern. I just... I need you to understand me when I tell you how important you are to me. I need you to believe me when I say it. You are not a burden. You are not too much for me. If everyone else makes you feel that way, so be it. Fuck 'em. Don't treat me like everyone else because saying this, voicing all of this to you, it has never been me but I know that this is what you need to hear so I'm doing it.... Please." He has his eyes closed as he speaks.

"That was the most romantic thing anyone has ever said to me," I admit out loud.

"I don't care if I'm romantic. I'm right," he admits.

My chest is still humming with desire that I know will go untouched tonight.

"You're right. I'm sorry," I admit. "I want... I want to let

THE RULES OF YOU AND ME.

people in. I want to do that, it just takes some... adjusting. I showed up here, didn't I? That's a step in the right direction."

"Can I get a few more steps?" he asks me and I brush my fingers over his chest, bringing my hands up to his neck and then his jaw.

"Hold my hand along the way and we'll see," I tell him.

He rolls his eyes but pecks my lips anyway, "Get in my bed... What do you want to do? Movie? Talk?"

"Are you willingly offering yourself up to talk? I swear I never would have thought that you—"

"'Brianne... We've been over this. I'm not a talker but I'm not really anything to anyone who's looking at me from the outside. Besides a football player—"

"Hot football player," I correct.

"Okay, fine. I'm nothing but a hot football player on the outside and that's what everyone thinks and I'm fine with that. I'm actually elated that no one knows any of the things that you know. Honestly, I'm happy to be learning. I actually like things I never liked before or thought I hated because I never had anyone to enjoy them with. Like yapping someone's ear off and I'm great at it because I learned from the best. I also like music and dancing and I love driving a car and I really freaking like spending time with a girl that I'm about to beg to be my girlfriend again for the millionth time because she's really cool and she smells like honey. I don't need or want anyone else to know those things. That knowledge is yours and yours only. So be it." He takes a deep breath after he finishes his speech and I cover my face.

"That was so cute," I laugh.

"Add it to the damn list. Now are you going to let me talk all night or do you want to do something else?" he asks.

"You made me feel a lot better," I admit and he blushes.

The hard cold exterior of Parker softens and melts as he

363

smiles. I climb on top, moving my hands up to his face. His eyes search mine and I keep my lips together, not wanting to say anything that might ruin this. I don't want to be rejected if I want him. If I need him right now in a way he's not ready for. I know he wants the label. I know it matters to him but I also know that I don't want it yet. I want him in every other way.

"You look like you want something, tell me." He tilts his chin up as I straddle his lap.

"I want you," I admit, my words are soft on my lips.

"I thought—"

"I know... I wanted to move slow and I regret ever asking for that. I do..." I admit.

He replies with a kiss, soft at first then harsh and needy, and then, I'm a puddle in his hands. I lean forward to take control of the kiss but he moves me so quickly I almost don't know what just happened. I look around and he smirks.

"Throw me around, why don't you?" I ask.

"You like it," he challenges.

He's right. I want to be nothing more than a damn rag doll when I'm in Parker's bed but I don't need him knowing that. My cards can't all be played at once. I need some edge over him. His hands hold onto my waist and he raises his eyebrows as if asking for permission.

"If you're going to ask if this is okay, the answer is yes. I don't care what this is either, I just want it. You. Something," I admit and he shakes his head.

"You should never agree to something if you don't know what it is," he tells me.

"But it's you... I'm safe with you, always," I fight back and watch his eyes soften to a degree I've never seen.

He tugs at my leggings and I let him, lifting my hips. I lean forward with the expectation to completely strip but he moves

THE RULES OF YOU AND ME.

me again, flipping so he's under me. I put my hands on his chest and shake my head.

"You're trying to give me whiplash," I fight back.

"I'm trying to give you an orgasm, actually," he fights back and my jaw drops.

"You're supposed to be shy and mysterious," I urge.

"And you're supposed to talk a lot but I plan to change that too in a second. Now can you make some room for me please?"

He inches my thighs further apart and I watch as he dips, moving his body between my legs. I've never in my life felt more exposed. I've also never in my life sat on someone's face but I don't think embarrassment is supposed to be the initial feeling.

"Parker, you don't have to if... I mean it's not something that you—"

His tongue is the first thing I feel and my words are replaced with a gasp, a low, barely sensible one that doesn't even register in my brain. The only thing registering is pure pleasure and it's coming from something absolutely sinful. It usually is the opposite. My mouth is the busy one and his is usually rendered speechless. But right now, there are no words. No way to speak when he works me the way he is right now. He's making love with his mouth, his lips, his tongue, even his breath.

Parker's lips are slow and teasing but at the same time, giving me any and everything I could have asked for. I don't feel exposed anymore, I feel seen. I feel like Parker has done everything he can to know how to make sure I'm satisfied because I damn sure am. I shudder, my legs tensing when he brings one hand around the back of my thigh so he can grip me and hold me where he wants me. He takes his other hand, bringing it under, working his fingers and his mouth in tandem. His tongue flattens against me, his fingers pushing inside of me. The speechlessness is done for because there's no way I can keep the moan inside.

For only a second, I think about the other people in the surrounding rooms, but the thoughts are gone when I feel Parker's fingers curl inside of me. I shake, my body almost losing its control and composure all at once.

"Please..." I beg him, wanting release. *Needing it.*

I throw my head back when his tongue moves, unrelenting, needing. I pant, my breath so unsteady I might as well be running a damn marathon, then it's over with. My pleasure turns blinding, white hot. I squeeze my eyes shut and feel my body react, my walls clenching around Parker's fingers, my mind turning to absolute mush. I try to keep my hips still as I fall apart and Parker helps, holding me exactly where he wants me as he buries his face between my damn legs like he's got bills to fucking pay. I breathe heavily and Parker moves up, bringing himself back to a sitting position. He smirks.

"What are you, proud?" I ask.

"Um, yeah?" he asks.

"You should be... My turn," I mumble, my body still reacting, but not enough to make me incapable of inciting pleasure.

"You don't have—"

"I said I wanted you and I got you in a way, but I want you in this way too... I don't have to, but are you really going to look at me and tell me you don't want your cock in my mouth?" I ask, keeping my voice sweet.

"I don't think I could make it believable if I said I didn't want that, but I don't need it. I don't need you to—"

"Do you want me, Parker? It's not about necessity..." I admit.

"I want you, Brianne. Always," he admits, his hand moving to my face so he can drag his thumb over my cheekbone.

"So, let me..." I start to move and he just watches, the hunger in his eyes so prominent and only growing when my hand slips under his waistband.

THE RULES OF YOU AND ME.

It's dangerous. Feeling him, feeling for him. Anything with him because it's all new territory... It's all something I've never felt before. Fire, burning for someone, caring about them and their pleasure, wanting nothing more than to be with them, especially when I need someone. I push the thoughts away, and focus on him, just like he did for me.

CHAPTER 30

I CAN SEE YOU (TAYLOR'S VERSION) BY TAYLOR SWIFT

Parker Thompson:

I walk through the open door of Brianne and Bellamy's apartment. There's noise not only blasting in here but pouring into the hallway. Though their apartment is far more expensive than mine and much nicer, it's still in a college town on Halloweekend. There's a party on every floor of this apartment building. I feel slightly dumb being actually dressed up and even more dumb considering the only reason I agreed to do so was because I listened to Xander and Nico.

Nico was the most adamant that I wear a costume, specifically one where I'm not wearing a shirt to show off my best assets in his words. I take a deep breath as I push through the crowd, all of my roommates following behind me. I barely make it inside before I'm swarmed. Attacked is honestly a better word for what's happening right now.

"PARKY!" Bellamy jumps on my back and Lawson is now attacking from the front. I open myself up to them knowing there's no fighting it despite the normal lack of physical touch I prefer. I lightly shove the two of them off of me and take in their

369

outfits. Bellamy is a... firefighter? I nod at the outfit, that's definitely what he is. And Lawson is... A douche? I furrow my brows at him.

"What are you supposed to be?" I ask. He scoffs and slaps his hands at his thighs.

"Bambi! Baby, come here." I hear him call his girlfriend over.

Sienna makes her way through the crowd spouting an insane amount of laughter, Kamryn trailing behind her. Sienna is in a pink bodysuit with neon leggings underneath. She's... some sort of Barbie doll. Oh... Ken. He's Ken, I get it now. Kamryn approaches me, pulling me in for a hug.

"Hi, Parker!" she cheers.

I can smell the alcohol on her breath, just like Bellamy's. Kamryn pulls away and I see the spots on her all-white bodysuit. The white thing hugs every inch of her and it dips low too. I keep my eyes up and respect her and Bellamy by not looking past her neck. The dog ears and the makeup solidify the fact that she's supposed to be a Dalmatian. Her and Bellamy's costumes sync together in my head now, too. I wish I could have planned something with Brianne. Speaking of her... I look around and I notice Xander still by me. He eyes me and then leans forward and I wonder what the hell he's doing until...

"Is your sister going to be here tonight, Archer?" Xander pulls off the perfect douchey attitude and I roll my eyes at it despite the fact that for once I'm happy for his interference.

"Ew. Are you trying to hit on my—"

"Shut up, Bellamy, let hot guys hit on your sister. Seriously, what do you think? That she'll be a prude forever and not date or fuck or—"

"Kamryn, baby, you're right, I get it but please think of your choice of words please," he sighs.

THE RULES OF YOU AND ME.

"Fuck, fuck, fuck." She bounces around him and he rolls his eyes.

"B is... Oh fuck no."

His eyes catch and all of us, including Sienna and Lawson, turn. I see exactly what he was saying that to. Brianne fucking Archer looks absolutely and devastatingly perfect. She's normally the person to wear looser fitting clothes, casual and fun because when she's at dance or cheer she's not able to do that... So seeing her here, right now... My mouth starts to water and I feel like I need to take the dog ears off of Kamryn and wear them myself because that's what I'm acting like.

She's wearing a tight corset bodysuit that fits her like a second skin. Her tits are... Her body is... Everything is fucking perfect. The body suit comes up over her hips, accentuating her waist and her perfectly muscular thighs. She's wearing fishnets and boots. She's also wearing a satin maroon robe with a sailor hat on. Dakota stands behind her shirtless with black pants on. He's wearing a bow tie, suspenders, and bunny ears. Hugh and his bunny but reversed. She looks—

"God, I want to kill her sometimes," Bellamy mumbles.

"Do not say anything rude. She looks hot," Kamryn tells him.

"I'm not going to, it's just... Hard." His jaw ticks and mine does too.

I get it to a degree, wanting to protect her, but that shouldn't mean he hides her and shames her which is exactly what he does. He makes her feel like she's an object which is so unlike Bellamy. He doesn't see it the way anyone else does. He sees it as being a big brother or a protector. I wish he would find another way to do that.

"What was your name?" Bellamy leans into my roommate.

"Alexander. Xander." He holds his hand out to Bellamy even though they've met on a few drunken occasions. Bellamy takes his hand and pulls him in.

371

"Don't fucking look at my sister tonight. Any other day, sure, but not tonight," he yells over the music and I clear my throat.

"Alright, how about a drink, Bell?" I ask him, pulling him away from my friend and wanting to throttle him all in the same move.

"Hey, guys." I hear her voice and chills instantly coat my body. She looks at her brother. "Dalmatian and firefighter, cute. Xander, a skeleton, cute. Parker... Sexy cupid, I like it. Lawson, what are you supposed to be?" Brianne asks and I look to see him sigh and then reach around to turn Sienna. She turns and smiles at Brianne.

"Ahh! Bri, you look so pretty!" She smiles and then Brianne nods.

"Barbie and Ken, amazing."

She gets it now, just like I did. I still haven't moved past Brianne calling me sexy. Yes, it was in the title of my costume but that's a minor detail. A win is a win.

"You look good, B." Bellamy pulls his sister into a hug and I'm glad he can try his best to keep his thoughts to himself.

She's stiff as she hugs him, still cold. He hasn't told me anything about the fight they had, but he has no idea that she has.

"Thanks." She pulls away and shifts, keeping her tone clipped. Her eyes hit me very quickly, but I see the plea in them. I nod.

"How about the drink?" I ask Bellamy again.

"Please. Come on Lawson." Bellamy brings him with us and we ditch the rest.

Xander disappears right away.

"What was that about?" I ask, waiting for Bellamy's explanation.

"What? Bri?" he asks me and I nod.

THE RULES OF YOU AND ME.

"That wasn't the usual greeting I see between you two," I add lightly, not wanting to seem like I'm prying.

"I fucked up a few days back... She's barely been staying here and has been avoiding me since," Bellamy sighs.

I furrow my brows, mostly because I didn't think that was the response I was going to get. I know she hasn't been sleeping at her house because she's been sleeping at mine. Waking me up in the middle of the night, needing me to hold her so she doesn't have anxiety attacks over this entire situation. I hate it for her but there's nothing I can do besides be there for her... Or this, talk to her brother under the guise of a concerned friend, not a concerned... almost boyfriend. I cringe at the thought.

"Yeah, he definitely fucked up," Lawson agrees.

"What did you do?" I ask, playing dumb.

"Me and my sister never fight. I don't know how to have a conversation with her or how to... Talk about problems because we don't have them. Ever. But there's an obvious disconnect between us and I'm not fucking cool with it. I hurt her feelings really badly because I started to say something and... I think she thinks I was going to say my parents would be disappointed in her if they were here," he finishes and I shift, knowing that's exactly what she's upset about.

"Well, what were you going to say?" I ask him.

"That they'd be disappointed in us knowing we got as close as we did and we're fighting over something so small right now. That this wasn't us at all... My parents would be over the fucking moon at the things we've individually done. I don't want her to think that I think that..." Bellamy takes a drink from his solo cup and I shrug.

"Talk to her," I tell him.

"I've tried but one thing about Bri is that she loves to talk, but the minute you mess it up or hurt her in any way, she's really great at being quiet. She needs to process things differ-

373

ently. I don't know. It's usually better if I wait for her to come to me. That's why this conversation even happened. She came to me and we got into it." He shakes his head.

"She's going to be fine. Bri is just swept up in college just like the rest of us were. Was Brianne your first priority your freshman year at SPU?" Lawson asks him and Bellamy sighs.

"She was still insanely important but I know I probably wasn't the greatest brother," he admits.

"Has she said anything during your dance class things?" Lawson asks me and I shake my head.

"She seemed more quiet and focused on Thursday, but we don't really talk except about what I need to do better. She's kind of bossy," I tell them, lying completely about how she felt, definitely not about the bossy part. Bellamy smirks at my last words.

"I miss being as close as we were. It's a huge fucking downer. This year has just taken a big blow to our relationship and you're both right, we just need to talk," he tells me.

There's loud cheering from the living room. I turn over my shoulder to see Brianne on the dining room table with Kamryn as well, the two girls dancing and singing loudly with the rest of the dancing group around them. Leah Ashley is laughing, dancing with Valerie and Brianne reaches in front of her, taking Dakota's hand. She sings the words of Calling All The Monsters to her best friend and she looks happy again—that true happiness I know she has pouring outside of her that gets dampened so fucking often.

"She looks happy right now," I tell Bellamy.

"Because she's with him... Anytime I ask her where she's going and she mentions going to see her boyfriend, she gets this fucking look. I've never seen her like this over a guy. It's weird," he tells me.

THE RULES OF YOU AND ME.

"What do you mean?" Lawson asks, having not heard this yet either I guess.

"I mean that she's actually into a guy as more than an accessory," he jokes. "She's dated guys and when she does normally, she just has them at arm's length for whatever she needs. She's just not... She's not a relationship person. Friendships or boyfriends or anything. Not since our parents passed. It's like she's never trusted anyone to get close to except for me," he informs both of us.

I wonder if there's a slight jealousy there, but the thought is falling from my mind the second Lawson opens his mouth.

"Then maybe she's falling in love," Lawson tells us and I hope my cheeks aren't burning fucking red like my chest is right now.

He's never seen her like this like she's falling in love... *Is Brianne falling in love with me?* Is it that serious for her? Because if it is, there's a huge reason as to why that's going to be a problem and he's standing next to me right now. I take a deep breath, not wanting to give myself away. It's also hard not to run through Bellamy's words again. He is the only person she trusts. Ever. But now there's me and I don't take that lightly.

"Is that Bellamy's sister?"

I turn to see one of our teammates standing next to me. He's wearing a ripped-up white shirt smeared with fake blood. I have no idea what he's supposed to be, but he's going to be gone and away from me in two seconds depending on what he's about to say.

"Yeah," I speak out coldly.

"Isn't she a freshman? Hanging out with Kamryn Hart isn't a good idea, even if she is dating Bellamy," he laughs and he's speaking to another teammate of ours, not me anymore but I still heard him.

"What the fuck is that supposed to mean?" I ask, turning him toward me.

I don't even remember his fucking name. Jasper, Jude, Jack? Who fucking cares.

"Chill out, dude. I was just saying if she hangs out with Kamryn she might pick up on some of those tendencies and start whoring around a little when her brother isn't looking." He starts to drink his drink and then stops.

"You know I wouldn't mind it if I got some secret action. She's hot," he tacks on and I grab him.

"Do you want to fucking repeat that? Say it out loud again so I know I fucking heard you right," I bark, holding his shirt in my fist and he looks confused and flustered now. "I said say it again, Jack."

"My name is James," he argues.

"I don't give a fuck—"

"Wow, calm down, Parker. What's going on?"

Lawson is the one who is trying to remove me from the situation, and Bellamy is right behind me too.

"Do not speak on Kamryn again and never fucking put Brianne's name in your goddamn mouth like that either. You wish you could bag someone even close to either of them." I break apart from Lawson and put my finger on his chest. "Say something like that again, especially about Brianne and I will end your career," I say the words low enough that the others don't hear. Just the boy in front of me.

"It was just a joke. Sorry." He holds his hands up in defense.

"You're a fucking joke," I spit the words out as he walks away.

"What the hell was that about? I have never seen you angry enough to fight so what's going on?" Bellamy asks, trying to get me to look at him.

"He said some stuff... about Kamryn and your sister. It

THE RULES OF YOU AND ME.

pissed me off," I shake my head, trying to not get angry all over again.

"What the hell do you mean he said shit about Kamryn and Bri? What the fuck did he say?" Bellamy's anger wells and Lawson stands between both of us.

"No. You're not getting angry and ruining the party. Parker handled it, just how you like, with his words. Didn't you Parks?" Lawson asks.

"If he touches your sister I'm going to rip his throat out," I tell Bellamy.

"Alrighty then," Lawson sighs, not getting the answer he wanted.

"I'll be first in fucking line. God, if he says one word to me he's fucking done on the team. Benched the rest of the season," Bellamy tells me.

"No, he just said it to me because I'm the quiet one. No one thinks I care about that shit or that I won't tell anyone," I explain.

"Well, thank you... For standing up for them."

Bellamy puts his arm over my shoulder and I flinch at his touch. *It wasn't for you. It was for her.* I think the words and want to say them out loud. I want to just tell him everything right here, right now, but I know I'd be the one getting the cold shoulder from Brianne if I made that choice for us without her input and probably a punch in the mouth from Bellamy.

"I need some air..." I tell him and break off, not waiting for a response.

I go through their apartment and head up the stairs to get some space. I run my hands through my hair and turn back around knowing there's nowhere to even go up here. I just—

I almost run directly into Brianne when I turn back around.

"Shhhh." She yanks me into her bedroom and I almost lose

377

my footing at her strength. She shuts the door and locks it and I look behind her.

"They're going to notice we're both gone at the same time," I tell her.

"Dakota and Xander are on brother duty," she tells me and I shake my head, turning away from her.

"What's wrong? Why are you mad? Did I do something?" she asks quickly.

"I really really like you, Brianne." I turn around after blurting my feelings into the air.

"I... I really like you, Parker." She lets a whisper of a smile grace her perfect lips and I stare at them.

"I'm mad that I can't like you in public or outwardly. I feel something and I don't want to scream it from the rooftops but it would be nice to tell someone not to talk about my girl instead of saying 'Hey, that's his sister, shut up.' It would be nice to get to stand next to you without pretending you don't exist," I explain.

"I'm sorry..." She gets smaller at the admittance. "Soon... We can tell him soon but we need to really figure it out. We can't be stupid about it," she explains.

She sits on the end of her bed and I stare at her, the excitement and feeling in my chest starting to vibrate.

"Does this mean you'll let me call you my girlfriend?" I ask her.

"Are you asking?" She smiles.

"I've been begging for weeks," I clarify.

"I don't know. I feel like it would be almost rude to ignore my rule list when it's hanging right there," she explains, nodding her head to a piece of paper push-pinned to her wall.

I walk around her and toward the list. I take it off the wall and scan her room until my eyes land on a pen at her desk. I grab it and write another rule.

THE RULES OF YOU AND ME.

10. Ignore rule number 5 and 6 in relation to Parker Thompson. He is excluded. - Parker.

"There. No need to feel bad." I hand her the list back. "And for the record, it wasn't the tequila that made your clothes come off, it was me. Come here."

I reach for her and bring her to her feet, breaking the space between us. I feel so wrong doing this here when I know her brother is below us and he can't know right now. But she feels so fucking right. She extends her neck and tilts toward me, giving me every ounce of access to her lips. I kiss her indulgently and she sighs at the touch and the kiss. I melt. God, my restraint is fucking thinning. Not tonight. Soon, but definitely not tonight.

"Boyfriend... I don't have a good track record with those," she whispers the second we break up.

"Then fuck all the past boyfriends and we can pretend I'm the first," I tell her.

"You just want the satisfaction that I'm solely yours," she laughs and I nod.

"Wrong. I don't want to own you or make you mine... But I damn sure will keep pieces of you, just for me," I mumble, debating whether or not I can handle kissing her again or it will make me melt into a puddle on her bedroom floor.

Girlfriend. I've never had a girlfriend. I've never had someone or something that's considered mine, that I can consider a part of me. Someone is actively choosing me. This is mine. It's ours. It feels fucking spectacular.

CHAPTER 31
THE ALCHEMY BY TAYLOR SWIFT

Brianne Archer:

I clap my hands at Parker, keeping him in rhythm. Though he still looks wobbly like a baby deer during most of the moves, the goal of all of these lessons wasn't so he would be an incredible ballet dancer. It was so he would be a better football player. I know him. I know that for the past few weeks, he's been itching to be the center of attention on that field. Part of me wonders what kind of person I'm going to see under those bright lights the second he's back in the game tonight.

Coach Corbin's allotted time for Parker to do lessons with me is up. He should be ready to be back on the field by the coach's standards. So that's why we're shoving in one last rehearsal today before the game. I hate the thought of not having these little lessons with Parker, but I love knowing he'll be doing what he loves now. I smirk at him, sweat glistening on his arms and his skin.

"Stop smirking at me like that, it's not funny," he mumbles, stopping the movements even though we aren't supposed to be done.

381

"I'm not laughing." I approach. "Hey, talk to me," I urge, crossing my arms over my chest, standing against him so I touch his chest.

He keeps his arms criss crossed over his own chest so I release mine, wrapping them around his broad back. I rest my chin on his crossed arms and stare up at him.

"The pressure is on tonight. I've been working with you for weeks now and if it doesn't show on the field then Coach is going to... Well, I don't know what he's going to do but I know he's not going to be happy. This could be it for me," he explains and I shake my head.

"I doubt a lot of things, but I've never doubted you or your ability on the field, Parker. Coach Corbin didn't pull you from games because you weren't good at your sport. He did it because he knows you can be better and there's no fixing what wasn't working if you're still trying to use it while you fix it. That's why you were out for a few weeks. I didn't put this much work and effort into you and this because I thought you were a lost cause. It's obvious how much you want this and that alone is why you're going to kick ass tonight, P... And your doubt is also an insult to my abilities. I whipped you into shape," I tell him.

"I need this," he explains.

"Sit down," I nod to the ground.

"We're supposed to be going over everything to make sure—"

"We didn't need this extra rehearsal. You just wanted it. Sit down. Now," I urge him.

"Bossy," he grumbles.

"Stubborn," I fight back.

He sits down, his back against the mirror. I sit diagonally from him, my legs crossed and my hands in my lap.

"What do you need? You said you need this. What is this?" I

THE RULES OF YOU AND ME.

ask. "Is it Coach Corbin's approval? To show everyone that you did it? Do you need to win or—"

"I need football," he tells me and I nod.

"Why?" I ask.

"Because it's the only thing I've always had. Because I wouldn't be who I am without the sport and the discipline. My strength, my agility, my tiny bit of people skills, and my drive, all come from football. I can't let that go. I won't," he explains and I smile with a nod.

"That alone is why none of this pressure matters. You know what this sport means to you. You know who you are and that's someone that's more dedicated to this sport than anyone I've ever met and I've met a lot. I believe in you..." I tell him.

A slight smile hit his lips, but it seems like he's fighting it. Then, he leans forward and pulls me to him by the back of my neck.

"Thank you." His words are soft and then so are his lips as he kisses me.

I smile against him, still not fully used to the feeling of him kissing me this way, freely and whenever he wants to. I would say whenever I want him to, but I always want him to kiss me. I haven't fully dove into the feelings I know I have for Parker, mostly because they scare me. Last weekend I agreed to officially be his girlfriend, with a title and everything. That's not a word I take lightly. I told myself I wasn't going to be in any actual relationships until I was a thousand percent sure. I was positive that feeling wouldn't come until far later in my college career. This hit me like a truck. Parker hit me like a fucking truck, metaphorically and literally.

This entire week we've spent, we've done so enjoying each other's company. The thing that's different with this is the sweetness—the care and compassion in everything Parker does.

383

I didn't expect him to be so... delicate. I didn't really expect him to be anything but especially not this. He's soft, sweet, and kind in every way. I've never had anything as simple as this, slow-paced to an extent I've never felt but also never been so okay with. We haven't had sex. He wants to wait and I want him to be comfortable. We've been exploring each other in other ways that aren't physical mostly and that's also new for me.

Despite how okay I am with the pace of everything, I'm also desperate to have him in the way we had each other the night of my birthday party. I want Parker Thompson in ways that I can't even speak out loud without blushing. I'm not ashamed of that, but I don't know what his plan is or what his intention is in waiting, but I'm excited for the moment. I want it so damn bad. He breaks the kiss from me because his phone is ringing. He groans.

"What?" he asks, his demeanor and voice changing drastically. "I'm with Brianne and even if I wasn't, I have my truck here. No, Xander. No," he groans again.

"Does he want to talk to me?" I ask and Parker nods.

"Hi, Xander!" I take the phone.

"Is Leah going to be at the game?" he asks me and I smirk.

"Leah is the cheer captain so she has to be at the game unless she's sick or dying," I tell him.

"Is that a yes?" he asks and I laugh.

"Yes, Xander. Leah is going to be there," I tell him.

"Cool, where should I sit so I can have the best view of her?" he asks and I roll my eyes.

"You're weird. Just talk to her, Xander," I tell him.

"Are you crazy? Leah would kill me if I talked to her again. I was at the bar she works at and... Well, never mind," he tells me and sighs. "Tell Parker I'll see him at the game and to play the shit out of that damn field. Bye!" He hangs up before I can say anything.

THE RULES OF YOU AND ME.

"What's going on with Xander and Leah?" I ask.

"No fucking clue. They talked at the Halloween party. He told me that, then he said he went into the bar she works at. Honestly, whatever it is, I have a bad feeling. Xander is like... like a tattooed teddy bear," he tells me.

"Leah is all work, no play, especially since she and my brother ended last year," I explain.

"Is that weird? Being friends with her?" Parker asks and I shake my head.

"No. She's completely moved on. Though I don't understand what it feels like to be bitter over a breakup, I can try to. If she has no bad blood with them, I don't either. I respect Leah, honestly. She's scary but she's also so fucking cool. Did you know she's staying another four years here so she can go to graduate school?" I ask him and he raises his eyebrows.

"What for?" he asks and I shrug.

"Fuck if I know but she's really determined. She also keeps everyone in line in such a special way. Like, yes, we fear her but if I ever needed anything, I know I could go to her. She would kill someone for me or kill me if I deserved it honestly. She's like... like an older sister."

I smile at him and he shrugs.

"She scares me," he admits and I roll my eyes.

"All women scare you," I joke.

"I'm not replying to that statement. Let's go. Warmups are starting soon and I don't want to be late and give Coach Corbin a reason to bench me."

He stands up and holds his hands out for me to hold. He gets me off of the ground and we head out with all of our things in hand.

385

Parker Thompson:

"You ready?" Bellamy snaps me out of my own head as I stand in the tunnel, waiting for the music to start.

I don't feel normal right now. I don't feel like I usually do before a game. My focus is there, my nerves are mild but present. I'm opening my senses up for the first time since I really started playing the sport. Normally at this point, I'm doing everything in my power to tune out my teammates' hype and the crowd's chants. The cheerleaders are nothing but background noise and the band is just vibrations. But I feel it all. I hear it all. I accept and welcome it and feel the buzz of energy they all give inside of my chest, like a hornet.

"I'm ready," I tell him with the most confidence I think I've ever spoken with.

Coach did what he did because he really believed in me. He wanted me to succeed. I'll be damned if I don't do just that. Our entrance song starts to play and the energy inside the tunnel starts to brighten and burst at the seams. I start bouncing and shaking my hands out, ready for this entrance, feeling like it's my first ever. Bellamy chants and hypes us all, and then we're off, running out of the tunnel and onto our field, our home.

I look up for once. I look out toward the lights and the crowd and the students screaming and cheering. I do what every single other person has always indulged in and I start waving and pumping my hands signaling for the crowd to be louder which honestly, I don't think is possible but I can try. I focus in front of me, seeing Bellamy meet up with his sister for their infamous handshake that's gone viral on just about every social media platform at this point. The brother and sister duo that everyone looks up to. Little does everyone know how tense it's been between both of them. As I approach, I hear the tail end of their convo.

THE RULES OF YOU AND ME.

"Fly high, baby sis," he tells her and she salutes him.

"Throw lots of balls, big bro," she jokes and I smirk. "And you."

She's talking to me now, which shocks me. I never expect her to talk to me or interact at all when we're in front of anyone else, especially not Bellamy.

"Yes, ma'am," I take off my helmet and look at her directly, not letting anything distract me from her perfectly made-up face.

"Remember everything I taught you. Elongating. Core is everything. Breathing. And most importantly—"

"Confidence," I finish.

"They grow up so fast." She jokingly fans her tears away and I shake my head.

"Don't forget to tuck in your tail... That's important too and... And I need to shut up, you've got this," she tells me, nodding her head.

"Thank you... For doing this, for helping," I once again add the small thanks on even though it's much more than something small inside my head.

"Stop thanking me, especially before the game. You could totally suck," she tells me.

"Thanks for the vote of confidence," I raise my eyebrows.

"You don't need it."

She's looking at me like she loves me and that alone is making this all the better. I can definitely do this.

"Baby B!" Leah Ashley calls and Brianne starts jogging backward.

She's got her normal uniform on with the exception of the long-sleeve high-neck shirts underneath and the tights on her legs so she can stay warm. Leah Ashley gives me a look and nods her head to Brianne as if she knows something she shouldn't. I look up above to the stands, my eyes scanning for a familiar face.

387

I spot the hockey jersey pretty easily considering he's in the second row. I nod my head up to him and she looks, her eyes seeming to find him just as easily. She turns back to me and I give a soft shrug. Two can play that game, Leah...

"You know nothing, Thompson!" she yells.

"Neither do you, Ashley." I jog toward Bellamy as I yell at her.

"What was Leah going on about?" Lawson asks and I shake my head.

"She was mad at me for apparently distracting Brianne," I tell them.

"And what did Bri have to say?" Lawson asks me expectantly, also speaking to me like he knows something when he has no clue.

"She was reminding me of everything I learned from her the past few weeks because she's been teaching me... If you forgot." I clap my hand on his shoulder giving him a serious look and he shrugs.

"Hey, both of you stop fucking around. This game is the deciding factor if we move on and we're playing our biggest competitors in the Pacific. So this is huge, don't fuck it up by messing around."

Bellamy puts his helmet on and I take a deep breath because he's right. Of course, Kirkland West here in Washington is a huge competitor of ours, but out of the entire West Coast, the only college team that can even compare to our turnout rate for NFL players and winning seasons would be California Sun College and State University.

When I was growing up in California, I had thought that would be where I would end up if the scholarships and football teams lined up, but I ended up getting a better offer from Seattle Pike. The thought of moving to another state far away from everything I grew up around seemed more perfect than anything else. Now, I kind of miss it, but I can't think about that right now. What I need to think about is making not only Coach Corbin proud of my improvement but Brianne too. Because if I don't kick absolute ass tonight, then this was all for nothing. I feel different. I feel new on this field like I was reborn to be here at this moment, but that doesn't mean it will show.

Lawson, Bellamy, and I walk to the center of the field with Coach Corbin on my right and we meet the captains of the CSCSU team at the center. Their uniforms are orange and black, bright and in your face. I stare down our opponents, not feeling intimidated in the slightest.

"Home team, heads or tails?" The ref asks and Bellamy starts to speak but Lawson puts his hand on his chest.

"Parks, heads or tails?" Lawson asks me and I smirk.

"Tails," I say, my eyes still locked on the opponents in front of us. The ref flips the coin and holds it out between us.

"Tails. Ball goes to Seattle Pike," The ref tells us and we break.

Bellamy claps and pulls me in by helmet.

"You've got this, Parky. Let's fucking go."

He slaps the side of my helmet and I return the gesture. Adrenaline is reigning free inside of my chest, my mind, and my entire body. Confidence is pouring out of me on every end. I have never felt this on top of the world while on this field and I can't believe I've allowed myself to miss out on this...

It's the other team's ball right now meaning offense is on the sidelines watching, looking at the close score biting our fucking nails. I watch the game in front of me, keeping my energy up, the adrenaline still not ceasing but my fear creeping in slowly.

We're in the last quarter and only up by seven meaning the

turnaround could be quick and end this entire thing with one play. I turn over my shoulder, looking at the girls on the sidelines right next to me. I search for Brianne, just like I've done all game, a confidence booster if you will. She's my reason to beat the hell out of our opponents. She's up in a stunt with Dakota. He's the only one supporting her and despite the training I have, I still have no idea how someone can do what he does. It's impressive and intense. I watch as she shows her personality, doing the cheer from all the way up there. She prepares for her landing and I watch it happen in slow motion. I watch her push before she's supposed to and I see his hand slip.

Brianne starts to fall and Dakota does everything in his power to make sure she's fine. Though he definitely breaks the fall, she still ends up on the ground. She rolls over on her back and Bellamy and I are already on the way over to her. The short distance is made and I'm crouched down to the ground.

"Are you okay?" I ask.

"B, talk to me."

Bellamy is across from me, near her head. I'm by her knees. She leans up on her elbows, Dakota standing between both Bellamy and I. Brianne looks at me, then at her brother, and sighs.

"You guys are dramatic," she mumbles.

"I'm not being dramatic, falling from over ten feet in the air isn't something to just ignore, B," Bellamy chimes.

"Every time one of you gets tackled, do you see Bri running out to the field to ask if you're okay? No, because it's your job to be out there, just like it's our job to be here," Dakota chimes from above as he stays standing. I stand now and shake my head.

"No, your job is specifically to catch her and support her," I tell him, a glare breaking my face.

"Oh, really? Are we going to play this game right now, big

THE RULES OF YOU AND ME.

shot?" Dakota asks and Brianne is up now, standing between us with Bellamy behind her.

"Stop it. I'm fine. Dakota, thank you for breaking my fall. Bell, Parker, thank you for checking on me. I'm okay," she tells me and I see the rip in her tights, the small red patch on her knees from the fall.

"You're hurt," I mention and Bellamy looks.

I hear whistles behind me. We all turn to look at the field and see the intense play, the fact that California Sun is about to touchdown and I shake my head, anxiety settling in my chest.

"Parker, go," Brianne tells me and I shake my head.

"And what?" I ask, knowing this is it.

"Play defense. Cornerback is similar to Wide Receiver. I know you can because we've all seen you play that position too on occasion, you've flipped your entire football career. Tell the coach. Now," she tells me.

"I'm not going to go and tell my coach to—"

"Coach!" Brianne yells and I swear my face is the brightest red it's been.

"B, what are you doing?" Bellamy follows her and so do I, knowing there's nothing I can do to stop it but maybe I can somewhat detonate the situation.

"Coach Corbin." Brianne approaches him and he turns slowly, looking at Bellamy, then me, and now Brianne.

"Is there a reason you're interrupting me while I speak to the other coaches, little lady?" he asks.

"Put Parker, I mean, Thompson in. Now. On defense. Pull your corner and put him there, I'm telling you," she instructs the professional football coach like it's her damn job.

"And why the hell would I do that? Better yet, why should I be taking that advice from you?" he asks.

"Because you have trained Parker in a lot of things, but I am

391

the one who has been drilling and instilling dignity and grace in his everyday technique on this field. If anyone can turn the game around right now and get the ball back in your possession or stop this from being a tied game, it's him. You've had him play defense before so put him in, Coach. Call the timeout before it's too late." He just stares at her and then he looks at Bellamy.

"I'm sorry, Coach. Bri maybe—"

"Call the damn timeout!" She raises her voice and I raise my eyebrows at her.

"Thompson?" he asks me.

I'll be damned if I don't have the same confidence in myself that she has in me.

"I want to go in. Let me..." I tell him. "She's right," I agree.

Coach blows his whistle and signals for a timeout.

"You've got more balls than half my team. Now get back over there with your team, Archer," he tells Brianne and she smiles.

"Thank you, Coach," she chirps and heads off to her cheer team who are all staring at her in disbelief right now.

Coach pulls our right side cornerback and places me in as the right side is my best side. I'm on the field now, not in my normal position, but no less confident than before. I breathe deep and heavy. I engage my core with the rest of my body. I tuck my tail in, just like she always reminds me. I remember to be long, take up space. I tell myself every single thing Brianne has instilled in me the past few weeks and the second the whistle blows I snap into action.

We're 1st and 10. Instantly, there's a collision, and I hear the smack of pads and helmets against each other. I backtrack, stepping as far into the endzone as I can, keeping my eyes scanning. I see number 16 on our opponent's team out of the corner of my eye opening himself up and I jump into action, my legs strong as they connect to the turf. I jump directly in

THE RULES OF YOU AND ME.

his line, my back connecting with his chest, the ball connecting to my open hands and into my arms. Number 16 crashes to the ground and I run, having picked the ball. I dodge and shove my way through the initial wall of guys in front of me, my heart beating loudly in my ears as I charge the field.

One of our defensemen tackles our opponent to the ground directly in front of me and I leap, jumping over the collision to avoid it. I roll off of my next teammate, taking the left instead of the right field, looking and running toward any opening until finally there's no one surrounding me. I'm clear and I'm charging for the endzone on the opposite field. I hear the announcer screaming as I run, chanting every single yard I make. I hear the crowd around us louder than they were when we first entered the stadium tonight. I charge, not even slowing down until my feet touch the spray-painted turf that's blue and gold. I don't stop until I read Hornets under my feet. I look at my feet, breathing hard. 99 yards. I just ran 99 yards in one pass, no one touching me while I did it. I smile and laugh at myself, having this moment for me and only me before I look up at everyone and flex, knowing how cliche and silly it may look but also not giving a damn. I fucking did that. I spike the football onto the endzone turf.

I'm attacked as I show off and hype the crowd even more by my teammates. That play, that moment, is going to be replayed for fucking years. I imagine the faces of my coaches from high school seeing that on their TVs. I turn to the sidelines immediately, not caring about my coaches, the crowd, or anyone else. I see Coach Corbin screaming and cheering so loud his face is beat red. Normally, that color is saved for when he's pissed at us, but by the sheer look of him, I can see nothing but happiness. I jog to him and he yanks me to him by my face mask.

"That's my fucking boy. That's my boy!" He smacks the side

of my helmet and Bellamy and Lawson always give me taps and pulls.

Brianne is in the middle of a victory chant but I see the smirk on her face. God, I want to kiss that grin right off her damn face. I smirk to myself too and jump right back in, the ball now being ours after that play.

It's a whirlwind. We do another pass play and Bellamy doesn't even hesitate to pass the ball to me before anyone else the second I'm open. I score yet another touchdown in the last few minutes of the game. We went from only a 7-point lead to now a 21-point lead in a matter of a few plays. If I continue with my own confidence and view myself the way the people who care about me and support me the most do... Maybe things will continue to work out this way. Maybe just freaking maybe things could start changing for me.

The second the buzzer goes off and the game is ours for the taking, I don't even celebrate. Bellamy starts to pull me in and I shove past him and don't acknowledge Lawson. I push through every celebrating teammate I have and charge to the sidelines. I turn her from Dakota and instantly lift her with one arm against myself, hugging her as tightly as I can with one arm, my helmet in the other. She hesitates but hugs me back tightly, laughing as I turn us slowly. I let her go slowly and she looks at me with alarm and excitement.

"What are you doing over here?" she asks over the commotion. "You should be celebrating, you should be with them—"

"They didn't get me here. You did, Sunshine," I tell her and she shakes her head but then she's swarmed by half of the football team including Coach Corbin.

I'm shoved out of the way. I watch all of them hype up my girl, this win is thanks to her in the end. Bellamy and Lawson lift her up and put her on their shoulders. I smirk, watching the entire thing go down. I'm more than thankful for her, not

THE RULES OF YOU AND ME.

because of this win but because she believes in me more than anyone ever has. Because even if she doesn't see it yet, she's changing me... My life. I can acknowledge that. I can appreciate it. I can't let it go either. I need Bellamy to know soon before this blows up in our face.

CHAPTER 32
MADNESS BY MUSE

Parker Thompson:

I wash every ounce of dirt and grime off of me from the game and even after my second rinse, I still feel like I need to wash myself again. I walk into the locker room that's still bursting with energy, so loud it's like a siren is going off in here. When I walk to my cubby, Bellamy and Lawson both shove me and tap me, getting my attention. I smirk to myself and shake my head. *I did that.* I can be proud of myself for this accomplishment because it is mine. I had help, of course, but I put in the work and I had the desired outcome, thank God.

"You're going to be a god on campus. This was your moment," Lawson tells me.

"We all had a moment. The thing that sets us apart. The thing that sets it in stone that we're starting every game and that we're going somewhere after we leave here if it's what we want," Bellamy tells me.

"'You were always good, Parks, but this just set you apart. I've never in my career run 99 yards in one play. That was..." Lawson shakes his head, not finding words.

EMMA MILLER

"The way you leapt over that player like a fucking gazelle? If I knew your technique would have improved that much I would have asked Bri to do three lessons a week instead of two," Bellamy jokes and I smile.

"So, are we going to celebrate? Are we going to Haven or—"

"No, I've got plans already actually," I tell them and they exchange a look with each other, then look at me.

"Parker, are you seeing someone?" Lawson asks and I narrow my eyes.

"Why do you ask?" I mumble, pulling my shirt on my body, now in socks, underwear, and a plain white tee.

"Because you've spent an exponential amount of time having plans with other people and we know it's not your roommates, so who is it? You wouldn't answer in Vegas. I'm not letting you out of this one," Bellamy asks.

"It could be my roommates. We've gotten a lot closer this semester," I admit, getting slightly defensive.

"And though that's probably true, I know something is going on. Who?" Lawson asks.

"It's no one and nothing, just leave it at that," I fight.

"Just say yes if you're seeing someone. Say double yes if it's the girl you hooked up with at the beginning of the semester," Bellamy asks and I fight the urge to cringe.

This is so weird and he doesn't even know it. He'll find out and he's going to hate me for it. I'm being forced to talk to him about it when he has no idea that I'm talking about his sister. I just nod and don't speak, knowing if I don't give an answer I'll be here all night getting bombarded.

"Oh shit... Is it getting serious?" Lawson asks, sitting on the bench behind me.

"It's... something," I say, not wanting to give away any details. I do smile at the thought of us being serious. I want us to work. I need it with her.

398

THE RULES OF YOU AND ME.

"You're blushing." Bellamy points out and I shrug.

"Whatever. I like her. What else is there to say?" I ask, trying to play it cool so they don't continue asking.

"So, you're seeing her tonight?" Bellamy asks and I nod again, not opening my mouth.

"Thompson!" I whip my head around to Coach Corbin in his office, nodding his head for me to follow. Though I'm scared to go over there, I'm thankful he pulled me out of this conversation.

"He's not going to get mad at you. There's no way he can get mad at you after you just kicked ass that hard," Lawson tells me.

I'm not worried he's going to yell at me. I'm worried about the fact that he's calling me into his office in general. We've already celebrated this win as a team. He screamed and cheered with us. So, he wouldn't be calling me into his office for that. I pull my jeans on and pad myself over to his office, no thoughts in my head because if I think too much about it, I'll panic.

"What's up, Coach?" I ask and he nods at the chair in front of his desk.

I sit, feeling more nervous than usual in his office and he sighs.

"I'm more than impressed with what you did tonight, Parker," he tells me.

"Thank you, sir," I nod.

"I knew you showed promise when we watched your tapes from high school and I've seen payoff from the kid at that school but the person in front of me now and the person who played tonight, is someone who is going to be in the league for a long long time. Longer than I ever managed," he admits. "You remind me of me... The way you played is the way I used to play. I busted my knees, both of them, and never played again, but you... I wasn't going to let that happen," he tells me.

399

"Thank you for believing in me and helping. Tonight felt... Better than any game before," I admit.

"And you should celebrate that. You did good, Thompson. I think we both owe your ballet teacher some credit and a lot of thanks too. She seemed to take that job seriously."

I smile at the mention of her and all the praise from Coach Corbin. I watch his head shake and my smile falters. He rubs his hand over his slightly weathered face and shakes his head with a sigh.

"How long have you had a thing with the Archer girl?" he asks me outright and my jaw opens and hangs slack at the question.

I turn slightly, looking out to see where Bellamy is and Coach clears his throat.

"Bellamy walked out with Lawson a second ago, so answer me, Parks. How long?" He shakes his head at me and I shake mine.

"How did you... I mean, what—"

"I'm not an idiot. The first sign was the fact that I've never seen anyone go up to bat for someone the way she did for you tonight. She's barely reaching 5'5 and came at me like she was taller than Bennet. She drove for you and your confidence boosted with her there. I could have brushed it off as the fact that she helped you with your technique, until I saw you yell at that boy she cheers with. I notice everything. You were to her side before her own brother was, and he might not see what's going on but I'm not stupid and I'm not blind," Coach Corbin starts and I just clench my jaw, my body tense.

"You won a huge game for us, and yes, I'm giving you that credit because, after the way you played and the maneuvers you made tonight, you deserve it. You didn't want the recognition, the hype from your teammates, hell, if there was a trophy you

THE RULES OF YOU AND ME.

would've let it fall to the ground and turn to dust. You wanted her. I watched you ditch the crowd and the team and find her right away. And just now, I have coached you for three years and watched you from the sidelines for longer than that, and not once have I seen you smile... until I mention that girl."

He crosses his arms now, walking to the front of his desk. He rests back on it but doesn't sit.

"I don't know what I'm supposed to say," I admit.

"You don't have to say anything. If it's worth it, if she's worth it, then go all in. I know you and I know your past. I know how hard all of this has been for you. If this is your one, who am I to stand in the way?" he hesitates to continue and I finally look at him.

"It sounds like there's a but that should be at the end of that sentence," I continue our conversation.

"But, I assume Archie doesn't know..." Coach raises his eyebrows at me.

"She didn't want to tell him yet, sir," I admit.

"I won't let a girl come between my team even if that girl is as tough and good as she might be. Tell him before you end up ruining something here and however he reacts is on him. Don't bring that on my field. Archer is going to win The Heisman this year. I'm sure of it, which is a very high honor. I'm not letting that be tainted by this little love spell you and his sister have. If it's the real deal, if it's that important, then he needs to know. Understood?" Coach Corbin asks me.

"I understand," I nod.

"Do it on your own time. I'm sure it will be tough but it needs to happen," Coach Corbin tells me and I nod.

"I wanted to tell him before I took her on the first date, sir. I just wanted to respect her wishes," I admit.

"You're a good guy, Parker. She's lucky to have you and vice

401

versa. I do think it's more important that all parties are aware," he tells me.

"But Bellamy isn't a party that's even slightly involved in this relationship. His friendship with me is separate from his relationship with his sister," I argue.

"But to him, it doesn't feel that way. It feels like a betrayal. It's not a good idea hiding something like this. He's a big brother. He feels like it's his job to protect her. He'll feel like he failed the second he learns one of his close friends is with his sister. You just need to prepare for the blowup and do it soon," Coach instructs me.

"Why are you giving me advice?" I ask.

"Because I said I saw myself in you, Parker. You're a good kid who has had a challenging life and I think you deserve all this good, but you can't get it while lying and sneaking around. I promise. I'm looking out for my team, yes, but I was never lucky enough to have my own kids. So all of you, that's what it feels like sometimes like I have to look out for you when no one else will. I know every part of you. Archer lost his parents. Bennet's dad skipped out. You never... You've only had coaches step in and be that figure for you. If I can help, I'm going to try," he tells me and I nod.

"Thank you, sir," I nod and he does too.

"Go celebrate tonight. You deserve it."

Coach claps my shoulder and I smile to myself as I walk out of the office. I'll deliberate and decipher everything he said to me in there soon. I'll ponder on it and think about how to talk to Brianne about it but right now, the only goal I have is to find her and take her and all our friends out. I want to celebrate myself for the first time in my life.

THE RULES OF YOU AND ME.

Xander, Nico, and Andrew piled into the car with me and we all drove together to celebrate. Not to Haven, of course, because that's where Bellamy and Lawson are going to be which is exactly why I can't be there. It's also why I don't want to be there. I don't have to force the way I feel. I just feel it all. Elated, excited, happy. I'm just... in awe of everything that happened tonight. I don't know how to wrap my head around that considering I did it. I'm happy because of something I did.

"Did you ask Bri if Leah is going to be here?" Xander asks.

"Dude, what is going on with you and her?" Andrew asks.

"Nothing is going on with me and her... Yet." He tells us with a smirk.

"You're delusional. Maybe you should get some advice from Bellamy on how to handle a maneater of a woman. Leah Ashley is all bite. She's mean," I tell him.

"She is not mean. She's blunt. There's a difference," Xander argues.

"So you like her?" I ask.

"I like the idea of her," he tells us.

"So, what's going on?" Nico asks.

"Like I said, nothing yet. I'm just... trying," he explains.

"You're insane," Andrew shakes his head.

"Dude, you can't get your girl to commit to you," Xander argues.

"It's not about commitment. I have my own issues, okay? It's not all her. Diana is coach Roberson's daughter and—"

Instantly, Xander smacks his chest.

"What the fuck did you just say?" he asks, completely interrupting Andrew.

"There's no way.... Andrew, you're fucking the coach's daughter?" Nico asks.

"We haven't... I mean, we... No, but... It's really complicated," he answers but Xander's face is red as he looks at Andrew.

403

"I need you to say that again. Diana... The girl you've been bringing around for at least two months now... Is Coach Roberson's daughter? And you never wanted to tell us this information? What the fuck, dude!" Xander raises his hands and Andrew shrugs.

"You two are a mess," I mumble.

"You're dating your best friend's sister and he doesn't know. And yes, Bellamy is one of your best friends at this point whether you want him to be or not. In getting closer to Bri, you've grown closer to him too," Xander fights.

"Shut up," I grumble. "Don't put me in a shitty mood."

"Well, we're here, so there's no more time for me to try, unfortunately. You also never answered my question. Is Leah coming?" Xander asks.

"Why don't you text her and ask?" I look at him as we park.

"Um... I think I'm blocked" he admits and I howl with laughter.

He's a lovesick puppy dog. I'm in shock, mostly because Xander is team captain. He's the head man. The stories I've heard about puck bunnies and ice groupies... I'm just surprised.

"You're down bad..." I press my lips together and nod.

"So are you," he argues.

"I can admit it. You, on the other hand, are in denial," I tell him and get out of the car.

I watch as Xander turns his attention back to Drew.

"I'm not done interrogating you. You have a lot of shit to spill and—Wait, hey, Parks wait," Xander stops me.

"What's up?" I ask, climbing back into the car.

"What's going on with you and Bri? Is it serious? You didn't correct me when I called her your girlfriend..." he tells me and both Nico and Andrew are leaning forward between the seats.

"I asked her to be my girlfriend and she said yes..." I tell them.

THE RULES OF YOU AND ME.

"So she's your first girlfriend? Like a real girlfriend?" Andrew is smiling at me.

"Yeah... She is," I smile with closed lips and look at all three of them.

"And have you two... consummated the relationship?" Nico asks and I roll my eyes.

"Nico..." I glare at him. But all of my friends look at me expectantly. "Oh come on, are you guys seriously asking me that?" I shake my head and look out of the window.

Silence is loud in the car and I groan.

"No, we haven't. Not that it's any of your business, but I really care about her and how she feels and I don't want her to think that sex is the most important thing to me because it's not. We've done other stuff, just not sex," I tell all three of them.

"But, you really want to?" Xander asks.

"I'm a guy... and you've seen her and how perfect she is, obviously I want to," I answer quicker than I even expected from myself. My mouth spoke faster than my mind.

"You love her, don't you?" Andrew nudges me with his elbow and I shake my head.

I don't even know how to love someone... Or what it would look or feel like. I've never had that, not in any form. The closest would be coaches growing up and even that feels wrong to claim. So no. I'm not sure what I feel is love. I have this picture in my head that I'll know. There will be something special or defining that will show me that I do feel more for her than I had thought and I have no doubt that I will... But I don't think I can call this love... Yet.

"I don't think so... Yet. But she's... Guys, she's really important to me," I admit.

Maybe this conversation feels easy because I'm hyped up on adrenaline still or maybe I've finally moved past feeling awkward with the three people surrounding me. They know

405

enough about me that it would be pointless to even try to hide any of it, especially with Bri. She's a staple now, just like they are. Tonight I get to treat her like my girlfriend in public for the first time since she said yes. Not behind closed doors, in dance studios, or on the phone—it's real and in my hands...

CHAPTER 33
MUST BE DOIN' SOMETHIN' RIGHT BY BILLY CURRINGTON

Brianne Archer:

I dance on the floor that's practically bouncing up and down with the music and the beat. I laugh wildly, Dakota behind me and Valerie and Leah in front of me, all of us dancing together. Dakota takes my hand and spins me and we dance together. Celebrating tonight is going to be easy when we won like we did, when Parker killed the game as well as he did. The song starts to fizzle out and I start a train, holding Dakota and Valerie's hands, pulling them with me. Both of them reach back and grab Leah and we fold into line to run toward the bar. I hit the wooden top first and it's easy to laugh out loud right now. It feels easy and free and so welcome.

"Hey! Baby B." I look at Leah and she eyes me. I raise my eyebrows.

"What? Why are you looking at me like that?" I ask her.

Things aren't weird between Leah and me even with the things that happened between her and my brother. We just exist around each other. I see her as the estranged older sister I never had.

"So, it's obvious now that I was wrong in assuming you and Dakota were together, right?" She asks and Dakota, Valerie, and I all laugh.

"Well yeah, I tried to tell you," I tell her.

"So, Parker Thompson?" she asks and my lips part in shock.

I don't know why I expected anything else from her. Leah is cold and calculated in everything she does usually. She's perceptive, especially over all of us. We're her little minions. She says jump, we say how high. I'm not surprised she picked up on it, but I wonder in my head if it was something I did. If I was the one who showed my cards to her without knowing it.

"Your silence is speaking volumes, Baby... I would just tell her," Dakota chuckles.

"It's not that serious, but yeah," I lie partially.

It shouldn't be that serious, but to me, it feels like it is. It feels like it could be detrimental to me one day—that's how much it means.

"I asked Bellamy last year if he was worried about his sister dating one of his friends and he said you didn't mess with football players and never have... In my head, I thought about how it was probably his fault you didn't, not because you weren't interested. I guess I was right," she smirks and I roll my eyes.

"Parker is... It was an accident. I mean... We didn't purposely fall into this and neither of us are very sure of anything..." I notice Leah's eyes lift from me just like Valerie's do, looking behind me.

I furrow my brows and start to turn, but don't make it all the way before I feel hands on me. Parker is unashamed, and uncaring as he presses my back to his chest. He wraps his right arm around my waist, keeping me against him, and takes his left hand to turn my face to him, his hand grasping my jaw as he turns my face. I make eye contact with him and he kisses me, in front of anyone and everyone who's around. My first thought is

THE RULES OF YOU AND ME.

just that, 'He's doing this in front of everyone!' Red flags shoot sky high but instantly, come down when I know I'm safe in his arms with his friends and mine. His kiss feels so good that there's no burn from anything but the fire he's creating inside of me. He breaks away but keeps the distance minimal between our faces. I look from his lips to his eyes.

"Hey, Sunshine," he smiles, his eyes showing nothing but happiness, no regret.

"Hi." The word practically squeaks out of me, all the air in my lungs having dissipated.

"Not that serious? Yeah, okay." Leah breaks me out of my daze and I look over to her, the smile still on my lips.

"Hi, Leah." Xander pokes his head around Parker and waves, a very soft yet cheesy smile on his lips.

"Oh, dear God, not you," she grumbles and turns to the bar top.

I watch Parker as he looks at his friend and presses his lips together.

"Good luck, idiot," he jokes, then turns his face back to me. Xander follows after Leah.

"What took you so long?" I ask, most of the bar turning into background noise now that he's in front of me, completely fresh and new after the game.

He's in a crisp white shirt that hugs him perfectly and a casual pair of blue jeans. His hair is as curly as usual, but what's new about him is the megawatt smile he's showcasing right now. I'm starting to become more accustomed to seeing it, but I can't get over the feeling that settles in my stomach when I think about how I'm the one who caused it. I'm never getting over that.

"Coach Corbin needed to talk to me," he tells me, taking his seat at the bartop, not letting me have a single second before he moves me directly between his legs and closer to him.

"About what?" I ask. He leans over to the bartender, passing his card and then nodding to me.

"Her tab is my tab now and I'll take a double whiskey, Buffalo Trace," he tells him, confidence pouring off of him as well as a slight bit of arrogance.

I don't know why the room feels suffocatingly hot as I see him turn his smirk toward me, but it does.

"What was Coach Corbin talking to you about? How great the game went?" I ask, a smile wide on my lips.

"He knows about us," he tells me, leaning back over the bar to grab his drink.

My face falls, every ounce of happiness melting into liquid-hot anxiety all throughout my body. Why the fuck isn't Parker freaking out right now?

"He... He knows? Coach Corbin knows about us and he talked to you about it? And you're not freaking out or panicking or running around like a chicken with your damn head cut off? What the hell, Parker? You should have called me or told me earlier on so I could crowd control and prepare myself and not have a full-blown—"

A kiss cuts me off. I can feel his teasing smile as he kisses me. Despite the butterflies that erupt around my entire body, I pull back.

"No, not shutting me up with kisses, this is—"

He kisses me again and the sheer force and heat his lips cause almost makes my legs give out under me. I gather myself and pull back.

"Parker! You're not thinking clearly obviously! You—"

The weight of his third kiss is life-altering. I sigh into his lips, his warmth captivating and sweltering. I stop breathing and thinking. Then, he breaks the kiss for me and my eyes stay closed as I revel in the feeling I just experienced.

THE RULES OF YOU AND ME.

"I'm going to keep kissing you until you calm down," he tells me.

I just mumble, "Mhm."

He laughs at my response. I sigh as I open my eyes.

"I'm calm. For now," I tell him.

I still feel anxiety dripping through my chest, but I don't react to it, waiting for him to talk me through it.

"We're telling Bellamy sooner rather than later so there's no issue. Coach wasn't mad. He was actually happy for me but he said I needed to tell your brother. He also made me promise no matter what happens that I won't let it affect the team. I agreed. All is well in the football world," he tells me, his demeanor easy and calm.

"I think you're too calm," I tell him.

"I just don't see the point in panicking or freaking out when nothing is going wrong. No need to freak out if the issue hasn't arisen, right?" he asks me. I nod.

"Sure, whatever you say," I agree halfheartedly.

"How about you go relieve some of that stress and dance with your best friend?" Parker nods his head behind me and I look over my shoulder seeing Dakota dancing all by himself in the crowd of people.

I look back at Parker and smile.

"Go, I mean it," he smiles and plants a sweet and quick kiss on my lips. "Go now or I'll never let you leave."

His words are softer and my stomach heats at the timbre of his voice. I want him more than I want to breathe at this point. Sure, tequila makes my clothes come off, but honestly, Parker Thompson talking to me the way he does also makes me want to get stark naked in the middle of this damn bar.

There's something different about him. I've noticed a small change here and there in the past few weeks. But tonight, right now... the way he talked to his friend like he's as close to him as

411

ever, the way he kissed me in front of everyone without hesitation, the way he's talking to me and his calm exterior, it's his newfound and insanely sexy confidence. That's exactly what it is. I won't take credit for it but whatever has caused it, I want to cheer and shout. Parker was a five-star catch before, but now, there's not a chart for someone like him. Because physically, he's far more attractive with the sex appeal he exudes now—the confidence and the absolute fearlessness.

An overwhelming sense of happiness overcomes me. I feel... proud of him. I've always been someone who thinks of my friends or family as extensions of myself and my body and soul. When they win, it's a win for me. When they lose, I lose. When they hurt, I hurt. And right now, I feel like I've won the damn lottery with the way Parker is feeling. I couldn't be more proud if I tried.

"You have three more seconds before you're trapped here," he tells me, his eyes heated and warm.

"You say it like it's a bad thing," I tilt my chin up to challenge him.

"You and I have a habit of getting caught in bathrooms. Don't make that the talk of this group by letting it happen tonight. Go, have fun. Dance for me."

He lets me go, my sides feeling cold without the weight of his large hands. I step backward and then turn around, not looking at him as I charge toward my best friend, practically jumping on him to get his attention.

"Oh, you've got him wrapped around your itty bitty finger," Dakota tells me and I roll my eyes.

"Is he staring?" I ask.

"Hasn't stopped since you left his side and probably won't stop until you go back to him. He's obsessive without being possessive. It's intense, the way you can see how much he cares about you just by the way he's looking at you," Dakota jokes, and warmth invades every inch of me at the thought. I shake my head.

"You're being dramatic." I twirl, my hair spinning around me.

"You'll see it one day. Get over here." He takes my hand and spins me toward him and I laugh straight from my chest.

I search around the bar for Parker, still coherent, only feeling the slightest buzz from the alcohol I've consumed. Dakota disappeared which I know means he found someone he's interested in on at least a physical level. I noticed Leah at a table with Xander, her eyes on him like she would have rather died than looked anywhere else but knowing her, that means nothing. The second she leaves these four walls, that look won't matter.

I spot Parker laughing with Andrew at the bar. There's a pretty girl standing with Andrew. Drop dead gorgeous level pretty. I'm so mesmerized by the gorgeous blonde of her hair that I almost forget who I was looking for. I see Andrew nod his head and then I see Parker look over his shoulder toward me. He stands up, immediately leaving the conversation. He's got his whiskey glass in his hand as he approaches.

"You didn't want to come over?" he asks and I shake my head.

"I was going to but that girl is so pretty. Who is that?"

"Andrew's almost girlfriend that won't commit to his dumbass. Her name is Diana," he smirks.

"Hey, I almost didn't commit to your dumbass," I tell him with raised eyebrows.

I slowly back up as his chest presses to mine. He doesn't hesitate to follow until I'm wedged between him and the wall, no space for me to move, not that I want to. He leans forward into my space and I tilt my head up to him, not even hesitating to do so.

"You did though and now I have you right where I want you," he tells me.

"Where is that?" I ask.

"Pressed against me in the middle of a crowded bar," he tells me and I roll my eyes.

His lips brush my cheek and he leans down, his lips now brushing my ear.

"Do you like being here, Brianne?" he asks.

Though I want to tell him I'd rather be in private so I could do what I want to him, I don't. I just nod. I smell the strong whiskey on his breath. I like the smell of it and mixed with the warm smell of his cologne, it's intoxicating. I suck in a sharp breath the second his hand touches my skin under my shirt.

"What are you thinking right now?" he asks and my brain is fried, frazzled, and going in every direction. I shake my thoughts away.

"You smell like whiskey, I've never had whiskey before," I tell him, changing the subject.

"Do you want to try, Bri?" he asks me, backing up.

I nod my head and he tips my chin back with his finger, bringing his glass toward my lips. He tilts his glass and it goes in my mouth, warm and smooth, some of it dripping down the side of my cheek and down my neck.

"Don't swallow it, taste it," he tells me.

I close my lips, feeling the warm liquid drip down my neck, fighting the urge to combust with the proximity of him, the feeling of his damn hand, and the weight of his stare. He brings his head down to the opposite side of my face, his breath hot against my neck. I slowly swallow the burning liquid and breathe my words out.

"What are you doing?" I ask softly,

THE RULES OF YOU AND ME.

"Having a taste," he mumbles, then he kisses my neck, stopping the trail of whiskey.

My lips part with an involuntary gasp as his tongue travels up my neck against the trail of alcohol until he reaches my jaw. When his mouth leaves mine, I'm practically panting, but that stops when his whiskey-coated lips crash into mine. Warmth and absolute lust burst from every part of my body. I moan into his mouth as he kisses me. I pull him forward, my fingers now holding him by the waist of his jeans. I keep my fingers tucked into his waistband. He hums his approval and I can't handle this anymore.

"I can't do this tonight, Parker," I break off.

"I can stop. Just say the word," he tells me and I shake my head.

"I don't want to stop. We always stop, we never go further, I can't play this game tonight if it's going to end in us stopping before we..." I hesitate.

"Tell me what you want, explicitly, Brianne," he tells me.

"I want you. I'm ready. I want you, I don't want to wait. I don't want to be slow. I want fast. I want hard. I want you, Parker. Tonight, please," I tell him, my words shaking.

"I was planning on waiting... just a little bit longer," he informs me and my chest deflates at the thought.

I've never needed to be physical with someone. I've never needed anything along the lines of sex but I've also never wanted someone this bad.

"Then we need to stop whatever is happening now, before we go too far," I tell him, still trying to catch my breath.

I start to remove my hands but he catches my arm by the elbow, not letting me let go.

"I..." He seems to be fighting his restraint.

I look up at him finally, the devastatingly pretty color of his eyes almost brings me to my fucking knees. I clench my

415

jaw as I stare at him, fighting every urge I have to take it further.

"It's fine," I admit, not wanting to push him.

He shakes his head and sets his almost empty glass down on the table directly next to us.

"Fuck it," he mumbles, taking my face between both of his hands and crushing his lips against mine. "We're going home. Now, before either of us has a chance to drink too much. We're both remembering this. Nothing like last time," he tells me,

"Yes, sir," I mumble against his lips.

"Go tell your friends bye." He breaks apart from me and taps my ass as he turns me toward the crowd of people.

"I'll wait outside," he tells me and then he leaves me there, still trying to catch my breath. I'm still trying to wrap my head around how someone can affect me the way he does. Maybe I... Maybe I like him more than I thought I did... Maybe I like him more than I wanted to allow myself... I can't think about that right now or I'll be running away instead of going home with him. And all I want to do is stay in Parker's bed again tonight, especially if it's half as good as the first time.

CHAPTER 34

CONSTELLATIONS (PIANO VERSION) BY JADE LEMAC

Parker Thompson:

The Uber ride home was torture. The walk up my stairs was never-ending and now that I'm unlocking my door, I know there's not a soul inside of my apartment except for me and her... I walk through the door and turn right away, taking her in my hands. I kiss her. I indulge. I don't let up. I have barely let myself have her. I have been brushing my hand against hers in crowded spaces. I have caught her attention in a crowded room just so she knows I see her and I'm only looking at her. I have told myself to wait in this regard, in having her the way I've wanted. I'm sure of her. I have been, but I have waited for her to be sure enough to tell me what she wants and tonight, there was no denying the look in her eyes. There's no denying it right now because her lips feel like a fever.

I swear it's like I can feel every ounce of emotion she feels as she kisses me back. I let her take control last time, and as much as I love her taking charge, as much as I enjoy seeing her confidence and care for me and my body... I let it happen that way because I was nervous and anxious. I wasn't sure of myself, my movements, my thoughts, and my wants. I wanted her to take that ease away with the bold person she is. But it's my turn. It's my night. I lift her with ease and relish in the small gasp that escapes her lips when I do.

I carry her all the way to my room and she pulls me back to her by my neck, kissing me like if she's apart from me for more than a second, she's going to cease to exist. I've never felt wanted like this. Not sexually, emotionally, or physically. Brianne is an entirely new experience for me in every single way and I need to experience her now that we know each other. Intimacy is relative to whoever is partaking and though I've never been one to make emotional attachments, there's a part of me that feels far more connected and sensitive to every touch and kiss and breathe now that Brianne means what she does to me.

Exactly what that is, I don't know yet, but I do know that I would rather die at this point than let her go. Her back presses to the door and her head tilts back. She's out of breath, staring at me with wild blue eyes and I need her. We both breathe heavily, our chests battling for air as we stare at each other. I take one more second, letting both of us take all of this in.

"I'm asking you now, you're sure?" I mumble as I open the door and kick it shut.

"Positive. Don't ask again," she orders and I smirk as I set her down on my bed. I kneel in front of her and don't let my eyes roam anywhere. I stay locked in on her face as I remove her shoes.

"Look at me..." I tell her and she does.

Every ounce of the adrenaline I had during my game, which feels like it was years ago at this point, is rushing back to the forefront of my emotions. I let all the cocky, confident feelings be present. If I didn't want to ruin the moment, I would be

THE RULES OF YOU AND ME.

giving myself a pep talk in the bathroom right now. In my head will do, though. *Parker, you can fucking do this. She made it unforgettable last time, now it's your turn.*

"I'm looking," she hums, crossing her ankles.

"I'm kneeling in front of you right now. Do you like seeing me here?" I ask her and her eyes darken, the bright blue burning now. "I'm going to worship your body tonight. I'm going to make you cum," I tell her as I slowly stand, not touching her as I do, but placing my hand on her thigh once I'm fully standing. "And last time I was puddy in the palm of your hand," I tell her, not showing the fact that I'm freaking out internally as I speak to her.

I've never been one to use bedroom talk, but I have since Brianne because it's what she likes. And I like to please...

"Tonight, you're mine." I move over her now and she leans back on the bed, staring at me, the same burning fire in her eyes. "You love to talk, Sunshine, where are all those words now?" I ask her and she swallows deeply. "Speak. Out loud. I said you're mine tonight. Is that alright?" I ask her.

I slide my hand up her throat until I'm holding her jaw, a grip I know she goes insane for. She opens her mouth, a slight gasp escaping.

"Okay," she breathes out, her words more of a rasp.

"Okay?" I ask her.

"What do you want me to say, yes, sir? Yes, daddy, I will? You're hot and you're talking to me in a way you've never spoken to me, sorry if I can't find all the right words, or formulate—"

I fight the urge to laugh at her ramble and crush myself to her, thankful to have someone as on fire as the girl lying on my bed right now. I'm cool, icy, and collected most of the time. She burns me up, melts me down, and shapes me. I fucking love it.

I reach down between us and fold my hands under the hem of her dress. I yank it up as hard as I can, exposing her lower half to me without breaking the kiss from her. The second the air hits her, she gasps, our lips still touching but separated from their kiss. I tug her body to the very edge of the bed and finally look down to remove her underwear, but she's not wearing any. I look up at her face, her cheeks more flushed now than they already always are.

"What kind of game are you playing?" I smirk toward her and she's still trying to catch her breath.

"No games. I forgot to pack them in my cheer bag so I just... went without," she admits to me and I shake my head, sinking back down to my knees. "Parker—"

Whatever she was going to say dissipates into the air, just like her moan the second I flatten my tongue against her perfect pussy. Her breathing shakes the second I take my tongue from her base all the way to the tight bundle of nerves that make her whole body react. The second I latch my lips to her, she lets out the breathiest moan I've heard from her. Brianne is not a quiet person, not even slightly and it's one of my favorite things about her. My goal for the night is to make that true in bed as much as it is out of bed.

"Oh my god," she moans, her words spoken normally, breathily, messily.

I revel in them and keep working, rolling my tongue over her insistently until I feel the pure muscle in her thighs tighten and clench. I force her legs farther apart and stand, burying my face in her having no shame as I devour Brianne fucking Archer in my bed. I break my mouth from her and slide my fingers down the length of her pussy to gather her arousal. I slide my fingers inside of her and kiss her with my mouth once more, using my tongue until she's writhing under me. I curl my fingers and I hear the recognition in her moan and gasp.

THE RULES OF YOU AND ME.

"Right there. Fuck." She arches her back, the death grip of her fingers on my bed no more as they move to me, my hair.

She runs her hands through my hair and I savor the taste of her, the feeling of her on my tongue and contracting around my fingers. My dick is hard as fucking rock right now and I can barely contain the groan from my mouth when she tugs on my curls the second the walls of her pussy clench around me. Her legs tremble and her hips twitch and buck against me. I hold her down with my empty hand and hold my fingers still as she's moving herself against me now. I stand fully, watching her, seeing her react to me.

"Use my fingers," I tell her and she whimpers at the words.

I'm fucking done for. I need her. I need to feel her now. I restrain myself, letting her ride out this high despite the fact that I plan to give her more. I remove my fingers from her and bring them to my mouth, cleaning myself off. She breathes heavily as she watches, her cheeks blazing, her hair messy.

"Take that off," I tell her quietly, my mind focused on having her in every single fucking way.

I turn away from her and take my clothes off while making my way to my drawer. I pull out a condom and turn to her. She stares at me as I rip the foil packet open. Her eyes scour my body, hers completely naked now.

"You're bossy tonight." She scoots herself back on my bed, almost as if she's making room for me. I pull her back to me.

"You stay here. This is your assigned spot for the time being," I tell her and she smirks.

"I think I like it," she finishes her thought from earlier and I roll my eyes.

"Spread your legs," I tell her and she looks up at me expectantly. "Please," I add on, knowing her, knowing that's the word she was waiting for.

She does so with ease, exposing herself to me once again. I

adjust her so she's leaning back and then I adjust myself, sliding my dick over her, gathering her wetness on me.

"Fuck, you're so wet," I mumble, more to myself than her.

I look at her, leaned all the way back, propping herself up on her elbows.

"Come here," I mutter.

I place myself at her entrance and when she makes her way up to me, I slide into her while meeting her for a kiss. Every ounce of my skin tingles and burns at the feeling of her. She's everywhere all at once. Around me, on my lips, on my tongue. Her hands are on my shoulders and her moan is infiltrating the air and my mouth as I settle, her body adjusting to me again.

"So fucking tight," I mutter and she whimpers and squirms, trying to get me to move.

The feeling is already too fucking much. I waited far too fucking long to fuck her again. I've thought about it. I've jerked myself off enough with her in my fucking mind, but I haven't let myself have her and I need a second to let myself adjust to the feeling of her again. A feeling I never intend to forget for the rest of my fucking life if I'm lucky enough.

"Brianne... Sunshine," I breathe out and she kisses me but then she tilts her head down.

I kiss her forehead and she's keeping her eyes locked on us, where we're joined. I breathe out, gaining my composure again so I can move again. She breathes along with my movements, her soft noises and moans sounding every time I adjust myself inside of her. I slide all the way out, the warmth of her gone for only a second before I slam all the way back into her, sheathing myself inside. Her mouth opens wide and her back arches, but no sound escapes her lips. I stay there, buried inside of her until she speaks.

"Again, please," she whispers, pressing her forehead to mine.

THE RULES OF YOU AND ME.

I do what she says, over and over again, hearing the sound of our bodies joining, thankful no one else is home for the time being. I love having her like this, all to myself. All on my own. No ears. No life around us.

"Mine," I mumble against her lips, my hand on the back of her neck as I hold her to me.

"Yours," she confirms and I almost lose it.

I kiss her and pull out of her. I move as quickly as I can, and her body moves like it's nothing, weightless like a ragdoll. I flip her over onto her stomach. She squeals at the sudden movement. I don't even smirk at the adorable sound because I need to feel her again more than anything. I pull her hips to me, raising her ass from the bed. She starts to put herself on all fours but I push her shoulder blades down. She complies, her hands on the bed and the second I slide my cock over her entrance she grips the sheets, her breath gone again.

"Please," she moans into my sheets.

I don't even hesitate to comply. I slide into her all the way once more and she cries out. I can feel her pleasure as she clenches around me. I groan, holding her hips. Her ass is perfect, in the air and slightly red from my hands. I slide them over her perfect cheeks and trace over her perfect tight ass. She gasps and I pull out of her. She waits a second before relaxing and turning over her shoulder.

"Has anyone ever touched you there?" I ask and she shakes her head. I hesitate.

"But... I would let you. If you wanted to try..." she tells me. "Do you have lube?" she asks me and I nod.

I back away from her and get it out of the drawer beside my bed. I take some on my hand and when I come back to her, she gets back into position. I smooth the lube over her and put more on my fingers. I use my free hand to place my dick again and I slide into her pussy, her whole body not relaxing like it had before.

"Relax, Brianne..." I speak softly to her and her breath shakes.

I bring my free hand around her body, letting my fingers find her clit. She moans into the bed and melts slightly, the relaxation I was looking for setting into place. I wait before I slide my thumb over her ass, lubing it up. I slowly ease it in, only one finger and I keep my movements slow as I rock my hips into her. The moan she lets out is guttural and absolute music to my ears.

"Tell me how it feels," I instruct her.

"Good. It feels..." She moans again and brings her fingers to where mine are, taking over the job of circling her clit for me. I bring my hand to her hip and hold her in place. She pants, burying her face into the bed as she moans loudly, louder than she's been with me before.

"Good girl," I watch her.

I need to see her pleasure knowing it's all me causing it. She clenches both holes and I groan out into the room, feeling euphoria and pleasure build at the bottom of my spine.

"Again," she whimpers.

"You're such a good fucking girl, Brianne," I moan into the air, still fucking her, slow and steady, sinking myself all the way into her.

"Oh my god," she can barely get the words out of her mouth as I feel her cum on me again.

Her pussy pushes me out. Her body trembles, her bones turning to nothing as she falls to the bed, overcome by the feeling.

"More... More please," she cries, trying to move herself back up, but still feeling the aftershocks.

THE RULES OF YOU AND ME.

I turn her body to the side, and spread her legs, hooking one over my shoulder. I place myself again and rub my fingers over her most sensitive area despite all of her writhing with sensitivity.

"Greedy," I mumble to her, a slight smirk on my face, but it disappears as I slide into her again, pleasure building inside of me to the point of no fucking return.

"Only for you," I lose it.

Pressure erupts from the bottom of my spine all over my entire body. I moan, pushing as deep into her as I can and she shakes still, her orgasm still working itself out, still clenching around me.

"Perfect. You're perfect," I tell her, my upper half almost collapsing onto the bed.

I catch myself, my hands in the sheets, my dick still inside of her, twitching with pleasure. She breathes heavily just like I do. I stay only for a second longer before I pull out of her and move to discard the condom.

"Go pee this time, no more UTIs. Go," I tell her.

"Grumpy," she jokes, helping herself to one of my t-shirts in my clean laundry basket.

"For once in my life, I'm not grumpy," I joke, getting clean underwear for myself.

She approaches me before she leaves and tilts her face up to mine. I bring my hand to her face, my thumb tracing her cheek and her freckles, my eyes lingering by my mind choosing not to count them this time. I kiss her forehead, her temple, her cheek, then her lips. The way she kisses me back sends shivers down my body so I pull back before I push her back down to the damn bed...

She leaves my bedroom only wearing my shirt, not that it matters considering it swallows her whole. I watch her from my

425

bathroom until she disappears into the stall and I shake my head. *Is this luck or stupidity?* Is it both? I don't even care. If something feels as good and perfect as she does... It can't be wrong. No matter what anyone says, Brianne is mine. I'm for fuck sure hers. This is... This is a good thing. She's a good thing. One of the only good things I've had the pleasure of having.

CHAPTER 35
FRISKY BY DOMINIC FIKE

Brianne Archer:

I wake up not only wrapped up in bedsheets on the softest bed ever but also wrapped in limbs. Very large, very possessive arms wrap around me so tightly it's almost like they're afraid I'd leave. Part of me feels bad because, in my past, I have left Parker. Whether we have silly sleepovers that amounted to nothing but kissing and cuddling or... Or if we're talking about the first time we slept together where I ran out on him. I'm also happy to know that I won't be running out again, hopefully. I do try to loosen his grip so I can go pee. I wonder if an apartment filled with hockey players and a football player has good coffee. Maybe even a Keurig, if I'm lucky. Parker groans as I break away from him.

"Don't go..." he whines and I smirk and swat at his needy hands.

"I'm not going anywhere. I need to go to the bathroom," I tell him and he lets go with another groan, then he rolls over.

I get up, still only wearing his shirt. I take my mess of hair and actually throw the mop of it on top of my head. There are knots and tangles everywhere but that's a problem for another time. I sneak across the hall, leaving Parker's door cracked. There's a TV playing in the living room. I didn't even look at my phone to see what time it was. I need to check my phone to make sure my brother isn't freaking out on me for being gone and not answering him.

Ever since our fight, Bellamy hasn't really been on me the way he was. He has been more of a silent observer in my life. Every time we're around each other, it's civil. It's normal. I can laugh with him but it still feels tense and odd. It nags on me in the back of my mind, that me and Bellamy haven't resolved whatever this situation is. I make a mental note to talk to him before the problem festers and it bothers us forever.

I walk into the bathroom and there's a shower running. The way this apartment is set up, I know it was meant for student housing. The showers are in stalls, three sitting right in front of me. There are also toilet stalls and three sinks. It's like a community bathroom, but large enough for everyone to still have their own space. Parker doesn't share a sink. Nico and Andrew do. My toothbrush is on Parker's sink and my own face wash lives there now too. I've been over here and used this bathroom countless times. Even knowing Parker lives with three tall, hot, hockey players, never has this specific situation ensued where I walk in here during a moment I probably shouldn't have... but I really need to pee. I hesitate, then freeze the second the water turns off. I move to turn away but the person that walks out of the shower stall with a towel around his waist is not who I expected in the slightest.

"Dakota?" I ask and he stands there, still partially wet and half naked staring at me.

"Baby? What are you doing here?" he asks and I scoff.

"What am I doing here? I have a very large Parker-sized reason to be here. Why the hell are you, my best friend, here

THE RULES OF YOU AND ME.

right now? Naked, might I add," I tack the last part on and he shrugs.

"I don't kiss and tell." He starts forward and I stand in front of him, my mind reeling with possibilities.

I thought Xander was wanting to get with Leah. I'm sure it's not him because even if Leah isn't showing interest, Dakota would never jeopardize that possibility... Andrew has an almost girlfriend, I'm sure of that but almost isn't for sure. Maybe they aren't exclusive. I don't know Andrew's sexuality. It could be him or the most obvious candidate... Nico.

Nico is hot. Incredibly hot. He's around the same height as Dakota at 6'. He's built and broad-shouldered. He has perfect lips and messy spiked hair, shorter on the sides and longer on the top. He has pretty brown eyes and he seems really sweet. But the question is... Is this a hookup or more? With Dakota, he never shows how he's feeling in that regard. I press my hand to his chest, stopping him.

"No, you don't get to slut it up in a hockey player's bed and then not tell me all the dirty details," I tell him.

"And what about you? Miss Promiscuous, are you even wearing pants?" He pulls up the edge of my shirt and I'm still not even wearing underwear so I tug it back down.

"Not important," I smirk.

"Very important! You aren't wearing underwear!" he shouts.

"You're not either!" I shout back.

"I was washing myself which you should probably do considering the fact that you had a lot of dirty provocative fun last night, didn't you? Tell me," Dakota urges.

"You—"

"Oh, shit..." We hear a voice behind my back and both turn to the most gorgeous blonde I've ever seen in my life. *Diana.*

Dakota and I stare... Our eyes meeting hers, then glancing down to see her in her entirety. She's wearing Andrew's hockey jersey which immediately takes Andrew out of the equation in my head now too. Unless...

"Oh my god..." My eyes go wide when I look back at Dakota.

"No! No. Don't even go there," he argues.

"Where are we going? Because if it's with both of you, I'm in." Her voice is raspy, and the intention behind her words is very blatant. Now, it's set in stone in my mind. Diana is a hot little vixen. Dakota is the luckiest man alive.

"Andrew and her?" I ask him.

"Wait, Andrew and me what?" she asks, the rasp in her voice feeling more permanent instead of just morning voice.

She smiles, her perfect teeth showing. Dear God, I have never been nervous around another girl because of her beauty, but I'm nervous around Diana.

"You three..." I point between Dakota, her, and the door where Andrew probably is. Then I look at Dakota who is pinching the bridge of his nose.

"I think I would remember if he was in that bed last night," she clarifies. "But he was not... Just me," she clarifies and waves to both of us. "Speaking of, I don't think I've ever actually met either of you face-to-face in person. I'm Diana."

She walks forward, Andrew's hockey jersey rising on her body as she lifts her arm, revealing her mile-long legs. I look at her and snap out of it, extending my hand. I shake hers and so does Dakota.

"Sorry for her and for this. Usually, I'm not in a bathroom at 9 am being interrogated but—"

"I was not interrogating you!" I yell at him then whip my attention to Diana. "I was not interrogating him!"

"And if you were, what would it be about?" she asks with laughter in her voice.

THE RULES OF YOU AND ME.

"It would be... Wait, are you and Andrew.... together?" I ask her and she smirks, her eyes drifting to Dakota then back to me.

"You're never going to beat these interrogation claims," she jokes and we all chuckle softly. "But me and Andrew are—"

"Who the hell is yelling at each other in—" Parker stops in the doorway of the bathroom when he sees the situation.

"Hey Diana... Hey, Dakota," he nods and walks in toward me then stops, furrowing his eyebrows together. "Wait... What are you doing here?" he asks, pointing a finger at Dak.

"Whatever it is, I'll do it again if this is how I get to wake up every time," he eyes Parker then he looks me up and down. His eyes definitely don't miss Diana.

"You two make a hot couple." He compliments. "And you should drop the hockey dud and—"

"Thanks, but also, what are you doing in my bathroom naked?" Parker asks again.

"Hey Dakota, are you—" Nico walks in, sloppy bedhead and sleep clouding his entire being. He's very shirtless, and now much more awake when he sees the situation.

"It was you, wasn't it?" I ask Nico and he looks between me and Dakota.

"Me, what? Who brought Dakota home?" he asks and I roll my eyes.

"Duh! Did you sleep with my best friend?" I ask him, turning my body to him.

"What do you think?" he smirks and I let my jaw drop.

"Dakota! You bagged a hottie!" I jump up and down, clapping my hands. Dakota puts his hands on my shoulders to stop me from jumping.

"Awe, Bri, you think I'm hot? Hey, Parks, your girlfriend thinks I'm hot," Nico nudges Parker.

"For the record, we all think you're hot," Diana clarifies, her arms crossed over her chest as she leans against the sinks.

"Andrew! Your..." Nico stops his yelling and looks at her. Then, he shrugs. "Your Diana thinks I'm hot!" he clarifies, avoiding a title. Parker is looking at all of us, incredibly confused. He stares, looking between Nico and Dakota, then he shakes his head.

"Nico... You're gay?" Parker asks.

"Um... Yeah? How did you not notice?" he asks.

"I didn't know you could notice gay?" he asks and throws his hands up.

"I've also never brought a girl back here or had a girlfriend since you met me," he tells him.

"Okay, but..." He shakes his head.

"Why is it so loud in here?" Xander walks in, sounding the grumpiest I've ever heard him sound. *What happened last night between Leah and Xander?* "Hey, what's Dakota doing here? And why are you all in the bathroom together? Hi, Diana," Xander's voice turned almost shy when speaking to Diana like she's his coach or something.

"Did you know Nico is gay?" Parker asks. I nudge Parker.

"Hey, you can't just tell everyone, don't out him," I chastise Parker, and Nico sighs.

"You can't out me when I'm already out. Parker is just stupid." Nico throws his hands up now.

"Yes, I knew Nico was gay. We all know Nico is gay. That's why he lives with the hottest guys on campus," Xander answers.

"The hottest guys on campus are Parker, Bellamy, and Lawson. Football players are way hotter than hockey players," Nico argues.

"Ew, don't mention my brother," I cringe. All of them roll their eyes.

"Orgy? In the bathroom?" Andrew walks in, his hair is messy too like he just woke up.

THE RULES OF YOU AND ME.

"No orgy." Parker points to him. "What the fuck are we doing in here? Can we take this meeting somewhere else?"

"I was coming to pee and met new friends," Diana's eyes light up.

"I was attacked upon walking out of the shower," Dakota defends.

"Because you decided to slut around at my boyfriend's apartment! I have questions!" I argue with Dakota.

"You're not even wearing underwear right now and you have the audacity to tell me I'm—"

"He's my boyfriend! Obviously, I'm going to sleep with him. You have explaining to do! I want all the details," I argue with him.

"Wait, you're not wearing underwear? In an apartment full of men?" Xander asks. "Dude, that's like the biggest win. We make her feel comfortable. Also, high five for consummating the relationship" He holds his hand out for a bro hug to Parker. Parker just glares at him.

"Hey, Bri... Can you do that thing where you make Parker not grumpy for a little while?" Nico asks me.

"He can't be grumpy. He has a family now, look." Andrew motions around all of us and Parker turns to him like he's going to attack.

I take his arm and wrap it around me, pulling him from the situation.

"You're an asshole, Drew!" Parker calls out, dragging behind me. I smirk and look back.

"You're not off the hook, Dak!" I yelled at him.

"Neither are you!" he chimes. I slam Parker's door shut and smirk at him.

"Sorry for them—"

"I love it. Don't apologize," I cut him off.

433

"I'm glad you met Diana. She's really cool, isn't she?" Parker asks and I nod and shake my head.

"I just can't put a pin on the she and Andrew's situation like what they are and also why

Xander got all nervous around her," I admit.

"They aren't dating but they're kind of exclusive, I guess? All I know is, we all just found out that she's the hockey coach's daughter, and that's why Xander is acting weird. He thinks this could fuck over all three of them next year if this ends badly."

"If she looks like that, I would sure as hell like to see her dad," I look over my shoulder like I'm signaling to her and when I turn back to him, he's approaching me, his body heat radiating.

"No. Mine," he clarifies, staking his claim. He tilts my chin up.

"Why did you even come after me?" I ask.

"Well, normally no one is awake at this point so I was hoping...." He backs us up fully now until my shoulder blades touch the wooden door. "That no one would be in there so I could lock the bathroom door and eat my breakfast," he tells me. My face is hot as I stare up at him.

"Sorry that didn't work out for you..." I whisper.

"I can have breakfast in bed..."

He yanks me from the door and lifts me up just to plop me back down on the bed. I squeal and laugh then gasp the second Parker spreads my legs and does exactly what he said he was going to do. I don't know if I'm going to get used to this version of Parker Thompson. The confident, ever amused, always smirking, silly mood Parker. I love this version of him though. I hope he stays because this person... This is the person I can see myself falling for and that realization is almost crushing to me.

∼

THE RULES OF YOU AND ME.

I stretch on the floor of the apartment, keeping my body warm. It's Saturday and we were made aware this morning when I was still with Parker that the football team is flying out tomorrow morning for a Sunday game since they won last night. Leah told all of us she's not going to ruin our Saturday by making us practice, but she is going to tell us to keep our bodies stretched and ready for a full-out performance tomorrow and perfect form during all of our stunts, tumbling, and cheers. So I moved our coffee table and decided to stretch in the living room with replays of The Real Housewives of New Jersey. I like New Jersey the best because their accents are my favorite. I focus on the TV centered in a middle split and the door opens, Bellamy sauntering in and Kamryn right behind him.

Bellamy just nods his head to me and I give him a close-lipped smile. Kamryn waves.

"Hey, Bri," she chirps.

"Hey, Kam," I breathe out my words as I release my stretch.

I look between her and Bellamy, his eyes not meeting mine and I shake my head, turning back to the TV, not even bothering today with trying. If he's not going to resolve the fight, that's fine. I'm not making the first move here this time because Parker and Dakota are right. I'm not at fault here. I'm not forcing this to work, especially since it seems like he doesn't want to fix anything.

"Okay, this is getting ridiculous. Bellamy, look at your sister," Kamryn snaps.

I press my lips together and sigh, turning my show down and then I just pause it altogether knowing I'll miss far too much. Kamryn has a way about her where she can make people talk. She plays mediator a lot between Lawson and Bellamy when they fight like brothers. I've seen it right before my eyes. She's like a detonator.

435

"She's pissed at me Ryn, this isn't the time," he mumbles, trying to keep his voice quiet.

"Why are you talking about me like I'm not in the room?" I ask and he sighs.

"Things aren't good right now, B. You're not happy with me and I'm not going to make that worse, okay?" he asks and I chuckle a sarcastic laugh.

"Okay, whatever Bellamy," I shake my head and Kamryn grumbles.

"No. This is not how it's going to be. You guys are going to actually speak to each other and lay it out all on the floor. Bri, speak your mind. I don't care if you don't want to." She raises her eyebrows at me, mothering me to a degree I've never seen before. I hesitate and then I look at Bellamy and do exactly what Kamryn says.

"You were a dick the other day and you've been a dick since I started at SPU," I tell him and he clenches his jaw.

"I can understand the other day. I can give you that but I don't see how you can say that about me since you've been at SPU the past few months. I'm your brother... I don't know what you're expecting me to act like," he admits and I shake my head, standing up so I can sit on the couch now.

"I'm expecting the guy I grew up with. The guy who respects me the way he would any woman and not treat me like a child. I understand I'm younger than you. I understand that I have a lot to learn and work on, but treating me like some pet or kid is... It's not you and it never has been. I want you to protect me and be my brother when I need it, not because I'm wearing a short skirt. A skirt that all your friends and girlfriend also wear. How is it fair to try to hide me and tell me not to wear something and then turn around and like it when other girls wear that or think other people look pretty in things like that? It's not. It's barbaric and rude," I fight.

THE RULES OF YOU AND ME.

"Okay, I agree. I was being..." he sighs and sits down.

Kamryn walks into our kitchen, staying close enough to hear but still giving us space.

"Bri, I'm lost here. I am completely lost on how to go about you being... You being all grown up. You're falling in love. You're going on dates. You're..." He shivers. "You're having sex and you're drinking and partying. You're doing everything a college person is supposed to do. You're doing exactly what I was hyping up one of my friends to do a few months back and I was being a hypocrite. It's hard to see you in a light that isn't my baby sister but as an adult. I'm sorry. I'm adjusting. I'm growing and I'm—"

"Changing?" I ask and he nods. "The thing you accused me of instead of being happy for me," I point out. I cross my arms over my chest and glare at my brother.

"I don't like feeling like you're hiding half of your life from me. I don't like that you feel as if I've made it hard for you to talk to me or be open to me. I miss debriefing with you. I miss feeling like you were my best friend and my baby sister. Not my roommate so I'm sorry," he apologizes and I feel tears prick the back of my eyes.

"What you said the other day was too far. Everything you said. About our parents. Running to Dakota. Shitting on me like that was... It was below you. So far below you that I didn't even know what to say or how to respond," I admit.

"I wasn't going to say what you think I was. I was trying to tell you that Mom and Dad would be disappointed to know we got this close and are actually fighting over something so stupid. I would never in my life tell you that Mom and Dad are disappointed in you because that would never be true. Even if you were nothing, it would still be everything to them but you're not. You're independent and you're funny and you're someone to be proud of and I'm sorry you haven't felt proud or happy

437

with me," he apologizes again and I nod, feeling tears pool in my eyes.

"I don't like this either and I've been bothered by how far apart we feel and I'm sorry for putting distance between us. I just don't want to feel judged by my choices. I don't want you to be grossed out by me telling you about my issues or my encounters," I admit.

"I'm never going to judge you. I can't." He shakes his head and I nod.

"I'm sorry too," I admit out loud.

"Come here." He stands up and opens his arms to me and I stand up, hugging my brother, feeling like I can fucking breathe again. I don't know what life is like without Bellamy and I never want to. Even the small distance between us these past few weeks has been absolute hell on earth for me, even though I kept the distance on purpose, waiting for him to come to me like he did.

"I don't know how to fight with you. I'm not used to it," he tells me and I laugh.

"So let's just not," I tell him.

"Good idea. No secrets. No judgment. Let's be Bri and Bellamy like we've always been, not how these past few months have been. Deal?" he asks me and my heart sinks.

Secrets. None. But I've kept a giant one from him. A Parker-sized secret feels even more volatile right now. More than it ever has. I nod, silently and swallow back the anxiety I have in my chest.

"I'm never going to stay mad at you Bellamy," I admit, backing up.

"I thought I fucked up everything. I thought you were going to be mad at me forever," he jokes.

"No. I need you too much," I tell him.

I do need him, and now the true fear of losing him forever is

THE RULES OF YOU AND ME.

real in my chest and so damn heavy. He's going to blow up. He's going to hate me forever. Maybe... Maybe I should just stop seeing Parker now before it's too late. I cringe internally. It's already too damn late. I practically start drooling at the thought of him and I'm supposed to pretend he doesn't exist to fix and placate my relationship with Bellamy? Parker's words replay in my own head. He told me not to put everyone else's feelings ahead of mine. Not to constantly put other people's wishes first... but Bellamy is different. I can't just disregard that.

I should just tell Bellamy now before everything blows up. Originally, I wanted Parker to be with me but I think Kamryn being here is better. She can calm Bellamy down and I can explain better. I should tell him before things go too far and there's no turning back, I—

"Are you okay?" Bellamy asks me and I nod.

"Yes... Just thinking. Relieved is all," I lie, reality snapping back in when I look at my brother. *I can't tell him. Not without Parker. Not yet.*

"Me too. I love you."

Bellamy hugs me one more time and kisses the top of my head. I squeeze him back, more scared than ever now. I'll figure this out. I'll talk myself down. It'll be fine. I can't worry Parker with this. I don't want to annoy Dakota by talking about it again. He's fed up already having to hear me question my relationship with Parker because he's friends with my brother. I'm tired of it too. I just wish that Parker and Bellamy had never met. My life would be void of problems if that was the case but it's not. I have a platter of issues I need to figure out so I don't lose Bellamy or Parker. Because as of right now, the three most important people are them and Dakota. Living without them would be devastating...

CHAPTER 36
DIRTY LITTLE SECRET BY THE ALL-AMERICAN REJECTS

Two Weeks Later

Brianne Archer:

Sitting in the front seat of Bellamy's Jeep with Parker sitting in the back alone next to our suitcases and luggage for the weekend was not what I was expecting, but that's what we've got. I sit with a heavy feeling in my chest, still knowing that I was at Parker's apartment having a game night with him and his roommates. Bellamy has no idea where I've been or what I've been up to despite the fact that we promised no more secrets. He's been insanely open with me about Kamryn and his fears about his future, about how much he loves her, and how much he cares for her. He asked me if I was okay with her moving in with him after Christmas... If she says yes, of course. I told him of course. Kamryn is spending Thanksgiving with her parents in northern Washington. Bellamy and I are driving to our old home, now our grandparent's house...

It's late. We waited for classes to end for all of us and had a Friendsgiving with Kamryn, Lawson, Parker, Me, Dakota, Bell,

Sienna, and even Griffin and Jade came home to celebrate with us. It was really special, but now, we're headed home despite how late it is. Bellamy wanted to go tonight so he could sleep in his old bed. I look in the rearview mirror, once again seeing Parker back there, not paying attention to us but looking out the window at the neighborhoods that pass by.

I brought it up to Bellamy that Parker had mentioned some of his past during our lessons. He was beyond confused by it and how he was never aware. It's crazy to me that Bellamy considered him a friend and didn't know he was in the foster system. Parker is closed off with most everyone else so I guess it makes sense, but... I let that cat out of the bag. In a friendly way, I told Bellamy that I didn't like the thought of Parker staying on campus for Thanksgiving when we had plenty of room for him or anyone else who wanted to join. Bellamy was more than happy to invite Parker. Parker was not so happy with me for telling Bell, but I... I don't want someone I care about to be alone on a holiday.

So now, we're driving home and I didn't really think this part through. The whole of Parker meeting my family without being able to introduce himself as my boyfriend, but instead as Bellamy's teammate and friend. There's a bitter taste in my mouth at that, but it's my fault that it is this way. I told Parker that the holidays were special to me and Bellamy and I didn't want to jeopardize that, so we agreed to tell him afterward. After the holidays, we're going to tell him. I've promised myself that.

"Should I know anything before I meet your family?" Parker asks us the second Bellamy turns into the neighborhood.

"No, they're normal grandparents just like anyone's. Just act normal," Bellamy tells him and I want to smack Bellamy's arm.

There is no normal for someone who's not usually around family.

THE RULES OF YOU AND ME.

"My Gam is sweet. She's quiet, an observer. My PawPaw is kind and funny. He's sarcastic and jokes a lot so, yes, prepare for that. He can take what he dishes out, but I warned both of them that you never talk. They don't expect much, just kindness. Try to smile, I know you're not good at that," I joke.

"You're mean," Parker tells me.

"And bossy," Bellamy chimes.

"And you talk too much," I mimic Bellamy's voice and he smirks.

"How did you know I was going to say that?" he asks.

"Predictable," I smirk with a knowing smile.

Bellamy pulls into the house and Parker looks awestruck. I can understand it. Our house is... It's a privilege, to say the least, that we got to grow up here, even if it was without our parents. That privilege doesn't surpass me any time I think about this house.

"Welcome home, Parks," Bellamy tells him as we get out of the Jeep.

I reach for my bag but Parker snatches it out from my hands before I can. He pretends to be indifferent, pushing around me to follow Bellamy. I smile to myself, imagining what he's probably thinking or what he would say out loud if he could. He'd probably say, 'Brianne, lay a finger on that bag and I'm going to be pissed.' Then, I'd tell him I can do it myself. Then, he'd tell me, 'I know you can, but you don't have to.' I keep the smile etched on my face at the make-believe conversation.

"Bell? Bri Bri?" I hear my Gam's voice and perk up.

"Coming in!" I yell out to her.

The house smells just like home. I see straight ahead to my bedroom on the first floor. It's a branch out from the living room. Across from mine is the guest bedroom. Bellamy's room and my parent's old bedroom which is now my grandparent's bedroom is upstairs as well as another guest room that was turned into an

443

office and TV room for my grandparents when they don't feel like coming downstairs. So that means Parker will be staying right next door to my bedroom... Easy access that no one even knows about. We walk around the large staircase and surpass the hallway. My bedroom and Parker's makeshift room are on into the living room.

"Hi, Gam." I hug her so tight and barely break away from her before my PawPaw is hugging me.

"Oh, I missed you, kid." He hugs me so tight and I squeeze him tight.

"Who's this?" My Gam asks and I look over my shoulder. "You mentioned you were bringing a friend home, I didn't know your friend would look like a professional football player like the rest of them," she jokes and Parker's cheeks turn pink.

He doesn't often show emotion, especially not embarrassment because his face is a mask. But right now, he is and I can't help but smirk.

"Gam, this is Parker, one of my best friends," Bellamy speaks out and I watch Parker's eyes slide to me then back to my grandparents. He extends his hand to shake my PawPaw's hand.

"It's an honor to meet you both. I've heard so much from both Bellamy and Brianne," he tells them and I watch my Gam blush. I haven't seen her do that in years.

"Well, all three of you get settled in for the night. The rest of your family is coming in tomorrow morning for the holiday," Gam tells us and I smile.

"Goodnight, Gam. Night, PawPaw," I tell them.

"B, will you show Parker his room and everything? I'm really tired," Bellamy asks as our grandparents retire up the stairs.

"Yeah, sure. Goodnight, Belly."

I hug my brother around the neck and he squeezes me tightly.

THE RULES OF YOU AND ME.

"Night, man." Bellamy bro hugs Parker and then he leaves too. I turn and look up at Parker with a deep breath and he smirks.

"Lead the way, Sunshine," he whispers and I dip my head toward the floor.

"You can leave those bags there," I tell him, coolly, not sure who's listening.

I lead him through the living room and into the large kitchen. I show him around and tell him where the drinks are in the outside and inside fridge. I show him my favorite spot, the sunroom that's far too cold to enjoy usually, but my grandparents put a heater in it last year so it's not anymore.

"Did they put the heater in for you?" he asks me and I nod.

"I was so happy they did it too. This is where I did my homework. I ate all my meals here. My mom would do arts and crafts with us out here when we were kids. There's just a lot of fond memories here," I tell him.

I then lead him out and back through the living room and toward the very small hallway we passed on the way into the living room. I open the guest bedroom first. The house is pin-drop silent. I stand in the doorway as he walks in.

"Your room for the weekend," I tell him.

He sets his duffle on the ground and turns, my duffle still on his shoulder. "I can take my bag now if you want," I tell him and he scoffs, a smirk on his lips as if to say 'You're joking.' He nods.

"What, you don't want to show me your childhood bedroom?" he asks and I roll my eyes.

"This bedroom is far from my childhood bedroom. It's basically the same as my room on campus," I tell him, turning around.

"I don't care, I still want to see," he tells me and I open the door across the hall.

I open the door and turn on the lights, feeling like it's been a

445

million years since I've been inside this room. The last time I was here was the first day of school, and even then, I didn't go into my room. I look around and turn back to Parker. He's looking at everything too as he sets my bag down. I sit on my queen-sized bed and cross my ankles, staring at him.

"Was it everything you were expecting?" I ask.

"More than that," he tells me. I look at him expectantly as he slowly saunters toward me.

"I didn't like having to do that," he mumbles, nudging his way between my legs, standing with his knees pressed to the edge of my bed.

His hands brush my hair back and move to hold my face and jaw.

"Doing what?" I ask.

"Getting introduced to them for the first time as anything but yours," he whispers, his fingers dipping under my chin to tilt my face up to him. I press a smile into my lips. "Don't... Don't do that. I know it bothers you too," he tells me and I nod.

"It does, but not as bad as it bothers you. It won't be that way soon. We talked about this..." I tell him and he gives a single nod.

"I know we did," he answers gruffly and I see the tension in his jaw and his shoulders. This is how it's been anytime things have felt... Odd when we're around Bellamy. He leans down and gives me a sweet and soft kiss before backing away from me.

"Goodnight... Come wake me up in the morning," he tells me and I nod.

"Stay... For a little bit..." I offer and he freezes and sighs.

"You know that would be a horrible idea for a lot of reasons." He looks over his shoulder at me. I know all the reasons he thinks are horrible are the exact reasons that they would be great in my own mind.

"I think you've got a lot of tension that needs relieving..." I

THE RULES OF YOU AND ME.

change the timbre of my voice and watch even more tension and tightness seep into his already taut muscles. Perfect.

"There's three reasons right upstairs as to why we shouldn't," he tells me.

"And there's always at least two reasons as to why we shouldn't... But you weren't saying that the other day when you slept over without either of them knowing," I explain and he sighs.

"Brianne..." He raises his eyebrows at me, turning to look at me fully.

"Parker..." I kick my shoes off and take my jacket from my body as well.

"I'm... I'm going to my room," he tells me with his jaw clenching so hard after that I'm afraid it might break.

I watch him reluctantly turn and close my door. I stand up, walking forward, about to close that distance, and meet him in his own room but I stop myself in front of my closed bedroom door. He's partially right. It would be reckless for us to do anything tonight. His coming in here in the first place to kiss me was already a risk but...

The past two weeks since we crossed that line together it's been filled with... with exploration and passion and... And honestly, Parker hasn't given me or my poor vagina a break. Not that I'm complaining because he's a fucking champ in bed just like he is on the field but it's like something was unleashed the second we let each other win two weeks ago.

I've always enjoyed the act of sex. I've always tried to have fun and explore slightly depending on who I'm with. But comfortability is a huge part of that and I've never felt as comfortable with any of my past sexual partners as I do now with Parker. It's... It's easy to ask from him because I know he's more than willing to participate in anything and everything. And he's very much a giver in a sexual sense. He enjoys that

447

more than anything from the way he talks about it and caters to me. I've never had a sexual partner more... Honestly perfect than Parker. I bring my hand back from the door and decide maybe I should just rest tonight and- The door handle turns and opens.

Parker closes the door with his foot and kisses me with his hands threaded in my hair, tugging and pulling at the root in such a way that I might turn into a puddle in his massive fucking hands. It's a mix of panting and heavy breathing until my knees hit the bed and I slip down, my butt hitting my mattress. He follows, catching himself with his hands on each side of my body.

"You said—"

"I know what I said but I want you in the worst fucking way," he mumbles and kisses me again, sending electric shocks all the way through my body.

I wouldn't be surprised if lighting and stars were shooting out of me just from the way his body and lips feel against mine. I never falter when it comes to kissing him. My lips have a memory of their own and they've taken extra caution in remembering every perfect curve of Parker Thompson. The way he moves, the way he gasps, the way he bites and nips at me. The way he speaks against me when he's asking or begging or pleading. I could never forget it no matter how hard I tried.

"You know I can't have you the way I want you," he whispers, bringing his hands from the bed to my hips.

His thumbs press into my hips and I fight the urge to whimper from the pressure.

"Then what way will you have me?" I ask him.

"In a way that's going to make this weekend absolute torture until we can go back to my apartment..." he admits and my cheeks blaze.

I open my eyes and he tugs me from the bed and unbuttons

THE RULES OF YOU AND ME.

my jeans. He tugs them, not giving me a chance to even breathe before he's crouched down, taking them all the way off of me. He nudges me back to the bed and makes his way on it with me. He kisses me again and he groans himself at the feeling of my lips. Just his kiss is building pressure in my stomach and lower abdomen. I'm squirming under him, half his body weight leaned over me.

"Tell me," I urge.

"I want to touch you. I want to feel you," he tells me and I let out a rasped breath against his lips.

"Please," I mumble and he kisses me again, brushing his hand down my stomach and over my underwear.

I know he feels the dampness that built just from my own traitorous thoughts. I'd been wanting him but knew the likelihood was slim.

"Shhhhh," he tells me, his lips skimming mine, his finger brushing over my clit through the cotton of my underwear.

I fight every urge I have and he pushes my underwear to the side, letting his fingers explore me, touch me, and feel me until brings them to the most sensitive bundle. I let out the breath I was holding and he watches me. He always watches me, he treasures me with his eyes and I don't hesitate to recognize that. He moves his hand slowly and the second he plunges his fingers inside of me he covers my gasp with his kiss and I thank him for that. His fingers are dangerous and absolutely devastating to my mental and physical health.

He curls them and I can't help the physical reaction, I know he felt the way my body moved to his perfect movements. He moves, gaining leverage over my body. He uses his other hand and brings it down to me, moving his fingers in torturous circles over my most sensitive spot. I pant, fighting to breathe at the building feeling in my stomach. It's easy to feel with him. To let my body react in a way I've never known with anyone else.

"Come on... I feel you, let it go," he tells me, coaxing me to the edge.

I feel the pressure build inside to an all-time high and I hold in my moan, whimpering at the feeling. He takes the feeling as his signal, the contracting pleasure he can feel wrapped around his fingers.

"Watch me... See what I do to make you cum," he tells me and I open my eyes listening to him.

I watch his hands, feeling insanely inappropriate as I do but feeling the heat spread all over my body as I see what he's doing to me. He turns his palm up to the sky, curling his fingers and moving them faster. It's hard to not fall into oblivion at this point. It's hard not to snap my eyes shut and feel the crushing orgasm that only his hand is bringing me but I somehow manage to watch, and he manages to ring every ounce of pleasure out of me while I do. I am breathless by the time he retracts his fingers from me. He pulls himself forward to me and I reach for him but he stops my hand, and kisses my fingers.

"The second you put a hand on me there's no chance I'm going to leave this room tonight, Sunshine," he admits and I look at him with fire in my eyes.

"Maybe that sounds perfect," I tell him.

"I'd tell you that you might have hit your head or gone crazy because that's not happening," he tells me and I roll my eyes.

"You're such a good boy, aren't you?" I ask him and his eyes darken.

"So good that I'm going to think about you cumming on my fingers when I fix this issue..." He takes the hand he stopped and moves it down to his groin.

I palm the large erection and I know he sees the surprise on my features.

"And I want you to take care of yourself again tonight when

THE RULES OF YOU AND ME.

you get restless from that thought... That I'm across the hall wishing I was inside of you."

He leans forward and kisses me, then he's gone. I curl my knees to my chest and feel guilty. Not for Parker but for what we're doing. I feel guilty every single time. There's purpose in our passion. We aren't doing what we do without reason. The reason is that we can't keep our hands or eyes off of each other. I refuse to admit what that could mean. I refuse to say the word that I'm thinking in my mind when it comes to the man across the hall. Not until my brother knows. Not until he can understand that it's not fickle it's... It's love. I love Parker. So fucking much. I'm scared of that. Because that's not a word that I use loosely. It's not a word I throw around to anyone. I can name every person I've ever told that I love them. Parker isn't on that list because I haven't told him. Because I'm terrified to do so which solidifies my feelings even more in my head. But right now all we are is a secret. Not a love story. Nothing more than whispers and closed doors. Nothing more than that until we can come out with it. With all of this.

CHAPTER 37
I CAN'T LET YOU GO BY LEVI RANSOM

Parker Thompson:

I will never celebrate Thanksgiving with someone else's family unless I'm going as a boyfriend or husband. This past weekend was exhausting. Terrifying in so many ways, but more importantly, it was infuriating. Being with someone in secret isn't something I would wish upon anyone. I've never been public as it is. I don't want to scream and shout that I'm dating Brianne. It's the subtle things. Like touching her hand when we're standing next to each other, or kissing her temple when she makes me laugh. Hugging her even. To everyone surrounding us, we're not close, just acquainted. Little does everyone know, Brianne and I are far past acquainted.

I adore that woman.

I took my time decompressing the Monday we got back. I didn't go to classes. I didn't talk to my roommates. I didn't even want my phone to be on. That night I got a call from Bellamy with good news. The best fucking news anyone who's going into football professionally can hear. He's nominated for the Heisman award. Which is a no-brainer for Bellamy. He's the number 1 ranked player in the nation right now. He's breaking records every game. Bellamy Archer is a force on the field and that's always something I've known since I met him. He takes football seriously in a way that I do. In a way, I don't see most guys my age doing. Like Lawson, he's decided pretty recently he didn't want to stay in the sport after this season with the exception of coaching. He wants to teach. I was shocked, but then again I don't know him well.

Tonight Coach Corbin and the entire coaching staff are throwing a giant watch party on campus. The only person that was allowed to go with him to the ceremony was the head coach. So Coach Corbin and Bellamy are there right now most likely. I'm getting ready. Normally when the person from your school wins they show a shot of the team celebrating our teammate's win. Bellamy is such a good guy, especially to our teammates that it will be fairly easy to celebrate him if he wins tonight. Brianne is going as well as most of the cheerleaders. Kamryn is definitely going to be there considering she's practically part of the team being the head of the students that are working with sports medicine on the field this year.

I hope... More than anything I hope and pray that I'm where Bellamy is next year. It's not usual for anyone but the quarterback to win the award. But with my stats and ranking across the US, especially after the past two games we've had... I'm a potential candidate. Three others before me have won the Heisman in my position on the field. I want to be the fourth. I dream of it and I always have.

I pull my suit jacket over my white button-down and adjust it. The button down is loosely unbuttoned at the top which makes me feel less formal and that's just what I want right now. We're all supposed to look extra nice, this party was thrown together, but they had a feeling it would happen so the football staff prepared. We were all told formal. My bedroom door

454

THE RULES OF YOU AND ME.

opens and I look from the mirror to see the most gorgeous girl in the entire world walk in. My hands freeze on my suit jacket. She's in a light pink silk dress that falls off of her shoulders but is tight on her arms and her chest. The dress reaches the tops of her thighs and she's in heels, her body stellar, her makeup incredible, her hair flowing down her back.

"Hi."

She places her hands atop one another on my shoulder and she leans forward on her tiptoes despite the heels and kisses my cheek. I connect my eyes to the mirror to watch her do it. Her hair is in curled ribbons that reach the middle of her back and as much as I love seeing her hair up in that bun even though she hates it or her cheer ponytail... When she wears her hair down like this I'm a goner. I'm done for. And this color on her is one I'll never forget. If anyone else wore it I feel like it would be an insult to it. It was made for her.

"I..."

I wanted to say it. The forbidden words. Words that shouldn't be forbidden but feel like a betrayal if I were to say them before we're public. I love her. So damn much and when I see her looking this way. When I see her looking most ways, my first instinct is to tell her that I love her which is terrifying. Especially because I've never uttered the words to anyone. Ever. I never grew up with anyone to say it to. I never had a moment of peace to feel something so soft and subtle like love. Because it feels like that with her. Love feels like comfort and warmth. It feels rewarding in a way I didn't know was possible. The only downside is the fear I have that comes with it.

"You like it?" she asks me and turns, thinking I'm lost for words. I'm not lost for words. I know the exact ones I wish I had the courage to say.

"I really really do... Come here." I turn to her and put my hand on her lower back, pulling her flush against me.

She kisses me in the softest manner and I instantly itch for more of her. I put my mind in check telling myself to not get carried away at the thought of her. If I did we wouldn't make it tonight.

"You're breathtaking..." I tell her and she blushes more than she already is. Her blush favorite damn thing about her. I look at the speckles of freckles on her face and smile.

"Can I be your chauffeur?" Xander bursts into the room and my smile instantly disappears as I loosen my grip on her. "Bad timing?"

"Always bad timing when you're involved. No, you can't drive us. Go away," I bark.

"You're so fucking grumpy. Love me, please," Xander begs.

"No. Go away." I reach for my phone on the bed and Bri sighs.

"I love you, Xander," she tells him and my chest tightens.

She can say it so easily. I know that love is different depending on the person. I know the love she claims she has for Xander wouldn't be the same love she has for Bellamy or... Or hopefully me. I hope she loves me. But it feels unfathomable that someone could love me the same way I feel like I love her. It's hard for me to describe it or explain it. Even to myself. But I do know that I've never felt so exponentially safe around anyone as I do when I'm with her. And feeling safe. Like I could sleep for years and nothing could get me. Like I'm protected. Like nothing can harm me when she's holding me... I think that's... That's more than I can say for anything else in my life. That feeling claws up my throat. The threat of tears hits me for some damn reason.

"Your girl loves me," he teases.

"Fuck off," I mumble, keeping my voice low.

"You only want to take us so you can maybe see Leah, don't you?" she asks Xander, thankfully distracting him from me.

THE RULES OF YOU AND ME.

"Maybe," He tells us.

"Call her like a normal person. Or give it up, she doesn't like you," I tell him, grabbing my keys from my desk.

"Let's go, Sunshine. Come on." I tap her butt softly, and she and Xander shuffle out of my room in front of me.

"She unblocked me, but she told me to now use her number, either way, that's progress" he tells me.

"It doesn't count as progress if she did it to you to get you to shut up..." I tell him and he glares at me.

"Semantics. Anyway, have fun tonight! Don't kiss or make sex eyes. You guys are really bad with the whole sex eyes thing. Seriously, someone is going to notice." Xander follows us to the door.

"For the last time tonight. Xander, fuck off," I tell him and salute him with my middle finger as we pass through the door.

"That's not going to be the last time tonight! I love you, Pookie!" Xander calls after me and I roll my eyes.

Brianne starts walking down the stairs and I want to lift her up. She doesn't deserve to have to walk when she looks like that. Especially not down the shitty stairs at my shitty apartment. I fight the urge, knowing she'll call me barbaric or something of the sort. We made it out and she begged me to let her drive tonight. It's easier to pass off when she drives us places. Most people don't notice but if they do I'll say she offered since my car is a piece of shit. It's not really. But it is far older than hers is. So it equals out as a good excuse. She walks to the driver's side and I follow her, turning her around, pressing her back to the white Jeep.

"What are you doing?" she asks.

"Kiss me now before you can't..." I tell her and she looks at me. "Please." I tack on and she nods.

I close the space and the lush feeling of her sends my brain into overdrive. Kissing her is like sharing energy. Like lighting and fire pouring from her and into me. I'm addicted to the feeling. Now more than ever. She breaks our lips and then kisses me a few more times softly. And even if she's not kissing me, I don't want to let go of her hips, this material she's covered in is soft and buttery. I know just how good it's going to look in a pile on my floor tonight too. I kiss her, one last time and she laughs. I escape and move to my side, climbing into her Jeep, listening as she plays Taylor Swift. From the sounds of it, the first album. I've learned the difference in the past few months of being around her. I'd never listened to Taylor Swift before meeting Brianne Archer, but now I know more than I had ever asked for.

I'm happy to know everything about the pop star if it makes my girl happy though.

When we arrive at the banquet hall I get out of the car before it stops moving so I can make it to the other side before Brianne is fully parked. She gets unreasonably mad at me when I do this because it's unnecessarily dangerous for something so subtle. But I like the subtle things. They feel the most important to me. So I open her door and she glares at me. I don't help her out of the car knowing that we're not allowed to touch considering there are football players and cheerleaders alike swarming the building. Though some of the cheer team knows about Brianne and me, they were sworn to secrecy apparently. None of them had an issue with that, but according to her, they urged her to tell her brother. She takes my hand and squeezes it before letting go and walking ahead of me, the heels of hers clicking on the sidewalk. I watch her shiver and could yell at her for not wearing a jacket.

"Before you say anything, the jacket would have—"

"Ruined your outfit?" I ask her, already knowing her answer.

I could say the same thing to her. That she's going to get herself sick over something as silly and non-important as that.

THE RULES OF YOU AND ME.

She would argue that looking your best makes you feel your best. I like knowing her like that. Like she's a part of me in a way... I like feeling like there are no surprises but still finding them and being all the more happy to learn something new about her.

"You're stubborn," I mumble behind her as we near other people at the front of the building.

"And you're no better than I am."

She looks over her shoulder with a grin and I smirk to myself as I follow her. Her legs... Her skin, her fucking hair. I want to thread my hands through it. To wrap it around my wrist and.... I stop the thought. I need to be tame. And it's so damn hard with her. We walk in and she's swept away. The life of the party as always, even if she's faking it. But right now she's not. I can see her smile and I know it's real. Like gold and sunshine. I smile at the image of her and am nudged.

"Who are you smiling at?" Lawson asks me and I shrug.

"I wasn't smiling," I tell him.

"Yes, you were," he urges and I shake my head.

"Was not," I fight back.

"Were fucking too! Is your secret girlfriend here? Parker, is she a cheerleader... oh my god is..."

He stops, looking across the way. Lawson freezes, his eyes hitting the group I was looking at. I clench my jaw, liquid-hot panic seeping through my entire body.

"Don't," I tell him.

"I'm not going to because that would insinuate that you're secret fucking girlfriend is the only available option over there. Which is Bellamy's fucking sister..." He turns to me. I've seen Lawson angry before and the last thing I want is that anger directed toward me.

"Lawson, don't put yourself where you don't belong. Don't

459

make a fucking issue out of something that's going to be resolved without your help," I tell him.

Kamryn and Sienna approach, tension far too high for anyone not to notice. Then to my fucking dismay... Brianne approaches too as she hangs off of her best friend who to them is her boyfriend. I stare at Lawson, waiting for him to make a move and he clenches his jaw.

"What's going on?" Brianne asks, her eyes looking panicked as she looks back and forth.

"I don't know, why don't you tell me?" He looks at her then back to me and her face turns tomato red.

"I don't know... I mean I have no idea what you're—"

"Don't bullshit me, Bri." He snaps and I step directly in front of her.

"Don't be a dick to her, Lawson. Back up." Kamryn puts her hand on his chest and Sienna stands by her best friend, not her boyfriend.

"Why don't you seem at all surprised by this? She's with your boyfriend's best friend and—"

"Actually, no one has confirmed anything," I clarify.

"I don't need your confirmation you sick—"

"Wow! You need to calm down. Now, Lawson." Sienna steps in now and she shakes her head.

"What exactly makes it sick? What makes it wrong?" Kamryn defends and this was the last thing I expected.

"The fact that she's like our little sister? That's reason enough. She's a kid," he tells us.

"Exactly. Our. Mine, yours, Sienna, and Bellamy's little sister. Parker didn't come into this until far after all of us. His eyes don't see her the way you might. You watched her grow up, it's different. And she's not a kid. She's an adult. Just like him," Kamryn defends.

THE RULES OF YOU AND ME.

"Once again, why are you defending this? Did you know?" he asks and she scoffs.

"Unfortunately, most people with eyes could pick up on the fact that there was something going on. It took you long enough and has taken Bell even longer. I stayed out of it because it's not my business and it's definitely not yours," Kamryn tells him.

"And what about you? You're fine with your girlfriend—"

"He's not my boyfriend. Never has been," Bri tells Lawson, letting go of Dakota.

"What do you mean?" Lawson shakes his head.

"I'm not into Brianne like that. She's my best friend but it seemed like an easy way for her to... For her to be happy," he admits and smiles at her.

"Bellamy is going to—"

"Nothing. He's not going to hear about this because no one has said anything," Kamryn tells Lawson with that scary voice she gets.

"That's not fair to him. He deserves to know," Lawson defends and Brianne shrinks minute by minute. I shake my head.

"No one deserves anything from her actually. It's not his relationship. It's hers. She doesn't owe him a single thing. Every part of her she has given to her brother and her friends and even me has been by her own sheer will and kindness. We plan to tell him. We wanted to wait until... Until after the holidays so Bri could enjoy them with her brother and her family. We have a plan," I defend her, still partially standing in front of her.

"This is going to come between him and all of us now that we know. Did you think about any of that before—"

"Stop talking to her like she's a child. You aren't her dad. You're not even her brother," I tell Lawson and he scoffs.

"I'm supposed to protect her. And that's exactly what I'm doing, you're preying on—"

461

"You're overstepping. On a level that's going to get one of us kicked off of the team if you don't shut your mouth, Lawson," I inform him and he clenches his jaw.

"You are overstepping. Acting like Brianne didn't choose this. Or acting like she doesn't have a right to and that's unfair. And If they say they're going to tell Bellamy they deserve that chance. If you don't tell him by the new year then Lawson will. Does that sound fair?" Sienna asks and I clench my jaw.

"That's fair because we're going to tell him. And it's not about us tonight it's all about him. So none of this needs to be discussed further. And Lawson. I love you, just like a brother but Parker is right. You're not my brother. And you don't have any right to make me feel like I don't deserve to make my own choices. Everything with Parker has been my choice and you can't take that away. It's out of character for you to ever even try," she tells him and I watch his features soften.

"I'm sorry," he apologizes. "I am sorry, I just... Don't know how to look at you like anything but my baby sister," he admits.

"Try harder," she tells him and presses a smile to her lips.

She turns away from all of us and the tension slowly seeps out of me as Lawson turns away, shaking his head with Sienna in tow. I want to go after her, but I watch as Dakota takes care of her, ushering her away from everyone as well. If anyone beside me has got her, I know it's him.

"When did it start?" Kamryn asks me and I tense once more, forgetting she was even there.

I look over at her. She's in all black, a color I normally see her in. Her hair is sleek black as well and all of her is dark. She's tiny beside me, shorter than Brianne even when she wears heels. I shake my head at the question she asks and look away from her.

"Do you really want to know the details considering you're already incriminating yourself by walking into that conversation we just had," I tell her.

THE RULES OF YOU AND ME.

"Parker... You said you were going to tell him. I'm trusting that you will and you were right. If anything you were right, Brianne belongs to herself. She owes no one any answers or explanations to anything. I love Bellamy. God do I love that man, but he's protective over his sister to a fault. Even when he doesn't need to be. If you say you're going to tell him, I believe you. If you don't then we all know what's going to happen. Me understanding the relationship that's happening here is the easiest way for me to be a buffer if Bell flips his shit over this," she tells me.

"He's going to freak the fuck out," I tell her.

"He's going to be fine." She shrugs.

"I have more doubts than you could probably understand," I tell her.

"Do you love her?" she asks me and I clench my jaw.

"I'm not answering that question," I mumble.

"You don't answer any of them. Sienna told me she caught you guys in the bathroom at Griffin's going away party. Was that before or after you guys started talking?" she asks.

"Way before there were ever any intentions of even speaking to each other. Honestly Kam, things just... aligned. Yeah, of course, I thought she was gorgeous. Of course, I had eyes on her but...It's like we were pushed together in a weird way. And I'm not taking that for granted. But Brianne is right. Tonight isn't about me or her. It's about Bellamy and the fact that he's going to win his first award in his professional career," I tell her and she smiles.

"You're right. She's right... Maybe you should go check on her." She nudges my shoulder and starts to walk away. "Everything is going to be okay, Parks. I promise you." She looks over her shoulder.

"I'll hold you to that," I mumble and head off, looking for Brianne and Dakota.

I need to play this off as cool because it really is. We planned to tell Bellamy after the holidays. No this wasn't in the plan, but that doesn't mean anything. We're fine. I turn a hall, looking for the bathroom. As I head to them I turn my head down another hallway and see both of them standing there together. Dakota has his hands on her shoulders and she's crying. I curse under my breath and head her way.

"If you're going to upset her more, go away." Dakota steps forward.

"Since when have I ever been one to make her upset? Move," I tell him and she snaps.

"Hey! You two stop fighting over me, this isn't even the first time." Brianne glares between the two of us and then leans back against the wall.

"Look, you upset her more," Dakota chimes and I clench my fists trying not to react.

"I am so sorry I upset her more, I will fix it if you walk away and let me. Please." I keep my tone cool and he rolls his eyes.

"I made your caveman angry," he chimes.

"I have never wanted to punch you, but right now you're inciting that type of rage inside of me," I tell him.

He gives me a sarcastic smile and turns his attention back to Brianne. "I love you, find me after you finish with..." He sighs and walks away from us and I roll my eyes.

"Your best friend is the bane of my existence on occasion," I tell her and she chuckles but still has tears in her eyes.

"I'm sure he'd say the same about you." She smiles and I take her face in my hands and shake my head.

"No more crying. Everything is okay. Kamryn is like your own personal guard dog," I joke.

"This is serious. And unfortunately so infuriating. I hate being called a kid and being pictured as some baby, or incapable or silly and frivolous and..." She shakes her head.

THE RULES OF YOU AND ME.

"Don't do that. Say what you really mean," I tell her, knowing her habit of rambling on without getting her point across.

"I mean that if I was Bellamy's little brother. If I wasn't me then I wouldn't be seen as incapable of making my own choices. No matter how big or small they were. I wouldn't be told what to wear or act like or speak. I've never been able to put it into words until now, but that's what it feels like to me. Like my worth is dependent upon what parts I have which is so fucking shitty," she explains and I nod.

"I'm sorry... That he talked to you that way. You have an army of people sticking up for you, Sunshine," I tell her, tucking her hair behind her ears so I can hold her face and feel her skin.

"How did he even find out? What the hell just happened?" she asks and I nod slowly, trying to figure out how to tell her that Xander was right,

"So remember what Alexander said about the sex eyes thing?" I ask her and she smacks my shoulder.

"Parker! You were not staring at me with sex eyes! Were you?" She shouts and I shake my head.

"They were more like 'I love you' eyes..." I tell her, saying it before I can fully think it through. Before I'm even positive I should and she pauses, hesitating. I stand there with I'm sure red cheeks and a shocked look.

"I didn't mean to say that out loud," I admit.

"I..." She hesitates and looks... Scared and shocked just as I am.

"You don't have to say anything." I shake my head, for the first time feeling embarrassed for anything I feel for her.

I haven't felt this feeling since she ran out on me the first night we were together. The fear that something won't be reciprocated and I'm going to look stupid. But right now that fear is intense and poking through every part of me.

465

"But it's true?" she asks softly.

"That I'm in love with you?" I ask and she nods. "Yes, it's true. And that's how I was looking at you I would assume... But you were standing with Dakota and Leah, so when Lawson looked over he put two and two together and jumped to five, skipping four altogether," I explain and she leans forward, and brushes her lips against mine.

I don't understand why, what her reasoning or purpose is, but I kiss her. There doesn't have to be a reason to kiss her back, I'll do it no matter the situation.

"You love me?" she asks and I scoff.

"Why are you saying it like it's the biggest shock in the world? You say you love people all the time," I tell her.

"But you don't..." she admits and now my embarrassment skyrockets out of this building and high above the earth.

"I... I'm sorry? I don't know what I'm supposed to say here. You don't have to say anything in response, we can just leave it at that. This isn't how I planned to tell you or—"

"I love you... I'm sorry I should've just responded with that. God, I talk too much." She covers her face and I shake my head.

"Say that again?" I ask.

"I talk too much?" she asks and I sigh, taking her wrists and moving her hands away from her face.

"The former please..." I add.

"I love you," she responds and I smile, feeling the hottest fire I've ever felt burn inside of me.

It feels like something is tearing through me right now with how hard my heart is beating. This doesn't feel tender and soft like everything else has with her. Feelings wise with the exception of sex I have felt more than simple with her. But right now I feel more than simple. I feel like I'm on top of the damn world.

I don't know who kisses who. I don't know who moves to what person or when we pressed ourselves deeper into this

THE RULES OF YOU AND ME.

hallway but I'm lost in her. Kisses, nipping, breathing her in. I pull back and she puts her hands on my chest. I feel like I'm 16 kissing a girl at a school dance.

"I love you," I say again and she kisses me softly, quickly.

"I love you, Parker," she tells me. "And I'm mad at you because I told myself I wasn't going to say it until we told my brother."

"I told myself the same thing and that didn't work out," I tell her, my forehead pressed to hers.

"I can't stay at your place tonight," she says with regret in her tone. I break myself from her and kiss her cheek.

"Have a fun night okay? Celebrate. This is a big deal, don't worry about coming and being with me... Now or later. I'm just going to fold back so I can avoid Lawson okay?" I ask her and she nods.

"Meet me in my car when everything ends," she tells me.

She kisses my cheek and then she vacates the hallway. I wait, staggering my exit so it doesn't look suspicious. I look around the room for her first when I'm in the banquet area. I see her pink dress next to her friends and I'm satisfied with that, walking away from her and toward the refreshments in the room. Some water and some air and space would be wonderful but I can't afford the air and space with the broadcast of the awards happening live on a big screen right now. I take my drink and I become a wallflower once again, wishing I could stand with Brianne as the award show commences and they go through the nominees.

Bellamy Archer. They go through his stats from the past year. He is dressed in a midnight blue suit, and he looks beyond happy to be there. I watch as they make it through, and then everything goes quiet.

"This year's Heisman Trophy goes to... Bellamy Archer

from Seattle Pike University," he announces and our entire banquet hall is in shambles.

Screaming, cheering, chanting for their quarterback. I smirk to myself and almost tell myself to wipe the look from my face but I don't. As much as I would have denied being close with Bellamy this past summer or the beginning of the semester. We have grown closer. We are friends... and I'm insanely proud of him because this award is something hardly anyone gets the excitement to achieve. He's just that damn good. And that's something to be celebrated. I whistle out for him when the coaching staff videos us celebrating to send as a live update for the award ceremony.

It doesn't take a rocket scientist to know that Bellamy has his future set in the sport. Especially now that he's a Heisman winner. Things like this make the little issues so small. Because in the grand scheme of all of this, how big of a deal is it really that I'm dating his baby sister when he's an award-winning, successful football player? There are more important things in life than who's dating who and so on and so forth. Next year hopefully it will be me they're throwing this party for. Hopefully, it will be me who will get the chance to walk up there and accept that award. Bellamy thanks his family, namely his sister. Then he thanks Kamryn. That rush hits again. Will I get to thank Brianne? Will my future be similar to his? Or will I somehow manage to mess it all up within the next month by telling Bellamy everything...

CHAPTER 38
BEST FRIEND BY CONAN GRAY

Brianne Archer:

I burst through the doors of my apartment and Bellamy is already home. I charge the floor and jump onto him, attacking my brother. He's laughing I think. I can't hear, I can barely think. This is something my brother has dreamed of. I remember when I was young when we were all together as a family he would tell our parents he would win that award one day. He and my dad watched the award ceremony every year. He really cared about it. Even without it, Bellamy is going to be far more successful than most college football players ever will, but it's not about the success of it. It's about the fact that he measures himself with this award. This is something he's thought about for longer than imaginable.

"You fucking did it! I'm so proud of you." I squeeze him, feet off of the ground, my body embraced by him.

"It doesn't feel real, B..." His words aren't stable in the slightest.

"It's real! It's real and you're a Heisman winner and Mom

and Dad would be so proud of you," I tell him and then break off. "Pop the fucking champagne oh my god!"

I shake his shoulders and he looks past me. I turn and see the rest of the crew walking in, joining Dakota. My heart sinks at the thought... What they know. Parker walks in with them too, having decided to ride with Kam instead of me. I'm sure that went well... I don't miss the harsh look Lawson gives Parker as he passes by.

"Congratulations you fucking legend." Lawson steals him away before Kamryn can, bringing him into a bear hug.

"Give me my boyfriend." Kamryn rips Lawson away as if he's not already a foot taller than her.

"Your girlfriend just manhandled me," Lawson complains.

"You deserved it," Kamryn tells him, and Lawson moves to his own girlfriend.

"You guys look amazing..." Bellamy looks around, hugging Kamryn back.

I feel a hand on my back and I turn over my shoulder to see Dakota by my side. I don't know why I had to check who it was. Of course, it's not Parker... my chest is tight as my eyes meet Lawson's, judgment on his face toward me and Dakota. This next month is going to be hell on earth.

"What do you want to do to celebrate?" Parker's voice dances through the room and Bellamy shakes his head.

"I'd prefer to save the celebration for tomorrow... I'm tired," he admits and I yank Dakota up the stairs, unhappy that I can't go with Parker tonight.

We said what we did and can't talk about it or really decipher that. I know we will. Probably at our away game on Sunday. But... That doesn't mean it doesn't feel wrong not even saying goodbye to him.

"Bye!" I shout.

THE RULES OF YOU AND ME.

I haven't debriefed with Dakota in over a week, both of us having been wrapped up in all things hockey and football... I've seen him in passing two times now when I was heading into Parker's apartment and he was leaving. But I still have no details on that matter and I'll be getting them tonight.

"Nice to see you, Dakota!" Bellamy calls out.

"Congrats!" he shouts to my brother and then we're in my bedroom and the door is slammed.

"If Lawson continues to look at you and Parker or even me for that matter with those looks I'm going to get in a fight with a football player," he mumbles, pulling his suit jacket off.

"Lawson is annoying and not going to do anything. Especially not with you or Parker," I tell him, knowing damn well that if Kamryn or Sienna have anything to do with it, Lawson will stay in his place.

"And if he doesn't? He still seems grossed out by the fact that you're with Parker. That's annoying," he tells me as if I don't know that.

"Yeah, I know that. It's the farthest thing from okay, but he'll come around to the idea. I'm not worried about any of them knowing. Me and Parker are going to tell Bellamy and everything is going to be fine," I tell him.

"But—"

"Parker told me he loved me tonight." I cut him off and he is too stunned to speak. His mouth is hanging open, his last words disappearing from his lips, his eyes trained on me.

"He did not," he mumbles and I nod.

"He didn't even mean to. It was... It was really sweet," I admit.

"And you? Do you love him? What the fuck baby?" He freaks out slightly and I laugh.

"I haven't seen you in a week! I swear it's like after Thanks-

471

giving things just ceased for a while and I haven't had a chance to—"

"Okay I get it, so you love him back? You told him? Before you even told your brother?" he asks and I sigh.

"I feel bad about that part," I admit.

"And what about what your therapist has to—"

"Dakota," I snap at him and he sighs.

"I'm just saying... Maybe you should try to talk to her. To sort your feelings out. That helped you a lot when we first met and you haven't seen her in—"

"I chose to stop going to therapy. Bellamy doesn't need it. I should move on from everything. I'm doing that. I can sort through my own feelings I can... I'm doing fine. Am I not?" I ask him.

"Baby... you're fine, sure, but you should be better than fine. You know that," he tells me and I shrug.

"This conversation isn't about me and therapy. It's about me and Parker," I tell him, pulling the zipper of my dress down.

"And as much as I encouraged you, I don't think this is a good thing right now. I think you and Bellamy are fixing your relationship and maybe he needs to know before anything else progresses between you and Parker," he tells me and I scoff.

"Dakota, who's side are you on?" I ask.

"Yours, always. That's why I'm telling you what you need to hear and not what you want to hear. I'm your best friend, not your pet," he fights back and I take a deep breath.

"Okay, step back. Calm down. We don't need to get into a fight about this, we never fight. I'm going to tell Bellamy. That's already decided. And I will think about therapy. I just... I think I'm happy, and I'm trying to learn what that looks like for me," I admit.

"And I want you to figure that out too. I'm just trying to look out for you," he tells me.

THE RULES OF YOU AND ME.

"Thank you." I look at him in the eyes as I slip on a hoodie, letting it swallow me whole.

"Now, can we not fight and can you tell me what is going on with you and Nico Jang. Why have you been at his apartment as much as I've been at Parker's?" I ask him.

"Because... He's invited me and I've said yes." I watch him shrug and pull off his shirt and I notice the hickey's on his chest.

"And he's had you in his bed the entire time?" I ask.

"I think I like Nico... more than I'd like to admit," he tells me.

"Oh, shit. Dakota, are you going to settle down with Nico? Oh my god, are we going to date roommates?" I ask him.

"I don't know. I wanted to have fun my freshman year and I have but I also never planned to meet a guy, a hockey player at that, that felt like Nico does," he tells me.

"Nico is a sweetheart," I tell him, smiling at the thought.

"He is, but he's also very guarded when it comes to being with someone so I don't know. But I want to tell him I like him more than just... Just fun. Though I want whatever this is to be fun. I want it to be serious too I think," he admits and I clap.

"Yay! Dakota this is a good thing, why do you sound unsure." I shake his shoulders as he sits on the edge of my bed.

"Because he hasn't given me any insight into how he feels so I don't want to make myself look like an idiot," he admits.

"Well if he hurts your feelings or breaks your heart I'll put mouse traps in his bed when he's gone," I tell him.

"You might kill him," he laughs.

"The goal is to seriously maim and harm but never kill," I tell him. He curls himself under the covers in my bed.

"Does your boyfriend know I sleep in your bed with you when I'm here?" he asks me, turning over so he can look at me.

"It hasn't come up, but Parker trusts you," I admit.

"Sometimes it feels like he hates me," Dakota chuckles.

"I think you both care about me in different ways but to the same degree... So it's hard for you to see eye to eye sometimes. But he really does like you and appreciates you. I think he trusts you more than he trusts my own brother," I joke and Dakota sighs.

"Bellamy really has been putting in more effort to be a better brother though," he points out and I sigh.

"And I've been putting more effort into lying to him. AKA being a horrible sister," I finish his thought and he shakes his head.

"Falling in love with someone doesn't make you a bad sister. Especially since Bellamy never explicitly told you not to date his friends. But, keeping something as... special I guess, from him is what probably would hurt him, B," Dakota explains and I nod.

"I just hope that's the issue and not the fact that it's Parker. Lawson tonight immediately went to the big brother's defense and if Bellamy does that I don't know what I'll do," I admit.

"You'll get through it. And I'll be with you whenever you ask," he tells me and I smile.

"And I'll be with you for everything with Nico... Whatever that is," I tell him and then a thought pops into my head. An odd one, but a thought nonetheless.

"When I get married, will you be my Man of Honor?" I ask him and he laughs.

"Do I have to wear a dress?" he asks.

"No, just hold my flowers, my ring, and help me not have an entire mental breakdown," I tell him.

"And have the car ready if you want to escape?" he asks.

"Exactly." I smile and he does too.

"Go to bed. With your love confessions I'm sure you're not getting any rest if you see Parker tomorrow," he jokes and I shove him.

THE RULES OF YOU AND ME.

"Gross," I mumble, rolling over.

"I love you, Baby," he tells me.

"Like a brother," I reply.

"Like a sister," he finishes and I close my eyes, Dakota's warmth behind me as I drift.

CHAPTER 39

Brianne Archer:

December has felt like a flash. Like it should have lasted longer but didn't. Like my first year of college is disappearing before my eyes and nothing can slow it down and stop it. Looking back a lot has happened obviously. I've met friends and made a million memories. I have Parker. To say the least, that's a huge thing that's come from my freshman year.

Over the past three weeks, the boys managed to win every single game, bringing them to a zero-loss season so far. Not even in the bowl games. Not even with our strongest competitors. We are on top. I can say I expected it, but with the aspect of how many other teams stepped up this year, there was no denying they had a fight. After Christmas, they start training every single day. Working toward the championship they plan to make it to. There are two more qualifying games before we can be sure, but if I had to bet money on anything in the world it would be Seattle Pike University's football team.

My dance finals have all gone phenomenal. During the time I had spent training Parker, I used the dance space to train

477

myself in skills I had never learned before. I even paid my dance teacher for private lessons in hopes of gaining more than antici-pated. It's been the best form of therapy I could ask for being on that floor and leaving everything there. Anxiety dissipates when I dance like I do on this campus. It's more than I've ever been able to accomplish before now.

Dakota doesn't know that I've been lying to him... I told him I started my real therapy sessions with Madeline back so he would calm down about it and he has. But what he doesn't know won't hurt him. I haven't wanted to see my therapist for plenty of reasons but the main one being that I can handle myself now. If Bellamy can do it, so can I. Plus, I went long enough. I think I've learned everything I need to learn. I don't need it, but if it makes my best friend feel at ease then that's all that matters. He's happy right now with Nico. They work well together and since he told him how he feels they've been seeing a lot more of each other... Officially now. Which is incredible for Dakota and me because we get to hang out together while our boyfriends hang out with us.

Bellamy is up in northern Washington with Kamryn to meet her family for the first time. It's a big deal for Kamryn appar-ently. Bellamy told me he's the first guy that Kamryn has ever brought home and I told him to not fuck it up. He didn't appre-ciate that, but he and I both know there's nothing to worry about. Bellamy is like the picture-perfect guy to bring home to your parents. He's nice and kind and seemingly what every girl wants. I don't know what could go wrong. He won't come home until tomorrow. But Christmas is today. Right now. And it's the first Christmas I've spent without him. Without anyone actually.

I visited my Grandparents yesterday, but have spent all of today alone. Parker went home with Xander's family for this holiday. I thought that was sweet considering he never would

THE RULES OF YOU AND ME.

have agreed to that when I first met him. But the relationship and bond between them has bloomed into brotherhood instead of whatever it was before. It's sweet... Dakota is with his family. Lawson and Sienna are staying with his mom for the holiday, Sienna's mom is joining them from what I know. Which leaves me here all alone. But oddly enough I'm not devastated by that thought. I will celebrate with my grandparents and Bellamy tomorrow.

Then after that, I'm going to have to tell him about me and Parker. But for now, I get peace and quiet until that storm comes. I'm cooking right now. My own Christmas feast. My feast of my favorite foods and no one else's.

Chicken tenders. Mac and cheese, the white cheddar shell kind, cheese made from scratch because what else do I have to do? I have warm rolls in the oven and mashed potatoes too. Mashed potatoes are a comfort food that can never grow old in my head. I'm not going to eat all of this, but I'll have leftovers for Bellamy because I'm sure he's going to be hungry the second he gets home tomorrow. He's always freaking hungry. There's a knock on the door that startles me out of thought and I jump. I put my hand on my heart, catching my breath and then I look to the door with furrowed brows. Who? I put my wooden spoon down and go to the door opening it.

Parker. I stand there shocked as I look at him. He's in a deep green hoodie and black loose-fitting pants. His hair is pushed back and curled at his chin, his beard is perfectly tripped and his smile is electric. He's got a couple of presents in his hand and a duffle bag on his shoulder.

"Merry Christmas, Sunshine." He smiles and my jaw unhinges and my lips stay apart as I stare at him. He steps into the apartment and shuts the door as I back in, still staring at him. I put on my own Christmas sweater, hoping to feel slightly festive, but not expecting guests. I'm not wearing pants, only

479

underwear and white crew socks. My hair is drying as it hangs down around me and I'm sure my cheeks are flaming considering I'm not wearing makeup.

"Are you going to say something?" he asks, setting down his gifts for me and closing in to hug me.

"What are you doing here? You said you were with Xander and—"

"And I celebrated with his family this morning, thanked them so much for letting me be with them, and promptly left after lunch so I could make it here to be with you," he tells me, kissing the top of my head. "I would never leave you alone on Christmas," he tells me,

"I didn't need this. And we both agreed on no presents. I didn't get you anything... I mean I appreciate it but I wasn't expecting it. I mean obviously, I wasn't expecting it, duh. But I just. I never want you to drop your plans or make your friends feel like I'm—"

"Shhhhh." He brings his lips to mine and kisses away all the thoughts in my head.

Except for the thought of food, because my mac and cheese needs to be stirred. I press off of him with a groan and push past him.

"My dinner... Well, our dinner. Have you eaten? Are you hungry?" I ask and he meets me at the stove, bringing his arms around my waist, and lowering his head to rest on my shoulder.

"Chicken tenders and mac and cheese?" he laughs and I roll my eyes.

"When you're only cooking for yourself, it doesn't seem like a bad idea. It's not traditional obviously... But you know what, neither are we. Are you hungry or not?" I look over my shoulder at him and he smirks.

"For more than just food..." He kisses me and I smile.

THE RULES OF YOU AND ME.

"Later. Don't make me mess up my shells." I go back to looking at the stove and he backs off, sitting across the counter.

"How was Xander's family? Did you have a good time?" I ask.

"They took me skiing. I've never been skiing before," he tells me.

"And?" I ask.

"It was a lot of fun, I think you would like it too. It was weird though. Xander's family is... they're just not your normal family. It's like being with people who know everything about each other but there's no... No warmth. It's very different from being around yours. I mean they barely speak. They just sit on their phones. With the exception of Xander's sister who's really nice. He protects her in a way I've never seen from him. It was... It was just a different side of him. I almost felt bad leaving," he tells me.

"I can understand that. Aren't his parents super rich? Like lawyers or doctors or something?" I ask.

"His dad is a celebrity lawyer. Like public figures and shit and he's... Yeah, he's very disconnected. It was sad," he admits and I nod.

"I'm happy my parents were never like that. They were loaded. They worked really hard but never let that stop them from being good people or parents," I tell him.

"I'm sorry. I didn't mean to bring them up..." he admits and I shake my head.

"It's fine. My mom loved Christmas... That tree we have, all the ornaments are mostly hers. She had special ones from all the places she and my dad traveled. My grandparents kept the ones Bell and I made when we were young. But we kept the ones with stories," I tell him and I look over to the Christmas tree in the corner of our living room. Parker looks and laughs.

"Do you have a fireplace on the TV?" he asks and I smile.

481

"It felt festive, okay? I was trying to feel the Christmas spirit," I tell him.

I finish with dinner and both of us take ours into the living room and sit on the floor to enjoy it, presents still under the tree and the fake fire dancing on my TV. It feels warm. Cozy and comfortable. And now that Parker is here it feels more right than I expected.

"When does Bellamy come back?" he asks, not meeting my eyes.

"Tomorrow, but we leave for my house right when he gets back," I tell him.

"And how long will you be gone again?" he asks.

"Till we come back for New Year's Eve... Bellamy said it's important that we throw a huge New Year's Party for Kamryn," I tell him.

"Why?" he asks.

"Well because it's apparently her favorite holiday. I thought that was weird, but apparently, there's some interesting lore there. I don't know, I didn't really question him much. I just told him I'd help," I admit.

"We should have told him before Christmas." He looks at me now, setting his fork down and I sigh.

"I know but I didn't want there to be any reason for him to ruin the holiday," I admit.

"Well if we told him when I wanted to, he would have left for Kamryn's parents and had time to simmer down before today or tomorrow," Parker tells me.

"And then Kamryn hates me because I sent her boyfriend home with her in the worst mood ever," I tell him.

"He might not be mad." He shrugs and I scoff.

"Right... and if he is?" I ask.

"Then he better not say anything that might hurt your feelings because I'm going to hurt him. I'm tired of people dictating

THE RULES OF YOU AND ME.

you or me. Dictating our happiness individually or together. I love you, what's the issue there?" he asks me, focusing back down on our food.

"And I love you. But that doesn't mean he's just going to understand. He's going to be mad," I tell him.

"And he's going to be really mad when someone tells him before we have a chance," Parker informs me.

"I have Sienna and Kamryn on Lawson duty. Kamryn is going to let us tell him on our own time. I promise that's not an issue," I tell him.

"I don't want to talk about this anymore." He shakes his head and I nod.

"Good, neither do I. It's Christmas. Not Bellamy time." I tell him and he looks at me,

"I'm really glad I came back... this feels right," he admits and my cheeks heat.

I don't fight my smile, I let it through and nod my head.

"I'm really thankful that I don't have to be alone. I was completely at terms with it and honestly okay with the thought, but this is just better. I've never really been the kind of person who likes to be alone unless..." I trail off and he looks at me.

"Unless?" he starts. "Unless you're dancing. Right?" He asks, and looks away from me and back to his food.

"Unless I'm dancing, then I like being alone," I agree.

"I really wish you'd stop quieting yourself or not finishing your sentences around me. I really love when you get talking... You know that." His eyes share the smile his lips show.

I love that Parker smiles with his eyes when he's genuinely happy. His eyes are gorgeous as it is, but this way they're captivating.

"I know you do. It's just a habit," I admit.

"Break it," he urges.

"Cause it's that easy..." I joke and he smirks,

483

"Open my gifts, come on." He pushes his plate and mine away and I sigh, and tilt my head.

"We said no presents," I tell him.

"And you didn't think about the fact that I've never had a girlfriend... Or anyone for that matter that I've been able to buy gifts for. Christmas never really mattered when I grew up, so getting presents doesn't mean anything to me. Spending time with you is enough, but I was really excited to get you something..." he tells me. I press my lips together, trying not to sigh again.

"Now I feel even worse," I admit.

"Don't feel bad. Brianne, I didn't tell you I was getting you a gift because I made one and didn't plan to buy the other but when I saw it I couldn't help it. It's okay. Being able to do this for you is really what matters to me. It's enough," he encourages. I pout my lips.

"You're so sweet you make my freaking teeth hurt," I joke, grabbing the first box.

"You haven't even seen what's inside." He pulls his knees up, sitting with his arms loosely hugging his legs.

He looks at me with childlike excitement and I'm happy to see him so happy. I don't care what's inside the boxes. I put another small box out of the one I just opened and I pull the lid back revealing a locket. It seems vintage. I look at the intricate design of the gold jewelry, thankful that it's the same color as all my other necklaces and rings. He pays attention...

"Open it," he tells me softly.

I set the box down and do what he said, opening the tiny locket. There's a tiny note etched in Parker's boyish handwriting. I love you. I pout my lip and look at him.

"This is so sweet... Is there a story behind it? This locket?" I ask and he shrugs.

"I was with Xander and Andrew and there was an estate

THE RULES OF YOU AND ME.

sale that they said we should go to. I saw it and picked it up and the woman who was running the sale was this cute old lady. She said it was hers, that her husband had given it to her but replaced it with something apparently nicer years later... He passed away and she said that's what the estate sale was for... Anyway, I thought it was sweet. And I thought a locket felt like something I could see you wearing..." he explains and with each sentence, my heart warms.

"I also really liked the idea of being like that with you. Looking back on this years down the road hopefully. That you'll keep small gifts or I'll keep sweet things from you so we can tell people about it when we're her age. It's sentimental but... I just liked the idea," he admits and I nod.

"And the note?" I ask him and he shrugs.

"I didn't want to decide for you what was most important for the pictures. I thought you could choose who you wanted on each side. It should rest right over your heart. And I think your heart is big and full of a lot of people..." he admits.

"You're being extra sweet tonight," I tell him, my pointer finger drawing on the outside of the locket as I look at the messy handwriting inside.

"I'm feeling the power of Christmas," he jokes.

"There's no such thing," I fight back, closing the locket.

"Then it's because I just love you," he tells me and passes me the next box that's bigger.

"I love you," I tell him and lean forward, pushing on my knees.

He doesn't meet me in the middle, but he does let me lean into him to press my lips to his. I sit back, rip off the paper, and then rip the box open. Inside is a frame, and then a stack of something wrapped up in tissue paper. The frame is empty so I set it to the side for now. I look at him and he pulls out his phone and nods his head to the rest of the package. I see the first thing

485

in the stack and it's an old-school-style polaroid picture of us. I don't know how he transferred a picture of us to the Polaroid but it's adorable.

The picture is from the bonfire where we first met. We're not next to each other in the picture. We're sitting in the group, all of our friends. Leah, Dakota, and Val are surrounding me. Bellamy, Lawson, Kamryn, Sienna, Parker, and Griffin are all surrounding too. But there's marker circling me and him and pointing to a heart in the middle. I laugh at the small addition to the photo but my mind focuses on the Spotify code that has been stuck to the bottom of the Polaroid photo. He scans it to show me, and the song that pops up makes me instantly want to cry. Enchanted by Taylor Swift.

"Did you research music to pick this song out?" I ask him and he's blushing as he looks at me.

"Well, I've been doing better listening to your favorite artists... But I had the guys help me pick out all the songs," he tells me and I furrow my brows.

"All of the songs?" I ask.

I flip to the next thing in the stack and the picture is a selfie we took at the going away party for Griffin. It's just me, Kamryn, and Parker. I smile, forgetting we even took this picture. He scans the song for me. Overnight Sensation by BORNS. I put my hand on my chest and then look at him.

"Parker..." I don't flip the next picture.

"Just look at all of them, and listen to all the songs before you say anything. Do you know this song?" he asks and I shake my head. We listen to it and I want to kiss him the entire time I do. The sweetness of the song is overwhelming. I flip to the next picture and it's our first solo one. A picture from my birthday party at the cowboy bar. I'm holding my hat to my head and it looks like I'm laughing. Parker's hand is so low on my back it's practically on my ass. He's got an easy smile on his

THE RULES OF YOU AND ME.

lips and my chest warms at the memories from that night. He scans the code and the song Kinda Cowgirl by Stephen Day pops up.

I've never heard this one either but I instantly fall in love with Parker Thompson all over again the second I do.

The next picture is from our first date. It's us in his truck after our city date. The song is one of my favorites, Dive by Holly Humberstone.

I flip next and it's a picture we took in our kayaks. The instructor took it for us on our second date. I'm smiling harder than I think I've ever seen myself smile. I don't remember ever seeing this picture after that date. The song he picked is Treacherous (Taylor's Version) by Taylor Swift. I smirk at a second edition of my favorite artists in the world.

I see a picture next that Dakota had snuck of us. I love this picture. We're both in uniform, both of us smiling incredibly hard it almost looks like it could hurt us. It was right after Parker's first game back when he killed it like I've never seen before. The song for this picture is Waste The Night by 5 Seconds of Summer. I smile.

"Who picked this song?" I ask over the music.

"Nico. He has a crush on the guy in the band apparently? Luke or something." He shrugs and I smirk, flipping to the next picture.

I try my hardest not to cry. It's a mirror picture I took of us in my hotel room when we went to Vegas. We're both wearing slimy green face masks and Parker is trying to kiss my cheek in the photo. I love this picture more than words could explain. He plays the song Perfume by Del Water Gap and I smile at him. The insinuation as well as memories from the night and how hard Parker was trying to restrain himself makes me laugh out loud.

The last picture is from The Heisman trophy ceremony and

the song is Daydreaming by Harry Styles, my favorite song by him in general, which I know Parker knows.

The last picture in the stack is one from right before everyone left for Christmas. A few days ago when we were here alone, I set up my phone to take a picture of us in front of the Christmas tree. He's trying to kiss me once again and I'm smiling in a way I feel like I never see in most pictures. This one's my favorite out of all the ones we took that night. The song is Birds of A Feather by Billie Eilish. I cover my face after I set down the photos and Parker puts his hand on my knee.

"Do you not like them? I know the song thing is something you and your mom did but I think of you when I hear music... I just thought you would like it, most of the songs remind me of you but if you don't like it—"

I uncover my face and launch myself on him, kissing him harshly. His breath is gone, his surprise is so imminent it's overwhelming. His hesitation in the gift, making sure I liked it. His care for me constantly is something it's hard to wrap my head around. I feel like a kid around everyone. Like I'm small and less than important. But around Parker, I feel like I'm the entire universe. I don't know if this is something that will hold in my life. I don't know if this is something that will break or bend or...

He pulls me onto his lap, bringing his hand up my bare thigh, letting his fingers only linger under the hem of the oversized sweater I'm wearing. He breaks the kiss and presses his forehead to mine. I look at his eyes, even in the dim lighting the hazel glow they produce is stunning. He tucks my hair behind my ear and holds my face. He leans in one more time, stealing kisses with ease and haste, like he can't get enough and I realize now that my previous thoughts aren't acceptable ones. Of course, I don't know if this will break but I won't let it. I can't let it. The world around me would need to crumble before I willingly allowed Parker to slip through my fingers.

THE RULES OF YOU AND ME.

"What's your favorite Christmas movie, Parker?" I ask him and he shrugs.

"I've never seen any but the cartoon ones. Most of the kids I lived with liked those so that's what we watched. But I like the one with Rudolph and that elf. It was cute." He tells me. "What's your favorite?" he asks and I lean my head against his chest.

He leans back so I can lean further into him.

"That's hard. Christmas is my favorite holiday so I really love Christmas movies. I love The Santa Clause, they always made me laugh growing up, and the original Grinch movie too... But I think I'm the most fond of the Disney ones," I explain, images of Bellamy and me on Christmas flash through my head and I fight a smile, then I fight tears. I didn't realize how much I wish Bellamy was here... How much I wish... I stop myself.

"Which Disney ones? Was it some tradition or something when you were younger?" he asks and I pull myself up from the ground. I hold out both of my hands to him so he can get up too. We leave the present trash on the ground and I clean up our plates of food, still not answering his question, my mind thinking about Christmas growing up with all of my family.

"Bri?" he asks and I smile up at him.

"What?" I ask.

"Are you okay?" He approaches and I finish the dishes.

"Perfect... Do you want to watch a Christmas movie with me?" I ask, walking into my living room.

He follows and I sit on the couch, pulling my knees up. He finds his space pressed next to me, immediately pulling me in as we nestle into the cushions. I start to turn on a movie.

"I want to watch the Disney ones you were talking about," he tells me and I get that choked-up feeling.

I don't turn them on. I just set the remote down and sigh knowing I need to just talk instead of closing myself off. I am dealing with this, I don't need therapy. But I should still maybe just talk about it.

"It wasn't tradition. My parents were very lax people when they were home because every time they were gone on work trips they had to be specific and precise. On Christmas, we would open presents whenever we would wake up. You'd think I would have been the one to wake the house up, but it was always Bell. He never slept in, especially not on Christmas." I smile at the thought. Especially when I was older I never wanted to wake up on time.

"Sounds like Bellamy," Parker laughs and I feel the vibration of his chest.

"But we never talked about it before the day of Christmas. It was never an argument either. Because back then, when my parents were here, me and Bellamy would fight like cats and dogs. We fought about what color the sky was if it was the only thing to argue about. But on Christmas we never did. And we never discussed the movie but always ended up watching these. Mickey's Once and Twice Upon A Christmas. I preferred Twice Upon A Christmas, but he was indifferent. It was one of the only times my parents could have us in the same room without wanting to rip each other's heads off," I laugh.

"How the hell did you go from that to what you are now?" he asks.

"When you lose the most important people in your life there's nothing else you can do but cling to the people you relate to. We leaned on each other because we realized we're all each other has," I tell him, my mind wandering off to how it would have been for me if Bell and I hadn't gotten close after my parents passed.

"I'm sorry he's not here." Parker kisses the top of my head after he speaks and I shake my head.

"I knew it would come one day. People grow up, and life

THE RULES OF YOU AND ME.

becomes a big mess of planning, conflicts, and schedules. I'm not mad or upset about it because I really hope one day when we both have families we're going to potentially get to do that again, maybe they'll have their own movies they bond over. I don't know. But I do think one day the tradition will be reborn again," I explain.

I don't know if Bellamy and Kamryn want a big family with a lot of kids. I don't know if they're wanting dogs and a beach house. I don't know but I do know that they're going to do it together.

"We don't have to watch those, then. If they're reserved for—"

"I'd love to watch them tonight. More than anything actually," I tell him and tilt my head up to look at him.

He looks at me softly and I lean in, kissing the corner of his lip. I turn back to the TV and turn on the movie. I nestle into Parker, feeling the warmth of him and the season in general. My favorite time of year is made sweeter by him and fond memories of times I can't have again but can always relive in my mind.

"I love you, Brianne." His voice is deep and so soft. Just like his lips are when he kisses the top of my head.

His hand moves under my sweater to trace his finger over my spine, the movie playing now in front of us. I drift, my mind only partially focusing on the movie, but mostly on the feeling inside of my chest. I've never been so settled in life. So quiet and calm. I've never felt so right. I cling tighter to Parker at that thought.

CHAPTER 40

CAME TO THE PARTY FOR YOU (DEMO) BY LEXI JAYDE

Parker Thompson:

I push into the party, into the house I was at only a few days before with Brianne, cuddled on the couch that people are currently mauling each other on. I avoid that mess altogether, brushing past everyone dressed in sparkles, wearing insane accessories with the upcoming year marked on their glasses and headbands. There are noise makers going off already despite the fact that there's an hour until midnight strikes. Everyone is antsy I guess? I'm not sure. I've never been to a New Year's Eve party. Mostly because I was always told that it's a dangerous night to be out so I always stayed in.

Bellamy is throwing a giant party though, and a party at Bellamy's is an excuse to see Brianne so I'm here now, even if I am late. It wasn't my fault that I was late either. I was caught up with my stupid idiot roommates. All of them were holding up the entire process of leaving and making it here at a reasonable hour. Andrew had issues with his almost-girlfriend. Nico didn't know he was invited. Xander was constantly changing his outfit and his mind on whether he even wanted to come because he was apparently scared to see Leah. He wasn't even positive if she was coming. But as I'm walking into Brianne and Bellamy's apartment I see her right now, leaning against the wall, kissing someone. Great. I sigh and turn around.

"Dakota! Hey, where's B?" I ask her best friend who is wearing a sparkly mesh top that shows off far too much of him. It's very in character for Dak though.

"Wouldn't you like to know. Thanks for finally showing up big boy." Dakota pats my chest and I roll my eyes.

"Yeah, it wasn't by choice to be late, my roommates suck. Tell me where she is," I tell him.

"Why?" he asks, joking and poking fun as usual.

"Because I'd like to find her before I'm found by her brother or Lawson. She said she was telling him about us when she was at her grandparents and she's barely talked to me since she said she was going to tell him. I need to see her now," I urge and he nods his head behind me.

She's walking off of the balcony that is pouring in frigid air. Wearing something that she shouldn't wear in the cold like she just was. She's going to freeze I swear. I nod.

"Thanks. You look good, have fun."

I pull him in for a side hug and bound off toward Brianne, getting a full look at what she's wearing. I notice that it's not a dress, but a two-piece outfit. She's wearing all black, yes, but the sparkles that litter the strapless top and tiny skirt are a million different colors. The top pushes her up far more than normal, and the skirt takes mini to a new meaning. But she looks drop-dead gorgeous, her hair down again. I could actually thank a higher power for that... My fucking favorite.

I'm instantly pulled by Xander before I can make it to Brianne, before she even sees me. He grabs me by the front of my shirt and tugs me to the side of the living room. I shove him

THE RULES OF YOU AND ME.

off and press my hands over my chest, situating my clothes again.

"What the hell are you doing?" I ask him. He reaches for me again and I smack his hand away.

"Should I try and kiss Leah at midnight?" he asks and I roll my eyes.

"You're manhandling me in the middle of my girlfriend's house because you want to ask if you should kiss a girl who has no interest in you? Are you a fucking idiot?" I ask. "Actually don't answer that, it was rhetorical, I know the answer. Yes, you're fucking stupid. I need to talk to Brianne, right now actually." I start to walk away and he stops me.

"You're making it sound weird, it's not weird. She could totally be into me. She's warming up to me I promise," he argues.

"If warming up means she doesn't completely ice you out and insult you when she looks at you, then sure," I pick on him and he rolls his eyes.

"We hooked up in my car the other night," he spills and my jaw slightly hangs slack.

"You... I thought she hated you?" I mumble.

He nods his head behind us and my eyes follow his movement.

"What?" I ask. I see Leah there, no longer kissing the guy she was with when I first walked in.

"You see her? She's been looking over at me all night. Don't look at me, look at her, she's going to look over here." He nods his head and pays attention to me.

I watch her like he says to and I see it, just as he suggested. Leah turns over her shoulder and her eyes land on him, scouring him like he's her next damn meal. Then, she notices she's been caught by me. She stares ahead and I raise my eyebrows at her.

495

She just pretends I'm not there and that I saw nothing, turning back around.

"She actually did look at you... like she was actually interested, too. What did you do besides sleep with her? Hypnotize her?" I ask.

"I flirted with one of her friends in front of her," he tells me.

"And? That seems like the opposite of what you should do," I shake my head.

"Well, I told her friend I was going to flirt with her so Leah would talk to me. And the friend said it was a good idea. I wanted to kiss whoever that cheerleader was for being in on it." He nods and I narrow my eyes.

I feel like this was not going in his favor, that maybe it was a setup. But Xander is the kind of person who can't be told not to do something, he's got to learn on his own.

"Then go for it, buddy." I clap him on the shoulder and he starts to open his mouth but his eyes catch and he furrows his brows.

"Why is Brianne talking to Ashton Baxter?"

I look and see just that. Brianne talking to someone I've never seen in my entire life. But someone who seems to know her. Then the name clicks. Ashton, her ex-boyfriend who she had a history with. The most history out of all of her exes. Every part of me is rigid because I can't approach her. I can't say anything. I just get to stand here and pretend it's fine.

"That's her ex," I bite the words out and Xander's jaw unhinges slightly.

"Really? He's actually really nice. Considering you're who you are I would think Bri's type is the opposite of nice. Grumpy asshole seems more accurate," he jokes and I glare.

"They have a lot of history. She hasn't run into him the whole semester so why the hell does it have to be now when Bellamy is in the room?" I ask Xander.

THE RULES OF YOU AND ME.

"Maybe he's just catching up with her." Xander offers, but the second he does I watch Ashton's hand move right over to her hip, skimming and brushing the small space of exposed skin on her midriff. I flinch the second I see her struggle to get his hand off of her, and push him away slightly.

"Maybe not," Xander mutters.

"I want to kill him," I admit.

"Maybe not a good idea," he suggests.

Ashton leans forward, brushing his mouth against her cheek so he can whisper in her ear and once again, touches her. I flex my hand and lose my composure.

"Back off..." I step in, removing the guy who is just as tall as I am and just as big. I try to be calm and casual about it despite the fact that my hands are shaking.

"It's fine Parker, it's fine."

"No, I could see that it wasn't. You put his hands off of you and he put them back on."

"Who is this guy Bri? Why is he being a—"

"Don't finish that sentence, Ashton," she snaps.

"Did you fucking touch her?" I ask him.

"You don't know our history bro, seriously. It's fine." He seems drunk.

Now that I'm standing here, I know he probably means no harm. He probably doesn't get the cue that he needs to calm down. But that's not an excuse and it doesn't make me any less mad.

"I know plenty of the history and I need you to walk away from her now. Even if there is an ounce of history that doesn't give you permission to put your hands on her whenever you want, back off." I step up and Xander steps in.

"Hey, what's going on Parks?" Kamryn walks up too and I shake my head.

"Come on Kam..." Brianne takes her hand and I'm thankful both of them walk away when they do.

"Hey, Xander," Ashton nods to his teammate then looks between us and nods. "I see. You two are friends, aren't you? And you know Bri?" He asks both of us.

"You could say that," I nod.

"It's just best if you don't talk to Brianne Archer again," Xander nods.

"Oh, shit. Aren't you on the football team? I get it, she's your teammate's sister but I respect her, I promise. Swear." He holds his hands up and I clench my jaw wishing I could hit him just to get my annoyance and anger out.

"Ashton, you're going to get punched. Shut up. Stop being a fucking idiot or I'm going to rat you out for being here to Coach Elliot. He'll bench you and I won't feel bad. Go," Xander snaps and I watch Ashton walk away, annoyed by the intrusion.

I shake my head and sit on the couch, annoyed by the couple next to me making out. Annoyed and upset I can't do the same damn thing with my own girlfriend. I came here for her. I can admit that. Not Bellamy. Not my other friends. I spent far too long getting ready even though it really didn't matter.

I don't want to pass the time drinking. I want to be sober. For her. For us, so we can go back to my place. I clench my jaw, wondering why I even came in the first place. I've never been a fan of parties. I've never been a fan of any of this stuff. I guess I came thinking it would be our first outing as a couple, but it's not plausible especially since I haven't even had a single chance to talk to her about how her conversation with Bellamy went. My anger and annoyance is growing every second until I see Brianne walking back down the stairs with Kamryn by her side. I swoop in instantly.

"Can I steal my girlfriend for a second?" I ask Kamryn with alert eyes. Kamryn smirks and steps to the side.

THE RULES OF YOU AND ME.

"I'll distract him, you guys go," Kamryn tells me, and then she squeezes Brianne's arm.

"We can go on the balcony, no one is out there right now," she tells me and I do just that, walking onto the balcony alone, Brianne in tow.

"What were you and Kamryn upstairs talking about?" I ask her, a sinking feeling deep inside my chest after how this night has gone.

"I didn't get a chance to tell Bellamy," she blurts out and my lips part in disbelief. That sinking feeling really settles and sets in now.

"Please don't look at me like that..." she mumbles and I clench my jaw.

"I'm trying not to get mad right now," I admit.

I don't lose my temper a lot. Not ever actually because honestly, nothing has mattered enough for me to do that, but tonight everything is sitting at the top of my emotions. Like it's weighing on my chest trying to crush me.

"You left me to tell him all by myself, okay? I didn't want to do it in front of my grandparents and cause a huge fight or scene." She admits and I scoff.

"I didn't leave you to do anything. I've been trying to get you to be with me so we can tell him together for the past month and you won't let me... You're just fine with the secret. You're fine keeping me and this as something unknown and I'm not," I tell her and she sighs deeply.

"I don't want to keep it a secret, Parker. It's more complicated than that. I'd love nothing more than for everyone to know that I love you, but I am scared," she tells me and I nod.

"I know you're scared and I get that, but it's not an excuse anymore. He needs to know. I'm not doing this," I admit.

"What do you mean?" She furrows her brows.

"I'm not going to be your dirty secret anymore. Tonight this ends or we..." I stop myself, wondering where the sudden words come from.

I don't want that. I would rather it be a secret than not have Brianne in my life... I'm just so... Hurt. Hurt that it feels like I'm not enough. Not enough to tell her own brother about.

"Or we what?" She crosses her arms and shivers, her breath visible as she shakes.

"Come on, let's go inside you're freezing Bri." I put my hand on her shoulder and she shrugs me off.

"No. Or we what? This ends or we end? Is that what you were going to say?" she asks.

"Yes. It's what I am going to say. We tell him immediately or I'm done. This is important to me. It has been since the moment I knew I wanted to be with you which was far sooner than you. I'm fine being open with my feelings toward you Brianne. I don't want to feel like your best-kept secret because I want to feel important enough for everyone to know about. I don't feel that way to you right now. I don't feel important or more than a secret sometimes when I have to pretend in public and I can't see you when I want or call you when I want. This doesn't feel real." I admit.

"It is real. We are real, what I feel for you is real," she tells me and I nod.

"When I think about it, of course I know that. But it's about action, not words and empty promises. I can't sit here and force myself to be okay with this. I'm constantly telling you to choose yourself, but I'm not listening to my own advice. I waited until you were ready to date, I respect you, and I respect your boundaries, but I'm not respecting my own. I'm not doing this anymore," I clarify again, trying not to choke on my words.

They taste bitter in my mouth. I know how childish ultimatums are. They feel like acid in my lungs, but I have to do this. I know she won't back away from us... From loving me. Deep

THE RULES OF YOU AND ME.

down I know she won't do that to me or us and what we've built, but that doesn't mean I'm not terrified as I stare at her right now.

"Tonight is really important to Bellamy. I can't ruin his night or make his life harder with this right now." Her voice is just above a whisper.

"What about me? What about you? What about anyone beside Bellamy?" I ask her.

"This isn't about me or you, it's about—"

"Him. Yes, once again it's about him. But you're not understanding me. When is it ever going to be about you Brianne? What has to give for you to be able to see that you sacrifice everything good just to make him more important? It's not fair to you or anyone around you." I argue, finally letting the words off of my chest that I've held in for what feels like ever. She just stares at me.

"I don't have to sacrifice anything. I haven't yet. I've got you. I've got my friends... I..."

"You have me to what extent? Behind closed doors and through quiet phone calls just in case Lawson is near? That's not having me. Not the way... Not the way I deserve," I admit.

"You can't make me choose," she tells me.

"I never asked you to choose me over your brother." I clarify.

"Well, that's what it feels like." She crosses her arms over her chest and I scoff.

"Because you refuse to see the fact that if what you're saying is true, if you've never had to sacrifice anything then you wouldn't feel like telling him would be choosing between me and Bellamy," I tell her and she looks at me with tears in her eyes.

I don't want to say anything else. I hardly want to look at her because it hurts. Looking at her right now hurts, but I force myself to.

"We tell him tonight or I'm going home," I say it again.

501

"I can't do that to him... Not tonight," she whispers.

I want to argue with her. I want to keep up this conversation and try to get her to understand but I know there's no point. I know her love for her brother is blinding her from the reality of her situation. It is not my job to show her that, it's hers. That doesn't stop the choking feeling in my throat that's clawing its way up right now.

"I'm sorry Parker... I love you, I just—"

"You don't need to say anything else, Brianne, honestly right now I can't hear it, I just need to go home. I..." I take a deep breath. "I hope you can see what I see one day too," I mumble and walk away, leaving Brianne on the balcony, and heading for the front of the apartment, trying to leave.

"Parky!" Bellamy grabs me by the shoulders and I fake a smile and nod.

"I was actually just heading out, but thank you for inviting me and stuff," I mumble, trying to shove past him.

"Parks? What do you mean? What's up?" He asks, his voice laced with concern. There's nothing I can say to him about what's wrong because even in my anger I'm not going to disrespect Brianne's wishes like that.

"We can talk about it another time. Have a good night Archie," I mumble, brushing my hand over my jaw.

I shove past everyone and leave the party and the apartment altogether, wishing to be anywhere else. She didn't say it. She didn't say that she chose him, but she didn't have to. And I didn't want that. I didn't want her to make a choice between him and me. He's the most important person in her life and I get that. I wanted her to choose herself. And maybe my delivery was off, but none of that matters anymore considering the two of us are... I don't even know what we are.

CHAPTER 41

ILLICIT AFFAIRS BY TAYLOR SWIFT

Brianne Archer:

I walk into my apartment feeling like I was hit by a semi-truck. After Parker and I... Broke up, I guess... I don't want to call it that, but at the end of the day, that's what it was. A breakup.

I told Dak, tears definitely brimming my eyes at that point. He quickly rushed me out, and we proceeded to drink at his apartment in his room. I cried, then he made me laugh, then I felt better, but right now I feel worse. I feel alone, and sad, and sick to my damn stomach. I need to text Parker. To try and get him to talk to me in a different setting about all of this. Maybe I'll tell Bellamy today and then I'll go talk to Parker after and explain everything and hope he can understand... I look up after I close the door behind me and freeze.

"Bellamy? What's wrong?" I ask him, setting my bag down before walking over to him and Kamryn. Bellamy looks up and he looks pissed.

I never see Bellamy angry, not a lot until this year it feels like. Most of it has been caused by me...

"What's this?" he asks, passing me a somewhat crumpled paper.

I take it from him and see my rule list. My heart sinks and drops all the way down. I stare at it, trying to think about what I could possibly say or do. Kamryn has no idea what happened between Parker and me last night. Last I checked, Kam was on my side, but right now she looks insanely guilty as she sits next to my brother.

"Did you tell him?" I ask, turning to Kamryn right away, betrayal seeping through and Bellamy's head turns to her so quickly.

"You knew?" he asks, and now my heart is gone and stopped beating altogether. Great, I've completely incriminated Kamryn too.

"I..." she hesitates.

"It's not her fault," I urge.

"I'm aware it's not her fault, but if she knew that you were sleeping with one of my friends I would expect my girlfriend to tell me," he snaps at me and my mouth shuts, emotion clogging my throat.

"Bellamy..." Kamryn tries to smooth his tone but he shakes his head.

"No. I don't break or snap or freak out. I'm always the level-headed one and I'm not doing that right now. I didn't even know you left last night, I went to your room and this was just there on the floor. So tell me. When? When did this shit happen?"

He holds the list out and I question in my head whether or not I should spill everything or if I should... No, I can't lie to him anymore.

"My birthday, but—"

"Your birthday? What... I mean you... Bri, you've been with Dakota this whole time and... You've been lying to me? Seri-

THE RULES OF YOU AND ME.

ously this long and..." He loses his words and I open my mouth to argue but he doesn't let me.

"Were you ever really with Dakota?" he asks.

I look between him and Kamryn, chewing on my lip. I know there are tears pooled in my eyes. I know I probably look terrified right now.

"No, I wasn't, and I tried to tell you. I tried to at the beginning of the semester and you wouldn't listen to me," I admit.

"You've been lying this entire semester? Not just about him but about... About Parker too? Is that where you were last night? With Parker? I've been so fucking stupid. The lessons and this entire semester. God." He shakes his head and starts pacing.

"Bellamy I—"

"Call him right now," he urges.

"I can't. We broke up last night over you, I can't," I argue.

"Do it or I'm going to him, your choice," he snaps.

"Bellamy, she just said they broke up... Specifically because of this. You are being ridiculous." Kamryn motions to the mess that we are and her voice sounds urgent, like she's defending me.

"No, I'm not. I don't care if they broke up, it's not about that it's... I think I need to be alone with Brianne right now," he tells her and my mouth drops.

"It's fine," Kamryn cuts my words in half. I close my mouth. "I love you, please call me when this is... When you want to talk," she tells him firmly, she eyes me and I can tell how sorry she feels. "Text me if you need anything," she mumbles and grabs her things, leaving me alone with Bellamy.

"Call Parker, now," he urges once Kamryn is gone. I do what he says and Parker picks up right away. I suck in a sharp breath, not able to stop my tears or my emotions.

"What's wrong? Brianne?" His words are urgent and my

heart cannot calm down. "Don't go shy on me now, Sunshine. Tell me what's wrong."

I want to cringe at his words, mostly because they hurt. His instant need to care for me has me ready to fall to the floor.

"It's..." I look at my brother, the muscles in his jaw feathered as he stares at me with anger and disappointment. "Can you just get here, please," I mumble.

"I'll be there in 5," he tells me and then he hangs up.

"Bellamy I—"

"I really don't want to talk to you right now," he mumbles, his voice monotone and low.

"I'm sorry," I whisper, trying not to cry.

Kamryn kept telling me everything would be fine but it feels like it's all falling apart and I'm going to try and do everything in my power to make sure that it's not the end of a close relationship with my brother. Honestly my everything, the only part of my immediate family I have left. My chest fills with hot liquid panic once again as we wait for Parker.

"Did everyone know?" he asks me and I let out a shaky breath.

"Yes, they all found out, but they wanted to tell you, I just begged them not to. Don't be mad at your friends, please," I beg him.

"You don't really have any room to tell me how I should feel about this right now Brianne." He keeps his voice monotone and I stay quiet once again.

I don't have room to tell him that. He's right.

"I really can't believe you right now." He shakes his head and I've never heard this much disappointment in my brother's voice.

Fear. Deep, penetrating fear ignites inside of me and I clench my fists at my sides, feeling my nails break the skin on my palms the harder I squeeze. I need to calm down but the

THE RULES OF YOU AND ME.

apartment feels so small, my chest feels small, my head feels small. Falling in love with Parker has never felt this hard. Loving him has never felt angry or scared or panicked. And right now all of it feels like pain and fear and panic.

"Is there anything specific I need to know before he gets here?" he asks, actually looking at me right now.

"Bellamy, I really wish you would calm down before you talk to Parker about this. I love him and—"

"How can you love someone when all he's been is a secret this entire time?" he snaps at me and once again, I let my lips close shut out of shock and realization.

I shut down, and there's a knock on the door. I start to walk forward, and Bellamy opens the door, pushing in front of me.

"What is this?" Parker asks, looking at my brother with no kindness in his stare.

Parker was warming up to the idea of being close to Bellamy. They were on a level of friendship they hadn't been on when I first got to SPU, but all of that is gone right now.

"I have questions," Bellamy mutters and Parker scoffs.

"So you drag me over here to have me explain when you have all the information you need from her. What is it, did you want to embarrass her? Make me come here to make her feel like some little kid who's in trouble?" Parker instantly gets defensive.

"She is a kid. Parker, she's a fucking kid," Bellamy snaps and I open my mouth to argue but stop myself.

The tears come in a wave that can't be stopped now. They pool over my eyes and I wipe them away quickly as Parker looks at me, wanting so badly to come to my aid from what I can tell.

"She's not going to defend herself because you're her brother, but I will. Your sister is not a fucking kid and you're not going to drag her around like she is one. This is a line that you have no right to cross. Siblings or not, you have no right to treat her like this, not now and not ever," Parker argues and Bellamy raises his voice.

"She's my fucking baby sister! I have every right to cross this line, especially with you, someone who I saw as my friend, my fucking brother!" he shouts and Parker rolls his eyes.

"Don't pull that shit. I wasn't even close with you until after the fact. And even then I was included because of my status. If I was some minor player on the team or not in a position that needed to be close to you, I never would have been invited or included and we both know that." Parker snaps. Bellamy looks hurt now like Parker just hit him in the face.

"You slept with my sister and bragged about it to my face. You slept with my sister for what? To prove something to me? To piss me off?" he argues and the offense in my chest hits hard.

"Did you ever think me wanting your sister had nothing to do with you and everything to do with her? You have a force of a fucking human as your sister and you look and talk to her like she's nothing but—" Parker starts.

"Parker," I cut him off and he clenches his jaw and his fists.

"If it truly mattered to either of you in the way you're making it seem then why did it need to be kept from me? You both, both of you lied to my face more times than I can count and you—" Bellamy turns to me now, not softening when he sees my tears. "You promised me. When we talked things out, you promised you would tell me everything. That we would fix what was broken and instead you do this? You wedge something so wrong in between us and expect me to not hate it? You expect me not to be more mad at you than I think I've ever been?" He raises his voice and I break.

"Bellamy, you're the most important person in my life. I've never been more afraid to lose someone than you and I didn't tell you because I didn't want to lose my best friend over some

THE RULES OF YOU AND ME.

guy." I speak quickly and the words fall from my lips faster than I can think through them.

"Some guy," Parker mumbles, and I look at him.

"Parker—"

"No... You made your choice last night Brianne and that's fine. " He turns his attention to Bellamy now. "I have nothing left to say except the fact that you aren't all that you think you are. You're great at your sport, you're a good boyfriend to Kam but what about her?" Parker snaps, saying something I never expected him to say to my brother.

"Watch it, Parker." Bellamy's jaw ticks.

"No, I'm done. Your sister has come to me crying on your account. She has walked away from conversations with you with tears in her eyes. She's a woman. She's a dancer, she's a teacher. She's not a fucking object and that's all you've treated her like this entire damn year."

"You say that like you haven't used her and had sex with her for what? To—"

"You don't get to do that. You don't get to diminish this to just sex. You don't know anything no matter how damn smart you think you are. You want me to be confident, or speak up for myself like you asked, well you've got it. You treat your sister like shit and she deserves more than you have ever given her. She deserves to see herself in a better light and you dim that every chance you get, and—"

Before Parker can say anything else Bellamy is on him, his fist connecting to Parker's face. Parker instantly tries to defend himself and I know I need to step in before Bellamy gets hit too. My brother is not a physical person. He uses his words always. But never has he needed to argue over me. Not until now, and it's bringing out a different side of him that I've never once seen.

"Stop!" I scream the words out and step forward quicker than I've ever moved.

Parker wipes the blood pooling on his lips that drips from his nose and looks up at Bellamy. Part of me worries that he's going to hit him back but his eyes look to me and then Bellamy. He just shakes his head and stands straighter.

"Get out," Bellamy breathes heavily as he looks at Parker.

"I'm not leaving you with—"

"Go Parker. Just go," I tell him, hardly able to speak over my tears. A look of betrayal washes over Parker's features and my heart shatters more which I didn't think was possible. He shakes his head as he turns away from both of us, slamming the door behind him, and shaking the entire apartment.

Bellamy's hand is red and angry. His dominant, throwing hand, Coach Corbin is going to be livid. Lawson is going to be pissed. Everyone that we know is going to hate this situation. Not only did I potentially ruin my relationship with my brother. I ruined some of his friendships. I messed up his relationship with Kamryn. I feel myself retracting. All the things I had said I would do and say when the time came for Bellamy to find out disappeared. Every conviction I had to defend Parker and me is gone. Bellamy's words replay in my head.

How can I love Parker if all he was is a secret?

I wipe the tears from my eyes. I yell at myself in my mind. Stop crying, stop acting like this is the worst thing that could have happened considering you're not the one most affected by this. Bellamy is. Bellamy is losing a friend, and fighting with his others. He's fighting with me now. He's hurt too. His good hand is hurt and he has a very important championship soon, one we're all traveling to Michigan to play and cheer for soon. I've messed that up.

I really need to man up. To get over it. He's right. He's always right. Bellamy has never led me wrong, and him telling me what he has is... It's right. It has to be right or else I could lose him. I'm thankful no one is here. Mostly because I don't

THE RULES OF YOU AND ME.

need to hear Lawson say he told me so, and I can't handle the anger Bellamy probably has toward his best friend right now. Bellamy shakes his hand out and I stare at him.

"Can I help you? Please." I mumble. He clenches his jaw as he paces. He gives me a single nod and I go to our medicine cabinet in the kitchen. He pushes himself onto the counter with his other hand and I take out a clean dish towel and wet it, taking his angry hand, and pressing the cool towel to the harsh skin. Bellamy sucks in a sharp breath and I shake my head. I fight to keep my tears in.

"Kamryn should be the one doing this, she knows how to do it better... To set it so it doesn't get swollen and..." I let out a shaky breath, realizing once again that I fucked up worse than I had wanted to.

"Well Kamryn isn't here and I don't want to talk to her or any of my friends right now," he admits.

"It isn't their fault," I tell him, once again trying to clean his hand.

"It's everyone's fault who didn't step in to protect you from anyone like Parker. He... What he did was disgusting, how he acted was out of character for him." Bellamy shakes his head. I want to tell Bellamy it wasn't wrong. Parker is one of the most fiercely protective men I've met. He would defend me like his life depended on it.

"I made these choices, they were mine... And I'm sorry," I tell him.

"Stop apologizing," he demands and I pause.

"I can't lose you, Bellamy," I admit.

"Think about that before you come between me and everyone else I care about. You are first. Always, B. I care about you more than I can explain, but this is... It's a mess that I shouldn't have to clean or deal with." He bites the words out and I feel the tears escaping again.

"I'm sorry. I can't lose you over anyone. Friends, boyfriends I don't care." I've chosen him over myself most of the time. Because he's more important. The most important.

"So, what's going to happen then? With you and him?" he asks.

I start to clean with alcohol now, the split knuckles clearing with the touch. Bellamy once again sucks in a breath between his teeth. I feel a sting too from his question.

"Nothing. I tried to tell you that... He broke up with me last night because of you because he knew that... It doesn't matter," I admit, feeling hollow at the words. I wipe my eyes, and back away from his hand, trying not to completely lose it.

"Bri..." Bellamy softens. For the first time today, he does and I step back fully. My face is completely broken, not able to hide how I feel but I still try with my words.

"It's fine. You're right. I just... I need to shower and clear my head," I admit, speaking through my tears.

"B, come here..." He tries to get me to come back but I sneak away, heading up the stairs in our apartment.

"Have Kamryn wrap that when she gets back and talk to her. Don't hate her for my mistakes, please... And they were mistakes, he was... I shouldn't have done any of this," I admit, the words are burning like acid in my mouth.

No matter how they taste, they're true. They have to be if I want to keep my brother.

"Are we going to really sit down and talk about this?" he asks.

"There's nothing to talk about. You're right," I tell him again and he starts to talk again, but I lock myself in my room, sinking against the door until my butt hits the floor.

I cry then, letting it come out like I had wanted downstairs. This is my safe space to be sad. I can feel that here, but the second I cross the threshold of this room I need to be me. My

THE RULES OF YOU AND ME.

normal self. I don't want to think about our next game. Our last game. I don't want to think about the struggle it's going to be when I see Bellamy and Parker working together. If I know anything about either of them it's that this sport and winning this game is far too important to them to let their outside feelings get in the way. That doesn't mean it won't absolutely suck. But that game is a week away and it's a problem for then. I won't borrow that right now. All I'll do is stay here in this spot and feel everything and anything I want to.

CHAPTER 42

I GUESS BY LIZZY MCALPINE

Brianne Archer:

I haven't left my room in two days. Not to do anything except eat downstairs. I haven't seen Dakota. I have definitely not read the text Parker sent me. I haven't talked to Kamryn even though she came up here to wave a white flag toward me. She said she'd be around if I wanted to talk but I said no that I was fine. Because the thought of talking about all of it seems too painful. And I don't need that to get in between her and Bellamy and give him another reason to be mad at me. Because he is. He's not spoken to me. Bellamy has barely looked at me in the past two days when I've passed him or cooked my lunch and dinner next to him. It's like I don't exist right now and I want to scream but I don't. Because if I pretend it's okay, then it will start to feel that way once again.

Bellamy will trust me again.

There's a knock on my door and I peel my damp eyes from the TV across my room that I wasn't even actually focused on. I don't even know what episode I'm on. I force myself up, crawling out of bed and to the door. I open it, light seeping in

515

through the crack. I see Dakota, his face fresh, his hair clean, his face laced with concern. My heart lurches and instantly I want him to leave.

"Hey B..." he mumbles the words. "Can I come in?" he asks softly.

I open the door despite wanting to tell him to leave. I crawl back into my bed, pulling the covers to my chest. I just look back to my TV knowing there's no way to even really pretend I'm fine. I'm not, it's obvious and he knows me well enough that even if I did pretend he would see right through it.

"Talk to me. You've been silent for days. I had to find out what happened through him," he tells me, sitting on the edge of my bed.

"It doesn't matter. I'll be fine," I tell him, hearing my voice for the first time since yesterday.

"It does matter," he admits.

"No, Dakota, it really doesn't. Why are you here?" I ask softly.

"I'm here because Kamryn and Parker both told me to check on you because you've been MIA for two days and I'm the only one who can make you talk," he argues.

"Well, I don't really want to talk. Especially not if you're going to go gallivanting around and telling everyone how I feel," I admit, surprising myself with the tone of my voice.

"Baby... I wouldn't go telling anyone how you feel and you know that." He looks hurt by my words. Confused and hurt.

"I really don't want to talk about it because none of it matters. I should never have tried to be with Parker, that was a mistake because Bellamy is the most important and I let my relationship get in the way. He's just a dumb football player and these feelings will go away soon," I tell him, once again feeling nauseated by the words. The bile in my throat burns.

516

"You and I both know that's not true. Your brother doesn't get to dictate your happiness and—"

"And it's not your business Dakota. I get that you have a perfect family and parents and whatever but I don't have that luxury. All I have is my brother and right now he doesn't even want me so just... Fuck off. Stop pushing me and stop forcing me to feel the way you would about things. I'm not you and we're not alike," I snap, silence filling the room now.

"I said I didn't want to talk about it. Why can't you just leave me alone when I ask?" I speak the words softer, regretting everything I had said the second it hit the air.

But there's no taking it back. And honestly, pushing Dakota away is the easiest way to move on from the pain of all of this. Because I can't have Parker. I can't have everything. So I choose my brother. That's all that matters. Dakota won't ever agree with that.

"Got it, Bri..." He nods and pushes himself up.

I'm left alone again and thankful for the silence. But my chest feels cold. My body feels cold. I feel exposed and raw and completely done with everything. So I turn the TV and sit in the dusky darkness in my room, staring at the wall instead, reveling in the quiet.

There's another knock on my door and I hesitate to answer. The last time didn't end so well for me. I push up anyway, hoping it will be Bellamy, but deep down knowing it won't be. I don't even know how long it's been since Dakota left. I open the door and regret it instantly. Parker is standing there in a hoodie and sweatpants. I don't know what sound leaves my lips. I don't know why I feel like falling to the floor and why I feel like crying all over again. Instead of doing any of that, I stare at him blankly.

"Can I come in?" he mumbles.

"Bellamy is going to hit you again," I warn.

"Good, let him," he grunts the words out, his grumpy attitude shining despite the fact that it usually never shows around me. I don't open the door and just stare at Parker.

"Bellamy and Lawson aren't home. Kamryn called me and asked me to come talk to you so here I am, let me in." He mumbles, not seeming happy that he's here. I open the door, hating that I'm getting visitors in here like it's a fucking hospital. I once again crawl back into my bed, not aware at all of how I look, smell, or seem. I stay sitting up this time, pulling my covers over my criss crossed legs.

"What do you want?" I ask him.

"What do I want? Some clarity. Some closure. Something…" he admits.

"You gave me an ultimatum, you broke up with me. There's nothing to clear up. Bellamy found my stupid rule list, then he called you and you know everything else that happened," I tell him.

"And you're okay with that? With all of this. Is this really what you want?"

"I don't know what I want anymore," I lie.

"I'm sorry. For giving you an ultimatum. I don't regret what I said to Bellamy, but I am sorry for putting you in the middle of it. I know I wanted to say that. And I know I want to tell you that I love you, break up or not…" he explains.

"How can you love someone when all they are is a secret?" I ask him and he clenches his jaw.

"Did Bellamy tell you that? Or is that a thought you came to on your own?" he asks.

"It doesn't matter," I fight.

THE RULES OF YOU AND ME.

"Yeah, it does because everything that comes from your head is usually sound and fucking sane. That? What you just said was not sane or sound and it definitely doesn't sound like the Brianne I know," he tries to plead and I shake my head.

"Then I guess you don't know me," I speak the words softly, hating myself for saying them.

"Tell me what this is about Brianne... Tell me, talk to me. Please, Sunshine." I look at him the second he says the nickname and I see for the first time the tears in Parker's eyes.

My heart shatters. I fight the urge to cry.

"You can't call me that when you... This is what you wanted, you gave the ultimatum, and you wanted Bellamy to know even though I was absolutely positive this was how it would end. I know I can't do this. You know we never should have tried, you know we were bound to end up here," I admit.

"I didn't know anything about that, no. I knew that I wanted you and I was going to do anything in my power to make that happen," he fights.

"And I knew that if it came down to it. If I had to choose I would always choose Bellamy. Because he's all I have left. He's my family. My home. My best friend. I choose him. He cares about me more than anyone else ever could," I tell him, the point coming into play.

"And if he really cared the way you're claiming he did then I can promise you he'd never make you choose between him and anyone else you love. Because whether you want to admit it or not, I know that's how you feel about me," he tells me and I clench my jaw.

"What I feel doesn't matter anymore. Because I can't lose my brother. I refuse." I tell Parker, avoiding his eyes altogether.

"Then can you at least do something for yourself? You want to hate me? Fine. You want to pretend we didn't happen? Fine. Don't rot in your bedroom. Go out. Live your life. Because if I had to sit there and hear from Dakota that you refuse to leave here. That you ended your friendship with him and that you've skipped cheer practice because you've been in your bedroom. I won't stand for it. You're better than this. And if I know I'm part of the reason you lose your light, I'll never forgive myself. This wasn't supposed to be the end result," he fights.

"Yeah I'm aware it wasn't but it's what we have. I don't need this, please go," I fight.

"I'm sorry, Bri... That he's making you choose. That you feel like you have to."

He stands up and I almost choke on my breath at his words. The second the door clicks closed I pick up my phone and text Kamryn.

> Stop sending people to check on me. Stop acting like my sister or my mom. You're not either. I'm fine. Leave it alone.

CHAPTER 43
MAKING THE BED BY OLIVIA RODRIGO

January

Parker Thompson:

I sit in Coach Corbin's office, my arms crossed over my chest, my bruised face the only thing to show for what happened last weekend. Bellamy is sitting next to me in his chair, silent just like me, arms crossed over his chest just the same. He won't look at me or in my direction. He hasn't in the past week and as much as I wish I didn't care, I do. Having the Archer duo out of my life has created a hole that I didn't even know would exist if I didn't have either of them. As annoying as Bellamy could be, he was also a bigger part of me than I had realized. I don't regret what I said, but I do regret the way I said it. I hate how childish it all felt even if it was true. I'm better than that, and Bellamy is better than hitting me.

Coach Corbin has been standing in front of us, eyeing my face and Bellamy's hand for the past five minutes. He hasn't said a word. He has expressed on his face that he's not happy but that's the only sign I have of what's going on here or what is going to happen in this office today. I'm scared that I'm going to be benched for the championship game next week. This is all chalked up to being my fault in the end, but I also have more riding on this. Bellamy already won the Heisman. We know he's a first-round NFL draft pick in March. I don't have the same security in my career... I'm nervous as hell sitting in this uncomfortable chair right now and I'm not going to let it show.

"Is there a reason we're sitting silently?" Bellamy breaks the tension and Coach Corbin almost snorts with laughter.

"Besides the fact that I'm trying to figure out what to say to you two idiots?" Coach snaps and I stay quiet.

"I didn't do anything," Bellamy argues.

He's the coach's favorite. His pet. As he should be considering Bellamy alone has driven us to four back-to-back championships in the last four years. He deserved that spot. But having that means he's a bit of a smart mouth to coach which is far more than any of us would ever get away with.

"You didn't do anything? Are you really going to sit here and tell me that when you have a bandage on your throwing hand a week before our championship game? Your final championship game in your college career might I add." Coach doesn't glance my way at all as he speaks.

"Then why is he here if I'm the one in trouble?" Bellamy speaks in a lower tone now, like he doesn't even want to acknowledge me. He hasn't even glanced in my direction.

"Because you hit me," I mumble, my eyes glancing at him.

"You deserved it," he snaps and I clench my jaw to keep from speaking.

"Shut up. Both of you." He walks around his desk and leans against it. "Now, I told you that you needed to figure your shit out and you promised me you wouldn't cause any problems," Coach Corbin starts.

I don't look at Bellamy because I already know he's going to

THE RULES OF YOU AND ME.

be mad that Coach knew and he didn't. Just like he had no idea any of his friends knew either. He's been the only one out of everyone in his life who was in the dark about Brianne and me, and that's another thing that's been weighing on me. I know it's half of the reason Brianne feels like she does. Because she cares more about her brother's happiness than her own and it's infuriating.

"You knew?" Bellamy's voice is once again full of betrayal, just like it was when I was at their apartment after he found out.

"You don't get up and arms with me, Archer. Anyone with eyes and half a brain could have guessed that Parker and your sister were dating. You just didn't want to see it," Coach snaps and Bellamy looks taken aback.

"Of course, I didn't want to see it. He was my best friend and he lied to me. She lied to me, and even worse he bragged about it to my face when it was all a secret. I thought he was talking about being with someone else this whole time but no he was talking about my sister to my own face? That's fucked. You're fucked up. That's my baby sister and you..." Bellamy argues and I shake my head, stopping him from spouting any more nonsense.

"I didn't. I tried with everything in me to never talk about my relationship with your sister in front of you but you forced that, just like you forced everything else. I didn't brag about anything. I told you the bare minimum because the thought of talking about her without her knowledge or yours grossed me out. Don't blow this out of proportion more than you already have," I snap and Bellamy opens his mouth but Coach holds his finger up, silencing both of us.

"I don't care. I really don't. Bellamy you can scream until you're blue in the face about her being your baby sister, but she's not a baby anymore and as much as you love her, you are not her dad. You're her brother and you're all she's got. So you're right, you should protect her," Coach starts.

"Exactly," Bellamy agrees.

"You didn't let me finish," Coach interrupts Bellamy. "You should protect her from bad people. Assholes, and pervs at a bar. Parker is not a bad guy and we all know that, you included," Coach defends me and despite the coldness in my chest, I do feel a spark of warmth at his defense.

"I don't know him and how he is. Not like I thought," Bellamy admits.

"You do. And you can pretend you don't, that's fine. I need a promise right now. From both of you," Coach Corbin interjects once again.

"I need both of you to promise that the fighting stops here. You don't speak unless it's about the game. You don't argue unless it's for the betterment of the team. And you damn well don't let whatever idiotic feud is happening ruin our chances at the championship. Archer, I know you're mad at him, but Parker and almost every player out there has a lot riding on this win. Their future, their career. Yours is set right now. And you have earned that. I don't care who she is. Family or not. You will not let a girl get in between your team and that trophy," Coach starts talking to both of us, but ends with his eyes on Bellamy.

"I would never throw the championship," Bellamy promises with his words.

"And you. I don't care what personal things you're feeling either. You don't try to hash this out or smooth it over until after the championship. Not with him, not with his sister." Coach Corbin looks at me now.

"Not with my sister ever," Bellamy adds and I nod to Coach, ignoring Bellamy.

"I promise," I tell him.

"I promise too," Bellamy chimes.

"Good, get out of my office and get on the field for drills. Both of you are doing suicides today because you're idiots. Go." Coach motions for us to leave. I let Bellamy go first and then I stand.

"I'm going to get her back, Coach," I tell him and he nods.

"I'm sure you are. Just don't let Archer hit you in the face again when you do."

He finally smirks and I want to smile but I can't. I haven't since the matter and I don't think I want to. I'm going to focus. I'm going to practice. And I'm going to be the reason we take the championship trophy home next weekend. I want that on my shoulders, not everything else.

Brianne Archer:

I should be happier on my first college championship game. That should be something I'm jumping for joy over. But I'm standing on the sidelines next to Dakota who I still haven't spoken to. Not in two weeks. I'm stiff from the lack of practice and stretching I've been doing and I know Leah has noticed. And I'm undeniably tired. Not from flying to Michigan or the jet lag. Not from my lack of sleep because I feel like that's all I've done. I'm tired in my head from all the hoops I've been jumping through to convince everyone I'm fine.

I am fine. This is fine.

Seeing Parker and Bellamy play next to each other like nothing even happened is completely fine.

Seeing the fact that I feel like I have no relationship with my brother now. No boyfriend because what I felt was all chalked up to an ultimatum. It was all forced to end because of my brother. And now both of them are okay with all of this.

So I'm fine.

And right now, the clock is ticking down at an alarming speed. Bellamy has one second to make a decision. I should be excited. Adrenaline should be rushing through me as I watch my brother make the final pass to Parker on the field. I should be happy that Parker is using the precision and skill he learned partially from me to maneuver through the field. I should be jumping up and down and screaming my head off the second Parker makes the final winning touchdown of the football season. But all I do is watch, my ears ringing, all of it feeling like it's happening in slow motion.

The team practically tackles him to the ground and I stand there, watching everyone go absolutely wild with excitement.

And I feel none of that.

But I do hear my name. And I realize how I must look so I smile. And I cheer. And I pretend because I'm very good at that game. Especially the last two weeks. I see the team. I see the excitement. I see them lift Parker like he's on top of the world and I see them lift my brother too. The MVP's of the game, both securing this for our school and team. I look at them, and I swear I watch Parker's eyes scour until they land on me. He only looks for a second, but he does look. Part of me wants to believe he was looking for me. That he's wanting to come to me. But the other part doesn't want that to be true because the last thing I want is to talk to him right now.

Then my brother looks at me. He smiles and cheers and I try to emanate the same reaction for him. Because he's looking at me. And he's happy when he's doing so and that's all I've wanted in the past two weeks was for my brother to be happy when he looked at me. So I make it my mission to not even glance in Parker's direction the rest of the night despite the fact that it feels like second nature to do so.

CHAPTER 44

COWBOYS CRY TOO (WITH NOAH KAHAN) BY KELSEA BALLERINI

February

Brianne Archer:

I wait in line at the club alone, irritated with how long it's taken for me to even approach the bouncer. It's freezing out here and in perfect Brianne fashion of course I'm not wearing enough to keep me warm. But Bellamy didn't mind when I left. He said I looked pretty and that's a step forward for my brother. It's just about the only step forward he's made in the past month since he won the championship but it's something.

I've been making an effort to try and make plans with him. Sometimes they work but mostly they don't. He's busy. I get it. I'm not dumb. I know it's not only because he's busy. It's also because he's not even partially my brother anymore the way he was. The way we used to be is never going to happen again. I've come to terms with that even though it's been insanely hard to swallow. But I'm trying.

I've already had some to drink tonight. I Ubered here alone in hopes of an escape. I don't feel that yet. I approach the bouncer and hand him my fake ID and he looks at me instantly giving me a sinking feeling. He doesn't say a word but he holds his hand out, waiting for mine. I hand it to him and he draws a big X on my hand and I scoff.

"Get a better fake sweetheart," he mumbles but still lets me in.

Not that it matters anymore considering I'm a walking red flag now. I walk in feeling defeated even though I just got here. I sit at the bar, covering my hand in hopes the X isn't as noticeable. I wanted to feel. I wanted to drink and feel and I can't do that. I scour the place for another vice. Another guy. Another thing to occupy my mind. I prop myself up on the side of the bar, looking, and waiting until I'm approached by just the person I wanted to come. The guy I had been looking at for the past few minutes.

He's got darker skin, but it's reflecting every neon electric light that's bouncing around the dark club. His eyes are dark and all of his features are so precise I swear it doesn't even look like he's real. He's clean-cut. Perfect. Definitely not my type for that reason alone. But he's undeniably hot so he'll do.

"You look lonely," he says, taking his place next to me.

"Wanna fix that?" I ask him. His smirk is hard to miss.

"What's your name?" he asks. Small talk, my favorite.

"Brianne, and you?" I ask.

"Jackson," he tells me and I nod.

"Nice to meet you, Jackson."

The back and forth is so simple I want to scream.

"What brings you here then, Bri?"

He jumps straight into a nickname and I don't know why I hate it so much, hearing the nickname instead of my full name. But then flashes of Parker hit my head and I know exactly why and instantly want to be rid of those thoughts.

"Someone like you," I lie, choking down the urge to cry or

THE RULES OF YOU AND ME.

scream or just run away.

He's gotten closer and closer within the last few minutes and I decide to just make the jump instead of waiting for him, wishing for relief and reprieve from my own mind.

He kisses me back and his lips are perfect. Just like I had expected. But they feel wrong. I did everything as I was supposed to. Like I've done before. I leaned in, I touched him, I kissed him and it feels wrong. It's lacking warmth. Instead of fire, there's chill and there's not a single spark that hits my head, my heart, or my body. I don't need a spark... But I want one. And there's not one. He breaks away from me and I almost gasp at the lack of feeling. I tuck my hair behind my ear, wearing it down because that's always what people tell me looks best.

"Is that an X? How old are you?" he asks, almost disgusted.

"I'm 19," I tell him truthfully.

"I'm too old for you," he tells me, and I know he's still in college.

He doesn't look older than 23 but he's probably right. And I'm an idiot for even being here. Slightly intoxicated, and have no way to get more. Jackson walks away from me, not interested slightly and part of me is thankful because I obviously wasn't interested either. But I still feel hollow. I still feel sinking in my chest. I still feel like I want something... Anything. I go to the bathroom and directly to the sink. I scrub. The soap and hot water burn my hands. I scrub until the back of my hand is raw and sore and I feel tears in my eyes. I don't need an Uber. I don't need to kiss someone. I need to go home, but I have no one.

If I call my brother I'll be in deeper shit. If I call Dakota he won't pick up. I wouldn't pick up if I was him either. Leah is... She's someone I trust. I could call her. But there's a single person who has always told me to call them when I need them. And besides the fact that I should probably never call him again, especially when I've had something to drink... He's the only

529

person I want to be around right now. So I take his advice, and I call Parker.

~

Parker Thompson:

I've never driven faster in my life. Mostly out of fear. Panic. Absolute shock. When her name popped up on my phone I almost fell out of my bed. That's where I've spent the past month. Every day after class. After everything, I've gone home. I haven't celebrated my championship win much at all. Mostly because Bellamy will be there and I can't expose myself to his potential anger or glares or hatred. It's warranted. But we still managed to work together and win the championship. I hate being in my apartment because Dakota's there and it's a constant reminder just how awful Brianne is really doing despite how much she's trying to fake it.

She hasn't spoken to him since the beginning of January. He's hurt. He's not happy. And I can't talk to him about it because I'll feel all of that and more. I understand him though. He doesn't want to reach out to her out of fear of her pushing him further away. I've felt the same. But I also don't want to diminish or deter any progress she's made with Bellamy and rekindle their relationship. I can't be the reason for that again.

I pull up to a nightclub, a bad feeling sinking into my chest when I see her. She looks... frail. Her hair is down. I love it when she wears her hair down but it's hard to focus on how pretty she looks when she looks this sad. She gets into my car without a word. Her scent hits me like a brick wall. Fresh and clean. Like honey and citrus. I try my hardest not to lose it. Not to ask her a million questions or panic like I want to.

"I'm sorry," she whispers as I pull away.

THE RULES OF YOU AND ME.

"Never apologize," I tell her and I mean that. I'd rather her call me. Anytime she needs me. I told her that months ago, and together or not, I meant that... Even if seeing her this way hurts.

"I don't want to go home," she admits.

"I have to take you home," I tell her, wishing it wasn't true.

"I'd rather be anywhere else," she whispers and I hate this.

I wish it wasn't this way. I wish I trusted myself enough to take her to my apartment. To let her be there. But with Dakota. With our past. With Bellamy. I don't think it's smart. So I fight the urge to say yes.

"I'm glad you called me. I mean I... I told you to call me, anytime. But why did you... why did you call me and not anyone else?" I ask.

"You're the only person that I can call who doesn't hate me right now," she whispers, not even looking at me.

"No one hates you. Dakota misses you. And Bellamy doesn't hate you... You guys are... You're better? No?" I ask and she makes a noise that I think is a laugh but I quickly realize is a cry. A sob. My heart cracks open, my chest breaks and I clench my jaw, trying not to let my emotions flow.

"Bellamy barely looks at me. I can't try. I can barely look at him either because I'm embarrassed. I hurt him and... He's just busy. Always. And I want my brother back," she admits to me.

I know it's hard for her to do that too. Because we wouldn't be in this position if it wasn't for how much she loved her brother. I could reach over and wipe her tears. I could pull her into me. I could crush her body to mine right now if it wasn't for how fiercely she loves Bellamy.

"It takes time. I'm sorry Brianne..." I apologize, feeling like all of this is my fault.

Like I tried to do everything right and managed to do everything wrong. I ruined her strongest relationship. The only familial relationship she had left. And I'm an ass for that.

531

"That's why I called you... If you want me to be honest, that was why I called you tonight," she tells me. I look at her, glancing with confusion toward her.

"I wanted to hear you say my name. I... I missed you. I kissed someone. And it felt wrong. Like acid in my mouth and I... and it wasn't you and it hurts," she admits and it looks like it pains her to say it.

I feel tears in my eyes. I haven't cried. I haven't let myself. But seeing her like this. Hearing her admit that to me breaks me in two. I just know it was hard for her to admit it. I know how hard it was for her to say it. But I also know she feels like she has nothing to lose right now.

I wait to respond. Driving quietly, thinking through everything I can, deciphering what the best option is. Brianne cries silently in my passenger seat. I feel anger. Anger at Bellamy. At her brother who claims to care about protecting her, but is letting her feel like this. Unloved. Uncared for. Immensely sad on a level I can't understand. I'm angry at her and I'm realizing that now. Not at her specifically but the situation. That the one person I've ever truly loved can't choose or love me. That she actively told me she wouldn't. It's a pain I've experienced, but not on this level. And I'm so damn mad that she's in this situation at all. I'm mad at myself that I care more about how she feels right now than myself.

"I just feel like I'm spending my life missing everyone instead of living. Because somehow I feel like everyone is leaving or gone." She admits. Her parents. Those are the first people that come to mind. Her brother. Dakota. Me. I pause at the thought. I still don't speak as I pull up to her apartment. My chest feels empty at the thought. Leaving her here when she'd rather be anywhere else.

"Promise me you're not going to do anything stupid the rest of the night. Shower. Rest... You look tired." I tell her.

THE RULES OF YOU AND ME.

"I am tired." She admits quietly. The talkative, sunshiney girl is gone. She's there when she's in a room or a crowd. I've seen her in passing. I've seen her posts on social media. She's really good at pretending but I'm seeing right through all of it. Especially now. She's a glass window. I turn my body to her and she pulls her knees up, looking at me, facing me.

"I miss you too," I tell her, knowing it's not a good idea, but feeling wrong keeping it to myself.

I've never been one to think like that. That saying what I feel is better than not. But with her, I can't help it. I watch tears spill down her made-up cheeks. Streaks now through the blush and foundation. I wish she wasn't wearing any of that so I could see her freckles again. She hesitates. Then she leans into me, kissing me, and my instinct kicks in. The muscle memory I have of her, where to place my hands, where to touch her back it all settles.

But feeling the wetness of her cheeks and the timidness of her kiss brings me right back to this. To what we are. I reluctantly pull away from her.

"Brianne..." I mumble, tilting my head down. I want to kiss her. God do I want to kiss this girl again, but I can't.

"I'm sorry," she admits.

"I want to kiss you, but I can't do it in secret. Not anymore. Not again. And not like this. With you like this," I tell her. "I won't take advantage of how sad you are right now."

"You're not taking advantage of—"

"If I kissed you the way I want to then yes, I would. You're not thinking... and Bellamy is right upstairs. You... you can't have me and him both. Unless something has changed," I tell her.

"I choose my brother," she tells me again and my chest burns with anger once again toward him. With hurt toward her and everyone else in my life for not choosing me.

"And I'm trying to respect that choice. I can't..." I tell her.

"Thank you for coming to get me," she mumbles.

"I'll do it again and again... But you have to promise me you'll be careful. Going to clubs alone and—"

"Save the lecture, Parker. I know," she cuts me off and gets out of my car, leaving me alone.

I drive home in silence. No music because even that hurts now. One song, any song I have on my phone reminds me of Brianne Archer and right now especially, it's too much for me. I go through the motions of going upstairs. I go into my apartment. All of my roommates and Dakota are sitting in my living room, waiting up for me. All of them are aware of what I was just doing.

"Is she okay?" Dakota is the first to ask.

"No. But physically, she's home and safe," I tell them.

I feel the tears in my eyes. I feel the hurt that I've harbored over all of this in my chest.

"What happened?" Xander asks.

"She's hurt, sad, and alone. And no one cares. I mean, no one that can care, no one in her life right now is actively giving a shit," I tell them.

"Let me guess... She called you because she misses you?" Dakota asks, knowing her just as well as I do.

I hesitate before I nod, not wanting to spill the details. I wipe under my eye feeling a tear pool over. I clear my throat and shake my head.

"I'm just going to go to bed. Thanks for waiting," I mumble and don't give them a chance to respond before going back into my room and locking the door behind me.

For the first time in all of this, I cry. I stay silent. I don't do anything but watch the wall in front of me and let myself be sad over losing the love of my life over someone and something so fucking trivial.

CHAPTER 45
I'M TIRED OF HEALING BY NOAH HENDERSON

March

Brianne Archer:

Bellamy is now a drafted NFL player. Bellamy. My best friend. My brother. He's moving to New York City this summer to play for the Giants with his girlfriend. And I won't be going with him. My brother will leave, and be over 2,000 miles away from me, the farthest we've ever lived from each other since I was born.

And he's over the moon.

I'm happy for him. I really am. But being here. Being in Washington alone and without him... Letting him leave me in a few months when we're still not fully rekindled in our relationship makes me want to cry. It makes me want to break down. It makes me want to call my therapist. But just like everyone else in my life. I haven't talked to her in far too long. I haven't answered her checkups. It's too late for me to want that.

Bellamy is celebrating right now with all of his friends. Griffin came back for his drafting. So they're all out right now.

And I wanted to be out too so I did just that. To a place all on my own of course because I can't party with my brother. He invited me, but I know he didn't mean it. It was obvious it was out of pity. And I'm drinking for an entirely different purpose than he is. He's celebrating, I'm mourning. My brother's relationship with me will officially be dead by the time July rolls around. It will be over along with everything else in my life. Part of me wonders if I should even continue at SPU. If being here has done anything for me but ruin my life.

Dance is the only normalcy I have. And even that I feel like I'm failing at. I could dance anywhere. I don't need this. Especially with Bellamy leaving. The thought is so sad it hits my chest. So I order another shot. Then another. And another and then the bartender tells me I need to go home and I tell him I have nowhere to go. I'm escorted to the front of the bar, wobbly on my feet. I drove here tonight. That wasn't smart of me, especially now that I can't drive home. I could ride in an Uber, but that would be dangerous for me. I can hear Parker in my head, telling me to be careful and safe. This wasn't careful or safe.

"Who can I call for you?" the guy asks, seeming more concerned than annoyed.

"I..." I hesitate.

Not Bellamy. If I ruined his celebration he'd be mad. Not anyone that's with him either... I can't call Dakota. I can't call Parker after what happened the last time. I won't do that to me or him again. It hurt too bad and I fell into a spiral for a few days after that. I can't set us back like that. I think and I think and I remember the rule list that ruined my life and I know just who to call. The only person who has ever in her life told me to call her when I'm drunk or need help besides Parker. I get sad thinking of Parker, sad and drunk don't mix well for me... They never have.

"Leah Ashley in my phone. Here." I hand it to him.

THE RULES OF YOU AND ME.

"She bartends down the street... Are you sure?" he asks, seeming hesitant like he's had his own experience or two with her.

"She's my cheer captain, just call her..." I tell him, annoyed by the question. He picks up my phone and calls.

"Hey... Hey, yeah she's fine. I don't know her name. She's drunk and she needs a ride. Can you get her? We're the corner bar off 9th," he finishes. "Cool, thanks," he mumbles and hangs up then hands my phone back. "Denny is watching you, don't make a run for it, and don't get in your damn car," he warns and I do what he says, waiting.

I sit on the curb, waiting for Leah even though I don't even know what car she drives. 15 minutes pass and a bright red Camry pulls up next to me with the window unrolled.

"Get in," she barks.

I get up and feel like my big sister just caught me at a party, but I get in anyway. The second I open the car door, I notice we're not alone and panic settles in my chest, but quickly diminishes because it doesn't matter. Xander sits in the back of the car, looking concerned. I don't do anything but glance at him before sitting in the front seat. Leah is wearing a tight shirt that says The Bulldog which is the bar a few blocks away. I guess she was leaving work... We sit in silence while she drives away and then she breaks it. She shakes her head, her perfect blonde hair moving with her head. Seriously it's cut in a perfect line following her jaw and it barely sweeps her collarbones. She's gorgeous.

"Do you want to tell me what the hell you're doing getting drunk alone tonight at a bar you have no business being at?" she asks.

"The whole answer or the short?" I ask, trying not to sound as drunk as I am.

"Short," she snaps.

"I'm sad," I answer and she sighs.

"Well, we knew that," Xander mumbles. I don't know if the alcohol I smell is coming from me, Leah, or Xander.

"You stay silent." Leah eyes Xander in the back seat through her rearview mirror. "Fine, the long answer because that gave me nothing." She turns her attention back to me.

"Why is he here?" I ask Leah, motioning to Xander.

"Because he got drunk at my bar and pestered me for a ride home when I got the call about you. Unfortunate, I know, now talk," Leah urges, but the answer feels forced and fake.

"I ruined my relationship with my brother who is now moving thousands of miles away from me in a few months. He tries to act normal, he seems decently concerned about me but I pretend everything is fine because it's not his job to make me feel better when I'm the reason I'm even in this situation. And I put him in a shitty situation so I don't want him to bring it up either. I hate SPU because I'm depressed. I love Parker Thompson and I'm not allowed to so I've been pretending I don't love him which has made my life hell. Dakota and I aren't friends anymore because I'm a bitch and pushed him out of my life. And I should probably go back to therapy because I think it was the only thing keeping me sane but I ruined that too," I tell her, speaking in one single breath.

"And you decided getting kicked out of a bar was a better answer than not?" she asks.

"Getting drunk at a bar is all I do besides go to the dance studio and cry," I admit out loud and feel pathetic doing so.

"I want to hate Parker. I want him to be horrible and bad and disgusting and he's not. I didn't want my year to be this way. Without everyone I care about," I tell her, trying not to cry now. I'm angry. Angry enough to cry.

"Why don't you reach out to Dakota? Just to see how he's doing?" Xander interrupts again.

THE RULES OF YOU AND ME.

"Why don't you just tell me? Since you know, you see him all the time?" I ask.

"He and Nico broke up like two weeks ago so I don't—"

"Xander. Sh!" Leah cuts him off again and my heart sinks. Nico and Dakota broke up? Is he okay? Was it amicable or is he hurt and heartbroken and... And I don't have a right to know any of that. I cut him off in a horrible way and he doesn't want anything to do with me.

"Getting back to the point, you're supposed to be getting yourself ready for next season." She bites into me and I shrug.

"Well, what if I drop out and don't come back to SPU? Then what's the point?" I ask and she scoffs.

"You're not doing this to yourself. I won't allow it. And you're not going home to be a mess in front of your brother. If your goal is to be fine in front of him, this isn't the way to do it." She doesn't look at me as she speaks.

"Then where am I going?" I ask.

"My apartment," she mutters and I don't want to, but I have no choice right now but to agree.

CHAPTER 46

SONG: SUDDENLY OKAY BY BLAKE ROSE

Parker Thompson:

There's a knock on my bedroom door and I look at it, wondering if I should just pretend I'm asleep. It's 2 in the morning so it wouldn't be far off. But if it's Xander he's going to know I'm faking considering I haven't slept before 2 AM in two months. I close my laptop.

"It's me, I know you're awake," Xander talks but it's obvious his words are slightly slurred.

He walks through my door and I lean up, pushing my throw pillow off of my chest.

"What's up?" I ask, barely recognizing my own voice at this point.

"I saw her... Tonight," he tells me.

"Leah?" I ask, assuming since he's drunk that he was at her bar as he's done before. But he had a game earlier today so my confusion is prominent.

"Well yes, but that's not who I'm talking about. I'm talking about Bri," he tells me, and my muscles tense at the mention of her name. My entire body goes rigid.

"What do you mean you saw her? Is she okay, what happened? Was she at the bar Leah works at? With who?" I ask rapid fire and he waves his hand.

"Chill out dude." He comes and sits on the end of my bed.

"I'm not going to chill out, tell me what happened," I insist.

"I'm working on it... I was at The Bulldog where Leah works. I was helping her out on her shift and she was closing up, getting ready to bring me back here because I definitely couldn't drive, but right before she left she got a call from Bri. Some guy called, he works at Corner Bar. Bri got cut off from drinking anymore there," he tells me and my heart sinks to the bottom of my chest and stomach.

"What did you do? Why did she call Leah?" I ask, partially wishing she called me, but knowing she wasn't going to after the last time she did.

"I don't know. When we picked her up it seemed like it was her only option in her mind." He shrugs.

"How did she look?" I ask.

"Really sad..." He yawns and I shove him.

"Wake the fuck up, this is serious., I urge.

"Sorry, sorry... She looked fragile and sad and embarrassed. She barely talked but when she did she mentioned that she still loves you but she can't. That she has no friends, and she can't talk to Bellamy still," he tells me.

"Her and Bellamy aren't speaking? Still?" I ask.

"Not from what she said. I didn't catch half of it, after she mentioned being in love with you I got excited and zoned out, I had a game tonight, give me a break," he defends himself.

I chew on the inside of my cheek, thinking over and over again.

"The fact that she and her brother still haven't smoothed this over or tried to figure anything out is insane... I wonder if he

THE RULES OF YOU AND ME.

knows how bad she's doing. I wonder if he cares," I speak my thoughts, not thinking them through at all as I do.

"I'm sure he does care if he knows, but I doubt that he does. She's been trying to keep it a secret from him," Xander admits.

I let my head fall into my hands and I sigh wanting nothing more than to just scream. I still want her. Brother or not, breakup or not, I want Brianne Archer. The past few months without have been dull and so dry. I thought maybe there'd be some semblance of a chance but it doesn't feel like there's any hope now. I can't try and talk to her because all she's going to do is push me away. Dakota doesn't talk to her either so he's a dead end. I could try Leah, but she'd probably rip my head off if she ever saw me face to face for hurting Brianne or having any part in this.

"Thank you for telling me," I mumble.

"What are you going to do?" Xander asks,

"I have no idea. I feel like there's nothing I can do," I admit. Xander stands up from my bed on wobbly legs and I shake my head.

"Why were you even at The Bulldog tonight?" I ask him.

"Because even if she won't admit it to anyone else, every time I walk into the bar, I see her smile. It's really small but I notice... There's more between us than I can really tell you... She's sworn me to secrecy and I'll be damned before I break her trust," he tells me.

"I don't know. I don't want Leah hurting you," I admit, knowing Leah is not the kind of person to mess with.

"Is that you caring about me?" He jokes.

"Yeah, it is..." I admit.

"Who are you, and what have you done with Parker?" he asks and I roll my eyes.

"Go to bed, and take a shower, you smell like a hockey rink

and a bar mixed together," I tell him and he throws his middle finger up as he leaves my bedroom, leaving me with a head full of thoughts about Brianne Archer.

So much has genuinely changed since I met her—since I fell in love with her. The person Brianne met, the man I was before, never talked. I never talked to my roommates unless he had to. I never talked to my friends unless I felt the need to, which I never did.

The Parker who met Brianne was a fly on the wall that didn't have much but the person I see myself as now is different. I feel rich compared to what I was, even if I'm missing a huge chunk of myself with her gone. I'm still... different. Determination has been something I've always had, but I never allowed myself to vocalize it. I never had confidence and now I can stand up for myself, my friends... and for the woman I love. I'll be damned if I let the changes in me—the confidence, the sense of self, the compassion I carry—go away. I can't let it go. If I did, I can just imagine how disappointed Brianne would be and how disappointed I would be in myself.

The morning light is blinding as it pours into the apartment. There's a loud and stern knock sounding through my place. I run to the front door , toweling off my hair from my morning shower. The knock finally stops and I question why not a single one of my roommates could have answered this, but then again, I don't even know which of them are here right now. My heart races at the thought of it potentially being Brianne. I know it's silly, but I can dream and hope. I open the door and am faced with an Archer, but not the one I had been wishing for. I just stare at him, my eyes set on Bellamy, my hands frozen in place now by my side.

THE RULES OF YOU AND ME.

"Considering you look confused, I'm going to assume Bri isn't here is she?" he asks, and now my brows furrow, a small bit of anger bubbling in my chest.

"No, she's not here. Why would she be here?" I ask him. "We broke up, we haven't spoken since..." I think back to the night I picked her up from the bar, the night she kissed me, the night I can't erase from my brain.

"That doesn't matter. I can't find her and she hasn't answered a single text or call. I'm worried about her," he admits, his voice exponentially calmer now than it was the last time we spoke.

"I'm glad you're finally worried... But she's physically fine. She's with Leah Ashley," I tell him and now his brows are furrowed.

"Why the hell would she be with Leah? And how do you know? Are you sure?" he asks.

"Yeah, I'm sure. Leah picked her up last night, my roommate was in the car with Leah. She took Brianne back to her apartment because she was apparently very drunk and really upset," I admit to him, and his jaw clenches. He stares at me straight forward, his eyes searching mine. I raise my eyebrows and look at him as if to ask, what?

"Can I come in and talk to you?" he asks.

"You're talking to me already," I admit.

"Yes, but I want to actually talk to you, Parks... A real conversation that I've wanted to have for a month or two now," he explains.

"Is this conversation going to end with you hitting me like the last one did?" I ask him.

"That depends on if you say something hurtful again, but no, I really hope it doesn't," he tells me.

I hesitate, but then I open the door fully, letting him in. He steps through the front door and I nod toward the couch, hoping

545

now that my roommates aren't home because if they see him sitting here, at least two of them will jump into fight mode. The first is Xander. I sit in a chair that's angled toward the couch while Bellamy sits on said sofa. I stare at him, expecting him to say something slightly rude or out of pocket toward me considering the last time we spoke resulted in a punch to the face.

"I'm sorry," he speaks out and my jaw hangs slightly. I furrow my brows and shake my head.

"Wait, what?" I ask.

"I'm sorry... For hitting you," he says it again and I blink a few times.

"I'm... I'm sorry too," I admit. "Not for the things I said, but how I said them. And for lying to you."

"You shouldn't be sorry about the things you said, even if they did hurt me." he admits and there's nothing I can say.

My shock is written all over my face that he's even saying any of this at all let alone admitting I was right.

"Is... Is that all you wanted to say?" I ask and he sighs.

"No. I wanted to tell you... I..." He shakes his head and pinches the bridge of his nose. "This is hard for no reason. I have been waiting. For you or Brianne to talk to me first. I have tried to talk to her. The day all of this went down I tried to talk to her. When I first found out, right after you left I was livid... Then I saw her face and I have never seen her look so... lost and honestly hurt. I tried then, but she wouldn't hear me, kept saying I was right and that she was sorry so I wanted to give it a few days. I had no intention to talk to you until we sat in Coach Corbin's office and he made the point that you're not a bad guy... and I don't know why I needed him to say it but I did." He stops for a brief second and looks at me.

"Um... Thank you? I guess?" I mumble.

"That's not my point. My point is, the more I've waited and thought about it, the more I realized that I wasn't hurt or mad

THE RULES OF YOU AND ME.

that you and Bri were together. I was hurt that neither of you felt like you could tell me. I was hurt that both of you felt like you had to keep it from me. Not mad," he clarifies.

"It felt like you were mad when you punched me," I mumble.

"I was. Only because you were telling me all the things I already knew but didn't want to admit nor hear out loud. I was still pretending like it wasn't true. And I already apologized for that, I shouldn't have hit you," he admits and I nod.

"She chose you... Either way, she chose you, you win." I admit, still bitter and hurt by the words.

"I don't want that, though. If what she says is true and you guys really do love each other, it wasn't my place to make her choose between the two of us," he says and I scoff.

"Well, it's too late for that. She chose you and she said it multiple times. And to be absolutely honest, you might want to hit me again for saying this, but it's a shame that she chose you and you're not choosing her back. You don't deserve how much she loves you. Not at all," I tell him and he nods.

"I know that. Not the choosing me part but the fact that I don't deserve her. I'm trying though, that's why I'm here. I'm trying to be worthy of the love she gives me," he tells me and I sit up straight.

"I'm going to give her more time. I'm going to watch her closely and try to talk to her, but I'm not going to force her into a conversation or she's going to push me away even more. But I do know that no matter what happens I won't leave for New York without her and I having a conversation. I think the reason she doesn't want to talk to me is because she... She wants something she can't have, which is you, and she doesn't want to lie to me anymore. I think Brianne thinks that I would be upset if she still wanted a relationship with you," Bellamy admits.

"Why are you telling me any of this?" I ask him.

"Because I want what's best for my sister and at first I thought I knew what that was, but I was wrong. What's best for Brianne is me supporting her and not stopping her from being with someone she loves... Even if it does slightly gross me out when I think of it being one of my best friends," he speaks and I open my mouth and close it, still trying to process this.

"So you came to apologize and tell me you want me to date your sister?" I ask him.

"I want whatever she wants... Which I think is you," he admits.

"You do realize that you telling me this only makes me want to call her," I tell him.

"Yeah I do, but I know you're smarter than that and I know that you want what's best for her too if I'm assuming correctly. Brianne doesn't need you to come to rescue her, she needs to figure this out. She needs to stand up to me, and I'm going to open myself up to let her. She deserves to get it all off of her chest, to throw it all at me, but until she's in a place to do that, she's also not in a place to be with you or anyone else for that matter. Don't you think?" he asks. I nod.

"I do. But when she does talk to you, when you two have that conversation, will you tell me..." I ask, still worried about his reactions.

"Yeah, I will... But before any of that happens, I need to threaten you," he tells me.

"Threaten me?" I ask.

"Yes. If all goes to plan. If you and Bri get back together... If you so much as harm a single hair on my baby sister's head I will fly back from New York and I will end your football career. And if that doesn't scare you enough, I promise I'll bring some of my new teammates with me and they'll help. You so much as breathe wrong in her direction and you're done." I've never seen Bellamy be so serious in my life. All I can do is nod.

THE RULES OF YOU AND ME.

"I understand," I admit, trying to contain my excitement and fear for what could come of all of this.

"I also want to... To ask if there's a chance in any way that the two of us could potentially rekindle this... Our friendship. Before I move, please." He looks nervous now. I clench my jaw and nod.

"I'd love nothing more than to be your friend Bell..." I admit, feeling relief all over my body.

He stands up and I do too. I step forward and bring him in first, our hands clasping, then our chests touching. I hear a sigh of relief from Bellamy and my heart finally slows, knowing Bellamy isn't going to lose it again.

"Take care of her when I'm gone next year," he mumbles into my shoulder.

"I will. Always," I admit. We start to pull away and are instantly interrupted.

"You let go of my best friend, motherfucker!" Xander crashes into the room and I open my arms up, stopping my idiot roommate who is armed with his hockey stick.

"Chill! Chill! Xander, calm the fuck down!" I shout, grabbing the hockey stick and yanking it free from his hands.

"What the hell is the enemy doing in our apartment?" He glares at Bellamy.

"Apologizing," Bellamy admits behind me. Xander instantly relaxes.

"Oh. Well in that case, welcome, can I get you water? We have regular and sparkling," he smiles and I shove him.

"Go away," I mumble and Bellamy smirks.

"Good to know Brianne has an army on her side," he tells me.

"You have no idea," I agree and see him out.

Relief is a feeling heavy in my chest, but there's still fear. Stark fear is present in all of me, hoping that Brianne will see all of this for what it is. That she'll want another chance at us, with honesty and no secrets. But considering how her last semester has gone, I have no idea what Brianne wants anymore. I don't even know if she knows...

CHAPTER 47
DOWN BAD BY TAYLOR SWIFT

Brianne Archer:

It's the last week of March. And I have a new... Friend? Person? Life Coach? I don't even know what to consider Leah Ashley. At first she was a team captain. An acquaintance to say the least. We hung out in groups. I would go out with her and the team. I never got close with her because she's not the most approachable person. According to Bellamy and Kamryn, Leah used to be a lot different but the past year and half she changed a lot. Well a year and a half ago she broke up with my brother... I was fine with the word friend, but being excessively close with her was not on my bingo card.

It's only weird if I make it that way. The past two weeks Leah has barely left me alone which has driven me to absolute insanity. I don't need it. I'm fine. Am I sad? Yeah. Am I dealing with it? In my own way, yes. She's pushing me. In a way that I don't like. In a way that's starting to grind on me. She's at my front door right now. Waiting downstairs. But there's a knock on my bedroom door.

"B..." It's Bellamy's voice, my heart jumps.

I try to seem normal, not wanting him to notice any discrepancies with how I've been before. Today I don't feel like trying at all. I don't feel like doing anything except laying in bed. Leah would drag me from my mattress by my hair if I told her no. The past two weeks Bellamy and I have been more normal than ever. We've talked normally but inside it doesn't feel normal. There's a lot of unresolved feelings I haven't dealt with but I will. Once I'm sure he's not mad at me, I'll figure out how to deal with that. Until then, I have to keep pretending.

"What's up?" I smile at my brother and he looks wary.

"What's going on with you and Leah?" he asks, leaning against my door frame.

"I kind of told you before... That's why I asked you and Kam about her last week. No matter anything, she's my cheer captain and she's going to be my cheer coach next year," I shrug.

Now that Leah is going to get her masters at the program here at SPU they asked her to coach alongside our main cheer instructor. She agreed and will be moving up next football season.

"I'm captain of my team, I don't hang out with random people on the team constantly. What's going on?" he asks and I instantly get wary.

"Well we're friends. Does it bother you? I mean since it's her, does it bother you? I'm sorry I didn't think about that, I mean I did, but I didn't think it would bother you because you and Kam have cleared things up with her so—"

"Me and Ryn don't have an issue with Leah no. We're... civil and friendly," he shrugs. "That doesn't explain this new... thing. Whatever it is. When you asked I didn't think it was because you two were best friends." He refers to the past two weeks. I shake my head.

"She's just helping me prepare for next season. Keeping me

THE RULES OF YOU AND ME.

on track. It's fine. As long as you're fine with it," I tell him, keeping my voice light. I nod.

"Of course, I'm fine with it. I just want to make sure that you're okay," he tells me, letting me walk out of my door past him.

"All good." I nod again. I press myself into him for a side hug which is not as personal as we used to be. Two weeks ago Bell got drafted to the NFL. Since then he's been around me a lot more. Like he's... watching me in a way. I press a close-lipped smile toward him, and he angles himself to me.

"B..." he calls out and I turn before I walk down the stairs.

"What's up?" I ask, wanting to leave more than anything.

The tension is high. It's felt like this on my side for the past month, like there's too much that needs to be said but I can't break it in fear of messing up what progress we've made. The not-so-normal normalcy is killing me more than I thought it would.

"Are you doing okay?" he asks softly and my chest feels like it was just bombed and shredded.

I stare at my brother and contemplate breaking down right here and now, forgetting Leah altogether. But deterring him from his happiness... His success at the end of this semester. That thought deters me altogether. I can't dive as deep into the real hurt I've been feeling anyway. Not unless I want to disappoint him even further.

"Yeah. Really good," I lie and smile again.

He looks at me and I can't read his expression. But the closest thing I can compare it to would be disappointment. I turn before I can question it anymore. Leah looks uninterested as she waits for me by the front door.

"You're running late today," she chirps.

"You're in a bitchy mood today," I mutter and she sighs.

I was scared of Leah. Now she's grown into an annoyance

like a pimple that keeps coming back. Even if I do use the term friend, I use it lightly.

"Your sister is kind of an asshole," she tells Bellamy as we start to walk out of the door.

"Not to me," he smiles and Leah rolls her eyes and shuts the door.

"You should be more of an asshole to your brother," she tells me.

"I'm not taking advice from you about my brother. Didn't end well for you," I joke and she shoots me a side glare.

She's wearing her normal workout set. Always a shade of pink or a light color. I'm wearing all black today. A long-sleeve gym shirt with black biker shorts. Leah and I don't talk as I walk with her, my two long braids swinging on my back as we make it to the elevator then eventually her Camry. We get in and I cross my arms over my chest.

"Are you ready to talk today?" she asks when we get in the car.

"I'm not talking to you. I have nothing to talk about," I tell her.

"Nothing to get off of your chest?" she asks and I shake my head.

"Nothing. I'm doing great," I lie.

I have been banned from going to bars. I was told by Leah. She also told my brother. Saying if I went to a single bar with my fake ID that I would be kicked from the cheer team next year. So I've spent all of my time in my apartment, the dance studio, or with the bright and sunny Leah Ashley.

"Have you called your therapist?" she asks.

"Have you learned to mind your own business? Oh wait..." I pretend to realize that she's once again prying and she clenches her jaw.

"Brat," she fights.

THE RULES OF YOU AND ME.

"Control freak." I urge.

"I'm trying to help you," she fights back.

"And I'm trying to not hate you the more you force me to go to the gym with you and spend time outside of my apartment. I have perfect grades. I go to dance classes. What more do you want?" I ask.

"I want you to talk to me about Parker Thompson. About Bellamy... Dakota?" she asks.

"I'd rather cosplay a speed bump," I tell her.

"You're dramatic," she sighs.

"Good," I smile and she just keeps driving.

There's nothing to talk about. I'm working through everything on my own. I should call my therapist. But I haven't made the choice if I want to start fresh or reconnect with Madeline. I don't want to make that decision yet either. Dakota doesn't want to talk to me. I know that even without talking to him. I've been making sure he's okay... Through Leah. Through anyone who will talk to me about him. But the thought of reaching out to him and being rejected, it's not going to be good for my already rocky mental state.

This is the most normal I've felt around Bellamy since January despite the fact that I feel like I'm walking on eggshells all the time. And as for Parker I have done everything in my power to forget about his existence because the alternative hurts too bad. I tell myself I don't want him. I tell myself I don't care and I don't feel because it's easier than actually feeling and caring. Bellamy would never be okay with it. Risking Bellamy for Parker... The pain of having to even think those words is too much and it burns. I shove the thought out of my head before I break down.

"You're doing ankle weights today. And you need a weighted belt for lifting. I don't want to hear your arguments," she tells me. I have every urge to shove my middle finger at her.

"Have you been eating?" she asks.

"Have you been eating?" I mimic her words and she sighs.

"Answer me," she urges.

"Yes. I have been eating two full meals a day and small stuff for breakfast," I tell her, not fighting anymore.

I don't get it. Her fixing and oddly mothering mentality. It doesn't seem like Leah. I've never known her to be a caretaker, but that's exactly what this is. I'm not going to ask her either because she'll most likely give me a smart response. Leah brings me to the campus gym and I reluctantly follow her in. Starting with cardio, she makes me wear the ankle weights when I bring my run to a walk. I hate every damn second of it.

We stretch too. She forces me into a pilates style workout which I despise. I do enough during dance, I don't need more but she doesn't let up. I want to scream. I do what she says, continuing to work and follow her lead, my body tiring, my mind breaking down the more I start to sweat. It's hard to keep up a facade this way. It's hard to not act like I always do when I get clouded like this. But I don't really have to act any way around Leah because despite how I act, she can very well see through it which pisses me off more. I sit up on my mat, my knees pressing into the soft material. I open my mouth to talk but my eyes catch on him for the first time since the championship game in January.

Parker.

His hair is long. Long enough to be pulled back, because it is right now. The messy bun he wears is a look I've never been a fan of, but seemingly love on him. His eyes hit me. Like a truck. Like a freight train. And just like gravity, I'm drawn to him. It all crashes in. The feeling. The hurt. The overwhelming love I have deep rooted in my chest for him. I can't believe it's been this long without even looking at someone I loved. I love... I... I don't even know. His eyes drift.

THE RULES OF YOU AND ME.

"Hey Leah..." he mumbles then looks back toward me. "Hi, Brianne." He speaks my name and my entire body shifts, ignites, and melts. I want to scream. I'm choked up, incapable of doing anything but stare.

"Hi, Parker," Leah says and I feel like I did when I first met him when I could barely speak around without feeling like a squeaky toy.

"Hi," I try to speak above a whisper, but my voice feels like a ghost in my body.

"How are you?" he asks me. Not Leah. He's looking directly at me.

"I.. I'm.."

"She's good," Leah speaks for me and gives me a look.

A knowing look. Like she meant for this to happen and I don't look at her any longer, wanting to see him.

"I saw a flier for a dance recital... Are you in that?" he asks me and my lips part.

"It's my final. My two performances," I tell him.

"Good luck. I wish I could be there," he tells me and I nod and watch him start to walk away. My heart and my mouth speak before I can even think through my words.

"Why can't you come?" I ask.

"Do you want me to?" He turns over his shoulder. I hesitate, my lip shaking. He nods. "Text me. If you want me to... You can always text me. It was good seeing you. Bye Leah."

He finally turns his attention to her again and then he leaves, cool, casual and calm. I feel my lip shake again and I watch where he was, my mind reeling, my heart pattering and sputtering. Hurt laces its way throughout all of me and I want to scream. I turn to Leah with wet eyes and she raises her eyebrows.

"You knew he would be here," I accuse.

"I had a hint..." she tells me, continuing her workout and I shove her so she can't get up. She plops down right next to me and glares.

"I'm not doing this anymore. Fuck this," I tell her.

"Do you want to talk about it?" she asks, challenging me.

"Why do you care? Why are you doing this?" I fight, my voice tight and angry but quiet since we're in public.

"Because I was in the same position a year and a half ago. I made a mistake. I ruined something, and I made your brother hate me and it changed me. A lot of me. I didn't have someone to pick me up off the floor. I just made an idiot of myself. I'm not letting you do that. Talk about it. Talk to me Bri," she urges.

"So you can't date my brother and annoy the shit out of him so you choose me instead?" I ask.

"Your insults don't hurt me," she promises and I feel my tears pool over finally, crying for the first time in weeks.

"Is this what you wanted? For me to cry, for me to be hurt and sad again?" I ask her.

"Again? You've been sad and hurt, you just harbor it and it's going to tear you up. Say something," she fights.

"We're not friends," I fight her.

"I'm the closest thing to a friend you have right now until you grow up and talk to Dakota."

She shoves my mistakes in my face again and I groan, wiping my eyes.

"This is embarrassing," I fight, thankful the gym is close to empty right now.

"Love is embarrassing. We either finish our workout which I planned circuits for the rest of our time... Or we go and get food and you talk to me."

She gives me an option and I press my lips together. Do I torture my body or my mind... The more I ignore my mind the more torturous it will be. I didn't think it would be this bad until I saw Parker in person for the first time.

THE RULES OF YOU AND ME.

"Why did I have to see him for you to get me to this point?" I ask her.

"Because I can't have you breaking down when you see him at practice for the first time. I can't have you breaking down over a boy," she tells me and I bite my tongue.

"I'm not working out anymore," I inform her.

"So you'll talk?" she asks.

"Yes, I'll talk, Leah," I tell her reluctantly.

I sit in Leah's car, overlooking the ocean, just like I had when I was with Parker. Those were my stipulations, that we came here. And that I got to pick out where we ate. I chose McDonald's. Leah is eating directly next to me, staring at me as I eat.

"Can I get a chicken nugget down before you force me to share my deepest darkest secrets please?" I ask her.

She rolls her eyes and continues eating just like I do for a few minutes.

"I don't know what you want me to say. You know how I feel. I need to talk to my therapist, but I haven't come to terms with that yet. I can't seem to get on the right page with my brother. I don't know how to even try besides pretending I'm happy and fine but I'm starting to feel like he can see through that and he's going to push away the second he realizes half of the reason I'm feeling this way is because I'm quite literally helpless when it comes to how I feel about Parker. Because I've tried to tell myself I don't care. That I don't love him. That I don't feel the way I do and seeing him today solidified to me that I'm a horrible liar even to myself. You know all of this," I tell her.

"What I want to know is why you feel like you have to harbor all of this and keep it on your shoulders," she talks to me in the kindest tone I've heard from her.

"Because why would I put it on anyone else?" I ask.

"Someone like your brother?" she asks.

"He's moved on from most of his pain. His grief. His sadness. He moves on quickly and I can't bring him back on his own journey for my benefit," I tell him.

"I don't think you give your brother enough credit for his emotional capacity. How much he cares. And I also don't think you're really telling me everything," she explains. "I didn't know about your parents until months and months into dating your brother. And he brushed past it so quickly that I didn't even realize he had actually mentioned it."

"Because Bellamy misses them and he does it infrequently. It's an afterthought. He sees something and thinks... Awe, I miss Mom," I explain.

"And you?" she asks.

"And me, when I dance I imagine my mom watching and crying and it crushes me. When I look at the ocean I break when I know I'll never be able to sit in the sand with my dad. I could shatter at the thought of someone being my forever person and never getting to bring them around my mom and dad. And it breaks me apart even more that the one person I have loved. The one person I really could have imagined forever with was punched by my brother, the only person whose approval means anything to me. And that was my fault. I never should have lied to him, but that doesn't change how I feel. I miss my parents. I will never be able to fill that hole but I can't bring that to Bellamy," I tell her.

"You know Bellamy knows how you feel. Whatever you think he doesn't know he does," she tells me.

"He didn't know about Parker." I raise my eyebrows.

"Yeah, I don't know how. I noticed at your birthday that you wanted him and he wanted you," she mutters.

"I think you choosing for Bellamy what he can and can't

THE RULES OF YOU AND ME.

handle isn't fair. He's strong and smart and annoyingly perfect most times. He makes mistakes. He made a mistake doing what he did with Parker. I'm sure if you just talked to him then—"

"I can't because that could potentially make it worse," I tell her.

"It's already bad...." she informs me like I didn't know.

"It could always be worse. And I don't need that," I tell her.

"Just think about it. Next time he comes to you, think about telling him. Talking to him..." She shrugs.

"I'll think about it," I tell her. I make a split decision, realizing in these past few moments just how good this has felt.

"This year... After your brother, after all the drama with Kamryn that I had started. My parents fell into some really hard times and I had to pick up a job at The Bulldog. After losing your brother, even saying it sounds dramatic. I'm over it, but that doesn't mean it didn't hurt and that it didn't change me. I was dumb, frivolous and tried to do anything to gain control. All of this. All of the hard shit I've had to deal with, it made me grow up. And as silly as it sounds, I was lucky to have all of that happen to me as an adult. I can't even imagine going through heartbreak or severe loss when you did Baby. I don't think you give yourself enough credit for how much you've survived..." Leah talks with her heart and I look at her quizzically.

"Did you just compliment me?" I ask her.

"I'm serious, don't be a bitch." She rolls her eyes and shakes her head.

"I'm sorry about your parents... But at least you have a hot hockey player that wants you, that's a perk, isn't it?" I joke and she scoffs.

"Xander is the bane of my existence," she mumbles.

"But?" I ask, waiting for the rest.

"But nothing. There's... History there," she hesitates when she says the word.

561

"History? Like before SPU history?" I ask.

"History that I've sworn myself and Xander to secrecy on so don't ask. Either way, it doesn't matter. Even if he's the bane of my existence, his persistence is annoyingly cute in a way, and I want to open up to him again. Maybe," she admits and I watch her cheeks get red, almost like she's embarrassed by her words.

I don't push her on it, even though she might have pushed me to spill if the roles were reversed. That's why our weird duo works: Me and Leah aren't the same, but I'm really thankful for that right now. Even thinking about that is shocking to me.

I sit in silence, shuffling the ice around in my cup. I take a deep breath and sigh it out, looking over the ocean.

"I think I will talk to my therapist. Today I will send her a message," I tell Leah.

"Good... I'm proud of you," she tells me and I scrunch my nose.

"Ew, don't be weird," I tell her.

"I'm not being weird," she fights back.

"Yes you are, you're being nice which is weird," I inform her and she smirks.

"You love me." I feel ounces of heat seep back into my chest.

"Yeah, in a way I do. But not when you force me to go to the gym," I tell her.

"How else would I have gotten you to have a breakdown?" she asks.

"How do you not have a breakdown every day in that stinky ass building?" I laugh and she does too besides me.

I haven't laughed in months.... Not actually. But I am now and it feels so freeing.

CHAPTER 48

SOMEONE'S SOMEBODY BY LEVI RANSOM

Brianne Archer:

Madeline was eager to meet with me the second I messaged her so we set up an appointment for today, during the first week of April. I told Leah that my appointment was today. Just to follow up with her and let her know. So the past hour I've debriefed my therapist on what's been happening since I decided to stop seeing her before Thanksgiving. She's been listening well. Talking to me here and there. I swore once the hour mark hit that she would tell me we needed to meet next week but she kept me going, saying she booked us extra time, figuring we had a lot to talk about.

"I just feel like I lose everyone and everything," I admit out loud to her.

"Correct me if I'm wrong, but to me, it feels like maybe you push those away so you don't have to deal with them leaving first, Brianne. Dakota is the perfect example of that. Kamryn too," she tells me and I clamp my mouth shut. I did push them away. I did that.

"And you don't want to reach out to them because why?" She asks.

"They wouldn't forgive me," I admit.

"Or have you not forgiven yourself so you're convincing your mind that they wouldn't either," she tells me.

"Ouch," I mutter.

"I'm sorry. It's been too long. Our talks were always productive... I think you calling me again was productive," she tells me.

"I'm happy I did," I admit.

"Are you going to do anything about the other men in your life?" she asks.

"Only one other man is in my life. And I can't talk to Bellamy if I don't have a reason to." I tell her.

"Okay. We can revisit that if you ever feel like it... But today I think you've gotten a lot off of your chest. I think you're learning that healing isn't linear. From anything traumatic that happens in your life. And it's not the same. For anyone. Parker dealt with something similar to what you did in a very different way. But even his feelings are different from yours." She explains and I ignore the burn when his name is mentioned.

"Healing is horrible," I tell her.

"It's not easy, no..." She agrees. "For the record I think your brother and you would benefit from a talk." She tells me and I nod.

"Can I think about it?" I ask her.

"Of course... Can we meet again next week Brianne, is that okay?" she asks and I nod.

"I think that would be a really good idea," I admit out loud, my chest feeling a weight lift.

"Do you have any plans for the rest of the day?" she asks and I nod. I hug my knees to my chest.

"One of my easiest coping mechanisms is dancing. I have a dance recital in two weeks. I have one ballet solo as well as a contemporary lyrical solo. My dance teacher says it's my strongest style next to ballet. I decompress when I dance and I think that's what I want to do today," I tell her.

"I don't think you give yourself enough credit Bri. For how strong you are. And how well you take care of yourself even if you need help and guidance," she tells me and I feel my lips turn up into a genuine smile.

"Thank you. My... My friend Leah actually said the same thing last week," I tell her. Calling Leah my friend for the first time ever and liking the way it sounds.

"You should listen to your friend. I'll see you next week," she tells me and hangs up, leaving me to change and put my clothes on.

I skip the leotard and settle for a pair of tight spandex shorts and a cut t-shirt that shows my collarbone and shoulder because this is the only thing I actually prefer to dance in.

I turn on my music and scurry to the middle of the dimly lit dance studio. I prefer it darker in here, only a backlight from the hallway and the cubby holes in the wall. It feels better this way. The soft sound of the piano drives me. The deepness of the bass could shake the dance studio but it doesn't matter because no one is around.

The lyrics alone are always something I could move to, with or without choreography. The truth behind them and how I feel in relation. Part of me chose this song in hopes Bellamy would hear it when he came to my dance recital and would talk to me afterwards. But I can't bank on that... So I leave my feelings on the floor. I dance with passion and power, the choreography me and my professor mastered and created blending so well with the vocals and musicality of the song. I throw myself into it.

Dancing on the floor, in the air, in my chest, in my mind. My entire body is enthralled in the process.

My favorite part of the song picks up and I run on the floor, fighting each part of myself. The part that's too scared to ask for help. The part begging to be heard. The part wishing for someone. The part wanting to be alone and okay with that. The part of me that wants to be what I was when I had Dakota. When I had Bellamy. When I had Parker. When I had anyone but me. Healing is not linear. And even when I do heal I know the truth of these words will always hit. No matter what I will always want to be wanted. If not by anyone around me, by myself. And I haven't been feeling the want and need for myself until recently..

The song ends and I stop myself on the floor in my ending pose, my back rising and falling rapidly from the full out performance. I keep my cheek pressed to my knee, my body curled up in my final pose. I breathe that way, hugging myself for more reasons than just the one. Then a soft clap brings me out of my trance and I'm instantly scared of who will be standing there. I look up and into the mirror in front of me, seeing a familiar head of dusty blonde hair. I turn around in the dim light to see Dakota walking toward me in socks because he definitely knows better than to wear shoes in the studio.

"Mind if I sit?" he asks and I shake my head no, not able to speak. He snatches my water bottle from the front of the room and hands it to me.

"Is that for your recital?" he asks me and I nod again. "I don't think I've ever been around you when you've been this quiet. It's me, Baby..." He sits down next to me, pulling one knee up.

"Sorry. I just wasn't expecting you to... I didn't expect to see you." I admit.

THE RULES OF YOU AND ME.

"Well, I was getting tired of waiting for you to come to me. So I made the jump," he tells me.

"I heard about you and Nico... I'm sorry Dak," I tell him.

"We both agreed on it... It's not a never. It's just not now. Neither of us are really ready for a relationship and I'm honestly overwhelmed with life right now... That and missing you," he admits and my heart jumps. I relax from the dancer position but still hold my knees to my chest.

"That song was... It was a sad one," he tells me and I nod.

"It's beautiful though. And the lyrics are..." I hesitate.

"Exactly how you're feeling right now?" he asks and I nod.

"How did you know where I was?" I ask.

"I went to your apartment. Bellamy answered and looked relieved to see me. I think he's worried about you..." he admits and I nod.

"I'm starting to think the same thing as of lately which means my facade isn't working," I tell him.

"So I assume that means you haven't been talking to him?" he asks me and I shake my head.

"Not about anything we should talk about," I sigh.

"Which is what?" he asks.

"Kind of just what I was dancing about. I know a lot of what I think and feel is in my head. It comes from my own hurt and insecurity. But I... I have given a lot up for my brother. I have done a lot for him and I love him and would do it all again. But I also think that maybe I'm coming to terms with how unfair our relationship has been. Not by his doing, but by my own," I admit.

"That's a big step for you," he nods.

"Because you were right. My brother's feelings should never control my happiness. But my happiness should never come from any man... Friend, brother, or boyfriend." I tell him. "I do feel that way. Like I'm constantly battling on what I want and what I think I should want based on what others tell me. I feel wrong and confused and... and I've never been this unhappy or felt this unloved. The past four months have been the loneliest moments I've ever had," I admit.

"I've been so worried about you, B..." he tells me, and my heart lurches.

"I'm sorry. For pushing you away. And for lying. Because I didn't start going to therapy again like I had said. I started back today and I just... I shouldn't have treated you the way I did. And I shouldn't have doubted you either, that was why I waited to talk to you. I thought you'd hate me for how I acted," I tell him.

"You could never make me hate you, Baby," he smirks.

"I'm serious. Leah has practically forced me to heal and move forward. I ran into Parker and had a mental breakdown at the gym. I just... I've realized a lot of this was my fault. My mistake. But what made me happy? What I did to make me happy wasn't a mistake and I shouldn't look at it as that. What was a mistake was ever trying to go through a breakup without my best friend. I'm sorry," I apologize.

"I love you, B. I don't need you to apologize. I understand why you said what you did and honestly. I have never had a relationship with a sibling like you and Bellamy because I don't have a sibling... I'd never understand that commitment you have. I'm sorry I didn't respect your feelings on it," he tells me and I nod.

"I love you Dak," I smile at him and feel tears in my eyes once again.

I wonder when the hell all of this will stop hurting and when I'll dry out of tears but part of me thinks it'll never be. Pain is proof of healing. At least I hope that's what all of this is for.

THE RULES OF YOU AND ME.

"Are you okay? Really okay?" he asks me and I shake my head no.

He opens his arms and I practically crawl into his grasp. He hugs me tightly. The first real bit of human contact I've had in weeks and I crush Dakota to me. I also cry. And he lets me do just that. He holds me like he's done this type of comforting for me his whole life and I've never been more thankful for a person. Dakota is my someone. He has been. Him making the step for me to break our silence is more than I could ever ask of anyone. He's a better person than I could be.

"Can you make me a promise that next time you're hurt, which will hopefully be never, you'll ask for space and not bite my head off when I try to help?" he asks and I nod.

"Yes... I promise." I nod through my tears.

"Also promise me that if you need help you'll ask for it. That you won't let yourself struggle like you have the past 4 months. Thank god for Leah Ashley. I never thought I'd say that but seriously." He laughs lightly. I nod and sniffle.

"I promise... Also, I think I got tears and snot on your shirt," I tell him.

"It's fine, this wasn't my favorite shirt or anything," he jokes and we both laugh.

Fixing things. Mending what's broken and also making sure that I'm mending myself too. I do want to be happy but I can't achieve that without fixing myself first. Madeline was right. It's not linear. And if apologies are what's on my schedule today, I have another one to add to my roster.

"I need to go see Kamryn." I wipe my nose and Dakota stands and helps me off the ground.

"Movie night afterward?" he asks.

The relief I feel is a weight that's completely lifted from my chest. I smile with closed lips, unable to stop the emotion.

"I'd love to..." I tell him, trying not to cry.

Dakota hugs me again and leaves, so I go to my phone and ask Kamryn where she is. At our apartment, no surprise there. I grab my things and head that way, driving slowly to think about what I need to say. I drive silently, no music, no radio talk shows, nothing. When I pull up to our complex I take a deep breath and head up, not letting myself second guess my own thoughts.

"B, is that you?" Kamryn asks from her and Bellamy's bedroom.

"Yeah, are you alone?" I ask, dropping my bag. I open the door to my brother's bedroom and she sits on the bed, homework spread in front of her.

"Lawson and Bellamy went out. What did you need to talk to me about?" she asks.

I stare at her from the door, holding onto it for safety despite knowing I don't need it. Kamryn is always honest but she's never cruel. I feel like I need the protection from my own vulnerability. It has nothing to do with her. She sits there, her skin clean, her black hair in a high ponytail that still trails down her back. She tilts her head and furrows her brows.

"Is everything okay?" she asks me and I slightly break, my face falling. "Aw B, come here, what's wrong?"

"I'm... I was going to talk to you but I obviously can't do that. I just wanted to say I'm sorry," I admit, stepping into the room.

"For what? Oh my god, you have nothing to be sorry for, what is wrong?" She gets up, completely discarding all the work that was in her lap.

She gets up and approaches me. She's shorter than me, but not by much. She holds my shoulders and looks me in the eyes.

"For what I said when everything first happened a few months ago. For putting you in the middle of this entire situation at all. You're the best thing that's happened to my brother

THE RULES OF YOU AND ME.

and I almost ruined that. On top of it, I messed up the small relationship we built and what I said was uncalled for, I—"

"Shhh, Bri, take a deep breath. Come here." Kamryn hugs me and I hug her back, smelling her fresh scent.

She smells kind of like my brother, clean and fresh and so comforting.

"I understand why you feel the need to apologize so I accept it. But I just want you to know, I get it. You're dealing with your feelings. I'm a victim to the same damn thing sometimes. We... We usually snap at the people we love the most. I've definitely learned that, and I didn't take it to heart. Honestly it made me feel like a sister. Like a part of the family." She smiles when she pulls back from the hug.

"You look like you could kill someone, but you're actually really sweet," I tell her.

"It's my secret weapon, but only the good people know I'm sweet deep down. B, you're like the sister I was never lucky enough to have. I appreciate the apology, but it's not needed. I just want... I just want all of this to be past us," she admits and I nod.

"Me too. I've been doing a lot better," I admit.

"I can tell, but Bri—"

"That was all I needed. Just to apologize. And to say I love you. Thank you too," I tell her and she nods.

"I love you too..." She nods and I think about Bellamy.

If I should maybe do what Leah said and talk to him. If I should ask Kamryn... But the last thing I want to do is bring her into this again. So I just squeeze her shoulder and make my exit, waiting for Dakota to head over here. There's only so much I can fix... And some things take time. Maybe that's what Bell and I need. More time.

CHAPTER 49
YOURS BY ALEXANDER 23

Parker Thompson:

I straighten my suit jacket and fix my hair. I cut it, the man bun is no more but it is still long enough to flow back. I had let it grow just to see if I could. But the second I decided I wanted to go to her recital I cut it back to this length, the length I had when we were together. Because she said she wasn't into man buns. I remember having a conversation about that. It always made me laugh.

"Xander..." I call my friend and he leans into my room.

"Are you ready, Pookie?" he asks.

"I don't know. I don't think she's ready. For me, for us. Bellamy never texted me about them having a conversation but he has kept me updated. Saying her and Dakota are friends again. That she's been happier, actually happy. But she has no idea I'm going to be there." My chest heats at the thought.

"So, why are you going again?" he asks.

"Because, even if I can't have her, I'll support her. I know this is important to her so it's not about me but I still want to be there... I'll just stay unnoticed and unseen," I tell him.

"I honestly thought you might just try and move on... Now that everything is a little more calm in your life." He tells me and I look at him, furrowing my brows. I narrow my eyes now and he cracks into a smile. "I'm kidding. You're on your hands and knees for her," he tells me and I shake my head.

"Shut up. I have two words. Leah and Ashley." I give him a fake smile and he rolls his eyes.

"She hung out with me the night we picked Bri up from the bar," he fights.

"No, she didn't. She tolerated you," I clarify and Xander shrugs.

"You actually have no idea what's going on. Anyway, you need to leave now if you want to be on time. Not that it would matter considering she has no idea that you're there." Xander shrugs. I grab my keys and my phone.

"Can you let me know..." Xander follows after me..

"Let you know what?" I ask.

"If you have a magical high school musical moment where she sees you from the audience and you fall in love all over again and—"

"You're annoying me, goodbye," I cut him short and he groans.

"I hope you guys get back together so you're less grumpy."

I close the door in his face and head out.

I did exactly as I planned. The concert hall is packed with friends and family. I notice Dakota with the whole group of cheerleaders near the front. Leah and Valerie included. Then I see Bellamy and Lawson's head sticking out of the crowd with Kam and Sienna too. I didn't make myself known to either group, not wanting a problem or a scene. I sat on the balcony

THE RULES OF YOU AND ME.

area away from everyone so that I could make sure I wouldn't be seen by friends, family, or Brianne.

The lights go down and the first few dances are different trios and group numbers but I don't see Brianne at all. I look at the program and my fingers trace over her name next on the scheduled dances. The name of the dance is in French and I have no idea what it means. I assume it'll be a ballet piece. I get excited seeing stuff like this especially from her because I'm faintly familiar with the art. The tiny bit of training I had makes it fun to watch. More fun I should say. The faint piano starts, the music soft and light. My breath leaves my chest though.

I've seen Brianne in her dance clothes. I've seen her warm up in her tights and leotard. She's sent me photos in her all black with her leg warmers and warm ups on which she looks stunning in. But I've never seen this. She's perfect. A piece of art. She's wearing a soft blue tutu that stands straight out and shows off her toned legs that are covered in the softest pink tights. Her torso and chest are covered in diamonds and gems and it looks like her skin is covered in a sheer layer of diamonds and sparkle. It could be the lights or her makeup I have no idea. That's another part of it. Her makeup is done differently than she does in cheer or daily. She looks flawless. Airbrushed. Not even real. Her brown hair is secured in a tight bun and there's a crown atop her head.

She dances with precision I've never seen before. Not from her classmates. Not online. It could come from ignorance or just complete infatuation but no one does it like her. The way she moves is inspiring. Inviting. I watch as she leaps and turns and makes the stage her own in a tight and elongated way. Her tail is tucked, her body is elegant and long and she's done everything she taught me and then some. If I hadn't met her. Touched her, held her... I'd question if she was even real. She exits the stage and I instantly clap, bringing my fingers between my lips to whistle for her. Proud is an understatement.

Just as I had last time, I watch in silence once more, waiting and counting down the numbers until she's back on the stage. I noticed that this song is in english. It seems casual and modern which makes me question if this will be one of the styles she prefers. Lyrical. That's what she had called it. I know she said that was her favorite so I eagerly wait, wondering what she will be wearing this time. What she will look like.

When she emerges again she's angelic. Perfect. Her hair is partially down, the other half slicked up and in a ponytail. The blue sheen and sparkle is gone from her skin, but she's still ethereal in the stage light. She's wearing white flowing pants and a white top that has large bell-like sleeves. They flow, like waves. Like ribbons.

The song once again starts with piano. And the second she starts moving and the lyrics make their way to my head, and my heart I feel like I did that day when I found her in the studio. I feel like I'm intruding as I look at her, the way she moves like water and the facial expressions she emotes breaks my heart open. I follow her every move like it's the end all be all of my life and I'd do it again and again anytime I saw her dance. Brianne's body is made of magic when I watch it move in this way. I've seen it every single way, but seeing her do something she loves. Something that makes her who she is. It's far more enticing and attractive than I could even express.

I have no idea who she's seen. What she's done. Who she even is now. It's been months without speaking to her. And things can change in a matter of days. So months... Months are like a lifetime. But I want happiness for her. I want her to do this forever. To dance like she's giving every part of her to the stage and dance floor. I want her to have people like Dakota and Leah... She does a flip, one with no hands and she lands then

THE RULES OF YOU AND ME.

folds her body into herself, curling like she can't take it anymore and my chest clutches. I swear it's like I stop breathing altogether at the beauty that she is. That she'll always be. Then she's gone, exiting the stage.

There's silence over the entire auditorium. For a few moments no one speaks, no one even breathes, all of us feeling the same thing from that performance. I pause and then someone next to me starts clapping. Then we all do. We all move, clapping and cheering and whistling.

"She was beautiful." The little girl next to me tells her mom, tugging on her shirt. I watch the kid smile wide and I feel my chest tighten again, wishing I could tell Brianne about this moment. That she's going to have kids looking up to her for the rest of her life with the skill she possesses. I'm in awe of her...

There's another group number that happens after her performance and she's in this one. Smiling and working with the 13 other dancers in her company. That's what she said they were called. Not a team which she corrected me on very quickly after I had said it. Then everyone does their bows and she looks absolutely gorgeous as she waves and smiles a million dollar smile. Everyone gets up to leave and I head for the exit, instantly panicking when I get stopped up trying to get out of the hall.

It takes me what feels like forever to get down the stairs and into the auditorium lobby. But it's madness. Considering it was a recital for every single class of dancers at SPU there's a lot of family and friends packed into this lobby. I try to stay close to the wall and squeeze past everyone, but there's a hand on my shoulder and my chest fills with liquid hot panic.

"Parker?" The question in her voice makes my heart jump.

I could pretend I don't hear her but I know that she saw me. I slowly turn. Then she's face to face with me.

"Step outside." She nods and I do, turning around to walk right out the doors I'm next to.

Anxiety rumbles through me but I keep myself calm and collected on the outside as I turn, finally looking at her in full. She stands at the perfect height. The perfect height for me to reach out to her, to touch her face to run my fingers through her hair. I've never been affected by someone like this. When they haven't even said anything but my damn name. But I'm at her will right now. I'd get on my hands and knees and grovel at her feet if she asked. I show none of that on my face or in my body language. I just look at her and wait.

"What are you doing here?" she asks with wonder and surprise in her voice.

"You weren't supposed to see me. I just wanted to see you. To support you..." I admit.

"How would I know you were supporting me if I didn't see you?" she asks.

"Well, today isn't about me or anyone else. It's about you. I wasn't going to cause anything by being here... I just wanted to be here for you, Sunshine." I let the nickname slip out and I hesitate. "I'm sorry," I mumble.

"It's fine." She looks down, tension between us.

"Can I talk? Without anything holding me back... Just for a second?" I ask.

"Go ahead," she nods.

"You're so goddamn beautiful. And that was incredible. All of it. And I'm proud of you... How far you've come even since I saw you last semester you were... I don't know how to put it. But you were just perfect." I tell her and then I see her cheeks blush. I see her smile. And I see only a few of the reasons I fell in love with her. Which still sits heavy on my chest, not being able to say those words.

"There you are, B..." Leah Ashley walks out and her eyes hit me skeptically. "Bellamy is about to be out here. I think he and Kam wanted to take pictures." She tells her, eyeing me.

THE RULES OF YOU AND ME.

"You have to go," Bri tells me quietly and I nod, pretending it doesn't sting. "I'm sorry. God I'm sorry. Thank you for coming it... Seriously you don't understand what it means to me, but I don't want Bellamy to... I mean things are starting to be normal and..." She trails off and I clench my jaw, understanding.

She doesn't want her brother to think anything.

"It doesn't have to be like this..." I tell her and she shakes her head.

"It does... I'm sorry, Parker." She turns away from me and I kick myself for even being seen at all.

CHAPTER 50
RYDER BY MADISON BEER

Brianne Archer:

This wasn't my plan. None of this had been my plan. I didn't plan on trying my hardest to move forward. I didn't plan on feeling so much better about this entire fuck up of a situation. I didn't expect to come to terms with my feelings on everything. On my brother. On how he treats me, how this year has felt. How I haven't dealt with anything in my life properly. I didn't honestly think I'd find happiness at this school again, or at least not for a long time. I didn't plan on crying my makeup off after my dance recital or locking myself in my bedroom when it finished either.

I especially didn't expect to finally crack enough to feel like I have to talk to Bellamy, especially after things started to feel like they used to.

But I have to. I have to talk to him. I can't sit with any of this anymore. I've spent months coming to terms with how I really feel. I've gaslit myself into thinking I was wrong or crazy and finally, I've realized and sat with this and it's not fair to me. I don't deserve this. To feel like this. Parker told me once that I talk a lot but never say what I mean and that's what I felt like I've done all year. Not actually speaking my mind and my heart and asking for what I want. What I need from those around me. I walk down the stairs and I knock on my brother's bedroom door. Kamryn and Sienna are together tonight, meaning he's alone. Meaning this is the perfect chance to talk to him. Even if it does ruin the progress we've made.

If I don't do it now I won't do it at all.

Bellamy opens his bedroom door and furrows his brows. He's wearing a hoodie and sweat shorts. He looks showered and comfy. I probably look like a complete and utter mess right now.

"What's going on? Why are you crying?" He asks and I sigh then shake my head.

"Can I come in? Can we talk, please?" I ask, and without hesitation, my brother opens the door to me and allows me to walk in. He motions for his bed and I crawl onto it, criss crossing my legs. He joins me but sits with his back on his headboard and his knees bent. His elbows hang loosely around his legs.

"What's going on?" he asks and I let out a shaky breath.

"I've been lying to you... again. And I know I said I wouldn't do that but I did and I'm sorry. But I've lied to you since January and I'm sure you started to notice." I tell him.

"About what?" he asks, his voice gentle.

"About being happy. Or being okay. Because I haven't been happy. And I'm really not okay," I admit out loud to him and he sits there, staring at me. There's really no point in holding in my hurt or my tears because they're going to come either way.

"And not only that but I've struggled the past few years. With mom and dad. With you being gone and at SPU. With you leaving again to go to New York. I've had a hard time for years and have been too scared to tell you. I didn't want to hurt you or make you backtrack in your own healing and... And I'm sorry for lying but I can't lie anymore. It's too much," I tell him.

THE RULES OF YOU AND ME.

"Why? I mean why did you lie? Did you think I couldn't handle it?" he asks and I shrug.

"I don't know. You just seemed so okay. So good with everything. So well managed and I'm a train wreck. It felt wrong to drag you into that," I admit.

"You drag me into every single mess. That is what I'm meant for," he tells me softly.

"I was so scared of losing you that I ruined our relationship. God I made my own brother hate me and for what?" I ask.

"Even when I want to hate you I love you. I will never not love you B. Even when you fuck up, because you will again and again. You're all I have left... I'm never going to hate you," he clarifies and I sigh.

"And I'd like to add that what happened this year... It's not your fault. It's mine more than anything. You didn't fuck up. You lied to me and I... I'm sorry you felt like you had to," he apologizes. I furrow my brows, thinking there's no way. He couldn't feel that way, especially when he doesn't know how I really feel.

"What if I told you that I'm not over Parker... And that I can't see him without feeling like my chest is cracking open. Because I love him and I want to tell him that and I can't because I chose you. Because I can't lose my brother so I lost him and it hurts. Losing Parker hurts," I tell my brother, anxiety burning through my chest.

"I would tell you that if you love someone that much, you should tell them that. Because if someone had told me not to love Kamryn. If someone had asked me to not choose her I would have told them it was too damn late. I never asked you to choose B. I never would. Because I'm your brother, even when I'm not your first priority I know you're still choosing me. But I also know you can't help who you fall in love with," he explains

583

and I feel like I'm in a dream. I feel like I'm hearing things. Like there's no way this could be real.

"You can choose to lie. To hide and do things behind my back... which you did. But you aren't right now. You're talking to me about it. And as weird as it is that you're talking about my friend, it's not weird because I know I can trust him," he tells me and I shake my head.

"But a few months ago you said—"

"I wish I could completely erase what happened a few months ago. I regret a lot of what happened. How I reacted. I shouldn't have gotten so mad. I shouldn't have hit Parker. I talked to Parker. I talked to him and admitted that I think my hurt came from the fact that my best friend and my baby sister felt like they couldn't trust me. You especially because you trust me with everything, B. I was selfishly hurt by your choices and that wasn't my place. I forgave you for your lie long before this second. I've just been waiting for you to talk to me because you've shut me down every time I've tried," he admits.

"I didn't feel like I could trust you for that exact reason. You just did it again. You called me your baby sister. That's what I am. Baby this, kid that. I understand I'm young. I know that I've got a lot of shit to learn and even more to go through, but diminishing me or any young girl to just that. Being young and a woman, saying it like it's a bad thing... It's not fair, and it's so not you. I expect you to protect me, but to treat me like I'm not capable? To treat me like I can't be my own person with my own style or make my own smart choices? It's ridiculous. That's why I didn't tell you. It's not an excuse. There's never an excuse to lie to someone you love, but I did feel like I had no choice," I tell him.

"You're more than what I made you out to be and I know that. I never saw you as less than, or young and dumb. Maybe a little reckless but you're supposed to be that way. I just never

THE RULES OF YOU AND ME.

want you to make my mistakes, but I know now it's not my place to stop you. I can try to guide you, and if you make that mistake anyway it's my job to help you piece yourself back together. Even though I was the one who broke it, I'm still trying to piece it back together. Here and now." He admits.

"This entire year I felt... No, I've realized... Since Mom and Dad passed away, I have always put your feelings over my own. That's not your fault, it's mine. But it's made me into a very passive and submissive person when it comes to you. I let your feelings and your thought process be my guide which has led me to pretend I'm okay when I'm not. I always wanted you to see it. To realize it. You never did, but Parker saw right through it... I felt seen and understood and... And we tried to fight it. We never meant to fall for each other but it just happened," I admit.

"I'm sorry. I didn't do it directly but I'm sorry if I ever played into it. Your birthday. Vegas. Halloween. Anything. There were always moments when I questioned your integrity. I wanted to ask, but I didn't want to make you feel like I didn't trust you. I think the biggest takeaway from all of this is that we need to talk more... Be more open when we're thinking or feeling something. Because I don't want whatever this has been for the past few months B. I want my sister back," he admits and I wipe a tear away from my eye at the relief those words cause.

"I'm sorry I lied to you," I admit.

"I'm sorry I made you feel like you had to," he admits. "And I'm sorry I made you choose me, even if I didn't ask. I'm sorry I made you feel that way. Especially with Parker. With what he's been through I... I never would understand but I. I'm sorry, B."

"So what does this mean?" I ask.

"It means that we really are done with secrets and lying from here on out. That even though in a few months I'll be halfway across the country we're not going to let that come between us. You're my best fucking friend and I'm not going to let that go over anyone or anything. Guys, girls. Whoever. We're the Bri and Bell that we always have been. The annoying talkative sister." He chimes.

"The cocky, stupid older brother." I fight back.

"And another thing... I don't want you to think you're alone in your feelings. With mom and dad, I mean. You mentioned it earlier and as much as I try my best, I have only coped with my feelings, but I haven't moved on or worked past all of it. You started therapy again. It's got me talking to Kamryn and thinking about it and I think I should have probably been going to a therapist for years. Healthy or not, coping doesn't mean I'm actually understanding and working through what I'm feeling. When they passed away I... I felt like I had to be more. I had to do better and I feel exactly what you do. The fear I have of something happening to you B, it used to keep me up at night. I feel like that a lot. How my brain would rationalize protecting you was more me wanting to freeze the moment. Freeze you as my baby sister because I can keep you there, and little, and young and... And it wasn't fair. So I want to talk to someone, to try and hopefully understand myself better, and not let the people I care about get caught up in my own mental health struggles. You're not alone... And anytime you need to talk about it. Mom and Dad or anything else, I need you to call me." He begs and I nod.

"Thank you... For taking on a role that you were never meant to take on. For being the best person for me for years. As for Mom and Dad, I can do that. I can call you," I agree.

"As for Parker... I hope it means that you'll call him. And talk to him... Fix what was hurt," he tells me.

"Are you sure he won't be scared of you hitting him again?" I ask.

"I'm sure he was scared of that before I went to talk to him about a month ago," he admits and my jaw drops.

THE RULES OF YOU AND ME.

"A month ago?" I ask.

"Yeah. I went to his apartment looking for you, but really looking to have a conversation with him. The way he defended you and talked about you. The way he knew what he was saying could have really pissed me off, but he said it anyway because he didn't care about himself, he cared about you. I really got it then. What you mean to him. What hopefully he means to you. I can't come between that. Especially after Mom and Dad passed. I'll never be someone to get in the way of your happiness and stepping in front of Parker would do that." He explains.

"I just didn't expect you to be open to it and not angry," I admit.

"I stopped being angry when I realized how shitty it was of me to be. I realized how badly it was affecting you pretty early on. I tried. I should have tried harder. I wanted you to come to terms with all of this on your own so I let you. I waited until you came to me because I was afraid if I pushed too hard you'd never talk again," he admits.

"I don't know if I'd be able to live without ever talking to you again. Especially without Mom and Dad here," I admit, wiping under my eyes once again.

"We're the only people that will ever truly understand how this feels when it comes to each other. I know that others have lost parents or didn't have them... But not our parents. That's only us. I miss them. Every single day... Your feelings don't need to be pushed aside to spare mine. I'm a big boy. I'm grateful for you. That you did that, that you care about me so damn much B, but if you're hurting yourself to help others... Especially others that love you, then it's not helping them. It doesn't help me if you're hurting. Never," he admits and a tear slips out of my eye once again.

"I missed you so much, Belly," I tell him and he tugs me into him.

The misery and hurt from the past few months is thawed and melted. Both of our cold bodies are once again warm and I feel alive for the time being. My chest vibrates with a laugh despite the tears coming out of my eyes.

"I missed you... And I love you, B. Always I mean it," he tells me.

"I love you," I tell him.

The one person who's been with me through it all. Even if he's caused some of the hurt and pain. Even if he didn't know how to handle it or what to say or do he always figured it out. We both did. My brother means more to me than words can explain. I don't need anything from him. I don't need his approval but I still want it. I still look for it. And having it means everything. We're kids. Even when we're grown, when we're here like this, hugging and laughing and crying, we're kids again. Both of us surviving through everything we've been left with. I convinced myself I needed to survive alone, but being here now. Being with him, I know I was so damn wrong. I never should have doubted the bond we have. The bond we've built since we were too young to even know what we would face.

"Do I get to be in you and Parker's wedding though?" He cuts the silence with a joke and I laugh.

"I don't know if he'll even want to speak to me, Bellamy," I laugh.

"I would bet my life and my spot on the Giants that he will," he tells me and I laugh again.

"I'm scared," I admit.

"For what?" Bellamy pulls back from our hug.

"Well, I've only dated him in secret. What if it's all different now? What if we don't work?" I ask.

"If we went through all of that for the two of you to not even like each other then I'm sure this must have been a social experiment. And just to reiterate what I already told him... Looking

THE RULES OF YOU AND ME.

back on those months when I didn't know I should have... I've never seen you that free. You were outspoken in a different way and you were happy and... and you were like you are right now but happier. You're speaking your mind. You're realizing what you want and deserve and asking for that and nothing less. I treated you in a way I shouldn't have. I treated you like a kid and you were anything but. If what you were wasn't in love, then I don't know." He shrugs and I nod.

"I do love him. I know that. I'm sure of that," I tell him.

"And I should have listened the first time you told me that. You've never said that to me about anyone you've dated and been confident while you did. I know you love him. And I'm happy it's him. I really am. I'll have to get used to it. But it's not about me. It's your relationship, not mine. I did threaten him though," he tells me.

"I wouldn't expect anything less from you... Especially since he's your friend," I tell him.

"Get some sleep B. Rest and call him," he tells me and I nod but I don't get up before hugging him again.

"Never let me fight with you that long again. Even if I'm being stubborn and don't come to you first, please," I beg.

"I won't. I love you, B," he mumbles into my hair.

"I love you Belly. Thank you... For Parker... For giving me the chance to try this," I tell him.

"It was never my place to take that chance from you... All I want is for you to be happy. Always, B," he promises and I squeeze my brother tightly. Thankful to have him, even through the hard times.

CHAPTER 51

AFTERGLOW BY TAYLOR SWIFT

Brianne Archer:

I did what Bellamy told me to—went to bed and slept better than I have in months. I slept so long that by the time I woke up, it was almost 1 pm, but after my successful dance recital, I think I deserved sleep. I walk down the stairs of the quiet apartment.

"Bellamy?" I ask and there's no response. "Lawson? Kam?" I call and no one is here. I shrug and fill my water bottle in the kitchen, calling my brother.

"Hey B," he breathes out and I furrow my brows.

"Where are you?" I ask.

"We went to the beach. We came and knocked on your door this morning and I came in when you didn't answer, but you were knocked out and I thought you should sleep. There are plenty of weekends you can come to the beach with us... and Parker too," he tells me and my chest squeezes.

"Speaking of... Have you talked to him about... About us talking yet?" I ask.

"No. I didn't know if you were cool with that. He asked me to tell him," he explains.

"You can tell him. If you want to, I wouldn't be mad," I tell him.

"Are you going to talk to him?" he asks.

"Yeah, probably today at some point. I'm nervous though," I admit and Bellamy laughs.

"Leave it to you to be nervous. It'll be fine, B. Promise... Kam is waiting on me but I love you. I'll tell Parker," he promises.

"Okay, I love you," I tell him, my chest warm.

It's comfortable between us. The conversation isn't stiff and tense.

I walk back up to my bedroom and to my desk. The crumpled rule list that got me into heaps of trouble... Right next to it is the locket. The tiny little locket Parker got me for Christmas that I never even wore because, by the time I could have, we were no more... I pick it up and turn it over in my fingers. I put the little pendant on and walk to my mirror.

I'm still in my sleep shorts and shirt. I haven't even brushed the knots out of my hair, but I stare at myself in the mirror and toy with the necklace in my fingers. I open it, the tiny note still inside. I smile, not even thinking about it before I do. That's common with Parker though, involuntarily smiling. Not having to think about it before I do it. I go into my bathroom, run a brush through my hair, and brush my teeth as well. My heart swells when I look at my phone and think about Parker. Calling him for nothing but because I want him and I need him to come here and talk to me. I haven't had that freedom in months. It scares me. I'm going to have a lot to tell Madeline.

I pick up my phone and call Parker, not thinking about it more than I need to. If I think too much I'll never do it. The phone rings and rings and rings and then it goes to voicemail. I think about leaving one but decide against it. Maybe he's sleeping... Or maybe he's out. Or maybe he avoided the call because

THE RULES OF YOU AND ME.

he didn't want to talk to me after I told him to go yesterday. My chest squeezes at the thought of all the missed moments and opportunities I had with Parker. The months I spent away from him that I could have loved and explored him in. I pick up the phone and call him again, but the first ring there's a loud knock on the door downstairs. I leave my bedroom and clamor down the stairs, my phone still pressed to my ear.

I open the door quickly when there's another knock. The breath feels like it was knocked from my chest when I see Parker standing there, his illuminated phone in his hand. He looks at me with questions in his stare. Like he's waiting for an answer. If this is really over. He looks so hopeful and I don't know what part of him still kept that hope alive for the past four months... But I'm thankful for whatever part of him that was.

"I was trying to..." I hold up my phone and then hang up the call.

"Bellamy told me he talked to you so I got in my car and came here right away..." he tells me.

"He actually talked to me last night," I admit.

"And he didn't tell me right away?" he asks.

"I asked him not to. I was scared," I admit.

"Of?" He asks, stepping into my apartment.

"You not wanting to see me or talk to me or be around me..." I admit.

"All I have wanted to do for the past 4 months is see you, talk to you, and be around you Brianne," he admits out loud. "So if your talk went well, then please... I will beg you if I have to, come here." His words crumble off at the end, emotion clouding his voice. I move to him but he's already moving to me, crushing my body to his. It's like breathing for the first time after you jumped into the deep end. His hand threads into my hair, pressing my head into his chest. I breathe him in, the sweet smell of his cologne mixed with his laundry detergent. The warmth of his arms wrapped so tightly around me that I'm surprised I can even breathe. I don't want him to let go though.

"We need to talk," I admit.

"The last thing I want to do is talk." He admits and pulls back, looking down at me. He hesitates and then he brings his face forward, crowding my space. He waits, giving me a second to stop him but I don't. I don't do anything but wait for his lips to brush mine then captivate them. His kiss is electric, ultraviolet. I burn into him. I become nothing and everything and I can't put into words the feeling of the hurt and pain and heartache melting the second he kissed me. Everything I wanted to talk about has disappeared. It's gone out the damn window.

His body meshes with mine, and he lifts me up at the first inclination that I want to be closer to him. His hands press into the backs of my thighs as I wrap my legs around him, not letting up on my kiss.

"Upstairs..." I mumble and he doesn't respond, he just kisses me. He doesn't let up. He makes it apparent he has no intention of doing so either. Even when we're in my bedroom. Even when he softly places me on my mattress. Even when he climbs on top of me, pushing me into my sheets.

"We don't have to do anything, I just want to... I want to kiss you. I want to touch you I missed you, I-"

"If you don't take your clothes off, I might die," I tell him and he rolls his eyes.

"Dramatic," he mumbles and pulls off his shirt, discarding it like it has never mattered to him.

His tattoo makes my mouth water, images of all the times I've put my mouth on it, my lips, my tongue... I trace it with my finger, following down to the waistband of his shorts. He shivers, despite the fact he was trying not to.

"God, I missed you."

He loses all composure then. Not giving me a second to

THE RULES OF YOU AND ME.

react before he's tugging at my clothes, pulling them off of me. His lips are a flurry all over. His hands are just as needy, touching me anywhere and everywhere he can get them. I'm being spoiled on this bed, treated like I'm the only thing that's ever existed.

"I want you. Now, no playing around please." I tell him, not wanting anything but him. All of him. He goes where he knows I have condoms in my bedroom and comes back to me in a flash, already rolling it onto himself. I'm propped onto the edge of my bed. He meets between my legs and positions himself. I hold myself up with one arm, the other moving to hang over his shoulder.

The euphoria that instantly hits is almost shocking. The feeling of Parker after months without him. I've never necessarily cared about physical touch, neither has Parker. Our whole lives we have lived without caring to have a physical connection. Only making them every now and then, but none of them sticking. Since each other. Since I have been with Parker, physicality is one of the simplest ways we can communicate. Wanting him, touching him, fucking him. All of it. And being with him like this feels like the most natural thing in the entire world.

He groans, his body physically shaking and shuddering with his movements.

"You feel so good... I missed you. All of you," he presses his forehead to mine. Then our eyes meet and everything just clicks.

"I love you. So much," I mumble, everything crashing into me.

"I love you," he breathes, then he brings his lips forward, not letting up again, messy sloppy kisses.

Hasty but purposeful movements from his hips. The feeling of him as well as the feeling he's exuding to me, kissing me, kneading me with his hands. I crumble. I unravel and I know he

595

can feel me do so. He barely takes a second to tumble down the same path with me soon after, my body still not even done reacting to the orgasm. I can barely breathe when he removes his lips from mine, but that doesn't stop him from bringing both his hands to my face, holding my back my jaw, his fingertips grazing behind my ears as he pulls me in and kisses me again.

"I.... I adore you. So damn much, Brianne," he tells me, and my heart stutters and melts.

"We... We need to talk," I tell him, both of us still very naked and very out of breath.

"I figured that part was coming... I wanted this part first," he tells me and I find myself smirking.

He kisses my lips one more time, then again before he backs away from me. He picks up my clothes for me and hands them to me, not allowing me to even do that for myself. When I go to the bathroom he stays in my bedroom, getting himself dressed.

When I walk out of my bedroom he's waiting for me, his eyes trained on me, watching every move I make like he's scared I might run away or bolt. I furrow my brows.

"What's wrong? Why are you looking at me like that?" I ask and he opens his arms up for me. I move to him, letting him hold me again. I need it.

"You're okay? That wasn't too much?" he asks me.

"No, it was just enough," I admit.

"Do we have to talk right now?" he asks, holding me tighter. I hug him back and then pull away after a few minutes.

"We have to talk now or we'll never do it," I tell him.

He lets me go so I can sit next to him. I pull into my bed, wanting to feel comfortable and he moves with me, sitting with his back to the headboard. I cross my legs and fold my hands in my lap.

"I'm sorry," I start.

"Don't apologize, please..." He shakes his head.

THE RULES OF YOU AND ME.

"I don't usually have a habit of apologizing for things I shouldn't be sorry for. I have plenty of reasons to apologize to you, Parker," I admit. "Just because you're not mad or hurt anymore doesn't mean there's not something for me to say sorry for."

"Okay... Sorry for what then?" he asks.

"First for not telling Bellamy about us when you had asked and for making you feel like I wanted you to be a secret. Because you being a secret was the best and worst thing for me. I never wanted that. I'm sorry for outwardly saying something so vile. I chose him. I didn't. As much as I was lying to myself saying I did, I didn't. I just couldn't see anything past my brother and that was my mistake. I... I will never understand what you've been through, but I never want to add to that pain so I'm sorry if I did. You're not someone to give up on. You're not someone to discard. Now I choose my happiness, and I should have done that from the start. I will never make you feel like that again. Like I have to choose anything or anyone over you," I tell him and he looks at me with a straight face, but blush... He's blushing.

"I'm sorry for what I said to you when you came here to see me right after everything happened. I never should have been rude or mean to you... I've been apologizing a lot for my behavior over the last few months, and you're the last on my list. I know there's a lot of stuff that's unresolved but I want to work to fix it... If you give me another chance." I admit out loud. Of course, we just slept together, but that doesn't mean he wants me back. It means he missed me just like I missed him.

"If you don't think the reason I came here the second your brother texted me wasn't to ask you if we can try again then you might actually be crazy..." he admits and I look at him directly now.

"I'm sorry. I have been working on myself a lot. My feelings and how to deal with them because I deserve that... but you also deserve that. I'm sorry you were so alone all these months. I didn't know what to do and I felt like my hands were tied. I wanted to come to you... So many times Brianne," he admits and I nod.

"I know... I know you did. As much as I secretly wanted that during those times, I needed all of this. Everything that had happened when I spent all of that time alone. I learned a lot. I needed it," I tell him with a nod, he brings his hand forward, touching mine. He draws his thumb over my knuckles, only loosely holding my fingers between his.

"So what now?" I ask, breaking the silence.

"I beg you to take me back," he tells me and I laugh.

"You wouldn't have to beg.... All you'd have to do is ask," I laugh.

"Then can we please be Brianne and Parker again? Will you please be my in-public, not secret, very important girlfriend?" he asks and I nod.

"Yes." I reach forward, brushing my hand over his face. He rests his cheek in the palm of my hand, looking at me with the softest glance and my heart melts.

"I love you, Sunshine. So much."

He holds my wrist and then kisses my palm, bringing my hand down so he can hold it. His eyes scan my face, dancing over my cheeks.

"You're never going to be able to count them all Parker." I smile.

"But now I have way more time to try..." He admits and I don't have to work to smile, it just happens.

"I love you," I tell him, no fear in my words. No worry about who might hear. Who might come around and who might find out. I hope everyone finds out. Hell, I'll make sure of it.

CHAPTER 52

YOU AND ME BY LIFEHOUSE

Parker Thompson:

I walk into the tunnel. It's my first game of the season and the first game of my senior year. My heart is thundering in my ears and I let it. I don't tell myself to focus and to laser in like I always do. I don't allow myself to submerge those feelings. I allow them to motivate me and excite me. Because I fucking made it to this moment and I've worked for it forever.

Summer was a fucking breeze. How could it not be when you spend it with people you love? Brianne and all of her friends who have now morphed into mine. Leah Ashley is probably the coolest mean person I've ever met. Dakota likes me now, thank god. According to Bri, he's always liked me but I never believed that. The cheerleaders are my personal hype squad, not just the team.

Bri renewed her lease at the same place when Bellamy and Lawson moved out but her two friends moved in. Dakota and surprisingly, Leah. She apparently has never had a friend group she felt comfortable living with. Until now. Funnily enough, it's her ex's little sister. But life is funny like that, connecting you to

599

people you never thought you would connect with. Brianne and I are the perfect example of that.

Coach Corbin is the one that pulls me out of my thoughts. I'm the team captain this year. Not the quarterback. Me. Of course, there are other people who count as captains, but there's one head and I was trusted with that position. Coach said he couldn't see it being anyone else this year and the honor didn't pass me by as something small.

"Get 'em. Kick ass, Thompson..." Coach Corbin holds me by the face mask and I nod.

He slaps my helmet and I jump up and down, taking on Bellamy's job of hyping up my team, making them more than ready for the rest of the damn season. Losing Bellamy and Lawson has been a hit, but we've managed and are ready to take this team to another championship.

We run out of the tunnel, our traditional song playing like it does every single home game, and I feel it—that I'm home here. But no matter who is staring, cheering, or screaming, I still scour every single person surrounding me until my eyes find hers. Bright and blue and so damn gorgeous. A ray of light. Human sunshine. She's smiling like her life depends on it and it's real... That's the part that never escapes me, feeling how real her happiness is.

The girls are in new uniforms this year, all white with gold and yellow detailing. That damn pleated cheer skirt on her is going to be the death of me. This is the one thing I am going to have to try to not get distracted by tonight. Because as much as I have my head in the game, it's hard not to let someone as ungodly perfect as Brianne distract me from my sport. Dakota lets her down from her stunt and she stands there, looking directly at me as I slowly pass.

"My lucky number 13! Good luck!" she shouts at me.

I take my helmet off and blow her a kiss, watching her catch

THE RULES OF YOU AND ME.

it. Somehow, her smile brightens and my heart shakes. On the sidelines, I see a handful of familiar faces, and excitement courses through me.

Bellamy and Kamryn. Lawson is here too. I didn't expect it, even though they told me they might show because Coach Corbin begged them to. I approach them first, ignoring my responsibilities. Bellamy pulls me into a bear hug and I hug him back.

"You ready?" he asks, shaking my shoulders.

"Of course, he's ready. If he loses, we'll kick his ass," Lawson jokes and Kamryn elbows him.

"You've got this, P," Kamryn nods and I hug her tight.

I missed them. All of them and it's only been two months since they moved.

"BELLY!" I hear Brianne behind me and I move out of her way, having to go line up anyway.

I turn over my shoulder and see Brianne almost tackle her brother to the ground. He's bigger and bulkier now that he's training with the NFL but she still almost takes him out. I laugh, watching her excitement at seeing her brother. I'm thankful he's here.

The coin toss goes our way. The first half of the game goes our way, but not without a fight. The new lead quarterback has been trying to figure out the team dynamic... But here and now, the ball is hurtling toward me. I charge the ball, jumping to get it in my hands, feeling greedy to have my gloved fingers touching the skin. I run faster than I ever have, diving through defensemen on our opposing team, securing us a first down on the 10. I stand and bounce my hands, getting a reaction from the crowd. We set up and I pull my teammates in, signaling for our next play, knowing good and well I need to be the one with that ball. Everyone is on the same page.

Once we line up, my head does that thing. I hear nothing

601

but a thrum, my heartbeat in my ears. A very dull roar of the crowd. Then, the ball snaps and I'm running and it all screams out in my head, igniting my fire. The ball hits my chest and I tuck it and run again, fighting through the defensive line until I'm on the spray-painted grass and hearing ear-shattering screams. My first touchdown of the season.

The sounds blow around me, the school band blares across the stadium and I shove through my teammates and toward the sidelines. Already almost off of the sidelines and on the field is Brianne. I grab her face, both hands pressing to her cheeks and I bring her in and to my lips for a kiss. It's just as precious and perfect to me as every single one before it. She pulls back and then we bring our hands together, performing our handshake, something she asked me to make with her for the season since she won't be able to do it with Bellamy this year. I said I would if she promised to do it with me after my first touchdown in a game. It was an easy agreement.

"Get your head back in the game, Thompson," Coach Corbin snaps from the sidelines.

The older man is pretending to be a hard ass, and most of the time he is. But I do see the hint of a smile on his lips as I jog backward.

"Once I get rid of one Archer, I have another one on my back. What's next?" Coach Corbin asks, throwing his hands in the air.

I watch Brianne roll her eyes at him and I smirk at her subtle attitude that she always has on when it's game day. I notice Bellamy on the sidelines with Kamryn and Lawson. Kamryn is looking at me, giving me a huge thumbs up, but I look at Bellamy who is staring at his sister with the happiest smile I think I've ever seen on his face. A year ago I never would have believed he'd be happy for her because she's with me. I never would have even dreamed I'd be with Brianne in this way at all.

THE RULES OF YOU AND ME.

But I did dream it. It was hard not to when she's involved because she's a dream in and of itself.

But the funny thing about dreams is that you either fall in love with them or you fall out of them. My whole life I never really knew which one I would be. Most would have assumed I would have fallen out with my dreams and gone more practical. As of right now, where I am, I'm thankful I didn't. I'm thankful I chased and fought and won. That little kid in my mind, the one that used to just sit and stare. He's jumping for joy every time I'm around her. Every time I score a touchdown, or I hang out with my friends. Because finally, I'm giving that part of me what it deserves. I learned that it's not silly or frivolous, but a necessity... Always.

EPILOGUE
MY GIRL BY THE TEMPTATIONS

Brianne Archer:

The second the plane landed about 15 minutes ago I was bouncing up and down in my seat and tapping my toes every second with anxiety. We're all in a group chat. Me, Bell, Kam, Lawson, Sienna, and Parker. They said someone would be here to pick me up, but they never told me who. I don't even know if it will be one of them or someone random. I've never been to the Boston airport, but there's a first time for everything.

Three years ago Parker graduated from Seattle Pike with not only a degree, but a Heisman trophy, a lot of new records, and a rookie spot on his hometown team, the San Francisco 49ers. I was actually more than happy he would be moving just down the coast instead of across the country, but I wasn't at all happy to be at SPU without him or my brother... It took a lot of learning, being there without them. Growing up with my best friends, watching new friends come, and old ones graduate. Watching people fall in love, break up, find love, find themself. I did all of that too, except for the breakup part. Parker and I never did that again.

604

THE RULES OF YOU AND ME.

After I graduated, I packed my bags and moved south to California into Parker's absolutely lavish apartment. I mean... I mean insane. Life altering. I had visited him when I was still in school, but he moved before I could protest, somewhere bigger. A place for both of us. I've been living there for a year now. I struggled a lot with what to do with my life the summer after I graduated. Parker said to do what I loved the most, which would be dance. I wanted to. Always. But dancing professionally doesn't pay well unless you really break into the scene. He said money didn't matter and I hated the thought, but ultimately, Bellamy talked me into trying.

I'm thankful I did. I've been professionally dancing with the San Francisco Ballet Company for the past year. I've also been content creating, mostly dance stuff as well as football behind-the-scenes content when I can sneak it with Parker. All of that combined has made it to where people notice me and want me to teach them. To come to their studios or judge at dance competitions. I've been flying around non-stop for the past few weeks just to teach master classes and answer questions for college students. I was in their shoes a little over a year ago and here I am now, living a dream I never thought possible.

Parker said that dreams were funny because they can be something made up, or something that can materialize if you work hard enough. If the stars align. I think dreams happen with luck and timing. And I'm really damn lucky the timing was right because I wouldn't know where I'd be if it wasn't dancing. Or in Boston, finally getting to see my brother and Kam after a few months, Lawson and Sienna after a long time, and Parker after weeks of FaceTime calls and screens. We start leaving the plane and I make sure to get off in a timely manner so I'm not stuck behind the slow pokes. The second I'm off, I'm racing to baggage claim and then I'm walking where the pickup is and I see an entourage, the whole crew standing in front of me.

I'm thankful there was no gap. No years apart like I thought there would be. First was Sienna and Lawson's wedding. I was a guest, Kamryn was the only bridesmaid, and Bellamy was the only groomsman. It was a very quiet ceremony, they got married at a vineyard and we all got drunk on wine after, including Lawson's mom which was a sight to see. We always met up for Christmas, even if it was late or early. We also tried our best to meet up for both Bellamy and Parker's NFL games. My favorite games were when they played each other. They came to see me at SPU as well, always welcomed by Coach Corbin.

After that was Bellamy and Kamryn's wedding. Which as expected was a huge party. They got married in Washington on a Ferry Boat. They set sail, married with the sunset in the background, and got everyone drunk off wine, but lots of tequila for me and Dakota. Every single teammate of his was there. I was a bridesmaid at the wedding and Sienna was the maid of honor. I could have kissed Kamryn for picking out the prettiest baby blue for us to wear. She said it reminded her of the color she wore on her and Bell's first date which was apparently on a ferry boat too. We had the night of our lives that day. I'll never forget it.

But finally after years of trying we're meeting in Boston. Lawson gave up playing football to coach an award winning high school team and Sienna still plays her sport and was called to this city. It was always in Lawson's head I think that he didn't want to continue to the NFL and from what I can see, this career looks and feels really good for him. He's always stepped up with his teammates and seemed like a leader. So him coaching and teaching, it just makes sense. As for Sienna, I watch all of her televised games when I can and have become a huge fan of lacrosse, especially when she plays. We're here for one of her lacrosse games, and Lawson has finally gotten Bellamy and Parker at the same time to come

THE RULES OF YOU AND ME.

and meet his high school football team and coach them alongside him. It's the very beginning of their training season, so they are going to think Lawson is the coolest coach ever. That's definitely going to go to his head. But seeing all of them now, none of that matters. I just care that I'm with them. I leave my bags only a second behind me and Parker is the first to hug me, per usual.

"Hi, Sunshine." His lips brush my ear and his hand is brushing my hair down on the back of my head.

"Back off. You get to see her more than I do," Bellamy's voice echoes behind Parker, and he quite literally pulls him off of me.

"Hey, I will—"

"If you two get in a fight at the Boston airport where there is quite literally paparazzi taking photos of all of us right over there, I will never hear the end of it from your coach Bellamy. You better stop." Kamryn snaps and I smirk, ignoring Bellamy altogether and pulling Kamryn into a hug. Over the years Bellamy and Parker stopped acting like friends and really started acting like brothers. They fight and snap and argue, but they love each other more than I could explain. That's how I feel about Kamryn. She's the sister I was never lucky enough to have on my own. Sienna is like the cousin I never see but when I do it's like no time has passed.

"Get your ass over here." Lawson and Bellamy practically bear hug me to death together and I don't care. I let them squeeze me until I can't breathe.

"Where's Dakota? And how's Leah?" Bellamy asks me about my two best friends.

"Let's talk about that in the car that's waiting for all of us, get a move on." Sienna claps her hands and we all move in, Parker being the one to grab my bags.

"Did you pack your closet?" he mumbles.

"You and I both know there's far more in my closet than those bags," I smirk.

"Dakota is in LA. He's got some huge influencer event thing he's planning. Honestly, I didn't understand what he was saying when he was explaining it, but it looked cool. Leah is still in Washington, she finished school with a graduates." I tell them. Dakota decided he wanted to start somewhere new when he graduated with me, so he did. He moved to California too and started working as an event planner. With his personality he's made it easy for himself, booking things left and right. And if Dakota is good at anything it's planning. Leah had one year left of her graduates degree after I left SPU, so thank god that's finally over with.

"I miss him," Kamryn pouts.

"I don't," Parker mumbles, running his hands through his chin-length hair. I roll my eyes at the constant battle between Dakota and Parker. They love each other but definitely at a distance. Parker I've learned doesn't like sharing me when we each have the time. I'm absolutely fine with that thought.

"Where are we going first?" I ask.

"We're going to my practice. I pushed it back to come pick you up from the airport you brat," Lawson jokes and I scoff.

"One of you would have been fine!" I snap.

"You deserve the best, B." Bellamy nudges my shoulder and I shake my head with a sigh, but I still keep a smile on my face. I lean my head against Parker's shoulder and smell the light scent of his cologne, feeling at home for the first time in weeks. I know I'm going to have to tell him and Bellamy all the things I've been doing the past few weeks once we settle down in Sienna and Lawson's apartment tonight, but for now, I enjoy the peace and quiet while we drive to the high school Lawson works at.

The high school is giant. I've heard him talk about it, and I've heard Bellamy say things too as he visited his first year in

THE RULES OF YOU AND ME.

the NFL, but this is still more than I expected. The car brings us to the football field and then Bellamy leans his head in, telling the driver where to take my bags while we're here.

There's apparently a sports medicine program here and Kamryn is going to talk to the students in that, the football assistants on the field, and such. She's excited because she's been working to get her graduate degree all these years so she can work in the NFL. She has to be at the top of her class considering how hard she works and how smart she is.

Lawson offered to have me talk to the cheerleaders there as I cheered all four years in college, but I said I would feel like a poser considering I stopped cheering last year when I graduated.

We all make our way to the field and there is an assistant coach already warming the players up on the field that is smaller than the one at SPU but not by much. I'm shocked by how nice this school is. Considering their sponsors dump money into the football program I guess it should look like this. Lawson jogs forward and announces to his team who he has behind him, but before he can even say it, I see the excited faces of some of the players. They already know who the two people I'm standing by are.

"I brought my best friends to practice today, and I've been trying to get this to happen for years so today you listen, you learn, and after you can ask as many questions as all your little heart's desire, but until then, you focus. Understood?" Lawson snaps and they all nod in unison, looking at Lawson like he hung the damn moon.

"Heard," the team echoes.

"Go on, introduce yourself." Lawson claps my brother on the back, Sienna, Kamryn and I take a seat on the bench, watching the three idiots together.

"Do I really have to do that?" Parker asks Lawson and he sighs.

"Well if you learn one thing today guys, it's that the NFL isn't going to make you any less shy," he jokes and I smirk.

"I'm Parker Thompson. I play starting wide receiver for the 49ers," he introduces himself.

"And I'm Bellamy Archer, I play starting quarterback for the New York Giants," he tells them.

I look at Kamryn and she's already looking at me, a smile on her face.

"What?" I ask.

"It's just sweet. How you look up to him. And also how much you love Parker just with your eyes," she tells me and I shrug.

"Well, we've been through a lot already. It's hard not to love him when he's stayed true to himself... And you two have no room to talk when you both have weights on your ring fingers," I mumble to both Sienna and Kamryn.

"That's what happens when you marry good ones. Besides, you're next," Sienna shrugs and Kamryn winks at me which only confuses me.

Do they know something I don't? Kam stands up when the football assistants make their way onto the field with full water bottles.

I stay with Sienna, watching Lawson coach and Bellamy and Parker just have fun. They teach and play football with all of the team. It's cute watching the young players look at my brother and boyfriend like they've never seen anything cooler. Like this will be the best thing to ever happen to them. After the practice ends and the players ask their million questions we all head back to Sienna and Lawson's penthouse apartment that stuns, to say the least. Both of them have done extremely well

THE RULES OF YOU AND ME.

for themself, especially Sienna being a professional on the biggest Lacrosse team in the US.

We went to dinner and it felt... It felt like home. Like everything I always crave when I'm away. There's never a shortage of laughter or warmth when we're all together. It's easy for us to mold back into the shape of our friend group. None of us feel like outsiders or the odd man out. It's just right. It makes sense... Even if there are people that stop Bellamy and Parker for pictures every now and again. Something I still am not used to.

But now we're back in the apartment, Parker and I in one of the guest bedrooms, readying ourselves for tomorrow, Sienna's big game. Everyone else has snuck off into their corners of the apartment and I'm happy to finally be alone with him. After weeks apart. After so much time without feeling his fingers brush over my face.

"You look tired, Sunshine..." he mumbles and I nod.

"I am, but I haven't seen you in weeks... I missed you," I admit.

"I missed you," he tells me for the first time.

"You looked really happy today with Lawson's team... It was really sweet actually," I admit, and he pulls me closer to him while we lay in the queen-sized bed, staring at each other.

His skin is warm against mine and I missed it, the way he feels pressed to me, the warmth of his touch and his breath fanning over me.

"I was happy. I am happy... I like talking about what I'm good at. I like playing with Bellamy. I miss it." He tells me.

"I miss seeing you two on the field together," I admit.

"Rumor has it... He hasn't told you yet because he doesn't want to get your hopes up, but I think that he might get traded... He might be moving, Brianne," he tells me and I sit up.

"Are you serious?" I ask and Parker nods. I push him back, leaning over him.

"But we still have a while before that decision could be made... I'm just happy I got to see your face when I told you. See your smile..." He whispers, and then his fingers start tracing over my freckles. He's never gotten to count all of them. But to this day I catch him trying. Every time he does, my heart melts.

"I don't think you can count that high..." I admit.

"I don't care." He leans forward, pressing a whisper of a kiss on my lips.

"We should probably go to bed," I tell him.

"I think we should get married," he blurts out, and I shake my head, almost falling out of bed at the confession.

"Pardon?" I ask.

"I'm serious..." he whispers, kissing the pads of my fingers.

"And I am too. What did you just say?" I ask, thinking back to hours earlier what Sienna had said.

"Marry me... While we're here in Boston," he tells me.

"What in the... Parker? Do you even have a ring? I don't have a dress... Is this... I mean have you thought this through?" I ask.

"Yeah. I have since the second I graduated and had to leave you in Seattle. I thought about it every single day. I actually already talked to Kam and Sienna about the possibility. And I do have a ring. I have the ring your mom wore, Bellamy got it from your grandparents and gave it to me a year ago. He gave me his blessing with it. It's in my suitcase I can—"

"Parker!" I raise my voice.

"Shhhh." He covers my mouth and I push it away.

"You're insane? I... I mean, you... We...." I panic.

"We don't have to. You can say no." He shrugs.

"I want to say yes. Wait, yes. Of course, yes... What are we going to do? Why is this the way you asked me?" I laugh.

"Well, I imagine we elope while we're here with our family," he tells me.

THE RULES OF YOU AND ME.

"But what about—" I start. He barely lets me get a word in.

"Then when we go home we can have a reception and a ceremony with everyone else... That way Dakota, Leah, Xander, and everyone else can be present too. You can have bridesmaids and a really pretty dress and anything else you want. But—"

"Yes. Okay, yes. But why now?" I ask.

"Well, I've been wondering when it would feel right. And right now, right here after a few weeks apart it felt right. You feel right. Like sunshine." He traces my lips and I kiss his fingertip, my eyes welling up.

"Parker you are the sweetest, most romantic, most—"

"Oh shut up you kiss ass..." He kisses me then, stopping my words and I smile with his lips pressed to mine.

"Leah is going to be so mad and Dakota is going to be pissed at me. We had a rule. We'd be each other's best man and best woman at our wedding ceremony. That was the one rule I had!" I urge.

"Well, I think the past few years are proof that neither of us are very good at following the rules. Especially if the rules keep me away from you." He tells me, his lips whispering on mine.

"I love you..."

I feel my lips turn up into a smile and I watch his eyes immediately soften. Parker hasn't changed much. He's shy. He's grumpy. But he's still the kindest, biggest-hearted man I've ever met. I know my parents would love him. I'm happy my brother does. And I'm happy I found the person that I never knew I always needed. Connecting with him, committing to him, and choosing him... Though they were rocky at times, they were the easiest decisions I ever made. I'd never regret Parker. Never in my life. So I kiss him again and again and again, never tiring of the feeling.

ACKNOWLEDGMENTS

Saying goodbye to the SPU universe was not something I had planned for. Of course I knew it would come, but it doesn't feel real. In all actuality, though I've written two other books before this one, not including my fan-fictions. This is really the moment I've felt like I truly did it. Finishing a book is always hard, leaving the world is hard. But I didn't have to do that until right now and the tears are welling up in my eyes as I type this out at the bar that I also work at. I will never be able to let go of this school, these characters, and every damn emotion I've felt writing them. So much so that I've already started a silly little spin off series... *Hello Leah Ashley!*

There's a lot of thanks to give, first and foremost to the Brianne's of the world. I find myself in her category to some degree. Constantly being told to be less of myself, be quiet, be less dramatic. Be someone you are not to make others feel comfortable. To the girls who "talk too much." But never say what they truly mean. I hope you find yourself, I hope you find your Parker. And if no one else has said it yet, I love you, I love the words you say and the thoughts you speak. You are exactly who you need to be.

To Sabrina, always. My editor, my friend, my confidant, my mentor in so many ways. My true and honest life saver. This would have never been anything without you here guiding and helping me. Bellamy, Lawson, Parker, Kamryn, Sienna, and Brianne as well as all of the others would be more of a mess than they're supposed to be if you weren't here to help me raise them. I adore you for that, always.

My husband because not only do I get to include his music, but I get to include snippets of his love and cuteness toward me in the words I write and the romantic scenes I portray. You mean the world to me in ways I'll never be able to explain, in this life and every other.

To Kassandra for making my dreams come true while working for herself in her amazing small business, and also another job on top of it. Also to her husband for helping her create these covers.

One of the biggest thanks I can give is to my other job. I've always felt an overwhelming sense of thanks for them for supporting me while I try to make my dreams a reality. I wrote The List of Things in secret mostly, none of my management team really knew where I was going with my life. The minute I told them I was publishing a book, Amanda, Maurie, Courtney, Jess, Autumn, Taylor, Ayanna, Marlie, Bri, Morgan and many others immediately bought my book, not knowing if I could even write a decent sentence let alone a book. I will never be able to repay that blind trust and support, but I will forever be thankful for that.

Not only the management and staff of my job, but so many of the regulars that come in to take a load off. All I could have been to you was a server or bartender, yet you made me into something more and that is a miracle, and such a dream. To Paula for being my number one fan. To the tennis girls for jumping back into the reading scene just to support me. Clint for stepping out of his comfort zone to read my book just because he thought it was cool that I wrote it. The many people who listen and learn about my publishing journey because you care... And to the many many regulars who may not read, but bought my book anyway just to be a support for me. You all mean so much to me, and your support fills me up more than words can express.

To Alaina and Heather who are both truly my sisters. Even if this genre isn't the one you normally choose you suggest, support, and absolutely love me through all. To the rest of my family as well, words aren't enough, but I love you will do for now. A million times thank you.

And to my Cherry babies. My readers from the start. Thank you for constantly adoring, creating, suggesting, helping. You are everything I could need and want. It makes me want to cry thinking about the unadulterated support you have shown me since 2020. I cannot wait to continue this journey, and thanks to all of you most of all, that is possible. Writing is my dream and passion and I hope that you can feel that through all of these words. Thank you. On to the next world friends! I love you all.

ALSO BY EMMA MILLER

Jump into the SPU series and read the stories that came before Brianne and Parker!

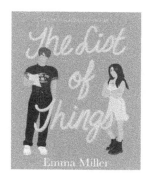

Thank you for reading The SPU universe!

ABOUT THE AUTHOR

Emma Miller started as a writer on Wattpad with over 20 million reads combined on all of her works. Some titles include Cherry, Roots, and The Stylist series. Emma loves writing but has been an avid book reader since she was young thanks to her parents. When Emma is not writing , you can most likely find her at a concert. Emma is married to her wonderful husband Levi Ransom who is a musician. Emma and Levi live in Georgia with their fur children Zeppelin and Jovi, two adopted cats who are fat and happy. To connect with Emma, learn more about her upcoming work, and more, check out her social media platforms.

@emmakmillerrrr

www.ingramcontent.com/pod-product-compliance
Lightning Source LLC
LaVergne TN
LVHW091509210125
801766LV00013B/120